MW00744247

This book would not exist if not for the support of my wonderful husband Mike, to whom I am forever grateful. Every writer needs someone to believe in them, and he has always encouraged and believed in me. (Thank you, love.) I also want to thank my children, Brennan, Dylan, and Erin, for tolerating their obsessive mother when she insisted on quiet ("This kitchen is my office!"), or when she wasn't paying attention because her mind was in the clouds. Thanks for loving me anyways, guys. I love you all, so very much.

I also need to thank the following people for helping me bring this book about: Robert Runté, Editor-in-Chief of Five Rivers Publishing (and a wonderful writer in his own right), for coming to the first reading I ever did of *The Tattooed Witch* and offering me his enthusiastic support , Lorina Stephens, Publisher, for stepping outside the genre box and for being the rare and lovely woman of vision she is, Sally Harding, agent extraordinaire, and Rachel Letofski, literary assistant, both of the Cooke Agency: their help in bringing this book (and me, as a writer) to its fullest potential must be recognized, members of the Cult of Pain Writing Group — Nicole Luiken and Barb-Galler Smith, especially, for their early revision suggestions and support, and Jena Snyder for telling me years ago over sushi, that I should try my hand at writing a novel.

Last but far from least, I must acknowledge the One who has always been there for me, who, when I asked years ago, "What should I do with my life? Help me find something to do that's worthwhile!"— accompanied me every step of this journey, showed me the joy in writing, helped me hone my craft, lifted me up during the dark moments, and finally, gave me this answer.

Chapter One: Host Maligno

IN THE FURTHEST corner of the gilded bed chamber belonging to
Alonso de Santangél, High Solar of Granad, Miriam Medina stood as
still as a porcelain vase. Only the occasional blink of her eyes and the
even, slow rise and fall of her breasts betrayed her presence, although
the priests in the room knew she was there. She had watched the
dawn come, had marked how the sun spilled through the crenellated
glass, how it had cut bright patterns across the floor. Her assistant's
tunic clung to her like a damp tent, as heavy as the velvet drapes on
the windows. Sweat trickled between her breasts. A potted oleander
bush, heavy with blossoms, shielded her from view. To her reckoning,
she had been banished to her corner for five hours now. In this place,
Miriam Medina knew it was better to be ignored.

  She breathed through her nose and tried not to gag. Beneath the
powdery scent of the oleander, the room stank of old men. She could
smell her own sweat, too. The heat of the day was not the only cause.
The priests had rounded on them when she and Ephraim had arrived.
Their open hostility startled her so much that she had stepped on

her father's hems. *A woman! In the High Solar's chamber? What are you thinking, Doctor Medina?*

She is a drudge, nothing more, her father maintained. They both knew it for a lie. And then she had been banished to this corner as if she were no more than a child. So demeaning, considering Ephraim knew her true capabilities.

You're at a loss, Papa. One touch and we'll know what ails the High Solar.

No. It's too dangerous.

But you said so yourself—you don't know what ails him!

I have my suspicions.

And they are?

They don't matter. I will deal with it.

And if he dies, what then? They'll blame you. And then, what will happen to me?

It had been an unkind thing to say, a selfish thing to say, but it had been the only way to move him. Against his better judgment, he had agreed.

You'll do nothing until I call you, Miriam.

Yes, Papa.

You'll stay out of the way and not dare to move.

Yes, Papa.

And if I call you—that's 'if' Miriam—you'll determine the trouble. Then you'll return to the house and stay there until I come home.

It wasn't fair, this pretense they were expected to maintain. She considered the room full of priests. These old men—they lived one way but preached another. Wasn't it Sul who had said, 'Hide not your light beneath a bushel, but place it on a candlestick, so that it giveth light to all the house?' Hers was a unique gift, but if she ever displayed it openly, they would accuse her of congress with demons.

If he would just call me. She closed her eyes to suppress her impatience and ignore her thirst. In spite of the sunshine, the bed chamber was littered with enough candles to light a nave. What the High Solar needed was darkness and solitude. Ephraim had suggested it, but the priests insisted that their patriarch needed the blazing protection of Sul all about him. It mattered not if the heat contributed to his demise.

A small page in white livery appeared in the doorway. He held a steaming bowl of broth in his hands. Earlier, Ephraim had turned away Alonso de Santangél's breakfast. The monks had tried to feed him, but he had spit up the gruel. Clear liquids only, Ephraim maintained.

With a nod, Ephraim beckoned the boy forth and accepted the broth. The monks in front of her shifted, affording her a better view of Alonso de Santangél.

She caught her breath.

Without his robes of office or a miter upon his head, he was a much younger man than she had assumed, about thirty years of age. A tonsure of blonde hair ran about his head like a crown. He had the face of an angel—beautiful in a stern sort of way, although at the moment, the visage was marred by pain. His bare chest was well muscled for a man of the cloth. He looked as if he spent his days scything grain.

He was handsome! The realization came as a shock. What business did a Prince of the Church have in being so attractive? And what business did she have in finding him so? Surely, it was a sin to think of him that way, although there were far too many sins as it was.

A flush rose to her face. She had seen naked men before, surreptitiously, through slatted shutters. None of Ephraim's patients had impressed her—all flabby bellies and flaccid penises, but this one; he would be different, as perfect as any sculptor's model, his thighs well-formed and his loins...she took a deep breath, thankful that the priests' backs were turned to her.

She set aside her attraction with a rigid self-control. She had studied the body's drives in Ephraim's medical books. It was logical to feel this way. She was a young woman reacting to a striking, albeit ineligible, man. She eyed the priests about her. At least Alonso de Santangél wasn't old and dried out, as these others were.

Ephraim set a spoon to his lips. She held her breath—*please, Your Brilliance, keep it down!*—and chided herself. She was reacting like one of those stupid girls who pressed themselves against the bricks and swooned whenever a conquistador rode by. Would she be so worried about the High Solar if he weren't so good looking? She knew the answer to that. She would not.

Alonso de Santangél accepted another spoonful, and then abruptly, he choked and coughed. She bit her lip. All around her, monks muttered in dismay. Ephraim thrust the bowl to the page and reached for a cloth. He leaned Alonso de Santangél to his side and helped him wretch up what little he could. Bloody spittle bubbled from his lips. She held herself tightly, knowing she could not rush to his bedside to help.

A Luster monk approached to help. Ephraim waved him off. "Leave it." He glanced to where she stood at the back of the room and beckoned her to come. "My assistant will clean it up."

She blinked. Gods, had she heard him right? He motioned to her a second time, so she dropped her gaze and strode through the priests with her hands clasped. Let them think she was no more than a servant reserved for the most odious of tasks. Alonso de Santangél loomed into view. *He is wonderful*, she thought as she drew alongside him, *like Sul after the Passion.* Without a word, she dropped to her knees and thought of the Goddess Lys in her incarnation as the Pietà, Mother of the God. With great care, she swabbed Alonso de Santangél's face. His flesh was a mottled red. Her attraction fled as fear for him took its place. She wanted to cradle him, to ease his pain. He lifted his suffering gaze to regard her. His eyes were as blue as a summer's sky. It took all of her strength to refrain from laying a soft hand against his cheek, to reassure him that she would do all in her power to help him. She caught a hint of sweetness beneath his breath. That was wrong. Why should his breath smell sweet? Abruptly, he choked and gagged. When he subsided, she wiped his chin and allowed the tip of her forefinger to touch his face.

A tongue of fire shot through her, burning her throat and turning her stomach into a molten churn. She fought the grey that engulfed her and swallowed. Her legs buckled, but since she was already on her knees, no one noticed. She curled her finger back into her fist and forced herself to breathe.

Trembling, she wiped his mouth as gently as she could, keeping her fingers clear. She couldn't afford to lose herself. Gods, what had he been given? She ran through the list of possibilities. Alonso de Santangél watched her with sunken, wild eyes, his pupils like dark beetles scuttling in a grave. One thing was certain; she and Ephraim couldn't leave him alone. Someone in the Solarium had done this, perhaps one of the priests in this room. She tucked a strand of her black hair into her kerchief. Her fingers twitched. Ephraim watched them intently.

Poison, she signed, knowing the awful truth of it. *Monkshood or oleander.*

Her father's eyes narrowed. He glanced at the soup. He reached into his bag and withdrew an envelope—medicinal charcoal for toxins.

"Take that away," he told the page, indicating the bowl of broth, "and on pain of death, don't touch it." He stared hard at the lad, knowing the proclivities of young boys. "From now on," he told the breathless assembly, "no food or drink passes the High Solar's lips that I don't prepare."

"But what is wrong with him?" demanded the Solarium's Exchequer. He looked like rabbit about to bolt for its hole.

Ephraim tipped the charcoal into a cup of water and set it to the High Solar's lips. "It's a sensitive matter, Luminance. When His Brilliance is stable, I'll share my diagnosis with you in private." Her father was no fool; the last thing he would do would be to air their suspicions publicly. He coaxed Alonso de Santangél to drink. To Miriam's relief, he kept it down.

"You must have some idea," the Exchequer pressed. "Is he contagious?"

"No. What ails him isn't due to any humour of the air, nor is it a god-sent punishment. He is sick through no fault of his own." Ephraim eased Alonso de Santangél to his pillows. "I want this room cleared. His Brilliance needs peace and solitude if he's to recover."

The Exchequer frowned, less bothered now that he was unlikely to catch a plague. As the priests grumbled, Alonso de Santangél captured her gaze. His eyes bore into hers as if she were his last link to life. His fingers trembled. He lifted a shaking hand as if to touch her.

A harsh clatter of boots came from down the hall. The tramp grew louder. Miriam pulled her gaze from Alonso de Santangél to see what army had arrived. A stark figure in black and white stood framed in the chamber's doorway. She ducked her head to hide. Gods! Ephraim had said that the Grand Inquisitor had left for Madrone that morning, but here he was.

Flee, her instincts told her. *Run and don't look back.*

This was the man that all of Esbaña feared as much as they did a god-sent pestilence. In three major cities, thousands had died smelling the stink of their burning flesh. *La Puraficación de la Fé*, he called it, a purification of the faith. He had given the town one week to come forward and confess its sins in an Edict of Grace. Most people attended. She and Ephraim had not; Ephraim's grandfather had been Juden until the family converted fifty years ago. The conversions made little difference to the inquisitors; they didn't believe them. Now, it was too late.

"What is this?" Tor Tomás demanded. He swept into the room, his boots striking hard against the marble. No one said a word as he stopped before her. She lifted her head to meet his gaze, hoping she looked as benign as a lamb. His eyes were a strange colour, so yellow as to be reptilian. He wore no tonsure as the other priests did, but had shaved himself bald, as if to impress Sul with his greater sanctity. His head resembled a cracked egg. A thin line cut across his face—an old scar, she realized. His only other ornamentation, other than the official Brand upon his chest, was a tiny hoop in his left ear. He looked more cutthroat than priest.

Ephraim cleared his throat. "This is my daughter. She cleans for me, nothing more."

"Monk's work."

"I take the sputum to my residence to study, Radiance. She knows how to collect it."

Tor Tomás dismissed the excuse with a wave. His fingers were long and thin, the nails uncut. Something dark and ruddy rimmed their bases. "She has no business here. She taints the very air."

"Forgive me, but I beg to differ." Ephraim stood his ground. "Even the medical college in Zaragoza allows that women have their place. I can vouch for my daughter. She's received no schooling, save for what little I've shown her. She's no threat to anyone, least of all, the High Solar. I would not have her here, if she were."

"How long has she been here?"

"Since early morning, Radiance."

"And *why* did you bring her?"

"As I explained, she collects...."

"You're lying. You brought her here because you thought she would be needed. Why is that, I wonder?"

"I don't know what you mean."

"You weren't at the Edict of Grace."

"I've been with His Brilliance all week."

"That doesn't excuse your daughter."

The silence was palpable. She felt the weight of the priests' scrutiny fall upon her. In seconds, someone would point a gnarled finger at her and accuse her of witchcraft.

"She is unmarried," Ephraim said quickly. "I don't allow her to travel or stay alone without a chaperone."

She walked through Granad as she pleased, although mostly to visit the market to buy supplies for the house or their pharmacopoeia. If the priests asked anyone who knew them, they would uncover the lie.

Alonso de Santangél groaned. The focus in the room shifted. Tor Tomás pursed his lips. "How is the patient?" he asked dryly.

"Not well. I've administered a tincture," Ephraim said.

"You prepared it yourself?"

"Of course. I wouldn't trust any woman to handle it."

She closed her eyes. Another falsehood. Fortunately, the Grand Inquisitor didn't question it. He studied Alonso de Santangél for a moment and then snagged his cheeks between his thumb and forefinger. "He doesn't look well," he said, handling him as he might a melon in the market.

The High Priest sputtered to life. His arms shook as if he had no more strength in them than a man twice his age. His hands flailed. He wheezed and choked.

"Radiance, please." Ephraim set a restraining hand on the Grand Inquisitor's wrist.

The inquisitor released his fingers as if he had touched something foul. He locked his strange yellow eyes with Alonso de Santangél's blue ones. The two men regarded each other with such loathing, that anyone with a whit of understanding could not fail to notice.

"This is terrible, my Brothers!" Tor Tomás announced suddenly. "Your Patriarch is dying!" He pointed at the Exchequer as if to accuse him of negligence. "Luminance, you can't allow him to leave this world without administering the Holy Unction. I have with me, a shipment of wine from Madrone. Let a cup of it be used for his last rites."

"Radiance, there is still hope," Ephraim began.

Tor Tomás dismissed him. "You've done quite enough, Doctor."

"But I can save him! Wine is the last thing he needs right now. He needs...."

"He doesn't need absolution? What kind of heresy is this?" He glared at Ephraim as if he had suggested they drain the high priest's blood from his veins.

"I don't mean that! Of course, we all need absolution...."

"Step aside, Doctor Medina. You aren't the only one who knows impending death when he sees it. Our brother doesn't need a physician. He needs a priest." He snapped his fingers. A Luster monk rushed forward with a goblet of wine in his hand.

"Not that." Tomás waved him off. "The rare vintage I brought from Madrone. Ah, there it is." One of his retainers stepped forth with a bottle in his hand. The man was as huge and as grim as block of granite. His black and white habit barely passed his knees. Tomás tossed the goblet's original contents to the floor and ignored the gasps of shock from the clergy. He broke the bottle's seal.

Ephraim stepped forward. "Please! Not yet, I beg you!"

Tor Tomás ignored him and poured fresh wine into the cup, topping it to the brim. "Great Sul!" he cried, holding it aloft for all to see. "Your shining son, His Brilliance Alonso de Santangél is soon to depart from this world. Let him not descend to the perpetual darkness you reserve for all sinners! Lift him up, Holy Sul! Grant him an eternal place at your side, ever radiant and ever strong, free from the stagnant waters of mortality!"

Miriam watched as the sun caught the rim of the glass. The harsh scintillation blazed like a star. Tor Tomás brought the goblet down and passed his hand over it in blessing. From where she sat, she saw a pale powder fall from his fingers. Before she could speak, the inquisitor pressed the cup to the High Solar's mouth. Alonso de Santangél raised frantic hands to prevent it from touching his lips.

Stop! she wanted to cry, but Ephraim had already done so. The Grand Inquisitor ignored him and pried the High Solar's mouth open. Alonso de Santangél had no strength to prevent it. He swallowed—one gulp, two. Wine splashed over his face and gushed from his mouth; there was no way he could not drink. He choked, gagged. In defeat, Miriam folded in on herself. The sacrament went on forever. The priests and monks looked on with distress but did nothing to prevent it.

Finally, the goblet was done. The wine had spilled down the side of the bed and had stained the sheets. Splotches of it spattered her face. She watched dully as Alonso de Santangél went into convulsions. His death was violent and hard, as one might expect for a man in his prime. She closed her eyes, couldn't block the sounds of his agony. She wanted to clutch him, send her apology flying after him: *Your Brilliance...Alonso! Forgive me! I couldn't stop him! I'm so sorry!* Her throat tightened into a knot, her limbs stiffened into stone. She couldn't afford to weep. The priests in the room watched in uneasy silence, their expressions grim. At the last moment, she opened her eyes to capture a last shred of Alonso de Santangél before he died. To her horror, he stared at her as a drowning man might, as if she were the last tenuous hold he had on life. She winced, wondering if those blue eyes registered what she was—a girl of seventeen, smitten for the first time and at the worst possible moment in her life, a girl devastated by his dying. With a violent shudder, his head slumped to the side and he gave up the ghost.

She wanted to scream. Tears streamed down her cheeks, but she made no sound. Alonso de Santangél had been stolen from her. Now, he was inextricably lost. The clergy lifted their hands and made the starburst of Sul. Their leader, His Brilliance, Alonso de Santangél, and youngest patriarch to ever have served the faithful in Granad, was dead.

Ephraim helped her rise. She stood, feeling broken, as if some part of her had fled. Ephraim looked as if he had shrunk inside his robe. He set a trembling arm about her shoulders and drew her away. They passed through the chamber like phantoms in a bone yard.

As they reached the doorway, a strident voice called out, "Stop them! Don't let them escape!"

Ephraim dug his fingers into her arm. She had been waiting for the Grand Inquisitor's shout, as had he. A tramp of footfalls rushed up behind them.

Her father stepped in front of her to protect her from the guards. "Why are you stopping us?" he demanded. "We've done nothing wrong!"

Tor Tomás confronted them. "Done nothing wrong?" he repeated. "I disagree. You bring a woman into the High Solar's presence. You allow her to approach him on his sick bed. He dies. You and your daughter are under arrest for the murder of Alonso de Santangél, High Solar of Granad."

Chapter Two: Potro

THEY WERE FORCED down a long hall and pushed down a narrow set of stairs. Unlike the main floor of the temple with its white marble facades, there was no ornamentation here. The walls looked as if they had been hewn from bedrock. They passed thick doors with barred windows, all monks' cells at one time, but judging from the moans emanating from them, not now.

"What is this place?" Miriam demanded. They had come to a large door.

"Interrogation Room." The large monk shoved her into the vault. He was a barrel of a man, at least twenty stone's weight and over six feet tall. He slammed the door behind her.

She grabbed the grill. "Where are you taking my father?" she shouted. They marched Ephraim down the hall. She strained her neck to see, but the dark swallowed him.

She spun on her heel. The chamber was large. Numerous torches had been set into the walls. Three chairs stood behind a table with quills, ink, and vellum. On the far side, a wooden pallet rested on thick legs at a forty-five degree angle. Lines of rope dangled from its sides. Across its width, slats of wood lay. Each slat terminated with a large screw.

Her heart lurched in her chest like a bird caught in a net. Not taking her eyes from the contraption, she forced herself to breathe.

A *potro*. She had never seen the damage it could inflict, but she had heard of it. As the screws tightened, the ropes bit into one's flesh. Bones broke and tendons popped. People said whatever they were told to, to relieve their pain. But why torture her if the Grand Inquisitor was already convinced of her guilt?

The answer flared in her mind like a spark on tinder. He might accuse her, but by law, the Crown required confessions. Thus, the vellum and the quills.

A tramp of boots came from down the hall. She backed away from the door as if it might attack her. The same beefy guard who had imprisoned her earlier opened it and stood to one side as the Exchequer and another priest filed in—a secretary to record her confession, no doubt. Before she could run, the guard grabbed her and marched her to stand before her judges as they took their seats. She cringed as Tor Tomás appeared in the doorway. He paused as he beheld her, his snake's eyes bright.

She flinched. The guard held her firm. His touch was anything but reassuring, but there was something unexpected in it—he wasn't the brutal thug she thought him to be. He was unhappy with the proceedings. Why? As he released her, the fleeting impression was gone. The secretary smoothed the roll of vellum, took a quill and dipped it into an inkwell. The Exchequer stared at her, his expression sour. As for Tor Tomás—he lounged in his chair, but his glance burned.

A hot flush rose up the back of her neck. His regard was not that of a cold, desiccated cleric arguing the finer points of canon law. He stared at her as the men in the square did, their lust as obvious as the bulges in their hose. She held her head high and ignored him, a foolish stance, but it hardly mattered what she did. From the faint smile touching his lips, he knew it, too.

"Your name?" The smile disappeared. He was all business now.

She met his gaze boldly. "Miriam Medina."

"Medina? A Juden name, is it not?" The Exchequer glanced between the secretary and Tor Tomás as if he had just realized it. They waited for her to confirm it.

She lifted her chin. "My family is devout. We are *Conversos*."

"As all *Conversos* claim to be. Still, your father kept the family name," Tor Tomás pointed out.

"As we are required to do, by law."

"Miriam is *also* a Juden name. If your family is so law-abiding, why did your parents choose a Juden name for you?"

She said nothing.

"Do you and your father attend the Solarium regularly?"

"We pay our tithes."

"That's not what I asked."

"We maintain a shrine to Sul at home. We can't always attend services. My father is often called to assist the sick."

"Your mother's name?"

"Mari."

"Not a Juden name. Her surname?"

"I don't know it."

All three blinked at her. "How can you not know it?" Tor Tomás asked.

"She died when I was three."

"Even so, I find it hard to believe that you wouldn't know her name. Surely, your father told you. How did she die?"

"An illness of some kind, I think."

"You think and your father's a physician." He turned to the Exchequer and secretary. "Maybe he poisoned her, too. What were the details of her death?"

"I don't know them."

He set a long finger to his lips. "Was there some scandal involved? Some reason your father would disassociate himself from her? Was she Juden, as well?"

"We are *Conversos*."

"Yes, yes. How old are you?"

She glanced away. "Seventeen."

"Seventeen and unmarried?"

"My father never arranged it." Ephraim had, but she had refused all three suits. Every time she had tried to talk to the mayor's son about the town's growth, he said her interest demeaned her—she was too pretty to be concerned about such things. The head of the Silk Guild's nephew rubbed his thighs and spoke to her breasts. The third was a widower three times her age with a daughter two years younger than she. After one too many pats on the knee, she told him he was a lecherous old panderer who should marry someone his own age and leave her alone. He called her a shrew. After that, the suits stopped. She decided she didn't need men and would remain a spinster all her life.

"You're a virgin?"

She frowned. It was no business of his.

"Answer the question!"

"Yes!"

He regarded her without saying anything. His gaze drifted to her breasts and lingered on her hips. Her face grew hot. He shifted in his seat. "How did you kill Alonso de Santangél?" His voice returned to normal.

"I didn't kill him."

"But your father did."

"My father hasn't killed anyone."

"Yet you practice medicine alongside him. Perhaps you made a mistake."

"I didn't...." A trap. "I do not practice medicine. I only help him clean."

"Perhaps you assisted in killing the High Solar."

"I didn't murder him." She regarded him through narrowed eyes. He had dropped the powder into the wine. The certainty that he had killed Alonso de Santangél resounded in her heart so loudly that it might have been a bell tolling from a tower.

"Am I allowed to ask you a question, Radiance?" She didn't wait for him to answer. "Does the god speak to you directly?" The Solarium taught that only saints heard the voice of Sul.

He nodded stiffly, unsure of where she was going. "He sends me impressions."

"Then if the god speaks to you truly, you know who really committed the High Solar's murder."

His eyes flashed. She had accused him covertly and he knew it. The Exchequer didn't notice. He waved his hand in dismissal. "This is getting us nowhere. She isn't about to confess unless we put her to the question. Set her on the *potro* and be done with it. We have a Requiem to arrange."

The small flush of victory curdled in her gut. She wanted to bolt, but the guard was behind her. Tor Tomás held up his hand and smiled coldly. Why had she been so rash? He would punish her even more severely, because of it. "Not yet, Luminance."

She swallowed. He was breathing more heavily, now. "With one so young, we must be...indulgent. By all means, go and arrange the High Solar's interment. Take Brother Diego and the guards with you. I'll finish the interrogation on my own."

Her heart hammered in her chest while her head yammered warnings. If they left, there would be no witnesses. What *were* those marks on his fingernails? He could be capable of anything. She didn't want to be alone with him.

The Exchequer fidgeted. "I wish it were so easy, Radiance. Unfortunately, we can't go. The Crown expects us to stick to proper procedure. With the High Solar's demise, it falls to me to act as spokesman for the Solarium. Granad must remain above reproach. As protocol dictates, I will stay awhile longer."

Tor Tomás bit off the words. "*If* you recall, Luminance, I established those procedures. Under their most gracious majesties, I have the authority to change them at will."

The Exchequer remained unruffled. "Of course, but revisions take time. We'd have to assign a scribe to pen them, and then send them by the fastest horse to Madrone. I wish we had that luxury, but we have a funeral Mass to perform. We can't leave Alonso for long. Not in this heat."

Tomás leaned back in his chair. "Let us continue with the questioning. Do you bear any birthmarks or unusual blemishes?" The hooded snake of some new emotion lifted behind his veneer. He was calm again.

She did bear one birthmark, a tiny dark crescent that lay between her breasts like a curl of hair. A moon mark, Ephraim had called it when she was little. She hoped her tone conveyed a lack of interest. "No."

"You're sure?"

"I am sure."

"What about tattoos?"

Tattoos were associated with forbidden knowledge. She didn't have any, but her mother had had. She scoffed. "Of course not."

He smiled at her, a serpent cornering a chick. "So, you know what tattoos are?"

"I've seen them." Why had she been so brash earlier? It would have been better to play the fool.

"Where?"

"On a man who visited my father. A sailor. The mark was infected. My father treated it."

"What did it look like?"

"I don't remember."

"How did he treat it?"

"A...a poultice."

"What kind of a poultice?"

Too great of an understanding of herbs would confirm her knowledge of medicine. Maybe it was too late for that. She had convinced him she was no fool. Drat, her blasted tongue! "I don't know."

"Again, that dreary response, you don't know. Let's leave her for now, Luminance, and speak with the father. Barto, watch her." He rose from his chair. The henchman nodded.

The three priests filed from the room and closed the door behind them. The guard was her one chance. She approached him as she might a tame bear. "Your name is Barto?"

He frowned at her and looked away. It was against the rules to speak with prisoners.

"Please. They'll hurt me. You know this." She plucked up her courage and set a hand on his forearm.

"Get off!" He pulled his arm away, but it was enough. The touch confirmed what she knew. She reminded him of someone.

"Do you have family somewhere?" If she could appeal to that sense of connection, she might turn him.

He refused to look at her. She thrust a finger at the *potro*, as if to accuse him of setting it there. "You'd let them do *that* to your sister, Barto?"

"I don't have no sister."

"Your mother, then?"

"She's dead."

"I'll be dead if you don't help me! Please! You must!"

He turned his back on her.

He was too big to straddle. She would have to talk her way around him, to coax him. Who did she remind him of? He wouldn't have a wife. As part of the Grand Inquisitor's retinue, he wouldn't have the means to maintain a mistress, either. "Please, I'm innocent, Barto. I...I am only seventeen! I'm too young to die! You must believe me! I didn't kill the High Solar!"

He looked pained.

"Please, I beg you! Do what's right and let me go."

He laughed. "And have my *cojones* torched for it?"

He might as well have slapped her. Fury found its way up from her throat like coals spewing from a pit. "So, you'd let them burn me instead? What kind of a man are you? You're a coward! You're *all* cowards! I hate you!" She flew at him, rammed his chest with her fists.

His face twisted with anger. He shoved her aside. "I ain't no coward! Shut up!"

A harsh staccato came from down the hall. Someone running. The door to the cell burst open and Tor Tomás rushed in, breathing hard.

His face shone with triumph. "Your father claims he never treated anyone with a tattoo! Which means you *lied* to me, Witch! I suspect you know all about them, that you're hiding a few yourself! Hold her, Barto. Let's see what kind of a creature she really is."

She drew back in alarm. Her heart pounded in her ears. "I don't have any tattoos!" she insisted. If they stripped her, they would find the birthmark. They would put her on the *potro*. It was only a matter of time before she told them everything—how she did more than assist Ephraim, how she prepared his potions, and worst of all, how she sensed others with a touch.

"Don't stand there like a fool! Seize her!" Tomás's words set Barto into motion. She backed away from him but kept her eyes on the two of them, looking for a break in their front. With Barto on her right and Tomás on her left, they hemmed her like hounds on a doe.

Her fingertips bumped the far wall. She made a mad dash past Barto, but Tomás lunged and caught her in his horrid hands. He swung her around and slammed her into the table. Quills flew through the air. His eyes were feral, he stank of wine. He pushed her down, grappled her breasts. She screamed and kicked him only to win a blow to her head. The pain stunned her. She choked in shock.

"What are you hiding, Witch?" His lips nuzzled her ear. His lust felt as greasy as blood. He drew back his arm and struck her again. The blow shuddered through her cheekbone. She bit her tongue. She gasped and turned her head away, fearing another strike. Something hard prodded her between the legs. She didn't have to guess what it was.

"Stop!"

She couldn't see who had shouted, but whoever it was had enough authority to stay him.

"This is highly untoward! There is no need!" The Exchequer was discomfited by the display of violence. "You can let the girl go. The doctor has confessed."

The words rang in her head. Ephraim had confessed? Why would he do such a thing? *Papa, what have you done?*

And then she knew. The answer flattened her like one of Tomás's blows. Ephraim had lied to save her. *Oh, Papa,* she thought, *you haven't spared me. You've only made things worse!*

"He's admitted his guilt, although he maintains his daughter is innocent. I see no need for us to proceed further," the Exchequer said.

"There *is* a need." Tomás's weight crushed her. She lay trapped between his arms. "She's a witch. She has a tattoo, I think. At least one, maybe more. I was about to search for it."

"Be that as it may, there's still the Mass to perform. You can leave her for now. Once we're done, you can deal with her as you see fit. She isn't going anywhere."

His mouth brushed her ear. "I want you to think of something while I'm gone," he whispered, like a lover suggesting favours. "Have you ever heard of a device called 'The Pear', little witch? It's an interesting tool, shaped like its namesake. One inserts it into bodily cavities, like so." He drew away from her and held his hands as if in prayer. And then he spread them into a 'V'.

She knew what had caused the blood stains on his fingers.

"Are you coming, Radiance?" The Exchequer waited at the doorway.

Tomás ignored him. "I can't wait to see how my toy affects you. But of course"—he touched his crotch briefly; she doubted that the Exchequer saw—"you can always beg for the alternative."

He smoothed down his habit. His intentions were clear, his plans for her delayed, not done.

Her legs threatened to give out from beneath her. As Barto locked the door behind them, she slid to her knees and lay where she fell. Her cheek throbbed where Tomás had struck her. She barely noticed it, chilled by his words. He would return in a few hours and rape her, perhaps do worse things. She turned her face into the flagstones, choked to keep from crying, and utterly failed.

Chapter Three: Grimoire

SHE ALLOWED HERSELF ten minutes of misery before she sat up and wiped her face. Crying solved nothing. There had to be a way out, a way to escape. If Ephraim had confessed, what had they done to him?

She glanced at the *potro* and stood shakily, hating the thing. Now that she was alone, it didn't terrify her as much as make her want to tear it apart, kick it to kindling, and smash it to pieces against the walls. She felt the same way about Tomás. She hated him more than she thought she was capable of hating anyone. He would rape her, of that she was sure. He had set 'The Pear' in her mind, a mental assault, but he would use it on her, too. He was convinced she bore tattoos. He had wanted to check her for them. Why? She thought of her mother, dead, so long ago.

Mari had borne three tattoos: one on her belly and two on the soles of her feet. They had been placed to be hidden from public view. Mari had warned her to never speak of them.

But why, Mama? They're so pretty!

Some people think them witch marks, my Miri.

Are you a witch, Mama?

Some would say so.

Her parents had shared a smile. Most people in Esbaña considered the Diaphani a race of witches. Was that why Tomás wanted to search her for tattoos? Because she looked Diaphani, as her mother had been?

They were a strange folk, her mother's people. Witches or no, they kept to their own. As a young girl, she'd seen them in the markets, but she couldn't remember seeing them of late. Had they been targeted by the church, like the Juden and the Moori? Once Tomás returned, it wouldn't take long before he forced the truth from her about her mother. He would also learn of the grimoire.

She'd found the book when she was eight. Ephraim had hidden it in a false bottom beneath the lowest shelf of his wardrobe. She had never confessed her discovery of it to him, nor had he ever told her of its existence. She had read it from cover to cover. Much of it showed how to cut tattoos for beauty, strength, and speed, for curing diseases of the flesh, bowels, bones, and teeth, for the correction of pregnancy and birth complications. A smaller portion dealt with spiritual gates, tattoos that enhanced communication with the Ancestors and the Divine. The smallest section spoke of dark magic, including the resurrection of the dead.

Superstitious nonsense, but damning evidence, even so. Come morning, Tomás would send guards to their house to confiscate everything she and Ephraim owned. They would find the book. The Holy Office wouldn't need their confessions. The grimoire would be proof enough of both witchcraft and murder.

She rubbed her arms. Why dwell on that now? A better use of her time would be to plan her way out of here, to talk her way past Barto.

But what if tattoos actually had power? A ridiculous idea, but judging from his interest, Tomás thought they did.

She went quite still. Was it possible they might work? She dismissed it, but the idea came again, as persistent as a fly. *What if...*she hardly dared think it...*what if the grimoire is my way out of this disaster?* What if she resurrected Alonso de Santangél? He could clear her and Ephraim. He would accuse Tomás, his real murderer.

For a long moment, she considered it. And then she dismissed it with a futile laugh. She was unraveling under the stress of imprisonment, eventual rape, and torture. As for tattoos, they hadn't saved her mother.

She rose and peered through the grill, banged her hand on the door. "Barto!" she shouted. "You have to let me out of here!"

She waited for him to appear, but he failed to show.

"Papa? Can you hear me?" Her voice bounced off walls.

She leaned against cold stone. With no other options presenting themselves, she was tempted to pray, but she had never found the faith for it. There was little point in turning hypocrite now. She didn't believe in Sul. She didn't believe in her mother's dark goddess, Lys, either.

The torches sputtered out, except for the lone one that lit the outer hall. She sat in darkness until a shadow appeared at the grill of her door. She shrank against the table, afraid that Tomás had come to finish his business with her. Barto opened the door instead. He beckoned. "Come."

So she had affected him! She didn't hesitate but ran to his side. He drew her from the cell. At his touch, she felt a fierce protection stir.

"My father," she said.

He shook his head. "Not him. Just you."

"But I can't leave him!"

"Look, you stupid girl." He propelled her forward. "I'm going to tell them you bewitched me. That's the truth. You have. I'll earn a whipping, but I'll take it. You want the chance I'm giving you? Your choice—either you go, or you stay for rape and torture."

He would take her back to her cell if she became difficult. They wasted precious time. She would have to leave Ephraim and find a way to save him later.

"Maybe Sul will save him, maybe he won't. Strange things have been known to happen."

"All right!" she said, terrified that someone might find them bickering in the hall. The grimoire was her only option. Madness!

The upper halls were vacant. Barto had timed her escape well. Most of the priests were busy in the nave, arranging the funeral Mass that would take place later that night. Even so, he was no fool. He led her along a circuitous route. As they passed from the Solarium proper, they skirted the cloister and entered a common room. A monk toiled there, his back to them as he stoked a great hearth. They skirted him and descended a narrow set of stairs that led to a low arched entry. Barto pushed her though the door. She found herself in a walled garden. Beyond it, a tanning shed stood beside a barn.

He pointed at an iron gate. "That's the way out. The Exchequer won't send the assessors to your house 'til morning. Go home, collect your valuables. Leave Granad tonight." He gave her a cautionary glance and shut the door.

She turned and fled.

She didn't remember how she found her way home. As she ran past white limed walls and down narrow, cobbled streets, she was hardly aware of the men who watched her pass from the shadows of their doorways. Overhead, their wives gossiped from balconies, but all she heard was mention of tattoos and grimoires. *Strange things have been known to happen,* Barto had said. Was that a sign? She didn't believe in signs. But if so, why was she running to find the book?

At her own iron-studded gate, she paused to catch her breath and listen. No sound emanated from the *carmen* so she fumbled with her keys and unlocked the doors. The courtyard was empty. She crossed it and entered the house. It was also dark and quiet, as she and Ephraim had left it.

With trembling hands, she lit a candle and climbed the stairs to the second floor. She made her way down the long hall that ended in Ephraim's bedroom. She set the candle on his night table and opened the heavy doors of his wardrobe.

She pushed his robes aside and felt for the groove in the bottom that indicated the false floor. She pressed a corner and the bottom lifted. Inside, cool steel met her fingers. She lifted the strong box from its place and opened the lid with shaking hands.

Inside, a strange collection of objects lay. The top half of the box was composed of wooden compartments with glass vials. Most of them were empty, save for one that held a half-full bottle of ink. Another cubicle held a small pouch containing needles and knives. She ignored these and set the wooden screen aside.

Beneath the screen, the grimoire lay, bound in burgundy leather. The cover had been embossed with a silver moon and opposing crescents. Inside the moon, an L-shaped hinge had been cut. It looked like a door with a latch.

She held her breath, remembering the first time she had opened the book. At eight, she had been inclined to believe in magic, but not now. Except, here she sat, with the grimoire on her lap. How to justify that? On page one, her mother had written:

> "I, Inara, Gate Keeper, dedicate my service to the Holy Pair.
> May they bless these Portals to enhance, heal, or ward."

For years, she had wondered who Inara Gate Keeper was. It finally dawned on her that Inara had been her mother's hidden, Diaphani name.

Beneath the dedication, Mari had penned:

> "Light to illuminate, Darkness to protect.
> Let no evil mar their effect."

Light and darkness. Her mother's references to Sul and Lys. Unlike the Solarium, the Diaphani revered both goddess and god. They were equally important, although the gypsies tended to favour the goddess. Miriam closed her eyes. She didn't believe in the gods. There were no Ancestors or life after death. But if that were so, why this inner drive? There was no explaining it, other than her need to save Ephraim. It went beyond logic, although reason still held its sway. She couldn't storm the Solarium's gates. No army awaited her command. There was nothing left, but to attempt the impossible.

"All right," she said. She felt ridiculous that she spoke to the dead at all. "If this is you, Mama, pressing me to save Papa, I'll try. But I don't think it'll work."

She turned to the last page of the grimoire and read the final entry: A Marking for the Resurrection of the Dead.

The resurrection spell was a *magnum magicae*—a great work—done under the direst of circumstances.

*Before attempting any great work, one must dedicate one's life to
the Goddess, her mother wrote. Only then will the magic take.
Lys is our divine Mother, our Protectoress and Guide. Without
her protection, there is likelihood of complications.*

Miriam shifted the grimoire between her knees. Mari didn't
elaborate what those complications were. She did, however, provide
a cross-reference as to how one might perform a dedication. Miriam
flipped to the aforementioned page.

Allegiance involved a tattoo, self-inflicted. The sigil was identical to
the rune on the book's cover—the full moon symbol with its crescents,
as well as the L-shaped key. She was expected to offer her life and
service to the goddess while performing the ritual.

In marking herself, she declared herself a priestess.

Tor Tomás already suspected her of witchcraft. One more mark,
natural or no, would make little difference. Ephraim had to be
rescued. If the tattoo served that purpose, then so be it. Where to
place it, though? The grimoire proposed a number of spots on her
body—all energy foci, it seemed: the middle of her forehead, the base
of her throat, over her heart or solar plexus, other places more private
and hidden. Her mother cautioned prudence, especially if the tattoo-
bearer dealt with non-Diaphani, those not of the blood. That same
old caution.

She freed her blouse from her skirt and bared her torso. She found a
knife and ran its edge through the candle flame to purify it. She lifted
it away and stared down at her middle. Now that she had come to it,
the idea of cutting herself turned her stomach to mush. It wasn't like
cutting a chicken for supper. She had to lay the blade against her own
skin, press the edge in so that it sliced through. She set the blade aside
and lay on the floor. Maybe it was better to place the tattoo elsewhere.
The idea of carving her forehead made her gag. She couldn't imagine
slicing her throat. Her sternum was not an option, too close to the
heart and lungs. There was nothing for it but to carve her stomach.
The skin was thicker there, at least three layers over muscle before the
blade struck her gut.

What if I close my eyes and just do it? She could feel her way, but there
was no telling if she copied the tattoo correctly. She had to watch

herself. A mirror, then. She stood on shaky feet and faced the glass in the wardrobe. She braced her feet and steadied herself.

With her blouse off and her upper half bared, she looked like a wild woman—the witch of whom she was accused. Her nipples stood erect from the night's chill or from fear. Her hair looked as if it had been tossed by a tempest, inky and storm-bound. The knife glinted in her hand.

She set the point above her navel.

With a sharp stab, she felt the flesh give. Her gorge rose into her throat. A mad woman stood in the mirror, gutting herself. Blood dribbled from the knife's point, drawing lines down her stomach and staining her skirt. Her vision greyed. She drew in a deep breath to clear her head. The cut burned like acid. She clenched her teeth and drew the knife up in a curve.

A strange coldness overtook her—mild shock, she knew. The grey receded but her head still felt light. She forced herself to breathe and managed to complete the first circle. As she finished it, she had an awful moment of imagining her intestines spilling through the hole. Her knees buckled; the temptation to drop her head between them was overwhelming. She forced herself to draw in a lungful of air. If she stopped now, she wouldn't finish. She had to keep going.

Her breath came harsh and fast. *The cuts are superficial. There's no need to panic,* she told herself over and over. The repetition helped clear her head. She finished the first crescent and then the second. Despite the blood, her replicas were good. She felt a rush of pride. If she could cut herself, she was capable of anything. She sliced the last incision—the lock to open the door. As she finished, her legs rebelled. She fell in a heap to the rug.

She was half done. She allowed herself a brief moment of calm and then unstoppered the bottle of ink. With a corner of bed sheet, she wiped the blood from her belly, then dabbed ink into her wounds. There was still the matter of the dedication. She didn't have the energy to make it flowery.

"Serve me and I'll serve you." She was too drained to care about a lack of respect. She didn't believe in Lys, but she was willing to be wrong. She gaped at the ceiling, trying to imagine the goddess hovering there. "I'll do whatever you require of me, as long as you bring the High Solar back to life. He has to save my father."

She had honoured her side of the bargain. Now it was Lys's turn. No divine voice spoke to her. She didn't expect one to.

She covered the tattoo with more cloth. Holding her belly, she read again, what was required to resurrect the dead. When her strength came back, she stripped the sheet into shreds and wrapped her torso. She had to reach the town's catacombs before the funerary entourage did.

She glanced out Ephraim's bedroom window. Over the tiled roofs of the town, the moon was rising in a gibbous crescent. At the Solarium, the Requiem would be underway. She had an hour at most.

She set her mother's grimoire in Ephraim's traveling bag and slung the pouch over her shoulder. She headed downstairs and retrieved what coin they had, as well as cheese and bread from the larder. She threw a cloak over her shoulders and drew the cowl over her face. It hurt to walk. The tattoo burned as she moved. She ignored it, stalked through the courtyard to the gate. She opened it and locked the door behind her. It was important to leave the house intact for as long as she could. As she set her hand on the iron latch for the last time, her throat tightened.

It had been a good house. She'd grown up, here. She and Papa had shared it, she'd learned to cook in it, had tended its garden. It had been their sanctuary.

It's just a house. She hated the lump in her throat. *There are more important things.* Her eyes stung. She set her forehead against the cool metal. *Goodbye,* she whispered.

Then she turned and hurried down the empty street. She rounded the corner and didn't look back.

Chapter Four: The Hill of Cats

THE MOON SHONE on the solemn procession as it emerged from the town's South Gate. At the head of the entourage, four black chargers pulled the death carriage. Behind it, Tor Tomás rode on a white stallion alongside the Exchequer and members of the Inquisitional Guard. Next, the sun priests marched in their habits of gold and white with temple banners waving and torches flickering in the night. The mayor followed on horseback, accompanied by his deputies and the heads of the guilds. Finally, in a ragged formation and bringing up the rear, straggled the townsfolk of Granad.

Miriam darted from where she had been waiting beneath a shaggy yew. The tree provided an excellent vantage point, but now that the procession was at the gate, she couldn't risk being seen. She retreated to the far side of the Hill and hid behind a tall tombstone. Only those who could afford it were buried in the mausoleum inside the bowels of the Hill. On the mount's crest, a large doorway to the catacombs shone like bone in the moonlight.

The jangle of bits and the crunch of wheels made her startle with every sound. As the horses' hooves scraped the gravel, she peeked from behind her headstone. The coach had stopped at the tomb's archway. The priests and the town's luminaries fanned out. Six Luster monks lifted Alonso de Santangél from his place of honour and hoisted his pallet atop their shoulders. With their hands clasped, Tor Tomás and the Exchequer followed the corpse bearers inside. She shivered, thinking of Tomás's fingers. She would never see a pair of praying hands in quite the same way again.

As the townspeople drew near her hiding place, she rose from her spot but kept her face hidden inside her cowl. No one paid her any mind. She was just another mourner come to pay her final respects. Out of the corner of her eye, she caught glimpses of the Hill's cats as they slipped behind statues or crept along branches. Their eyes flashed green and gold. Many of the town's people warded themselves.

Finally, Tor Tomás, the Exchequer, and the attendant priests emerged from the depths like grubs to the light. Without a word, Tomás mounted his horse and retreated down the Hill. The Exchequer and the death coach lumbered after him and the crowd trailed behind. Miriam returned to her yew tree and watched the dwindling multitude. No one looked back up the Hill. As far as the entourage was concerned, the dead kept company with the dead.

I'm a ghost, she thought.

The middle doorway of the Sun Arch was illuminated by guttering torchlight. A few brands had been left in their brackets to burn until they died. She steeled herself, fought down the old fear. There was nothing in there that could hurt her. She ran for the archway. Past the portico, a narrow stair fell. She forced herself down it and found another torch burning beside a heavy, iron-studded door. It would be darker beyond it. Small, enclosed spaces always were.

She hated the fact that she was already trembling. It was a ridiculous fear, this terror of being trapped in the dark. It didn't make sense; why should she suffer it? Would the girls she had scoffed at as a child laugh at her, now? She pulled off a shoe. If she propped the door, the light from the torch would show her the way out. She yanked it open and wedged the shoe in place. The murk was darker here, but bracing the door helped.

She allowed her eyes to adjust. In niches honeycombing the walls, bodies lay in stages of decomposition, their skulls and jaws gaping against clavicles, the threads of silk and gold dusty amid the bones. The room smelled of corpse-rot. She covered her nose and took a step. As she did, a lithe shape darted past one of the skulls. Her heart leapt into her mouth. She bolted for the door.

Stop! she told herself. *You have to do this!* Her hands shook, her heart pounded. *Besides, it was only a cat.* The idea of rats upset her. She forced herself to go on. She passed through a similar chamber, and then into another, much the same as the last. Another set of stairs led to a larger door with the starburst of the Solarium upon it. The smell of death was bolder here, putrid and cloying. The torch above her head guttered low.

Barbs of fear clawed their way up her back once again. She swallowed and focused on the door, set her palms upon it. It felt sturdy enough. It had barred this place for hundreds of years. It wasn't likely to collapse. She pushed on it, and it opened smoothly as if well-oiled. The light, however, seemed loath to seep past it. She tamped down her fear and stepped into blackness. An overwhelming stench assaulted her—a mixture of rot, lavender, and myrrh. She clapped a sleeve against her nose and took long, slow breaths through her mouth. They helped, but not much. Other than the sound of her heart thumping in her ears, the vault was silent. Her eyes watered. She choked again and fumbled for the candle she had stowed in her bag.

It took a few failures before she managed to light it from the outside torch. She cupped the tiny flame in her hand and returned to the final resting place of His Brilliance, Alonso de Santangél, High Solar of Granad.

He lay on a dais in the middle of the tomb. The monks had dressed him in a chasuble of white and gold. He was handsome even in death, although he smelled. She waved that unworthy thought aside. His eyes had been so blue. He looked as if he slept.

She propped her candle beside him and studied his face in the soft light. He resembled a saint, though no saint had the right to be so perfect. Had he ever wanted to marry? Had he not liked women? She didn't think much of the women she knew either, so she could understand it.

"I'm so sorry, Alonso," she said, testing his name upon her lips. She liked how it sounded. It was like music, like the wind soughing through the trees. *Ah-lon-so.*

What would life with him have been like? What if he hadn't been a priest, but a suitor...a husband? She would have lain with him, have shared his bed. He would have touched her, caressed her with as much sensitivity as a potter forming clay. Every caress would have linked them because of her gift. She would have felt what he felt. His desire would have set her alight. But now, only Death embraced him. And even if she brought him back....

She touched his cheek. His skin was cold and moist. She ignored her dismay and traced the line of his jaw. Strong and firm. A bit of stubbornness there, but what man was worth his mettle without it? She couldn't abide weak men any more than she could stupid ones. She gazed at his face and knew he'd been neither. Such a loss. She withdrew her hand and retrieved the knife and ink from the pouch at her side. She poised the blade above his forehead.

"Forgive me, Alonso. I must do this," she said.

If it worked, she didn't know for how long he'd remain animate or in what shape his mind would be. It seemed a cruel thing to do, to bring him back into a poisoned body, but if he did suffer, she hoped he would understand that his pains were to save an innocent man. He would want that. The town's people had spoken well of him. He'd been a good High Solar. All of Granad had turned out for his interment, something unheard of.

She recalled her mother's instructions:

Each letter of the Diaphani alphabet is not only a letter but a symbol of power. When you incise the letter with intention, you invoke divine change. The first letter you must cut is Dalet, which represents the Four States two for the goddess, and two for the god. As you draw Dalet, focus on the elements of water, air, fire, and earth. When you add the ink, you call the Ancestors to witness. Dalet is drawn like this.

She hated to cut him, but it was necessary. As she incised his forehead, she imagined flame, smoke, water, and mud. She muttered *Dalet* and inked the tattoo.

The floor shifted. Grey flooded the edges of her vision. In alarm, she grabbed the edge of Alonso's dais to right herself. Wafts of blackness coalesced before her eyes and dissipated into shreds. She fought for air. The hair on her arms prickled as if from sudden heat. Her mother hadn't mentioned these reactions—why were they occurring? Her vision cleared. Her sense of balance came back. Shock, she decided. How could she not be affected as she cut Alonso? In desecrating his body, she defiled her own.

The next letter is Lamet, its symbol the whip. Lamet is the goad of the righteous. Upon reanimating its flesh, the corpse will enforce its will. You must not allow this. As you ink the tattoo, use your right hand to do so, while your left mimes the lash. Lamet is carved like this.

To Miriam, *Lamet* looked like a hook, a disturbing image. She had to slice the glyph over Alonso's heart. Hooks bound the caught with the catcher, didn't they? An unsettling thought, but it made sense. She pulled at his surplice, but the heavy weight of it made it difficult to shift. She lifted it to cover his face and fought her sense of propriety. Surely, if she was going to undress him, he had a right to see. She dismissed her qualms. He was dead. He wouldn't care. When he was mobile, she would arrange his robes properly. Beneath the surplice, he wore a gown of one thread with no obvious seams. She slashed at it and then pushed the two halves aside to lay his chest bare. She paused to admire his form.

In death, his skin resembled cold marble. He was as beautiful as a sculpted angel. She took a deep breath and cut the second sigil into his waxy chest, thinking of how she had cut her own. They were joined now, in a macabre wedding of her making. Mouthing *Lamet*, she blotted the ink and mimed the whip.

This time, an icy breeze crossed the tomb's threshold, squeezing the air from her lungs. Her vision gave out completely. Some part of her knew she remained at Alonso's side. The odor of death intensified, coiling about her like a snake. She fought for breath and waited for her vision to return. If this was the magic manifesting, she should be reassured it was working. *Steady,* she told herself. Never again, would she dismiss those things that seemed a fool's fancy. Again, her eyes cleared, but she still saw patches of grey. With a shaking hand, she lifted the knife for the third pass.

The third letter, Vev, is the final letter; its symbol, the crossroads. Here is where the living meets the dead. Vev brings us to what we know and what we need to know. It is the end of one path and the beginning of another. It is cut like this.

The last letter resembled a scythe. Death's mark. The symbol of complete and utter transformation.

She fought for calm, forced her fingers to remain steady. The last thing she needed was for her nerves to ruin the sigil. She suspected she verged on panic. An hour ago, she hadn't believed in magic. Now, she wasn't at all certain what would happen once the spell took. Would he remember her, recall their locked gaze as he died? Had he felt the connection between them, as she had? Would he be angry with her for bringing him back? She had to trust Inara, had to believe that her mother would not have included such a working without mentioning further precautions. *I've done what I must*, she reminded herself. *I've dedicated myself to Lys and have followed Mama's directions to the letter. There is no stopping this now.*

Together, these three, Dalet, Lamet, and Vev, form the word Delev, meaning doorway, her mother had written. *Upon the body of the corpse, the word creates a portal for the spirit to return to the world of matter. From Dalet you will call it, through Lamet, you will hold it. Through Vev, it will answer to your purpose.*

Sweating profusely, she lifted the knife for the final tattoo. She could barely see Alonso beneath her. The last incision had to be made above his navel. A dark presence squeezed her now, threatening to blind her, drown her senses. Her skin prickled. Her imagination played tricks. The vault felt crowded as if invisible presences bore witness to what she did. Perhaps Alonso watched her as he approached life's brink. With her heart pounding in her ears, she cut the final letter, dribbled the last of the ink. *Vev*, she muttered. Ink welled over her hand.

Now, to call him. She set one hand back on his forehead, the other she left where it was. "Through these three, *Dalet, Lamet,* and *Vev,* I summon you, Alonso de Santangél, High Solar of Granad. I have opened the doorway, *Delev.* You will leave behind the world of spirit. You will return to the mortal sphere and answer to my need. So say I, Miriam Medina, disciple of the Lys. Come!"

As the last word left her lips, a dazzling brilliance burst from the darkness, knocking her to the floor. She cried out, startled that it would burn her, but she felt no pain. Instead, she'd been thrown into a vast, dark space, so immense that she couldn't determine the end of it. In the centre of that place lay a colossal, boiling star.

Within its flaming core, an ember sparked. She watched as it grew, turning into a fiery worm. The maggot thrashed on the curdled surface. Each wrench of its body sent a surge of radiance speeding toward her. As the first ring touched her, the phosphorescence burned like acid. She cried out in shock.

Her cry triggered a metamorphosis in the worm.

The lump-like body swelled, grew a head, two arms, and two legs. Soon, it bore a flaming chasuble and miter. The face was bloated and molten. With burning coals for eyes, it turned its face in her direction and marked her. Seeing her, it lifted its fiery arms and sped toward her with dizzying speed.

Whatever the thing was, it wasn't Alonso. She spun about to flee, but there was nowhere to run. Her feet found no purchase. She turned to face the monster and shrieked finding it upon her. She held up her hands to fend it off, but to no avail. As they collided, the impact knocked her senseless.

When she returned to consciousness, the fiery sun was gone. She floated, a lone ember in the dark. But there was also a new taint upon her, like that of soiled flesh. The stench of it settled into her nose, seeped into her pores. In dismay, she found herself overcome with the need to weep. She burst into sobs, each cry wracking her body with shudders of wretchedness. A small part of her knew this wasn't her battle, not her despair.

Stop! She attempted to gain control of her crying. She took a ragged breath. Words formed upon her lips.

Where am I?

Horror flooded her. The voice wasn't hers, but a man's. It was deep and resonant in spite of the fear that threatened it from the edges. Unfamiliar thoughts burst into her mind, bright shafts in the darkness—*I'm not burning! The torment is gone!* Then a revelation—he was in *her* body, not his.

No! she cried, crushed by the certainty of it. Life coursed into her limbs. She toppled and fell. He plummeted alongside her. They were two chicks dropping from the same nest.

They landed with a bone-jarring crash. Every part of her felt pummeled, bruised. She tasted blood and spat, disgusted at finding herself doing so. Her hands cradled her arms and brushed her chest. They cupped her breasts as if surprised to find mounds there. Mortification flooded her. She thrust them aside. The effort left her breathless. There wasn't room enough for the two of them.

Gods! What new madness is this? His attention shifted to her crotch. He explored new land.

Stop! she shouted.

He flinched, surprised to hear her voice. *Who are you? Show yourself!*

There was no way to show herself. He was in her, and she, in him. They were two souls locked together in the dark. She pushed at his presence. He formed a shield.

Don't crowd me! she insisted. He withdrew slightly, but only because one did that for women. If this was one.

Are you a succubus? Disapproval flowed through him like mud.

No.

What then?

I...my name is Miriam Medina.

Who the blazes...wait! I know you! You were at my bedside! Are you some kind of a witch?

Was she? One badly wrought spell didn't qualify her as one. *I don't think so.*

How did I come to be here?

His tone grated. He was too imperious, too demanding, as if she were the servant and he the master. To be fair, he was also upset and confused. *I brought you forth from death. You were supposed to animate your own body, not mine.*

So, you're a witch after all, but a bad one. You did this, why?

My father has been accused of your murder. I need you to intercede on his behalf.

He gave a short bark of laughter. *Oh, I will. Have no doubt about that.*

Good. The first thing you have to do is to reanimate your corpse.

He laughed even harder. There was an edge to it, like broken glass. *I don't think so. I'm not keen to relive that experience again.*

But you have to! For my father's sake! If you don't, he'll die!

No. There's only one thing I have to do, and that's to kill Tomás. I'll make it quick though, unlike my death which was slow and torturous.

He was mad. She could feel it now. His thoughts fluttered like birds in a fire. They crisped and burnt as he considered and discarded the ways he could murder the Grand Inquisitor. She caught an image of his hands cracking Tomás's skull. He would finish the job the scar had begun, expose the brain and let it slide like egg though his fingers. She gagged. *You aren't in your own body, anymore! Are you aware of this?*

Yes. You're a woman. I wear your guise. It can't be helped.

You'll send me to my death! I just escaped from the Solarium. Even now, the Grand Inquisitor searches for me!

Does he? That could work.

It won't work! If he catches me, he'll kill us both!

Not if I kill him first.

Did he expect them to return to the Solarium, seek out Tomás and finish him as easily as they might attend a Mass? She wanted no part of it. She would be the one making the killing strike, not Alonso de Santangél. And even if they managed it, she would still meet her death on a stake. The priests would be convinced that not only had she killed their High Solar, but the Grand Inquisitor as well.

She lunged at him as if she might push him from their perch. Again, that iron will held her in its unrelenting grip. She could no more move him than she could the temple. Alonso de Santangél might have been forced into death by poison, but he would not be manipulated again.

You are my one chance. His voice ground like iron filings on skin. *He won't get away with my murder. He takes an eye, I take a tooth. I shall have my vengeance.* She took a faltering step.

What kind of a man are you? She fought him as best she could. *You're supposed to be a priest, a man of the God!* Her shin slammed into a niche. Pain bloomed in her knee. Bones rattled down the wall. Alonso paused, but only for a moment before they were on the move again. Why had she ever found him attractive? He was a monster, all the more so because his evil hid behind a beautiful façade. He was no better than any of the other men she had known, except he was dead, and mad, and bent on using her to commit murder. Unless, of course, Tomás killed them first.

As they maneuvered though the tomb, it dawned on her that her fear of the dark had dissipated, replaced by a new terror.

They came to the first door. It opened onto the landing that led to the long stair. The torch had guttered out. She ascended the stairs to the outer world. Moonlight spilled about them in a cool, serene glow. The night seemed peaceful despite the thumping of her heart.

She wished she had never attempted the magic, had never found her mother's damned book.

Chapter Five: Luck or Madness

THE SOUTH GATE was locked for the night. To her relief, Alonso didn't force her to hammer on the gatehouse to demand entry. The guards wouldn't treat a lone woman with respect. Instead, they paused outside the town walls while he rifled through her memories like a fishwife counting the catch. She hated every moment of it, resented him for using her in the way he did. He ignored her anger and forced her to a section of the wall where she had played as a child. The hand and footholds where small, but she managed to climb. A wind sprang up. It began to rain. By the time she clambered over the top, she was drenched.

They made their way through the lower tiers of the town. The streets were quiet. No one wanted to be out in the wet. Even so, he kept her to the shadows and directed her along less traveled routes. They passed through the merchant's quarter, then past affluent streets where candles guttered behind streaked windows. After half an hour, they came to the temple grounds. She leaned against an oak tree and caught her breath. Above her, branches flailed. The rain pelted down. She drooped with exhaustion.

Once again, he goaded her.

I can't!

You will.

They'll catch me!

Move.

I hate you! You're no better than he is! She meant Tomás. She threw herself to the ground and clawed at the mud.

I'll forgive you for that, considering how upset you are. Get up! You won't fight me on this. Once again, she stood. Her hands and face were filthy, the grimoire's pouch, sodden.

How do you plan to get me inside? She wiped her dirty palms on her cloak. *Women aren't allowed in this part of the Solarium. Or did you forget?*

Of course not. Before them, was a low arched door. *That's the back of the Refectory. No one's about at this time of night. We enter and find our way. I know these buildings intimately.*

How comforting. Someone has to be watching.

No. The succentor is an old man. He'll be asleep, along with the rest of them.

She stumbled for the door. It opened with little effort. She stepped out of the rain and found herself in a corner of a dining hall. It was dimly lit with cresset lamps. On the far side, a black archway yawned. She headed for it, passing empty tables. Beyond the arch, a wide staircase climbed to a second level. She balked, guessing where they were bound.

I can't go up there!

You will.

She fought him all the way. Her feet were deadweights, although she was not so stupid as to make a sound. Her pulse pounded in her temples, she felt sick. At the top of the stairs, she paused, thankful he had the sense to wait before pushing her into the dormitory. Monks snored inside.

On the wall inside the door is a line of pegs. The brothers hang their robes there, so as not to crease them while sleeping.

She stepped through the doorway. In organized rows, men slumbered on low cots. The closest monk lay no more than six feet from her. He snorted and turned on his side. Without taking her eyes from him, she lifted a brown habit from its place and drew it over her head. A pool of light appeared at the doorway.

She flattened her back against the wall and held her breath. An elderly monk entered the room with a cresset lamp in his hand. He paused for a moment to get his bearings, and then he walked past her, limping. He turned his head this way and that.

She didn't move.

Brother Francesco! What is he doing up at this hour?

She had no answer for it, prayed that the old man would not see her. He continued on his doddering way, peering at those who slumbered at his knees.

When he gets to the far end, slip out the door.

He didn't need to compel her. As the monk reached the last row of sleepers, she grabbed a second habit from its peg and fled the dormitory. She flew down the stairs.

What's the second habit for?

My father! Remember him?

You've only two hands. You don't have room for it.

I am not tossing it aside! He'll also need a disguise!

He didn't force her to discard it. She tucked it into the pouch with the grimoire. They hurried down another long hall and into a kitchen. At the far end, a great hearth lay banked. She headed for a side table. Upon it, a clutter of utensils lay.

I want this done quickly and well.

She reached for a cleaver.

No! She pushed at him with all the inner force she could muster. They blundered against the table's edge. She lost her balance and wind-milled into the cutlery. A knife sliced her hand. Blood welled from her fingers. He swore an oath no priest should utter.

What right do you have? she demanded.

I have every right! I'm an important person, the High Solar of Granad. Tomás murdered me, not you! He will answer for it!

She hid the knife in her sleeve, then stumbled into a buttery where she retrieved a flagon of wine. *He'll have taken residence in my chamber,* he said tightly. *We're going there. Don't fight me. If you do, we risk discovery.*

I should have left you for dead! You're a monster!

I am what I am. My regrets for disappointing you.

Gods, had he sensed her earlier attraction? She sincerely hoped not. In any event, he disgusted her now. *What about my father?*

First things first.

She felt as futile as a canary battering granite. It was hard to understand him. When he didn't burn with anger, he was as cold as stone.

They made their way down a number of corridors. They passed through one of the cloister's promenades and came to the wing that held his old quarters. Luck was with them. They encountered no one, but she started every time they passed a pillar and her shadow flickered upon the walls. At his prompt, she released the folds of fabric from about the knife. She paused at the ornate vestibule outside his suite. From within their gilded frames, saints watched her accusingly.

Inside.

She opened the gilded door and slipped through, expecting to see Tomás rise from his bed. A lump lay in the middle of the sheets. She held her breath, set the flagon on the floor. They would no longer need it as an excuse.

One wrong move and her nemesis would awaken. Step by step, she drew closer to where Tomás lay. She doubted if he slept soundly. A man like him never would. He'd grab her, rape her, and then call for the guards to imprison her with her father. She didn't want to touch him. Her skin crawled as if from leeches. Fear turned her vision grey.

Kill him and it's over!

With a small cry, she plunged the knife into the lump and struck mattress. No body lay beneath the sheets.

She doubled over, clutched the knife. Her heart felt as if it might hammer itself free from her chest. For a moment, Alonso said nothing, although his sense of impotence was scorching. *He'll be in the dungeons, then,* he replied, furious with their failure. *More difficult for us.*

Once again, she was hauled to her feet. She retrieved the flagon of wine as an afterthought—his, not hers. *Stow the knife, Miriam,* he said. She didn't argue. All she could think of was her father. If Tomás was in the cells, he would know of her escape by now. He would be interrogating Ephraim. She felt sick, imagining what her father's agony on the *potro* might be.

They were half-way down a wide corridor when the temple's bells began to toll. The clangor forced her from her daze. *What's happening?* she asked him.

I suspect they've discovered you're missing. Step to the side and keep your head down.

She hid her face and pressed against a wall. Priests appeared from doorways. Monks milled about. A few began to run down the hallway while others shuffled in the direction of the nave. A troop of the Inquisitional Guard pounded past her, causing the monks to scurry like flustered hens. Fear for Ephraim and fear for herself battled for prominence.

Ignore the guards and keep moving.

She made her way to the stair leading to the cells and kept her eyes averted from any who ran in the opposite direction. As she reached the lower level, the dungeon was empty of clergy and guards, although the odd moan still emanated from behind thick doors. The door to her old cell stood open. She skirted past it.

In the next hall, another door stood ajar. If anyone remained inside, it might be because they didn't have the wherewithal to leave. Dread shook her like a terrier on a rat. She ran for the door, needing to see.

Ephraim was inside. He was naked and bound to a *potro*. Beneath the device, pools of blood stained the flagstones. The ropes had cut his skin to shreds. His eyes were open, but they were glazed. She ran into the room, dropped the knife and flagon. The pitcher burst into shards. As she released the *potro's* screws, the ropes slackened and Ephraim slid into her arms. His agony flowed across her body in rivers of pain. She nearly fainted from the strain of it.

Great Sul! I never would have.... Alonso also felt it. They aren't supposed to draw blood! I didn't invite them here! I was trying to get rid of Tomás and his ilk!

She ignored him. Ephraim stared at a lone candlestick flickering on the table beside them. The abrasions across his chest were the worst. His breathing was laboured, shallow.

"I've brought you a robe, Papa. I'll put it on you, and then you must lean on me."

"Miri?" He focused on her.

"You have to stand. Do you think you can do that?"

He nodded. As she lifted him, they nearly swooned from the effort.

"Two of my ribs, I think," he said.

She nodded, fumbled for the robe she had stowed in her bag. "Once we have the habit on you, we'll take our time." A lie, but he needed whatever hope she could offer. "We'll look like two monks."

"How did you escape?"

"I'll tell you when it's safe." She draped the habit over his head, held him as they navigated the neck and sleeves. He gasped, stared at something over her shoulder.

"Well, isn't this *cozy?*"

She spun about, recognizing the clipped tone before beholding the speaker. Tor Tomás smiled at them from the doorway. Barto towered at his back.

"Shut the door behind me, Barto," he said softly, not taking his gaze from her. "You needn't stay."

Barto avoided meeting her eyes. The heavy door clanged shut behind Tomás.

Miriam stepped in front of Ephraim. The knife lay where she had dropped it. She glanced at it. Tomás read the intention in her eyes.

"It's a mistake to think you can overpower me, but I'll give you the chance," he said. "I'll let you take two steps to reach it before I stop you. What do you think? Won't that be fun?"

"Miriam, don't," Ephraim said. "If you try it, he'll have his proof of attempted murder."

The inquisitor clapped his hands as if to applaud him. "Very good! You've outwitted me!" He glanced at the grill behind him. "Did you hear that, Barto? They're talking of murder. Write that down."

Barto grumbled from behind the door.

Tomás smirked. "He's an illiterate clod. He can't read or write. Still, he has his uses." He took another step toward her.

Kill him! What are you waiting for? Alonso cried.

She lurched for the knife. Her feet tripped on her robe and she sprawled to the floor. The knife lay inches from her grasp. As she reached for it, her elbow exploded into pain. Tomás kicked her. He drew his leg back to do it again, but Ephraim clasped him about the shoulders, giving her a chance to scramble to her feet. Tomás punched him in the head. He dropped like a sack of grain.

She ran to the desk, wanting to set it between them. Tomás watched her like a cat eying a mouse, his amber eyes bright. A small smile played upon his lips.

He pounced. She feinted to the right but dodged left, thinking to use the candlestick against him. He snagged her by the arm. Ephraim's blood made her hard to hold. Seeing his mistake, Tomás caught her by the habit and swung her to the floor.

He was on her before she could find her feet. She clawed at his face, but he knocked her hands aside and struck her face, stunning her momentarily. Pinning her, he hoisted her robe and skirt to her thighs. His hands made her recoil, she wanted to vomit. She kicked him and earned another punch to the head. He launched on top of her again, cutting off her wind with a forearm. He prodded her legs apart. Something wet and hard settled between them. Alonso howled and threw himself against the walls of her mind like a rabid, caged dog. Something bright and fierce flew through the air. Her head erupted. For a moment, everything went black.

When she came to seconds later, she realized the pain was not her own. Tomás lay upon her like a dead man, his erection, gone. With revulsion, she shoved him from her. Ephraim cradled his ribs and dropped to his knees. The candlestick fell from his fingers.

"Papa!" She reached for him.

"Did he...?"

"No." She shook her head.

Is he dead? Alonso's hate burned like lye.

She studied Tomás, wanting to spit. He breathed. *No, he lives,* she said. She turned her back on him. "Come, Papa. We have to go."

No! Kill him! Now, while you have the chance! Grab the knife and slit his throat!

She hardened. Why had she ever thought him noble, or kind, or handsome? He disgusted her. *I won't!*

You're in no position to disagree. Do it!

His will bore down upon hers, and something else—her own desire to kill. Tomás deserved to die. He was evil incarnate, a devil that pleasured itself on rape and torment. If she killed him, she would set the world aright. She would destroy a great ill, even if it meant committing a lesser evil. But therein lay the flaw. Who was she to judge? If she slew Tomás, she would also be a murderer. She would swim in the same cesspool he did. *No!* She pushed Alonso back. *If I kill him, I'm no better than he is. I'm a healer. Healers don't kill.*

I don't care what you say you are! He deserves to die! Kill him! His outrage churned about her like a tempest.

What right do you have? She felt his will overpower hers and it infuriated her. She fought back with the only weapon she had available. *Who are you to play the god, Alonso de Santangél? Are you Sul, now? Or has Sul abandoned you, knowing you for what you are? I saw you truly when I called you from that fire! You're a selfish, loathsome beast! A demon, like Tomás! Go back to hell!*

Ephraim stared at her. Had she spoken aloud? Mortification washed through her, but it wasn't her shame. It was Alonso de Santangél's.

I am not...I'm not that! His hold on her released. *I am not a demon. I don't know what I am! I have never forced a woman in my life. I am not in my right mind. Forgive me....* His voice trembled, faded out.

Ephraim looked as if he was about to fall. She rushed to his side. "What was that?" he asked.

"Nothing. We have to go." She set an arm about his waist and they headed for the door. It occurred to her that she didn't remember the way, nor did she know where the stables were. They needed Alonso. She bit down on her frustration. *Your Brilliance, where are the stables?*

Silence met her. Chastened, he had retreated to some remote corner of her mind to mope, but their link remained intact. Why were men so difficult?

Your Brilliance, you have to help us! She pressed her lips in frustration, knowing she couldn't have it both ways. Either she tolerated him or she didn't. As annoying as it was, she had to retract what she had said. *I was wrong about you being a demon. Obviously not, if you can feel regret. Please!*

She felt him respond like a man granted a pardon. His presence solidified. *I'll try. There is still the problem of the guard.*

She had forgotten about Barto. They opened the door and Barto stood there as if he had taken root.

She hesitated, trying to gauge his reaction. He had let her go before, but something in his demeanor had changed. Had Tomás given him a worse beating than he had expected? The giant glanced at Tomás lying unconscious on the cell's floor, and then at her. She was tempted to threaten him, but something told her that trying to intimidate him would be a mistake. The menace she presented wasn't in voicing the threat. It was in being a worse threat than Tomás was. She stared him down, knowing that if she flinched, it was all over. His nostrils flared like a bear's, and then the dull fire in his eyes dwindled. She and Ephraim slipped past him.

As they walked away, she waited for the sound of his footfalls, but they never came. At the bottom of the stair, she gave Barto a last glance. As their eyes met, his thumb and forefinger formed a crescent—a moon symbol. She wasn't sure whether it was a ward against evil or an acknowledgement of who she was—a powerful witch. He turned away and lumbered into the cell. Miriam hefted Ephraim up the stairs.

They kept their heads down and managed to swerve past a tight group of priests who glanced at them before returning to their discussion. One of them said, "He's talking to the doctor, while they search for the girl."

"Pray to Sul, they find her. If they don't, we'll be blamed."

"How can he blame us?"

"He'll say we neglected the wards."

"We've never needed wards before!"

"Yes, well, we've never had a witch breach the premises, either."

A pair of Luster monks strode toward them from the end of the hall. Ephraim stumbled against her. As she steadied him, she looked down. He had left a trail of blood behind them.

Don't stop. Keep going, Alonso said.

Miriam led Ephraim around a corner. A voice called after them. "Are you in need, Brothers?"

Miriam hazarded a backward glance. One of the monks had followed them. His companion trailed behind.

Miriam shook her head. She kept her grip on Ephraim and kept walking.

"Wait!" The taller monk strode toward them with his hands in his sleeves.

Tell them he's a flagellant!

Miriam didn't look at the monk. "He has finished a penance." She spoke as deeply as she could. "We seek the Infirmary."

"Great heaven, what did he do?" The second monk strode up to them. The first gave him a scathing look.

"We're part of the delegation arrived from Leod. Brother Salvatore was late for the interment, much to our prelate's displeasure. The penalty was twenty lashes."

"Ah, that would explain it. Very pious of him. Sul keep you, Brothers."

"And you." Ephraim slumped at her side. He was near to fainting from blood loss and shock.

Turn here, Alonso directed.

They had come to a narrow corridor.

This is a short-cut to the cloister. Once we reach it, we must be careful. The bells are about to toll for the Fourth Watch. The monks will congregate along the promenade for final Vigil.

Do they head to the Solarium or to a smaller chapel?

To the Solarium.

How far is it from the stables?

They're in the opposite direction.

The Infirmary?

Also in the opposite direction.

Miriam nodded. The priests would not place the sick in proximity to their animals. Her body felt thick, her mind, dull. It had to be three in the morning. If any of the monks lagged on their way to the Mass, she would have a difficult time explaining their direction.

As they climbed down a stairway leading to the cloister, the temple bells tolled again. Miriam hesitated, reluctant to enter the promenade.

With a moan, Ephraim's legs gave out from beneath him. He fell to the steps.

She knelt beside him. He had fainted. She felt for a pulse. It was weak, but steady. They had to reach the stables. Even if she allowed him a few precious moments to recover, she doubted he could walk much further. The bells continued to toll. Beneath their peals, doors opened and closed. A shuffle of feet drew near them.

The procession is about to pass by you. Stay where you are and don't move.

She set her arms about Ephraim, drew his head down, and hid her face against his cowl. Walking in twos, a line of monks strode past their hiding place. Footfalls also came from behind them. In terror, she rose and coaxed Ephraim to his feet. She drew him from the stairwell and into view of the passing procession, praying he wouldn't fall. Holding him upright, she kept her head down as two more priests emerged from their stairwell to join the line.

Follow the procession to that doorway. Step inside as the line continues. You'll find yourself in a small entry with another door on the far side. That way leads to the stables.

She murmured encouragement to Ephraim and pulled him over the lintel before he collapsed again. This time, she couldn't rouse him.

Leave him. Get a horse. Hopefully, he'll revive enough for you to heave him into the saddle.

I can't leave him! What if someone comes and finds him here?

That's a chance we'll have to take. Most of them will have congregated for the Mass by now. So far, we've managed. Luck is with us.

Luck or madness, she thought. She ran for the door.

She opened it and peered out, afraid of rousing any hostlers on duty. The rain still hammered down, turning the cobblestones slick. She dashed across the compound and entered the stable. The place was warm and smelled of horse. She waited for her eyes to adjust in the murk and scanned the stalls before her.

Every pen was empty. No horse nickered from inside the barn. In frustration, she realized that Tomás must have commandeered all the able riders to search for her. That explained the guard pounding past them in the Solarium.

Try the manger.

He directed her to it—a lower building adjacent to the stables. She expected goats and a few blinked at her from the straw, but a donkey also stood there, along with a flat-bedded cart in an adjacent pen. She coaxed it from its stall, slipped its harness about its neck, slid the shafts through the loops and attached the traces. A tarp lay over one wall. She grabbed it, thinking to use it as shelter. She also picked up a shovel and threw both things into the cart. She grabbed the donkey by its harness and led it to the door.

The beast balked, seeing the rain. She clapped it across a shoulder and tugged on it harder. Begrudgingly, it followed her into the courtyard. She ran back inside to retrieve Ephraim. As she dragged him along the hall, hysteria settled upon her like a flock of crows fighting over a prize. She felt the urge to laugh wildly. They would escape Granad in a donkey cart. The Inquisition would never catch them. The velocity of their speed would be dizzying. She and Ephraim would live to a ripe old age and never look back.

Steady now. His concern surprised her.

Why? I'm half-mad, anyway. I have a voice in my head and a tattoo on my belly. If Tomás finds me, I'll burn. How can life get any better?

You're not dead.

That sobered her. She dragged Ephraim into the courtyard and patted his face to bring him around. He was weak and in pain, but his pulse was even. He needed water, much rest. A pail of rain water sat on the doorstep. She lifted it to his lips. "Drink, Papa. You need this."

She splashed it across his lips and he came to. The water refreshed him enough so he was able to stand. He half-fell, half-collapsed into the cart. She threw the tarp over him and grabbed the donkey's reins. As the bells of the Solarium tolled again, she passed beneath the stable's arched gateway and into the outside world.

They trundled along dark cobbled streets. No candle shone from the town's windows, having been snuffed hours ago. She kept to the narrower byways, knowing that armed men, riding by twos, would have a harder time negotiating lanes not much wider than a cart. The South Gate lay the closest. She directed the donkey to it. They waited beneath a dripping eave as she considered the gatehouse. A dull light wavered from behind the barred window. A shadow passed it—one of the guards. She weighed the wisdom of waiting until dawn for the gates to open against chancing them now. She slapped the donkey with the reins and drew up to the gate.

The corporal on night duty saw her and stepped from the gatehouse. The rain pounded down.

"I need this gate unbarred," she shouted. Her cowl dripped with wet.

He squinted at her, trying to determine what wasn't right. "By whose order?"

"By order of Tor Tomás, the Grand Inquisitor."

"The Guard's been here, already. Why weren't you with them, then?"

"The Solarium doesn't discuss its business with all and sundry. Let me through!"

"I'll need to check the cart, first."

"No! Don't touch it!"

Too late, he lifted the tarp. He gasped as he saw Ephraim and the shovel beside him.

"Plague!" she shouted. Terror lent a shrill edge to her voice. "This brother is dead from it, you fool! If you value your life, you'll let us pass! I go to the Hill of Cats to bury him. If I survive, I return in five days! If not, I die alongside him!"

He dropped the tarp as if burned. "Gods!" he said. "Why didn't you tell me in the first place?" He backed away and withdrew the bolts from the great doors.

"Say nothing!" she warned as he pulled the gate wide. "If you do, the whole town will panic!" He nodded dully, looked sick. She slapped the reins and the donkey jogged through. She felt clammy, cold on the inside and out. Her hands stiffened on the reins. She felt no relief as the gate closed behind her.

The road twisted past the Hill of Cats and to the south. As they passed it, a forest of oak and scrub hemmed them on both sides. The rain hammered down so hard that it looked as if it fell from the ground up. Her back prickled with fear. At any moment, Tomás and his Guard might charge through the gates. Lightning cracked overhead. The donkey brayed in fear and trotted harder. Thunder rumbled; her nerves were at their breaking point, her instinct was to hide. She squinted through the rain. A side trail lay a short distance ahead. She drove the donkey to it and urged it into the woods. The wheels left deep tracks. She despaired as she saw them but hoped the rain would wash them away. After twenty minutes of branches whipping at her face and the wind howling overhead, the fight went out of her. They could go no farther. She jumped from the rig and pulled the donkey beneath a yew. She sagged beside a wheel and pressed her hands to her face. They had won their freedom, but for what? That they might spend the rest of their lives on the run? That they live like deer fleeing wolves in the forest? Above her, the storm grew wilder.

There was one place she could think of, one refuge where they might be safe for a while. They had to reach Gaspar.

She wiped the tears from her face. It was good to have a plan. It made her feel less vulnerable. She lifted the tarp to check on Ephraim and caught her breath. He shook with fever. She set a cold hand to his cheek. Delirium swept through her in a rush. His heart fluttered in his chest, too fast, too faint.

"No!" she cried. Overhead, thunder crashed. She climbed into the rig and dabbed at his face and arms to cool him down. He had to survive, had to hold on until they reached Gaspar. "Keep your end of the bargain, Lys!" she shouted at the angry sky, "or I'll...!" What would she do? She could do nothing, except stay with him and hope. In spite of her threat, she still didn't believe in the goddess.

I would pray to Sul, Alonso de Santangél said, *but I don't know what to believe in, anymore.*

Did he expect her to sympathize with him? Poor man, he'd lost his faith. She'd abandoned her home and was in danger of losing her father. The world was a harsh place. Lives were destroyed every day. Why should his be any different? *Do you know what you are?* she demanded, turning on him. *You're a man who feels sorry for himself when he's not terrorizing someone. I wish I'd never resurrected you. You're a burden I don't need! Go away!*

The rain beat down. He said nothing for a few moments. It annoyed her to find that she was waiting for him to respond.

I don't think I can.

She ignored him. Ephraim needed her. Those cuts on his chest would turn septic if she didn't treat them soon. Maybe they already were. She'd have to find something in the forest, in spite the night and the storm.

Would lavender help? My mother used to use it.

Where? she demanded.

There's a small clump by that tree.

She didn't bother to ask him how he'd seen it. Under his guidance, she found the plant, pulled it up by its sodden roots. She could pound it, press the mash into Ephraim's wounds.

Half an hour later, she had doctored him as well as she could. She pulled the tarp over them and lay beside him, exhausted. She needed a few hours of sleep. At daybreak they would make their way to Gaspar. Perhaps the rain would stop by then. She closed her eyes.

It felt as if she had only slept a moment. She awoke to Alonso shouting in her head. *Gods, Miriam! Wake up! Can you hear me?*

She knocked the tarp aside. Beneath a pearling sky and as unstoppable as death, the crash of heavy bodies pounded toward them.

Chapter Six: Heart Debt

JOACHÍN DE RIVERA was fairly certain she was the same beauty he had dreamt of three times before, but it was hard to tell. Her face was hidden by a cowl. *Push it aside, mi bonita,* he told her, *and then I will know.*

To his surprise, she turned her head as if to oblige him. The hood fell back. He caught his breath, a thing he did every time he saw her. He drank in her inky black hair, the softly curving cheekbones, her perfect lips. She was sleeping. It was easy to imagine waking her with kisses. Let that happen sooner than later. He willed the dream to show him more.

The view broadened. He frowned. The cowl she wore...a Luster monk's. She also wore the habit. Worse, she wasn't alone. Another monk slept at her side.

Joachín sputtered with disgust. Why would he dream of this if she wasn't meant for him? What did the goddess mean by it? He willed himself to wake but the vision held him fast.

In the distance came the pounding of hooves. His dream girl woke with a start. The other monk lay as if dead. She jumped from a donkey cart, grabbed a spade and held it high, her face taut. Two riders of the Inquisitional Guard crashed through the bush toward her. They hadn't seen her yet, but they would notice her in moments.

What did it matter if she was on the run with a lover? The monk was useless, unable to protect her. Joachin reached for his knife.

The dream shattered.

No! He clawed after it as if he might forge the disappearing bits together. He had broken the cardinal rule of true dreaming. Any interference on his part spoiled the dream. He turned away in frustration and knocked his head on a gunwale. His eyes flew open. He stared at the underside of a boat.

Gods! He rubbed his brow. A nightmare, except it was real. He sighed deeply, hoping she survived the guards. Perhaps another dream would show him. Pray to Lys she was all right.

He set his hands to the bottom of the dory and pushed it away. The beach was deserted as he knew it would be. The sea was calm, the morning, soft. He dragged the boat down the spit, slid it into the water and jumped in. He liked how the oars forced his muscles to work. A gull flew overhead, its cry lonely on the breeze. Perhaps it was an escort, showing him the way.

After twenty minutes, he estimated he was about a half league from the shore. There were no other boats on the water. Fishermen were a superstitious lot—to fish on the autumn equinox tempted Lys's wrath. It had been a rainy night, but now the sky was clear.

His glanced down at the red silk pouch he had set on the bench, and his throat tightened. Nine years, to the date. He should have known he would feel this way. His mother had died on his birthday. Today was his twentieth. He hated birthdays.

After a few more minutes of rowing, he glanced down the starboard side of the dory. The water was turquoise; the boat cast a wavering shadow. A reef lay not far below, rippling with colour. The wind died down to nothing. He lifted the oars and set them on the thwarts. He picked up the silken pouch and retrieved a dark braid from inside it. He kissed it once and then balanced on his feet with the grace of an acrobat. He held the braid out to the sky and the sea.

"Great Lys," he said, "accept this earthly remnant of your daughter, Estrella. Her body lies elsewhere, crumbled to dust. That it took me nine long years to bring this to you isn't her fault. The negligence is mine. Accept your daughter, for she never forsook you. Embrace her and welcome her home. Let her dwell in your realms, forever."

He kissed the braid again and let it fall from his fingers into the sea. As it sank, it unraveled. He thought of unseen fingers untying the plait, like a mother's hand pulling softly at a child's head. His eyes stung.

"Sleep in peace, *Maré*," he whispered.

He rowed to the shore without looking back.

When the oars struck the sandy bottom, he set them into their rowlocks and jumped into the knee-deep water. The waves rippled past him, scalloping the sand in arcs. As he hauled the boat onto the beach, something white and green tumbled past him in the surf. He reached down and retrieved a Dartura flower. None had floated in the kelp when he'd been out on the water. There had been no weed at all; the sea had been clear. He stared out to the place where he had dropped his mother's plait, and then tucked the blossom into his pocket. He left the boat where he found it on the shore.

He retrieved his horse from the thicket of myrtle where he'd picketed it at the edge of the beach. The village of Herradur wasn't far from the bay. He intended to visit the sun chapel that sat on a hill above the town. His stomach growled; the lukewarm mutton he'd eaten the night before no longer appeased. He needed coin to buy a meal. Every chapel had at least one altar piece of value, and every town, its dealer in stolen goods.

As he drew close, he considered the church. It was a typical white-stuccoed affair with a gold-domed roof and a one room cottage behind it. A gravel path snaked up the hill, leading to both buildings. It was early; none of the villagers were about. He doubted if the priest slept, but if he did, that would make his efforts all the easier.

He left his horse to graze by the path and paused inside the chapel's doorway. The priest was inside, setting candles into sconces. Joachín stepped back, but too late, the Solar turned and glanced his way. "Can I help you, my son?"

"No. You're busy. I'll return later." If he was preoccupied here, the house was vulnerable.

"I am never too busy for one who seeks the god." The Solar strode toward him with his hands tucked into his gold-trimmed sleeves. His belt tassels bounced against his ample belly. "You are soul burdened. I can feel it. Let me relieve your darkness with light."

The man was a charlatan, all priests were. "You're right," Joachin said tightly, giving in to the temptation to needle him. "I carry a great weight. Tell me, what is your view of a priest who serves only himself?"

The Solar frowned. "What do you mean?"

The memory, never far from his thoughts, burned in his mind's eye like a torch. A naked man lay sprawled over his mother's body, his robes of office in a heap by the bed. His back and legs were streaked in blood—not his own. "Tell me," Joachin continued. "Does the faith protect clerics who fornicate and kill?"

The Solar flushed. "No patriarch would do such a thing."

"But if one did?"

"Then he would be chastised and his ordination removed."

"*How* would he be chastised?"

"Do you have knowledge of such deeds? Are you accusing someone?"

There was nothing to be gained from antagonizing him. He needed to let it go. "Forgive me." He dismissed the question with a wave. "I know of no prelate who has done these things. I have only myself to answer for. I find myself wishing for a new existence. A life of service, perhaps." At any other time, the lie would have made him laugh aloud.

Disbelief flickered across the priest's wide face. "Anyone can atone."

"True. Still, I think I am called to the priesthood." That *was* the truth, but the fat Solar wouldn't see it for what it was.

"In what manner have you been called?"

"Dreams, mostly. Promptings. I felt an inclination to come here and talk with you. Forgive me if I was wrong."

The priest made a face. "Dreams are the purview of the dark goddess. They are sinful, ephemeral things. It's wrong to rely on them."

Joachin nodded. "So a seminary student once told me. I always wondered what became of him. Perhaps you know him?"

"There are many who serve in the Temple. What is his name?"

"I never knew it, but he bore a scar across his face. I'm certain he earned it while throwing himself in harm's way."

"I know of no such person."

Joachin nodded as if agreeing with him. The priest was lying. It took a liar to know one. "Good day to you, Solar," he said. "I'll think on what you have said."

"Sul be with you, my son."

"And with you."

He felt the priest's hard gaze on his back as he mounted up. The man was too clever, had guessed too much. He left the chapel's environs and made his way down the hill. Maybe better pickings would be found in the town.

Chapter Seven: Close Call

MIRIAM CLUTCHED THE shovel. She felt as if she were shrinking and expanding at the same time. An image fluttered through her mind: she was a hare, paralyzed beneath a hawk's gaze, a mouse waiting for cruel claws. Any minute now, the guards would spot her. They'd guffaw and leap from their horses, wrench the spade from her hands and throw her to the ground. Alonso lurched back and forth inside her like a trapped lion. She wanted to scream at him to stop.

Something tore her from the inside. There was a moment of icy cold. She swayed, felt faint, but righted herself. Alonso had fled. The pain of this final betrayal was too much. She wanted to cry. She hated the guards and she hated him. She gripped the spade hard. She wondered, after raping her, if the guards would leave her for the scavengers in the woods.

There was a crack and a shout. A covey of partridge burst into the air, their wings a blur as they scattered into the trees. The first guard swore, the other laughed. "It's only birds," he said.

"Damn horse nearly threw me. Almost pissed myself."

The second sniggered, reached into a saddle bag and withdrew a flask. He unscrewed it, took a swig, and handed it to his compatriot. They glanced about the woods and wiped their mouths. Miriam didn't move. Her brown habit camouflaged her. By some trick of the light, the spade didn't catch their eye.

"Let's go. There's nothing here."

"What about the tracks?"

"Old." He waggled the flask. "Besides, we're empty."

The second one shrugged. They headed back to the road. Miriam sank to her knees. She lay in the wet grass and stared at the sky.

Are you all right?

He was back. She was too numb to care. She closed her eyes.

They've gone.

She ignored him. If she sat up too quickly, she'd faint. *How did you do that?* she asked finally.

The birds?

She nodded. Her tongue felt thick.

*I...I couldn't let them hurt you. I didn't know what else to do, so I jumped at them...*Alonso's voice trailed off. She caught a flash of the inferno from which she had called him. He'd been afraid of returning there but had risked it to protect her. *It seems we're still joined,* he pointed out.

Ephraim groaned.

She climbed to her feet. She hadn't checked on him since waking. She stumbled to the cart and stared down at her father. His face was tight with pain.

She clambered into the rig, yanked up his habit and regarded his wounds. Despite the lavender she'd set into them the night before, two of the gashes were pus-filled.

That doesn't look good, Alonso said.

It was worse than that. If she didn't treat them with something stronger, the infection would travel up his bloodstream. She applied more purple mash to Ephraim's wounds and took up the reins. They had to reach Gaspar soon, and without being seen.

Chapter Eight: Herradur

To all appearances, Herradur was a poor town. Joachin had few scruples, but one he maintained was to leave the simple folk alone. There was nothing wrong with honest labour when fortune failed to provide. He could muck stables or pitch hay, whatever was necessary. He was tired of sleeping in the bush.

The inn was typical of all the buildings on the Costa del Cobre—two stories high, stuccoed with lime and roofed in tile. Nets lay heaped against one wall. Barrels were stacked against another. The place smelled of fish and beer. He tied his horse to a post and entered the building to find the innkeeper. The interior was dark, the hearth banked low. A back door led to a kitchen. Beyond it, chickens strutted in the yard like grand dames on the streets of Madrone.

A girl came through the far doorway, carrying a basket of eggs. She wore a homespun skirt and a faded blue blouse. Her hair was swept into an untidy bun. She stopped short when she saw him.

"It's *siesta*," she said. "We don't open for an hour."

He swept off his hat. "I want work. For a meal and a place to sleep."

She set the basket of eggs on a table and came toward him, taking in his face and clothes. He kept his hands on his hat and allowed her to inspect him. She carried herself with a brashness he liked. He suspected she had protection close at hand or there was nothing that could be done to her that hadn't been done already. She set her hands on her hips.

"Pepe's busy." She nodded at the staircase that led to the second floor.

"You speak for Pepe?"

"I speak for myself."

She wasn't a whore then. In most taverns, the women were. "So, you hire on Pepe's behalf?"

"I'll ask the questions. What can you do?"

"I can mend nets or gut fish. Pluck chickens or muck barns. Whatever you need."

"Do you dump night water? Air bedding?"

He nodded. Not his favourite tasks, but he'd do them.

She thrust a finger at him as if she had bested him. "Ha! Too late. Already done."

"Alas, for me, then." He set a hand to his heart as if she'd broken it.

She smirked. "How do I know you won't run off the minute I feed you?"

"Tell me your name and I'll stay."

She shrugged his charm aside, but he could tell from her face that she liked it. "I have fish that need gutting and filleting. In exchange for those, I have eggs and bread."

"Fine. But tell me the most important thing."

"What?"

"Your *name*." It never hurt to be on the good side of one's employer.

She pursed her lips. "Inez. Follow me." She led him through the kitchen and into the yard.

He set to work gutting and scaling. After an hour, she fed him fried fish and eggs, with bread on the side. The bread was stale, but he'd eaten worse. Pepe appeared at the back door and glared at him. His hair was oily and long. There was some resemblance between him and Inez. He wondered if she were his daughter.

"You can sleep in the stable above the horses." Pepe jerked a thumb at the barn's loft. Joachin flexed his hands. His effort was worth more than a night in the straw, but he wasn't about to argue. As Pepe disappeared, Inez came out with a mug of ale.

"For thirsty work." She set down the cup.

"It's done." He indicated the mound of fillets that lay in a large bowl. The slops sat at his feet in a pail.

"If you want to wash, there's a trough in the barn."

He nodded, took a long drink. It would be good to rinse away the stench and the road grime.

Inside the barn, horses nickered from their stalls, including his Fidel. Inez must have retrieved him from the front of the inn. The horse shook its mane at him. Joachin pulled off his boots, tore off his shirt, and climbed out of his pants. From an overhead rafter, several hens eyed him as if appraising his form. He grinned and saluted them. Outside the barn, a shadow hesitated and then passed. Inez, he realized, stopping to peek at him through the cracks. He smiled, hoping she liked what she saw. Most women did. Chances were good he wouldn't sleep alone.

An hour later, he was clean and dry. He'd taken the liberty to wring out his clothes, and then don them while they were still damp. The smell of grilled fish and bread made his stomach grumble. He headed for the kitchen and paused in the doorway when he saw Inez there.

"You never told me *your* name." She set more mugs onto a tray.

"Juan," he replied.

"Ha! Juan. The name a man gives a whore."

"José. Forgive me. It's an old habit."

She nodded. "Come into the bar, José, or whatever your name is. Sit at that table over there. I'll bring you ale."

He headed for the table she indicated. Despite the afternoon heat, a fire burned in the hearth. A few fishermen drank in a dim corner. A pock-faced youth strummed a guitar. The tune was familiar—an old *Sonea* he recognized. Several girls appeared on the balcony and ambled down a long stair. They had painted their faces and wore bright dresses. Women for hire.

One of them, a ratty-haired blonde with ample hips, glanced his way. A younger girl—a brunette—also noticed him, but the blonde shoved her aside. A pecking order was in force here. Herradur was the same as everywhere.

The blonde sauntered toward him. Without waiting for an invitation, she dropped onto his bench. Her skirts billowed like sails. "I am Carmella. I dance here. Do you dance? You look like you might."

He shrugged. "I pass at it."

She nodded, as if he'd confirmed her opinion of him. "Where are you from?"

"Here and there. I grew up in Taleda."

"Ah, Taleda! Then you know how to dance the *Taltell*. I've always wanted to learn it. You must teach me."

He smirked. "I doubt I could teach you anything."

She laughed coarsely. At the bar, the brunette struggled against a man who pulled her toward the stairs. His skull cap marked him as a whaler.

"Let go!" she cried.

Pepe came out of the kitchen. "What's going on?" He glared at the girl as if she were to blame.

She yanked her arm from the whaler's grasp. "He doesn't have enough."

"So, he'll come back when he does, won't you, Rufio? We don't give it away for free, my friend."

Rufio glared at them. "I'll be back," he told the girl. "Then we'll see who has the upper hand." He stomped from the inn. The girl spat after him.

Carmella turned to Joachin. "Such a fuss and all for a *puta* just broken. Rufio could do better elsewhere." She ran her hand up Joachin's thigh and squeezed it.

"Carmella—get!" Inez stood behind them, holding two mugs of ale. Without a word, Carmella rose from her place and made her way to the other side of the room. Inez slammed the mugs onto the table.

Joachin shifted uncomfortably. "She approached me. It wasn't the other way around." He suspected his chances with her were dwindling.

Inez sniffed. "It doesn't matter. She is what she is. You can't fault a cat for its claws."

"If it makes any difference, I prefer honest women." He studied her appraisingly. "You're not like the rest of them, here."

"No." Across the room, a fisherman pulled Carmella onto his lap. Inez made a face. "My father keeps them around for business. I put up with them. They put up with him."

"Pepe's your father?"

"If you can call him that."

He sipped his ale. Life here couldn't be easy. Other than marriage, women in Esbaña had few options. He hoped no one abused her. "No one bothers you?"

She sat beside him. "No. They know better unless they are strangers. Then my knife shows them."

"Convincing friends, knives."

She nodded. "So, what brings you to Herradur?"

He shrugged. She nudged him with an elbow. "Oh, come now. Everyone has a story. What's yours?"

Across the bar, the guitarist had struck up a *Sorida*. The dark-haired girl was swaying to and fro with her eyes closed. He wondered if she'd taken something. "I came to pay a heart debt," he said softly.

"Whose?"

"My mother's."

"I'm sorry to hear that. My mother's dead, also. Nine years, this month."

"A coincidence."

Her eyebrows rose. "Your mother died nine years ago, and you're paying her heart debt, now? Why have you waited so long?"

Instead of feeling irritated, he felt a strange compulsion to talk. The morning had resurrected painful emotions. It didn't matter what he said. He'd be gone in the morning. "I was young. She was murdered when I was eleven. I ran away from it, did what I could to survive."

"Your father didn't avenge her?"

"He died when I was nine."

Her eyes widened. "So, you seek a death debt. Who murdered her?"

"A scar-faced priest. I don't know his name."

She narrowed her eyes. He suspected the temple was given little respect in Herradur. "I haven't seen such a one in these parts," she said.

They shared a meal and several jugs of wine over the next few hours. By the time night had fallen, the bar was full. The villagers were exuberant. A day without toil restored their energies. The extra coin in Pepe's coffer improved his mood as well.

Two more guitarists joined the first and Carmella, finding a moment between customers, leapt atop a table to dance. She wasn't half bad, Joachin considered, as she attempted a tricky *Perdiza*. The dance mimicked the foot drumming of the red-legged partridge. She raised her skirts to show off her legs. Fogged with ale, the patrons hammered their appreciation, but their clapping threw her off-tempo. She swore, lost her place and kicked at their heads. Most weren't too drunk to duck out of the way. Pepe roared her down, and the small brunette jumped up to take her place.

"I want to see a *Taltell*," Carmella demanded as the girl danced. "I've never seen one." She pointed at Joachin. "He says he can do it!" Her claim brought shouts of encouragement from the crowd. Carmella pulled him to his feet. Inez glared at her, but she didn't object.

"I'm out of practice," Joachin said. "I haven't danced in awhile."

"Show us how it's done!" A stout fisherman clapped him on the back. He was one of the ones who had nearly won himself a kick to the chin. "Carmella's stale. She needs new tricks!" Roars of laughter rose about him. Carmella lunged at him and missed.

"I don't dance on tables." His mother had done that. He refused to do it on principle.

"Clear him a space!" Tables were pushed aside to make room. The dark girl was shooed away. Joachin looked to Inez for support.

"Go!" she shouted, giving in to the crowd's enthusiasm. "It doesn't matter if you dance like an ox. It'll give them something to talk about."

He wasn't much comforted by her encouragement, but he wasn't so drunk that he couldn't dance either. He thought of Estrella, his mother. She'd been the best dancer in Taleda, had taught him how to dance before their lives fell apart. He couldn't afford to be unworthy of her. Let him dance in her memory.

"I see I'm outnumbered," he said. The crowd crowed in approval. He turned to the guitarists. "Can you give me a measure in repeating eights? Something like a march, in a minor key?"

The middle guitarist strummed a few notes. "Something like this?"

Joachin nodded, took his place in the circle they had made for him. The crowd quieted. He looked down at his feet, hoping it would all come back. How ironic that he should remember his mother in a place like this. But he wouldn't think of that, now. She was his mother, first and foremost, beautiful and talented, before she turned whore. She'd done what she had to keep them alive.

He let a few bars go by. Then slowly, he brought up his arms and snapped his fingers to the beat, his feet stepping to the *entrada*, the opening. Knuckling the tables or clapping their palms, the crowd took up the rhythm, their accompaniment insistent and martial. He added to it, his toes and heels beating first in time, then in counter-time. As his body remembered, his confidence built. He held himself tightly, always keeping the basic tempo but experimenting with doubles and triplets. Soon, there were gasps from the crowd. He executed a series of sharp turns, and then, when he could hold back no longer, he exploded into a flurry of footwork. He thought of the scarred priest and his mother. His feet hammered into the floor. A mug dropped, and he smashed it beneath his heels, his face florid as he ground it to dust. Finally, after an execution so rapid that the crowd could barely follow it, he came to an abrupt halt. He stood, panting heavily. Then he slapped his chest, a gesture telling them that he was done, but he bowed before no man.

The crowd surged to their feet and howled their approval. Hands clapped him on the back. They entreated him for more. Carmella screamed and reached for him, but Inez was there, sliding into his arms. "Where did you learn to dance like that?" she asked, leaning into his ear. She smelled of oranges.

"My mother." He ached at the thought of her. His passion lay too close to the skin.

"You must teach me to dance like that," Inez murmured. "Later. Tonight."

And he knew she wasn't speaking of dance at all.

Chapter Nine: Dream Woman

DESPITE HER HARD front, Inez turned out to be a kitten in his arms. For awhile, he wasn't sure whether she was a virgin. She reacted to him with a reluctance coupled with desire that made him wonder if she'd been ill used. Finally, he accomplished his goal and brought her to satisfaction. Startled by her own pleasure, she stared at him in surprise. Her eyes rolled back and she clutched him tightly. He rocked to his own climax and then slumped beside her, content and replete.

She said nothing, but lay beside him, watching his face as if committing it to memory. Sleep threatened to overtake him, so he pulled her into a cozy embrace. She traced a finger along his jaw. "Go to sleep," he whispered, grabbing her hand.

She sighed, wriggled free of him and turned on her side. Not wanting her to feel rejected, he threw an arm over her and drew her close. He felt her settle, relax. Her breathing leveled out. Sleep overtook him then, and he knew no more until he heard the screams.

He jerked awake. Inez sat beside him, staring at their door, their thin blanket covering her breasts. More shouting came from without.

Furniture crashed and splintered. There were shrieks. Joachín jumped from the bed and grabbed his pants.

"Don't." Inez reached for him.

He frowned at her. The disturbance came from a room two doors down. It bothered him that he was the only one investigating it. A woman pleaded. Someone growled. There were more thumps. Whoever was being struck cried out again.

"It's not your business!" Inez called from their doorway.

He lifted his heel and kicked open the offending door. The thin wood splintered. Inside the room, Rufio, the whaler, had drawn back his fist. The brunette huddled at the end of a bed, shielding her face with her hands.

"I'm not done with her yet," Rufio said gruffly.

Joachín threw himself at the whaler and rammed him in the chest. The wind rushed from Rufio's lungs. With a crash, they landed in a jumble of arms and legs on the bed. The girl scrambled away. Rufio aimed a kick at Joachín's ribs. He rolled aside, but not before it caught him in the kidney. He punched Rufio in the solar plexus. The whaler grunted and leaned in close. He bit down on Joachín's cheek.

The pain was agonizing. A red veil obscured Joachín's vision. He no longer saw the room, the girl, or Rufio. Instead, he grappled with a priest. In his fist, he held a knife.

The man's face was bestial, ruddy, as if lit by an infernal glow. Joachín slashed at him, once, twice. The priest swore, clapped a hand to his face. Whatever gnawed at Joachín let go. The knife disappeared. All he wanted was to pummel the beast beneath him to a pulp.

"José! Stop it! Get off!"

Someone yanked him aside. Whoever lay beneath him no longer moved. The red haze faded from his mind. He tasted blood and saw through one eye. The whaler lay beneath him, his face a mash where his teeth had broken through. Joachín's knuckles were shreds.

"You have to get out of here!" Inez said. "If Pepe sees what you've done to Rufio, he'll kill you." She leaned into the hall. "It's all right! It's settled!" A far door slammed. She turned to him. "You have to go."

He stood, feeling as if he had been trampled by a bull. His cheek throbbed. The dark girl had fled, he didn't know where. Inez grabbed his shirt and hurried him to the kitchen where she dabbed at his cuts.

He brushed her ministrations aside. "This is a bad place." He clasped her by the shoulders. "Come away with me." He didn't love her, but that didn't matter. He would take care of her. The inn was no different from the *bordello* that had claimed his mother. With Inez, it would only be a matter of time.

She pushed his hands aside. "I can't."

"You mustn't stay here."

Her glance slid away. "This place is as good as any."

"How can you say that? Someone may not take your knife for an answer. Pepe may not always protect you. You'll become another girl, just like the rest of them."

She looked at him, incensed. "I'm no whore! I run this place."

"Your father runs it."

"I've as much say as he does!"

"So you turn a blind eye to Rufio?"

"His money is the same as anyone else's."

He stared at her, stunned. And then the truth of who she was hardened him. "So, you're not a whore, but a whoremonger, then. No better than your father." The tenderness they had shared was gone. He grabbed his hat. "Sul keep you." He strode from the kitchen and into the yard.

"You think you're better than us? Better than me?" she shouted at his back. "You're *basura*, garbage! Go to hell!" She slammed the door behind him.

He retrieved Fidel from the barn. The blanket Pepe had left him was draped over a stall. He stole it. His conscience didn't bother him in the least.

From Herradur, the road climbed steadily. The land lifted from the sea in dark, mist-shrouded hills. A three-quarters moon made every bush, tree, and stone stand out in sharp relief. Autumn was upon the land with the promise of winter to come. Joachín shivered and considered the need for warmer clothes. Perhaps he could pick up a cloak in Velez, the next town on his search.

After an hour of riding, he estimated it was four in the morning. The moon dropped to the west, about to set. He was an hour from Velez. The gates wouldn't open until dawn. He reined Fidel off the road and found a dry spot beneath an almond tree. He slung out his blanket, pulled off his boots, and tried to ignore the throbbing of his cheek. Eventually, sleep claimed him.

His first dreams flashed by, a jumble of images from the recent past— his mother's braid dropping into the water, Inez's angry face as he left her. These weren't what he wanted to see. His mother's heart debt was paid, but the death debt remained. *Show me the priest,* he willed.

Sometimes he could call the true dreams, particularly if his need was strong. Inez's face faded to black, a good sign. Experience had shown him that the dark canvas was a preliminary to true dreaming. Once the vision formed, he made note of the time of day, the locale, the people—these were the clues he had to follow.

An image took shape. With anticipation, he watched it build.

It turned out to be his dream girl again, the beauty with the black hair and heart-shaped face. His throat tightened. He was thankful she'd escaped the guards, but why did the goddess keep showing him this? He watched impatiently. The girl was applying a mash to her paramour's wounds. The paste was a pale purple. Lavender, it looked like.

He prickled with resentment. He had assumed they would meet. After the second dream, he had looked forward to it, expected he would be tongue-tied when they did. She was the perfect woman, a veritable angel, a promise to him from Lys. That she traveled with a man twice her age and a monk at that, changed everything.

Her face crumbled. She was trying not to cry. Tears dribbled down her cheeks. "Please, Papa," she said, "you have to hold on!"

The words struck him like a slap. Hope and remorse chased themselves like butterflies in his chest. This man wasn't her lover. He was her father. They were in disguise and on the run. The Guard was after them.

The dream faded. He stared at the stars through the almond's branches. She needed him. Why else would the goddess show him her plight? She *was* his future as much as his mother's murderer was his past. In the darkness, his desire for both burned hotter than the gash on his cheek.

Chapter Ten: False Convert

JOACHÍN WOKE AT dawn, cold and damp. His cheek throbbed, but he ignored it. Pain was a part of life. He was impatient to move on, but let Fidel browse on the grass. He feasted on almonds from the tree and stowed a few handfuls in his saddlebag.

Mounting up, he thought of his mystery girl and where she might be. The oak forest suggested north. Since he was heading that way, she had to be travelling south.

The sun rose and turned the sky a glorious peach. He set her out of his mind and thought of the scar-faced priest. The man who had killed his mother had been a seminary student, but he wouldn't be, now. Velez had both a Solarium and a seminary. The school kept records. He'd need a better excuse than the lie he'd told the Solar in Herradur.

After an hour's ride, the town appeared on the horizon. It was bordered to the east and south by cliffs, carved by the River Gemilla. A bridge spanned the water from the road to the town. At the town's highest point, white spires lifted like spears, surrounding the

Solarium's broad dome of gold. To Joachin, it resembled a great eye peering at heaven. He wondered if Sul appreciated the scrutiny.

At the south gate, the guards ignored him as he rode by. Months ago, he'd stolen a saddlebag from a mail carrier. Messengers were as common as labourers. He looked as if he was on legitimate business.

He trotted from the gate and headed into the town proper. Soon, the low lying houses on the outskirts gave way to the market. He skirted it and made his way to the temple, guessing the seminary would be located nearby. He found the smaller, grey building tucked on the periphery of the Solarium's gardens. Students walked along hedged paths, looking harried or in deep contemplation. Joachin dismounted and tied Fidel to a tree.

A student tripped down the steps from the main entrance. Joachin intercepted him. "I'm looking for a particular priest. I believe he once studied in Taleda."

"Talk to Luminant Theo. I'm sorry, but I'm expected for noontide service." The student sprinted across the gardens, his hems flying. Joachin climbed the steps and entered the seminary.

Inside the rotunda, a huge multi-rayed Orb hung. It looked built from solid gold, but from past plans to steal one, Joachin knew it was only gilded wood. A patriarch in a grey trimmed habit stood beneath it, talking quietly to a student. Joachin waited.

The apprentice nodded and left. The priest glanced his way. "May I help you?" he asked, quirking an eyebrow.

"Yes, I hope so." Joachin mopped a hand across his brow, hoping he looked confused.

The prelate beetled his brow at him. "Are you lost, my son?"

Joachin snapped his fingers. "That's it." He turned to stare at the Orb as if dumbstruck. "But now that I'm here, I think I've found my way."

"I don't understand."

Joachin regarded the priest earnestly. The tale he was about to spin relied on how well he told it. He put on a doleful face. "I've had an unusual experience, your Brilliance. Does the seminary ever accept those with a sincere desire, but no connections?"

"Oh, I'm not so high as to be titled Brilliance," the priest said. "I'm only a Luminant, but your words intrigue me. What's happened to you, my son?" His glance drifted to the mark on Joachin's face.

Joachin touched his wound, as if surprised to find it there. "I seek clarity, Luminance. I've had a visitation from the god. I know it sounds incredible, but I can put no other meaning to it. You're a busy man. Perhaps I should come back when it's more convenient."

The priest blinked. "If you've had a true calling, there's no better time than now to discuss it. What kind of a servant would I be, if I didn't enlighten you on Sul's behalf?"

"Your generosity humbles me, Luminance."

"What happened?"

"Well," Joachin began, pleased that his fabricating sounded plausible so far, "I was riding my horse from the village of Herradur, passing Sul's chapel, when a force struck me from my mount and threw me to the ground. I was terrified I'd encountered a demon known to frequent the place. But instead of being dragged to hell, as I well deserve, I beheld a brilliant light. And from that light came a mighty voice."

The priest's eyebrows rose like gulls lifting to the sky.

"And the voice said, 'Go to the town of Velez. There, you will find a priest to assist you.'"

The priest stared at him, open-mouthed. Abruptly, he closed it. "Assist how?"

"Well, that's the strangest thing." Joachin scratched his head. "I'm to seek a scar-faced priest. *He*'s to teach me the ways of the god. I must serve him and Sul, without any recompense, so I might atone for my sins. I've no qualifications or money to pay for tuition, Luminance. But I'm afraid that if I don't serve Sul, he'll send me to the demons. Do you think this was a true encounter or an hallucination?"

The priest wrinkled his brow. "It *is* unusual, but it just so happens that we *do* have a prelate here of your description. He has a diagonal scar across his face. Perhaps he's the one you seek."

Joachin went very still. "Perhaps so. Where can I find him?"

"You don't have to find him. I'll take you to him. Maybe he's also had a vision. It's been known to occur. Come."

He followed the priest down a long marbled hall. They made a number of turns into smaller corridors before descending a broad staircase. Finally, they came to a low arched door. Joachin slipped his knife from its sheath and hid it behind his back.

They waited politely as the priest knocked on the door. "Arturo!" the priest called. "You have a visitor!" He turned to Joachin. "He's a bit deaf, so he may not have heard."

A scuffling came from behind the door. When it opened, a wizened monk stood there, dressed in brown. Spatters of ink dotted his chest as if a quill had exploded. A diagonal scar ran from his left eye to his right cheek. "Hello, Theo," he wheezed. "Come to see me?" He squinted at Joachin.

"Yes, Arturo," Luminant Theo confirmed. "This young man was told by Sul to serve you. You're supposed to teach him everything you know."

"What a remarkable thing!" The old man smiled sweetly at Joachin. "My prayers have been answered! God bless Sul!"

"Well, Sul is the god, Arturo," Luminant Theo reminded him.

"Yes, of course!" The monk waved an ink-stained hand. "Well, come in, my boy. What's your name? I should know it if we're going to work together."

Joachin slipped his blade back into its sheath. "I must see to my horse first," he said. "Is there a stable?"

"There's one behind the seminary," Luminant Theo said.

Joachin turned away and strode down the hall. He didn't wait for the old men to follow.

"Shall we wait for you at the entrance?" Luminant Theo called after him.

Joachin lifted his hand in dismissal.

Chapter Eleven: Caspar

THE URGE TO relieve her bladder was overwhelming. They had come to the edge of the woods. Miriam peered through the screen of trees that separated them from the road. She was hungry, but that wasn't the worse thing. The dull ache that had begun as soon as the guards left was now painful.

Your torso hurts, Alonso pointed out. *Maybe you should apply some of that lavender to yourself.*

The problem wasn't the tattoo. She headed for a nearby thicket, too embarrassed to explain. He blundered along with her.

Do you mind? She shooed him away as if it might stop him from following her, a futile gesture. He wasn't outside her body, but in it. Unless he could leave her again, he'd witness every bodily function she was required to make.

Oh! He finally figured it out. *I'm not sure I can.*

You did it with the birds! She cradled her belly.

Yes, but I was....

He was going to say 'panicked'. She clenched her jaw. Her eyes closed at the same time, not her doing. He was experimenting. She danced from foot to foot. *Alonso!*

All right! I'm trying!

She felt a tightening, followed by an unpleasant stretching sensation. Suddenly, her body thrummed like a plucked guitar string. She yelped, afraid she had lost control. Fortunately, everything stayed dry. They were still joined, but less so than before. *Hurry!*

I'm sorry! This is new for me! If I try again, perhaps a bit harder.... She throbbed, and then, he was beside her, a cool shadow. There was some overlap, but he no longer inhabited her like one Rustti doll inside another. She sucked in her breath.

There's a cord between us, he said in amazement. *Actually, there are two. Yours is silver. Mine's a darker grey.*

Fascinating! Privacy!

Oh, of course. Forgive me. I'll wait over here.

She wasn't sure where 'here' was, but she knew he no longer dwelt inside her, closer than breath. She did what was required. Having her body to herself was a relief.

Afterwards, she took a moment to check her tattoo. Two of the cuts had puckered beneath the blood and the ink. Other than dabbing them with lavender, there was little she could do. They had to scab cleanly. She left the thicket to check on Ephraim. His tremors had lessened, but that wasn't always a good sign. It was possible he was growing weaker. They needed to risk the road to reach Gaspar.

Who is Gaspar?

He was in her head again. Now that her need wasn't so pressing, it didn't bother her so much. *A crofter who supplies us with hard-to-find herbs.* Gaspar was much more than that, but she didn't want to explain. She stepped from the trees to survey the road in both directions. *How far can you move from me? It would be helpful if we knew where the Guard was. Can you check the road ahead?*

I'll see.

This time, the separation wasn't so dramatic. She felt her back tighten, her skin stretch, and then came that familiar 'pop'. Her body vibrated like a string. She waited impatiently. After a few minutes, he dropped back into her like a pigeon returning to its roost.

I went around the corner. He sounded breathless. *After that, I grew light-headed.*

It wasn't faintness that he felt, but anxiety. She let it pass. *Perhaps with practice....* His voice trailed off and then he rallied, as if sensing her perceptiveness. *There's no sign of the Guard. How far away is your crofter?*

She wasn't sure. There was a tiny traveler's shrine on the main road. After that, a trail led to Gaspar's hut.

I'll see if I can find it. She caught his intent: he would not have her think him a coward.

The 'thrum' of his leaving took less time than before. Perhaps they were growing used to it. It was disturbing to know each other's minds, but on the other hand, it saved explaining everything. She hauled the donkey by its harness and coaxed it onto the road. Without Alonso, she felt more vulnerable than ever. He was an imposition but also a comrade in arms. His presence was reassuring.

Make up your mind, she told herself crossly. Now that they weren't at odds, she found him attractive, again. Gods forbid he should sense it. A day had passed since she had swabbed his face at his deathbed. Even in death, he'd been beautiful.

A tendril of smoke curled about her nose. She lifted her head in alarm. The air was clear, but the breeze brought news.

I found the shrine.

She jumped. His voice was so immediate, he might have shouted in her ear. *It's been demolished,* he said.

How far did you go? Is there a fire ahead? she asked.

About twice what I did before. I saw smoke above the trees, but I wanted to return to you. I'll go further if you like, to get a better look.

Don't. She sensed another departure. Testing his limits gave him a purpose, but without him, she was blind. *I'd rather you stay, awhile.* He might keep them informed, but if the Guard was no longer in the vicinity, she saw no reason for him to scout ahead.

Very well. We're safe for now, but I'll leave in a bit, just to make sure we stay that way. He settled beside her as if they were two companions on the road. That surprised her. She snapped the donkey's reins.

She was very aware of him, but also thankful for their separation. Perhaps he was of the same mind, knowing that they needed a certain amount of space for sanity's sake. There was still some overlap between them. Feeling curious, she focused on where she ended and he began. Her talent wrapped tendrils about him, felt his length and breadth. He was two heads taller than she and broader in the neck and chest. His hips were lean and his legs well-muscled and long. He held himself with an easy grace, more like a farmer heading to market on a sunny day than a priest hunched over a pulpit. He felt vital, strong, male. It was best not to dwell on it. She focused on the road.

Are you able to do that because we're joined or is it something else?

Embarrassment swept her in a tide. He'd been aware of her scrutiny the whole time. She may as well have groped him with her hands.

It's all right. I don't mind. His smile was a warm glow.

She wanted to die of mortification. He didn't mind? What business did a priest have in making such a remark? He'd been a professed celibate all of his life, hadn't he?

You feel intensely. More than I was ever able to.

She drew in a breath. *I'm sorry. That was unforgivable. I'm not used to this.*

He paused, to weigh his words. *I suppose it's something we'll have to get used to.*

She didn't know what to say.

But what is it, exactly? You have a way of feeling, of sensing....

Oh—he was trying to describe her talent. Safer ground, at last. She released her breath in relief. *I'm what is known as a sentidora.*

A what?

She smiled in spite of herself. *Some people have visions, others hear voices. I feel what others do when I touch them. That's all.*

Really?

It isn't madness or witchcraft. It's just...a talent. Like singing.

So you felt what I did as I lay dying. When you touched me with your finger.

He remembered that? How much had he sensed of her attraction? *Yes.*

He was silent for a moment. She reached for his impressions, but they were as fleeting as sun beams in a cloud. *How terrible for you to feel others' pain,* he said at last.

Another reprieve, thank heaven. *I recover quickly. It helps me work as a healer.*

You mentioned that before. So, you do that, too? Like your father?

I should clarify. I help him, but always under a premise.

Ah. The power behind the pulpit.

As if there were such a thing. He, of all people, should know what she risked in being what she was. Others had burned for less. *I wish. It was never that grand.*

They'd come to the shrine. It had been reduced to kindling. To one side, a decapitated statue lay—Saint Cecilia, it looked like. Ephraim had told her that many of the female saints were actually representations of the goddess Lys. The statue's dainty head stared patiently at the sky. It bothered Miriam to see it so. She didn't believe in Lys, but she didn't like the irreverence with which the statue had been dealt.

It has that significance? She felt Alonso's dismay. *If that's the case, the Guard has done this.*

But Cecilia is a recognized saint!

Tattoos go hand in hand with goddess worship. Destroy an image of the goddess, and the worshipper may appear to rectify it.

A chill clawed up her back in spite of the heat of the day.

Did you bear that stomach tattoo when Tomás questioned you?

No, why?

Maybe it doesn't matter. By now, the priests will have told Tomás of the tattoos you carved on me, anyway.

But how would they know about those? I thought the tomb was sealed.

No. For seven days, they return to the Hill to replace the rushes about my body. Tomás won't know how you did it, but he'll associate your escape with my tattoos. He'll conclude that you, or someone on your behalf, thwarted his plans. I pity the people of Granad right now. He'll suspect a conspiracy and search for a cabal. He'll see you as key. If he thinks you can give him the power to thwart death, he'll stop at nothing to find you.

She wanted to bolt, terrified that they would be discovered at any moment. *Let's leave this place.*

They found Gaspar's trail a short distance from the shrine. It showed signs of recent travel. In places, hoof prints had churned the ground to muck. As well, the smoke was thickening. *Are you sure there's no fire?* Miriam asked.

Silence met her. He had already gone ahead to check. She hadn't noticed his leaving. The donkey balked.

"What's the matter with you?" she asked, snapping its reins. She was tense again, now that Alonso was gone. The donkey dug in its hooves and refused to budge. She listened for sounds of approach. There were none. There was no bird song, either. She jumped from the rig and yanked at the beast's harness. "For Sul's sake, move!"

A whiff of something unpleasant snagged her nose. She recoiled. It cloyed, had a hint of charred feathers about it.

We have to go back. Alonso's voice was overloud in her ears, his mood a black cloud. She felt a tug at her elbow. *There's no help to be found this way.*

Why? What's happened?

Nothing you want to see.

Trepidation rose in her like a flock of storks out-flying a storm. She was seventeen, but no child. He had no right to shield her. *Tell me!*

A sob caught in her throat. His revulsion tossed her into a dark well from which there was no returning. *They've burnt a child. I found it, smoldering on a stake. I don't know where its parents are.*

She stifled a cry and ran down the path.

Miriam! Come back!

Tears streamed down her face. She had to see, had to be sure. Why would they do this? How could they have connected her to Gaspar?

The birds. The Guard had found the pigeon cote on the top of their house. Ephraim had sent a pigeon to Gaspar to ask him to bring lungwort for Alonso. Tomás would have freed them to watch where they flew.

She ran harder. Let it not be him. Please to the god, not Gaspar. As a child, she had been so sure he was a fairy, that he could grant wishes. She had crept up on him, captured him in her chubby arms. Granad had seen his dwarfism as a curse, but he was the kindest soul she knew. He treated every living thing with a deep respect, a reverence most people lacked.

Miriam, he's gone. There's nothing you can do for him.

She could do nothing? Alonso was wrong. If the poor soul on the stake was Gaspar, she would pull him down.

Ahead, the light brightened as the trees thinned. The smoke carved her lungs. She leaned against an oak and clutched at a stitch in her side. Her eyes streamed.

In the midst of a smoldering vegetable patch, a stake speared the sky. Upon it, a small black form arched like a bow. Beyond it, a hut stood, its walls painted with daisies, confirming for Miriam who the victim was.

She let out a wail and ran to the body. She couldn't get close; the flames were too hot. Not knowing what else to do, she ran to the cottage. The door had been left ajar. Inside, Gaspar's few sticks of furniture had been overturned. His herbs had been trampled underfoot. In one corner, a clove of garlic lay. She clutched at it as if it were his heart.

There's nothing you can do here. Alonso meant to be comforting.

Nothing I can do? I can bury him, Alonso! I brought this upon him!

You didn't. How, possibly...?

The Guard followed our birds. They flew here. I should have let them go the night I left Granad, but I forgot them! And now this!

It isn't your fault.

Whose fault is it then? Is it yours, Alonso? Let's say it's yours. All this began with you. With the Solarium, with the temple. Men of the god did this! Priests, like you! You keep us downtrodden. When we're different or we don't know our place, you torture and kill us! It's all about control! How can you suggest I not bury Gaspar? You of all people should understand this! Her words cut. He flinched under the verbal assault.

You've left your father on the trail. He sounded tired. *We have to retrieve him. The fire will go out soon. You can bury Gaspar later. I doubt if the Guard will be back. They've done their worst.*

He was right. She'd left Ephraim, a foolish thing to do. As for Alonso, his stoic martyrdom tested the limits of her patience. She had spoken her truth, had exaggerated his involvement, but if he expected an apology, he would have to wait. She had no time for male sulking.

I don't want that. He sighed. *Sometimes, I forget how young you are.*

I am not...! How dare he dismiss her accusations or simplify them! As if once she found a calmer piece of mind, she would see her outburst as a need to vent her pain and shock. She felt Gaspar's loss to her core. But then, so did he. He felt everything she did.

She stifled her retort. He was right; she *was* acting like a child, but she wasn't about to admit it. They both suffered. Let it be left at that.

As she dug the grave, she kept her head down and focused on shovelful after shovelful. Her throat remained thick, her eyes stung. She refused to look at the block of charcoal that bent from the pole. Instead, she saw rescued birds, a fox with a bandaged leg, a tiny rabbit, cupped in calloused hands not much bigger than her own. A puppet cunningly made, the clever manikin that moved by strings. Gaspar had fashioned it to remind her of him. For years, it lay on her bed, a cheery gnome to chase away the bad dreams. Her fingers formed blisters and bled, but she had welcomed the pain—a small penance for what her negligence had wrought. She would never forget him. He had been a small man, a half man, but his selflessness had been vast. His death was the world's loss. It was as if the rare beauty of a rainbow had been snuffed from existence, removed from the sky.

She stood by the hole, too sick to give voice to her grief. Alonso stood beside her. *I can say a few words, if you like.*

His reluctance was as tight as wet cotton. He no longer believed but thought it might give her comfort if he voiced empty prayers. She let the shovel drop.

Tears streamed down her face.

Don't, he said. *Despite what you think, you didn't do this. Tomás would have suspected anyone living this close to a shrine. It's as you said. If he can't control something, he destroys it.*

She lifted her head and took a faltering step to the stake. With trembling hands, she reached for Gaspar, touched what might have been his thin shoulder, now covered in black scabs. She began to shake.

Shhhh! You don't have to do this...!

His words set her ablaze. She would no longer tolerate anyone who told her what she could or couldn't do. Not her society, not her family, nor any outside imposition. She would only heed that inner compass that prompted her to act. *I have to!* she screamed. *Don't you see? It's all I have left to give him!*

She turned back to the pitiful crust on the pillar. Crying through gritted teeth, she snapped off an arm. She broke off the second. Then the head, the spine...when she was done, she filled the hole, tamped it down. Numb once more, she stumbled back to the hut to check on Ephraim.

Amid the space she had cleared, he lay on the floor as still as death.

For one heart-stopping moment, she thought he was dead. She stood stock still, as if ham-strung and about to topple. Some shred of strength she didn't know she had prompted her to scan his body for any hint that he still lived. His chest rose and fell shallowly. She caught her breath, fought off the grey. He breathed.

How is he?

She ignored Alonso and fell at Ephraim's side. She lifted his habit. The pus had returned, worse than ever. She wiped it away with her sleeve, crushed the garlic clove beneath a rock and set the pulp into the wound. Her hands shook. She had to get supplies for him. If she didn't, she would lose him, too.

The village of Batos isn't far. About an hour from here if we stay off the road. Do you have coin?

She nodded, thankful that she had had some foresight, after all.

I'll be back soon, Papa, she promised, looking down at him. She covered him with her habit.

Too tired to think, she stumbled from the croft.

Chapter Twelve: El Lince

THE MISUNDERSTANDING AT the seminary put Joachín in a foul mood. He had no money, no leads. His cheek bone ached. The gods mocked him. How was he to pay his mother's death debt if he couldn't find her killer? His stomach growled. He headed for the market.

He left Fidel with a hostler with the promise that he'd pay for the horse's upkeep once he returned. It wasn't long before tents flapped about him, each one more colourful than the last. All about him, geese honked, melons spilled, hawker's cursed, and fish stank. Children ran everywhere. Mothers scolded. One kiosk offered fine wines, while its neighbour sold overripe tomatoes. Disorganization reigned. Joachín approved. Chaos suited his purposes.

Something brushed his hip. He reached down and grabbed an urchin with a dirty face. To his surprise, the girl looked Diaphani, or perhaps half-Diaphani, as he was.

"Choose better marks," he warned her, keeping his face out of spitting distance. "My wallet's empty. I have nothing." With impatience, he released her. She twisted into the crowd.

He strolled down an aisle and side-stepped a flock of chickens. Ahead, a heavy-set man haggled with a woman at a tanner's booth. He wore the latest fashion, a velvet cloak trimmed with fur. The object of their contention was a black leather vest.

Joachín ambled over to take a better look. The waistcoat was striking. On each panel, twin lynxes stared at the viewer. Their ears quivered with anticipation, their eyes sized up the prey. He felt an immediate affinity with them. He had to have the vest.

"How much?" the burly man asked.

"Twenty *soltars*," the woman replied.

"Too much. I'll give you two."

"Don't insult me. Fifteen."

"Five."

"Go away. I don't need your business."

"Seven. My last offer."

"Twelve."

The *patrón* reached into his money bag. "I have eight *soltars* in my pouch. That's all." He laid the gold coins on the counter, one by one. Joachín glanced at the purse and wondered at the woman's sense. The bag bulged, but her eyes were on the money.

"Highway robbery." She presented the man with the vest and scooped up the coin. He stashed the vest under his arm and walked away.

Joachín followed him, knowing that the right moment would present itself sooner or later. Out of the corner of his eye, something blue and yellow flitted between the tents. It kept pace with him and his mark. Joachín paused, pretended to glance at a display of baskets. The flutter of blue stopped. He moved on. His shadow resumed its pace.

The man stopped at a gold dealer's booth. Joachín unsheathed his knife. The fool's purse was of the softest suede—a mistake when hard leather would have protected his coin better. A slice through the bottom, and whatever lay in the bag would be his.

The flutter of blue and yellow darted in front of him, as haphazard as a butterfly. It was the Diaphani girl who had tried to steal his wallet earlier.

"*Ser! Ser!*" she cried, clinging to the man's coat. "A *pentine* for me, so I can buy a sweet! Please, *Ser!*"

She glued herself to his knees. He tried to kick her off. "Let go, filth!"

Joachin went to his assistance. The girl glared at him as feral as a weasel, but something in her eyes made him reassess. She was *helping* him. With a deft slice of his knife, the coin was no longer in the man's pouch but in Joachin's pocket. The girl swore at him, and snatched the leather vest from the mark's hands. In seconds, she was running away from them.

"Grab her!" the man shouted. "She has my vest!"

"I'll get her!" Joachin chased her past a flurry of tarps and faceless people. She darted around a corner and into a narrow gap between two booths. She wasn't breathing hard by the time he caught up with her.

"You look Diaphani," she said by way of greeting. "I didn't see it at first, but I think you are."

He ignored the comment. "How much do you want for that vest?"

"Maybe I don't want to sell it. Maybe I took it for my father."

He gazed at her with sympathy. What was she, nine years old, ten? Likely, an orphan. What she needed was food. He fingered the *soltars* in his pocket. There were at least a dozen of them in there, as well as eight *linares* and a few *pentines*. "I'll give you a *linare*," he said, feeling generous.

"Three," she countered. "One for my mother, one for my father, and one for me."

"Two."

She regarded him with suffering eyes. He recognized the look. He'd used it himself at that age.

"Very well, three."

She handed him the vest. "Don't let anyone catch you," he said, as he paid her.

"No one catches me. I am too fast."

"*I* caught you."

"Because I let you."

He waggled a finger at her. "Even so, a thief can't be too sure of herself."

She squinted at him. "How did you get that cut on your cheek?"

"Don't ask personal questions."

"What's your name?"

He looked down at her small, impish face. "Names are valuable things," he said, not wanting to lie to her for some reason. "I've already paid you three *linares*. You don't need my name."

"Then I'll call you *El Lince* after those cats on your vest."

The moniker pleased him. He grinned at her despite his better judgment. "Be careful, Little Cat." He turned to go.

"Goddess keep you, *El Lince*."

He spun about to warn her—no one in their right mind acknowledged the goddess openly—but she was gone.

He spent little time in the market, knowing their mark would call the constabulary to search for him and the girl. That would protect her. The guards would look for an adult and child team. He bought what he needed: a thicker coat for the coming weather, food for his belly, and enough hard-tack to keep him for a week. He retrieved Fidel from the paddock and they trotted for the North Gate. There was still the matter of his dream woman. He may as well go along with what the dream had shown him. Since he had no firm direction for finding the scar-faced priest, north was as good as any.

After a few leagues, he reined Fidel off the road and headed into the woods. He had no desire for a stint in jail, or worse—death by hanging, so he never spent the night where he had committed a theft. The forest was a much safer place.

He found a sandy spot, ringed by olive trees and not far from a stream. There would be no bonfire tonight. Flames drew unwanted guests. Twice, he thought he'd gained a clue about his mother's killer. The priest in Herradur knew who he was, but as for the archivist in Velez...what a farce that had been. Bloody priest could be anywhere.

He bit down on a piece of salt pork harder than necessary. His cheek flared with pain. He swore, clapped a hand to it, and drew away pus.

He should have killed Rufio when he'd had the chance. Cupping his cheek, he headed for the stream and scanned the forest floor as he went. What he needed was bruisewort, but he doubted he'd find any this far south. There was still the Dartura flower in his pocket.

Dartura was both a healing and a dream herb. He'd never used it because his prescience came naturally, but as far as the bite on his face was concerned, it might help. He dabbed his cheek with a petal. The pain ebbed, a good sign. He left it on the cut and swallowed another for good measure. Might as well assist the healing from the inside as well as out. He headed back to Fidel and tucked the rest of the blossom into his saddlebag. He climbed into his blanket, feeling drowsier than usual. The flower was working. There was no point in fighting its effect. He drifted off, hoping to dream of the murderous priest. Surely, he and the goddess were of the same mind—that he should find his mother's killer and end him.

Chapter Thirteen: Batos

WITHOUT THE CART, the trail was easy to travel. Even so, it took Miriam the better part of an hour to reach the bridge that led to Batos. It consisted of a double arch with stone abutments on either side. She tethered the donkey to a bushy willow and hauled herself up a muddy embankment. Her shoes caked with mud, her arms were soon streaked with grime. She reached the bridge and crossed it to the hamlet.

Batos looked to be a mining town. Although the inn was a lively place, she suspected most of the villagers were at home for their supper. Two children ran past her. She hailed them. The boy kept running, but the girl turned around. She stared at her with wide eyes. Miriam knew she looked a sight.

"I won't hurt you," Miriam reassured her. "Does a midwife live around here?"

The child pointed to a small cottage at the end of the road. A picket fence surrounded a prim yard. Beyond it, a trail snaked up a steep hill where goats browsed. The girl ran after her brother.

Miriam made her way to the cottage and noted the well-tended herbs in the yard. The fence was meant to keep out the goats, but one had invaded the garden. As she passed through the gate, she shooed it away. It leapt over the fence.

The door to the cottage opened and a large woman filled the frame. She wore an apron over her plain dress and a kerchief on her head. From behind her, light streamed from a fire. "Who are you?" she demanded.

"Greetings, *Sera*," Miriam said politely, hoping that her deference might compensate for her filthy appearance. "I've come to buy herbs. I have coin."

"So you say?" The woman glanced about to see if she had come alone and then regarded her. "You're not from around here."

Miriam wiped her hands on her skirt. "No. I've been traveling. I need some supplies. My friend is hurt."

"Is he now? Well, you'd best come inside and tell me about it."

Miriam followed her within. The cottage consisted of two rooms. The largest held a table, chairs, and a wide hearth over which boiled a pot of soup. Beyond it was the bedroom. Bundles of herbs hung from the rafters. The place smelled of onions and stewed meat. On the table, a bunch of rosemary lay.

"His axe slipped," Miriam explained, "while he was cutting wood."

The woman's eyebrows rose. "If the cut's deep, it'll need stitching. You should bring him here."

"The wound isn't deep, but it is infected."

"Salvia's good for that. I don't have much this time of the year. It'll cost you."

"Salvia is an efficient extract, but garlic would do as well." Garlic was much, much cheaper.

The woman pursed her lips. "Something of an herbalist, are you?"

Miriam nodded.

"Where do you hail from?"

She fished a silver *linare* from her pocket and set it on the table. "I also need bandages and comfrey. A little wine if you have it. I think this should cover it all."

The midwife heaved herself to her feet. She went to a cupboard and retrieved the garlic and bandages. "You could use a little help yourself, niña." She pointed at Miriam's blouse. Blood stained the cloth.

"Oh, that's nothing." She scooped the bandages and garlic and thrust them into her pouch.

"Let me see."

"It's a bramble scratch."

"That's no bramble scratch. Don't be shy. You've paid me well. I won't charge you." She set her hands on Miriam's waistband.

"No, please." She pushed her hands away.

The woman ignored her and yanked up her blouse. The cloth came away freely, exposing her tattoo. The midwife eyed her accusingly. "As I thought! You're Diaphani!"

"No, I'm not." Miriam backed away.

"Yes, you are! You're a god-plagued Diaphani witch! How dare you come here? You steal my goats and blight my plants! Get out!"

Miriam ran for the door, the woman at her heels. "I'll set the men on you! And don't think to curse me, either! I'll hex you right back!"

Miriam ran from the yard. The midwife pointed at her. "Witch! Witch!"

The door to a nearby cottage opened. A woman glanced into the darkening street.

Get off the main road. Slip between the houses and find another way.

Miriam darted between the cottages. *But what if there's livestock?*

Better that than the villagers.

Behind the houses, she encountered a mule and a sow with piglets. The mule brayed. The sow charged her as she ran past, but it soon gave up the chase. After a dozen cottages, the houses ended. She faced an empty expanse between the hamlet and the bridge. She paused to catch her breath. *The midwife thought I was Diaphani.* She felt Alonso's assent. *Why are the Diaphani hated so much?*

They're outsiders. I suppose it doesn't help if the odd chicken or pig goes missing. There are no locals about. I think it's safe to run.

She was about to slip out from beneath the eaves of the last cottage when lights flickered beyond the bridge. Men on horseback emerged from the woods, carrying torches. She froze.

Hide! His fear made him shout louder than necessary. *Between the houses!*

She darted back between the two cottages, pressed against the wall of one, and hoped the chicken coop of the other might shield her. She stood in shadow, but there was no room to crouch. She turned her face to hide it from anyone glancing her way. She held her breath, not daring to breathe.

The first two riders approached. They slowed their horses to a walk. They dismounted and hammered on the door of the first house. The other guards trotted past, about a dozen of them in all. As the villager answered his door, there was a curt demand for entry, followed by the tread of heavy boots.

"Nothing there," one guard told the other. The two passed within feet of her and knocked on the door to the second cottage. Her heart skipped a beat as she clutched her pouch. The urge to bolt was overwhelming.

Not yet, Alonso warned.

Her skin crawled. A lone rider appeared at the edge of her view, like Death on a horse. He had stopped to survey the road. He pushed his hood from his bald head as if wanting to savour the cool night air. In the fading light, his scar gleamed like sinew on bone. Tomás. Her instincts screamed at her to flee. She closed her eyes.

Don't panic. He's about to ride past.

From further down the street, the midwife shouted. Tomás spurred his horse and trotted on.

Back now, Alonso said.

She needed no coaxing. Like a sparrow outflying a fire, she darted and stooped, praying that no one saw her. The donkey was beneath the bridge where she left it, but it was skittish and keen to be away. She drew it into the woods and skirted the river's banks until the hint of smoke told her they'd come back to Gaspar's. She entered the dark croft and found her father. To her relief, Ephraim hadn't died. His chest still rose and fell. She crushed the garlic and comfrey and dressed his wounds. When she was done, she took a deep breath and then left the cottage to stare at the rising moon. Exhausted from the day and from fear, she sat beside Gaspar's grave. Her throat tightened and her eyes pricked. She fought for breath. She would *not* cry. Not any more. Besides, she wasn't sure she had the strength for it. She was parched, cold.

Allow me. Invisible arms wrapped themselves about her shoulders. They had no more mass than a moth's wing, but oddly enough, they made her warm.

Where do we go? she asked him, wishing he had a shoulder she could lean on. *Where is safe?*

For a moment, Alonso said nothing. She wondered what he was thinking, but she was too tired to work it out. She gave up the effort.

When he finally spoke his voice was strained, as if a different mood had claimed him altogether. Before she caught it, he tucked it away. It seemed a thin shadow of longing, an uncomfortable yearning smoothed into submission as if it had never been.

I wish I knew, Miriam, he replied softly.

Chapter Fourteen: Dathura Dreams

JOACHÍN'S DREAMS WERE fragmented at first. In spite of his intention to find the murderous priest, he relived his life in the alleys of Taleda. Life in the brothel hadn't been pleasant, but at least he'd had regular meals and a corner to sleep in. After he had slashed the priest with his knife; the whore master had tossed him out. He had fought the rats for food until he learned how to steal.

His dream shifted. Now he regarded the urchin from the market. She gazed at him with solemn brown eyes. A sudden smile broke over her face. "*El Lince*," she said. "Come home with me." She held out her hands.

Her offer annoyed him. He had no home. His mother's people had never come to claim him after Estrella died.

They did not know. The voice floated into his awareness, coming from nowhere. It touched him with a holiness so pristine he wanted to weep.

He saw his own self-pity for what it was and shook it aside. "Show me the priest!" he demanded. "Then I'll find home!"

The sense of grace retreated. He regretted his temper. It had to be the Dartura. Usually, his dreams weren't so jumbled.

Torchlight. Brands jigged past him—men on horseback in habits of white and black—the Guard. Between two houses, his dream girl pressed her back against a wall. As the riders rode by, she turned her face so as not to be seen in the moonlight.

He's about to ride past. Don't move.

Another disembodied voice, but this time it was a man's and lacked the grace of the first one. Joachin glanced about. No one, other than himself, stood beside the woman. Had he heard the voice at all? It seemed more thought than inflection.

His dream woman closed her eyes.

Someone shouted from down the road. Joachin turned to the terrified girl. His lips felt like dead weights. "Who are you?" he mouthed. His face felt numb. She paid him no heed.

Something nicked him behind an ear.

He came fully awake and reached for his knife. To his horror, his body refused to cooperate. He couldn't move. He could barely open his eyes.

"No one you need to know," a dark shadow muttered. "One move, and you're dead."

He willed his hands to lift. All he managed was a facial twitch.

"There's something wrong with him."

Joachin forced his eyes to focus. A black shadow leaned over him. The lanky form was outlined by stars. "I think he's drugged." His assailant slapped him on the face. He raged inwardly at the insult.

A second hulk loomed over him. This one was more heavily set than the first. "His business. Makes ours easier."

"What's that on his face?"

"Who cares? Some kind of leaf."

"Do we kill him?"

The older one nodded. "We can't take any chances. He's come too close to the camp. Dead men don't strike."

A knife pricked his jugular. He closed his eyes and waited. The point hesitated and then withdrew. "He looks Diaphani."

In the darkness, his would-be killers stared down at him. The heavier one leaned in to take a closer look. He was a man of middling years. His eyes were deeply set and piercing. "Sul," he swore. "He does. Are you Diaphani?" He grabbed his chin and turned his head from side to side.

Joachin forced the word from his lips. "Half." It came out 'haph'.

"Maybe he's just saying that," the skinnier one said.

"No one admits they're Diaphani unless they are." The heavier one rose to his feet.

"What do we do, *Paré?*"

There was a long pause. "What we have to."

Joachin felt his neck constrict. Instead of a knife severing his throat, the two men hauled him to his feet. His legs refused to cooperate. They dragged him across the grass and hoisted him onto Fidel's back. The pommel dug into his gut. He wanted to vomit but didn't have the strength for it. They led him through the woods. Soon, he smelled wood smoke. Entering a small encampment, he heard muted voices. With gentle hands, his abductors lifted him from his horse and set him beside their fire. He slumped to the ground.

"Get Luci," the big man ordered. A small boy ran off on bare feet.

A number of people clustered about him, a forest of legs. One wore a familiar skirt of yellow and blue.

"*El Lince!*" she blurted.

Little Cat. These had to be her people. He never thought he'd set eyes on her again.

"*Paré*, what's wrong with him?" Her face filled his vision.

Someone pulled her aside. A skirt of deep indigo. "What's this?" a woman asked.

"We found him on the camp's periphery," the big man said. "I don't think he knew we were here."

A middle-aged woman knelt to regard him. She cupped his face with a calloused hand. She was dark-haired and tiny. Crow's feet spread about her eyes. Joachin felt his heart constrict. Had his mother lived to middle-age, she would have looked very much like her. The resemblance between them was striking.

"What's that on his face?" Little Cat asked.

"I'm not sure," the woman said. She plucked the petal from his cheek and smelled it. She stared at him with disdain. "Were you aware of the potency of this plant before you used it?"

Joachín said nothing. He was so tired. It didn't matter.

"He's falling asleep." She laid his head on the ground with a tenderness that surprised him. "We won't get anything more from him until morning."

"What do we do with him?" the big man asked.

"He can sleep in my bed," Little Cat said.

"Don't be ridiculous, Casi."

"I don't mind. He's the one I told you about, *Maré. El Lince.* The man who gave me three whole *linares.*"

"That's him? Are you sure?"

"He's Diaphani, *Maré.* No one's that generous to us. He has to be."

"He looks it." The youth who had held the knife to his throat confirmed.

"Lay him on a blanket beneath our *vardo,*" the woman said. "At least he'll stay dry if it rains."

"Is that wise? What if he wakes up?" the big man asked.

"He won't. The Dartura will hold him for a few hours, yet."

Hands lifted him and carried him to a caravan. They rolled him beneath it. Someone covered him with a blanket. The last thing he remembered was Little Cat smiling down at him and stroking the hair from his eyes.

Chapter Fifteen: Blood Tells

JOACHÍN AWOKE TO the aroma of food cooking on a campfire. Boiled acorns mixed with barley, it smelled like. Estrella had made a gruel much like it. Above him, a rustic ceiling of wagon lay. He lurched to his side. Two legs barred his view. A broad face leaned beneath the caravan to regard him.

"So, you're awake," the big man said. "There's breakfast, if you want it."

He glared at his captor. "I think I'll be going," he replied ungraciously. He clambered out from beneath the caravan.

The big man shrugged. "Your choice. You're a guest in my camp. It's tradition to offer hospitality."

"A guest." Joachín stared at him. The younger one had held a knife to his throat. They'd discussed killing him.

"You're half Diaphani, or so you claim. We don't harm our own."

No. But they banished them. His mother had been a prostitute. What would they say to that? He shrugged. "If I'm free to go, I'll be on my way."

"You're not leaving!" Little Cat appeared from behind the wagon like a sparrow flitting down from a tree. "I made you breakfast. *Maré* wants to talk to you!"

He took in her small face. There was no reason to feel a connection to her, but he did. It bothered him.

"Please!" She grabbed him by the hand and hauled him to the fire where her mother stirred a cook pot. Other members of the clan lingered nearby, listening, no doubt. Joachin allowed himself to be led. Soon, he stood before the woman. She handed him a spoon and a bowl of the steaming gruel.

"Eat," she said. "The food will take care of any residual effects from the Dartura."

He was ravenous. He shoveled the cereal into his mouth.

"I am Luci," she said. "You know Casi, already. You've met Guillermo, my husband, and Iago, our son."

'Met' was an interesting choice of a word. The silence lengthened between them, broken by the sound of his eating.

"Did you take the Dartura to treat that cut on your face?" she asked. "I suspect you weren't aware of its potency."

He shook his head. "I wasn't."

"Dartura can be a dangerous herb."

"I would have used bruisewort if I'd had it." He handed her the bowl. "My thanks."

"You say you're half-Diaphani," she said. "From which clan?"

"I don't know. My mother never told me."

"Your mother is Diaphani?"

"Was. She's dead."

"Oh. I'm sorry." Little Cat, Guillermo, and Iago had come to stand beside her. "What was her name? Perhaps we know it. If she died, we should honour her." There was something in her eyes. A hope, a fear, he wasn't sure.

"You'd honour a woman who was named outcast?" he asked. "Her people threw her out—*your* people. She married an outsider, my father. She was banished."

The woman lifted a hand to her throat. "What was her name?"

"What is it with you people and names?"

"Please! Tell me her name!"

"She was Estrella Montoya de Rivera. A Diaphani, a pariah, and yes, in the end, a whore! There! What do you think of that, *Sera?* After my father died, she had no one. *We* had no one!"

The woman let out a low cry. "Estrella! It can't be! Dear Lys!"

Guillermo caught her in his arms. Joachín turned to leave.

"No!" Luci called out to him. "Please! You mustn't go! *El Lince*, we didn't know about her. We didn't know about you! Iago, stop him!"

The youth barred his way, his hand on his knife belt. Other members of the clan hemmed him in.

"*El Lince*, give us a chance to explain," Luci called after him. "Hear me out. I'm your mother's sister, your aunt. We did *not* throw her out. She left us. She didn't want to stay."

He didn't believe her, would not. All his life, he'd known otherwise. His mother's people had banished her. It wasn't the other way around. "You're lying," he said, not caring about the consequences. The men glowered.

"Estrella left because of your father. Juan didn't like us. He was town's folk. He could live no other way. Your mother was so in love with him that she gave us up for him!"

His anger boiled over. "I don't believe you!" He clenched his hands into fists.

"Why would I lie? Juan loved your mother, but he didn't love us. He thought he was doing her a favour by making her respectable!"

He glared at the faces about him. What she said sounded uncomfortably true. Juan de Rivera had been a difficult man. He and his mother had met one night when Estrella danced in a tavern. Among the Diaphani, she'd been known as 'La Muneca' or 'Doll'. She'd been a celebrity among her own people, but after she married Juan, his father insisted that she conform to his ideas of propriety. No more dancing. And no more Diaphani.

He ran a hand across his brow, the fire of his passion, doused. "Perhaps what you say is true," he relented. "Forgive me. It's a belief I've held for a long time."

His aunt's expression softened. "How old were you when Juan died?"

"Nine."

"And when Estrella passed?"

"Eleven."

He knew what they were thinking. For two years, his mother had earned her living on her back. After she died, he'd been an orphan, left to survive on his own.

"I see Estrella's hand in this," Luci said without judgment. "She orchestrated this. Or perhaps the goddess did. Dartura is a goddess plant. You took it and are reunited with us. Destiny is at work, here. Welcome home, *El Lince*."

He remembered Little Cat's words from his dream. *Come home with me.* And the other voice: *they did not know.* Perhaps there was some plan he didn't see, some fate bigger than the rest of them. Deep down, he'd always wanted a family. He had always longed for a home.

"What should we call you?" Guillermo asked. "What is your Diaphani name?"

'Juan' formed on his lips and then, 'José'. His two most-used aliases. He found he didn't want to lie to these people.

His throat grew thick. "I am Joachin," he said, feeling overwhelmed.

Over the next few hours, he met the rest of the clan. Most of them were Montoyas, cloth merchants and dealers in indigo when they had it, although indigo was hard to come by. The clan's destination was a hidden valley near the town of Elysir, an ancient site sacred to the goddess. Every year, Luci informed him, the different bands gathered to pass the news, arrange marriages, and show off new babies. It was a time for reunion and celebration, an annual pilgrimage made by the far-flung Diaphani to honour their goddess and themselves.

"Of course, there are always squabbles," she explained as if they were a test to her patience. "In particular, the Ortegas and the Ferraras don't get along. Years ago, half the Ortegas' herd went missing. They accused the Ferraras of selling the horses to the Moori before Granad fell. Of course, the Ferraras denied it, but after that, they gave up tinsmithing for weapons manufacture. One doesn't do *that* without a lot of money."

She cocked an eyebrow at Joachín. It was clear which way she thought the river flowed. "In any event, it's important to set feuds aside, to renew old ties as well as make new ones." She squeezed his hand. "We Montoyas didn't have much to report, but now we do. You'll be our news."

Joachín's heart gave a queer little hitch. She reminded him so much of his mother. He felt at ease with everyone he'd met. *Blood tells*, he considered. They took it for granted he was one of them.

The plan was that he would travel with them to the site near Elysir. He would ask whomever he met about the Guard, who they called the Torch Bearers.

At their mention, Guillermo's face darkened. "There have been rumours that they've been active in the south. That's why I set guards on the camp last night, and how Iago and I found you. Last year, the Vargas never made it to the Womb."

"The Womb?"

"The site of our pilgrimage."

"They were arrested?"

"We aren't sure. Last we heard, they were in Madrone. But then they vanished. No one knows what happened to them. The only reason I let the clan go into Velez yesterday was because I had to unload raw cotton. But your talk of Torch Bearers worries me."

"I don't have a lot to go on." He didn't want to tell Guillermo about his dreams or his mystery girl. Not yet. Too much strangeness would alienate him. "All I know is that a priest killed my mother. It makes sense that such a one might rise in the ranks."

"Give me your hand." Guillermo took out his knife. He ran the sharp edge across his own palm and then sliced Joachín's. They pressed their cuts together. "There. Now we are blood-debted. If anything happens to you, I'll kill the priest on your behalf."

Iago bound himself to Joachín with the same oath. "We are cousins. We stand together."

Casi wanted to do the same but Luci forbade her. "Women already bleed," she whispered, drawing her away. "We don't make blood oaths. That's for the men."

"I'm as good as any man!"

"True, but we make babies. They can't do that. We must allow them their pride."

Casi balked. "I want a tattoo. Like yours."

Luci herded her into the *vardo* on the pretext of some chore. Joachín glanced at Guillermo.

Guillermo shrugged. "A woman thing."

"Most of the women bear at least one," Iago said, "Some of them, more."

Joachín had never seen a woman with a tattoo. His puzzlement showed on his face.

"It's a goddess thing," Guillermo said. "They use them to appeal to Lys. When you come to Elysir, you'll see our matriarch. She has tattoos all over her body. She's very powerful."

"Men don't wear tattoos?"

Guillermo shook his head. "Not as a rule. When a Diaphani woman carves herself, she dedicates herself to the goddess. In return, Lys grants whatever she wants for a price. Most women bear one—to ease birth pangs. They honour the goddess by bringing forth a child and being good mothers."

Joachín turned this over in his mind. As far as he knew, Estrella had never borne a tattoo. She'd been a good mother though, perhaps too good.

"It would have been dangerous for Estrella to have one," Guillermo said, as if hearing his thought. "The Solarium considers them demon marks. Juan wouldn't have allowed it."

One thing was certain, he had much to learn about his relatives. There was much to being a Diaphani that he didn't know.

Over the next hour, they broke camp. The clan never stayed long in one place. Too often they were accused of thefts for which they weren't responsible. As Joachín stacked bolts of canvas in the back of a *vardo*, he overheard Luci give Casi a tongue-lashing. Luci had come across Casi's cache of sweets.

"Did I not say you could beg but not steal?" Luci demanded.

"*Maré*, you're hurting me!"

"Did I not tell you?"

"You did! Let me go!"

"What if you were caught?"

"It's only jellies!"

"Jellies, jewels, it doesn't matter! We're Diaphani! Any excuse and the *gachós* will kill us! Your father or brother would have taken the blame!"

"The man didn't see me!"

"You're banned from the markets until I can trust you!"

"Joachín steals!"

He flinched. He didn't want to be a part of it.

"Joachín's a grown man. He can take care of himself."

"So, how come *Paré* and Iago caught him last night?"

"That's not the point!"

"Did you ever steal, *Maré?*"

Joachín glanced at Iago. He looked bemused.

"I did," Luci said, "and my mother took a switch to my backside for it."

"What did you steal?"

"It doesn't matter! Get into the *vardo* and quit pestering me with questions! Be glad I don't take a whip to you!"

"Can I have my jellies?"

"No!"

Luci pushed her up the stairs and into the caravan. She slammed the door behind them. There was more talk between the two, but it was muffled.

"She'll give them to her, later." Iago smirked. "She always does."

Joachín wasn't sure rewarding Casi's behavior was a good thing, but he understood it. It was hard to mouth platitudes when one was guilty of the same sin. If Luci was as Estrella had been, nothing went to waste. Not even stolen goods.

Guillermo found him. Together, they hitched up the wagon. "I wish you'd told me about the Torch Bearers before," he said.

Joachin frowned. When had he the chance?

"What I mean to say, is that I wish we'd run into you sooner. We've no choice but to ride through Elysir, now. I worry that we'll encounter the Guard." He was thinking of the clan, half of whom were women and children. If they ran into trouble, the men would fight. On the other hand, finding the murderous priest was the very thing Joachin wanted. Traveling with the Montoyas complicated things.

"We are blood-debted," Joachin reminded him. "If it comes to it, I die alongside you."

The words rang false for some reason. He would die if it came to it. But if that were so, why this lingering feeling of guilt?

It made him uncomfortable, so he dismissed it.

Chapter Sixteen: Matriarch

THE *CALIPHA* *PASS* was high, barren, and windswept. With few trees and little water, the crossing was as hard on the clan as it was on the horses. The clouds were building, as grey as wraiths. Anassa Isadore felt the *vardo* tilt as it began its descent. Despite the bundle of blankets she had cushioned about herself, the cold had settled into her bones. The jostling of the wagon hurt her more, but she endured it, as anxious as the horses to reach the warmer slopes of Esbaña.

The *vardo* lurched. She reached out to steady herself. From the caravan's roof, pots swung and spoons clattered. A box of nutmeg slipped from its cache and struck her on the arm. Up front, Lorenzo swore and shouted at the rigs behind to watch for the rut. Anassa fumbled in her pocket for a stick of willow. Tea would be better, but she didn't have the option to brew it. She winced as she bit down on the bark.

I am too old, she thought. *This journey will be my last.*

As the wagon descended, the horses found steadier ground. She napped until Lorenzo pulled them to a halt. The light inside the caravan had grown dim. She glanced out the small window set in the front of the *vardo*. Beneath an amber sky, a weed-choked trail split from the main road and twisted into an olive grove.

Lorenzo turned in his seat to regard her through the *vardo's* window, his big hands steady on the reins. He had been chewing his mustache, a thing he did when he was anxious. "We won't make the gorge, tonight," he said. "What's around here?"

"I'll look." She closed her eyes and focused on the land about them. Shadows solidified. Not far ahead, a dark patch lay amid the olive trees, a grassy circle that looked as if it might accommodate the clan. Beyond it, a stream cut through the grove.

"Is there a land owner?" Lorenzo asked.

"I'm searching." She saw a nearby cottage—a plain, white stuccoed affair with a red tiled roof. The place was dilapidated, in need of repair. Chickens nested in an unsheltered clump by the door. Pigs wandered through the yard without the benefit of a pen. The farmer was pulling onions from a weed patch.

"I've found him. He looks like he could use some help around here. The house isn't far, just up the trail." The olives hung thickly from the branches. She doubted if Lorenzo would offer to pick them. They needed to reach the Womb by the following day.

"I'll speak with him." Lorenzo ran a hand through his thick black hair. It hardly mattered. His dark skin and high cheekbones marked him as Diaphani. Either the land owner would allow them to stay or he'd run them off. She watched as he loped down the trail. One man was less of a threat than a whole band. Lys forbid that any of the other families had given the farmer cause for complaint. When one of them crossed the *gachós*, it hurt them all.

She waited and didn't leave the *vardo* for fear that the farmer might return with Lorenzo. The intricate patterns across her throat and arms would frighten him, convince him she was a witch.

Soon, Lorenzo returned and waved at the dozen caravans behind them, signaling that they had been invited to stay. She wondered what kind of arrangement he had made. Perhaps a trade of their spare salt sellers, although the peppermills were of greater value. Hopefully, he hadn't offered those. Diaphani custom held that if something was within one's means to give, it was ill luck to withhold it.

Over the next hour, she endured the shifting of the wagon as Lorenzo parked the *vardo*, fed the horses, and lit their campfire. She stayed hidden. The other wives brought her food. Their host turned out to be generous and wanting of company. He butchered a pig and shared it with the band. Pork was a rare treat. It had been a long time since she'd eaten it. As the men sat down to drink after the meal, she peeked from the window to watch them. It was hard to be shut away. She suspected Lorenzo had angled himself so she might observe them safely.

"So, do you have a wife, children?" Lorenzo asked their host. They had exhausted the subjects of the late summer weather and the state of the olive crop.

The farmer shook his head. "My wife is dead."

"Ah, I'm sorry to hear. Mine, also."

Lorenzo set a comforting hand on the man's shoulder. It surprised Anassa to hear him mention Kala, her daughter. Losing her had broken his heart. It had been worse for him than when her own dear Bruno had passed on to the Summerlands.

The farmer winced, took a sip of his wine.

"It's not something one easily forgets," Lorenzo said. "I'm surprised a man like you doesn't take a second wife. This looks to be a fine farm."

The farmer shrugged. "I might have wed, but it didn't seem right. Bonita and I built this place. Every tree has had her hand upon it. Another woman would be an intrusion."

Lorenzo nodded sagely. "If a love has been a great one, there is no replacing it." He looked down at his empty cup. "I'm out of wine. Rana!" he called.

Anassa watched as her granddaughter stepped from behind the circle of *vardos* where the wives and daughters ate. She retrieved a fresh jug from the back of a wagon and sidled over to the men. As she uncorked the bottle and poured the farmer a fresh glass, she kept her eyes downcast as a proper Diaphani girl should, but at the last moment, she lifted her gaze to stare at him boldly. Even from here, the girl's ability to attract was hypnotic. She trapped his attention like a viper mesmerizing a mouse. The farmer's mouth fell open. Lorenzo glared at her and shooed her off. Their host couldn't see Rana's breast tattoos, but they had their effect. Rana sauntered back to the women with a slight sway to her hips.

That girl is too brash by half, Anassa thought. The farmer tore his gaze away and gripped his cup. She felt sorry for him. He was embarrassed and worried he had offended Lorenzo. She had forbidden Rana to tattoo herself, but Rana had cut herself anyway. Lorenzo hadn't been pleased with the news.

A wind sprang up. Sparks flew about the camp. Anassa shielded her eyes. Beside a caravan, a bucket overturned. No one stood beside it. She focused on the place.

Near the pail, a shadowy woman appeared. She lacked colour and looked thin and grey. She darted across the compound to confront the farmer, but he paid her no heed. In frustration, she slapped him. Her hand passed through his face.

She fell back with a cry. Then, as if not believing she lacked the substance to strike him, she flew at him again, pummeling his head and shoulders until her fists were a blur. His expression crumpled, he cupped his face in his hands and cried.

Anassa stiffened with dismay. From the moment they could understand, Diaphani children were warned—in death, they weren't to linger but to seek the goddess's embrace. Those who didn't became as this one did, a half-crazed spectre that punished the ones they loved. Sometimes, the ghosts turned demon and fed upon the living. Anassa had encountered such a ghoul in Constantesh. It had nearly cost her her life.

"You must pass on!" she shouted at the ghost-wife. She wasn't sure she could reason with her, but she had to try. "He will come to you when it's his time!"

The ghost turned and marked her. Its eyes deepened into black pits and its mouth, an empty hole. The first barbs of its hatred came winging at Anassa like arrows in flight. She knocked them aside. The wraith screeched in frustration, coiled, and flew at her from across the camp with outstretched claws. As it struck her, it knocked Anassa to her knees.

The thing whirled past and gathered for a second blow. Anassa might have dealt with such a phantom when she was younger, but she was no longer in her prime. This would be a battle to see who had the stronger will. She was a seer. She saw the wraith. That made her vulnerable. She clawed at the bone necklace about her throat. Every knuckle belonged to one of her ancestors, all seers and daughters of the Tribe. Her mother's knuckle lay at the very end.

Maré! she implored. *Lys! Your strength!*

Power surged through her. She collapsed to the *vardo's* floor. The wraith fell back as if hitting a wall, but as quickly, it tore through the camp, screaming and passing through caravans like a hot wind. Anassa lay where she fell and checked for broken bones. Her head throbbed, but she was whole. She sat up painfully, thankful to be alive.

Lorenzo was at her side in a moment. "What happened?" he demanded. No one had forgotten the incident in Constantesh.

"We have to go. I'm sorry, I should have foreseen her. The husband is still grieving. And Rana...." She didn't finish the thought. Lorenzo was sensitive about Rana. The girl had tempted the farmer. It had triggered the wife's attack.

There would be no peace in this place tonight. The ghost was weaker now, but it would still affect them in disturbing ways. Even the most insensitive would be assailed by nightmares.

Without another word, Lorenzo signaled to break camp. He looked ill at ease, but no one questioned the decision. Soon, a dozen *vardos* lumbered from the grove and onto the inky road at a measured pace. It would be another cold night.

Inside the coach, Anassa lay aching amid her quilts. Rana had prepared her some willow tea, but she hadn't stayed to see if she drank it. "How far are we from Elysir?" she asked Lorenzo weakly.

He snapped the reins. "A day's ride. What's ahead?" He was anxious about thieves. A lone outlaw wouldn't be so foolish to stop them, but a band of cutthroats was still a risk. She gazed in each direction. Nothing followed them from the north. Little moved to the south, east was bound by high peaks. She scanned to the west.

West was foul. "What's west of us?" she asked.

"The village of Batos."

She focused on the sleeping town. Despite the late hour, the inn was alight. Shadows moved beyond candlelit windows. Outside, a dozen horses were hitched to posts. Each bore an expensive saddle.

On every face plate, a flame had been incised. She knew the mark. "Torch Bearers, Lorenzo!"

"Are they approaching us?"

She scanned the hamlet to see if any were at large. Other than the tavern, none were about. "No. I think they've settled in."

"We're never safe as far as they're concerned." He gave a shout and urged the horses into a gallop. Behind them, Clan Isadore followed suit. The *vardos* rumbled, jingling, and squeaked. Anassa wondered how anyone might miss their passing. Her head throbbed, she felt sick.

Lorenzo drove them hard all night. The stars shifted in their courses and the moon set. Dawn threatened, the road dipped. They entered a canyon and set their caravans beneath a leafy canopy of trees. Lorenzo posted sentries and didn't spare himself despite how tired Anassa knew he was. "No fires until we reach the Womb!" he told the camp.

Anassa drew her quilts about her. The Womb was half a day away. If they failed to reach it....

Enough, she told herself. Such thoughts brought ill luck.

Chapter Seventeen: Heartsick

"THH...THIRSTY...."

Miriam's eyes flew open. From their bed of straw, Ephraim stared at her bleakly. She was thankful to find him alive.

"Let me get you some water, Papa." She rose from their bed and retrieved the bucket Alonso had found the night before. Gaspar's well had been behind the croft. She cupped Ephraim's head and helped him drink. When he could take no more, she set him down gently.

"Where...?" He gazed at the rafters above them.

"In an abandoned hut I found." She couldn't tell him. The shock of Gaspar's death would be too much for him to handle. He frowned, on the verge of recognizing the place. She distracted him.

"Papa, I've been thinking. If we go to Qadis, we could buy passage on a ship, travel to Roma, and start fresh there."

He licked his lips.

"I know Roma is corrupt, but the Papacy is tolerant. The Juden have been granted sanctuary...."

"...not that."

"What then?"

"Snow."

He was worried about the Calipha Pass. On the highest peaks of the Sierra Nevaras, the snow rarely melted. Within a month, the pass would be thick with ice. "I think we'll be all right. We have a few weeks, yet. Can you eat?"

He nodded. She fed him small bits while cautioning him to stay put. She didn't want him to stand until necessary. After breakfast, she checked his bandages and applied more comfrey and garlic. As they shuffled from the hut, she tried to block his view.

"I know where we are," he said, glancing at the painted daisies on the walls. "This is...." He stopped short when he saw the burial mound and the stake.

"I buried him, Papa. He's at peace now." She said it louder than necessary, as if her insistence would convince him.

Ephraim clawed at his chest as if he couldn't draw in enough air. With a low moan, he sagged and fainted, became a dead-weight in her arms. "No!" she cried, struggling to hold him. Her knees gave out from beneath her. They fell awkwardly to the ground. She clambered over him and pressed an ear to his chest, praying for a heartbeat.

Chapter Eighteen: The Womb

BY MID-MORNING, LORENZO was anxious for the band to be on its way. At the end of the canyon, the trail branched. The main route led to the town of Elysir. The other, which was rocky and showed no signs of travel, dipped between cliff sides that leaned overhead. The trail narrowed to little more than a *vardo's* width. The band had reached the most dangerous part of their journey, the neck of the Womb.

Anassa insisted on driving the lead caravan. Lorenzo could barely keep his eyes open. Too tired to argue, he handed her the reins and climbed into the *vardo*. Soon, he was snoring. She slapped the reins and coaxed the horses forward. Jostling from side to side, the convoy followed.

After fifty feet or so, the cliff side on her left retreated. She kept the wheels of the *vardo* as close as she could to the cave wall on her right. The ground dropped away. Far below, the River Gemilla churned. With a prayer to the goddess for protection, Anassa led her people down the steep descent. As the coach lumbered out from under an overhang, the sun blinded her momentarily.

She kept her eyes on the horses as the vista spread before her. The valley was small and round and formed a deep cup. High cliffs bordered it on all sides. Only in late summer, was it accessible. In the winter, the place was a lake of ice. Diaphani myth spoke of the canyon as once being a cauldron of fire. Now, the River Gemilla wove through it, a bright braid glinting in the afternoon sun. No one, other than the Diaphani, came here. The Elysir locals maintained that the valley was a haunt of devils. Anassa caught a hint of sulfur on the air.

Snapping the reins, she drove the caravan to the bottom of the canyon where she regarded every rock and bush with love. So many memories it held—her marriage to Bruno, her birthing of Kala, her dedications to the Tribe and the goddess, the markings of her body. Here, her people lived without fear. Here, they danced and rejoiced. Here, they were free.

She directed the horses to their usual camping spot and clambered painfully from the rig. Driving the *vardo* had cost her. Her back ached. Everyone knew what was required of them, but she waved each family to their appropriate place. There had to be at least two wagon lengths between rigs. Her people weren't to think of themselves as a separate band, but as part of an entire Tribe. The mixing of wagons reinforced that idea. It also forced feuding parties to reconcile, if possible.

Lorenzo woke and took over the organizing. Freed from her duty, Anassa glanced about for Rana. Her granddaughter had traveled with Kezia to avoid her; what Rana needed was a firm hand, but Anassa didn't have the stamina for it. Lorenzo was of no help, either.

"She's not spoiled, *Maré*," he said the day before, after Rana had refused to do the laundry. "She's headstrong."

"She's stubborn and disobedient, Lorenzo. I'm too old to wash clothes. My back won't take it."

"I'll speak to her."

In the end, Rana conceded when Lorenzo reminded her that she would need to handle such tasks as a wife. Rana had her eye on Angél Ferrara. Angél was so handsome that many of the girls joked about groom-price.

"Tell me about Angél." Rana had dumped all of their clothes into the wash tub. "Is he still grieving? Has he found someone else?"

"Sort, like I told you," Anassa said. "Your father's clothes first, ours next."

"Fine. I'm doing it. Well?"

"I don't know, Rana."

"Use your sight to find out."

"The sight isn't used for that."

"Then why be a seer if you limit yourself?"

Anassa turned away. There was no point in arguing with her. Rana didn't understand why the ability wasn't used to spy on a suitor. No wonder Lys hadn't given her a gift.

She caught sight of her emerging from Kezia's wagon. The two girls looked like young birds set free from their cage.

"Rana!" She raised an arm to hail her. A pain shot through her shoulder. She winced. She shouldn't have lifted it so quickly.

Rana glanced at her with contempt. "What do you want, *Puri?*"

"Come!" She waved feebly. "I need you to help me to the pools."

"Oh. Of course." Rana liked the pools. "Kezia and I will join you. We could both use a bath."

The climb to the first cave wasn't difficult, but it would have taxed Anassa had she tried to make it on her own. The great mouth yawned before them, the smell of sulfur, strong. A steaming rivulet carved its way down their path like a slick, yellow tongue. As they made it to the top, they entered the grotto. Inside, the light was soft. The women descended a series of slabs until they reached the steaming waters of the first pool. A crack in the ceiling above made the water glow a vivid green.

Anassa shed her clothes like old snake's skin. Rana and Kezia kicked off their boots, untied their blouses and stepped from their skirts. With trembling hands, Anassa clasped each girl by the hand. As the warm water hit her legs, she groaned with relief. She sank to her knees and immersed herself to the neck. Rana and Kezia swam to a ledge on the far side of the pool.

Kezia pointed at Rana's breasts. The tattoos around Rana's nipples stood out like black thorns on roses. "Did those hurt?" Kezia asked. Her voice echoed softly throughout the chamber.

"I bled for days," Rana said.

"You think they'll affect Angél Ferrara?"

"They better. If they don't, I'll cut something else."

Anassa closed her eyes, wishing she could block out their voices.

"I hope Jaime Franco isn't married, yet. He's nice." Kezia sounded wistful.

Rana splashed her. "He dances like a pig."

"That's because he's a musician! Better with his hands!"

"Let him play with his tongue, for all I care. A man who can't dance, can't love. Look at Magdala Munoz. She thought Natal would bring her the good life, but he mounts her from behind, like a mule."

Anassa bristled. "That's enough! Remember where you are!" She glared at Rana, but the girl was already looking away.

Anassa forced her frustration to seep into the water. *I had such hopes for you,* she thought dismally. Rana had shown signs of a prophetic talent, but she wasn't the seer her mother had been. The Tribe needed a new matriarch, someone who could handle the role. If not Rana, then the goddess had to have someone else in mind.

But who? For the past fifteen summers, she'd asked that same question. It had to be someone strong enough to shoulder the responsibility, someone who understood that with power came a price, that the costs of privilege and status were duty and obligation to all.

Pray to Lys that this year, she would have her answer.

Chapter Nineteen: Confessions

EPHRAIM'S COLLAPSE HAD been from shock and not from an attack of the heart as Miriam had feared. She fanned his face as he came to and insisted he drink more water. He was in a precarious state, mentally as well as physically. She would have to keep an even closer eye on him.

At the River Gemilla, there was no help for it but to abandon the cart. On the far side of the stream, the bank rose steeply.

"You're going to have to ride the donkey," she told Ephraim. "Can you hold on, or must I tie you?" The crow's feet about his eyes had grown deeper, but his mouth was as stubbornly set as ever.

"You don't have to tie me. I'll manage."

He drew himself to a sitting position in the cart bed. She bit back on scolding him, hoping he hadn't done himself more hurt. His face turned pale.

"You're sure?"

"I'm not dead yet, Miriam." He reached for her hand and gripped it. "Let's go."

She helped him mount the donkey. The river rushed by.

As far as I can tell, this is the shallowest point, Alonso said. *The water might rise as high as your chest, but further on, it gets deeper.*

She nodded. There was no way to avoid it. They had to cross. As she stepped into the river, the current caught her skirt and swirled it about her knees. The breeze lifted, a wave sprayed her face. She sputtered, snatched the grimoire from her side and balanced it on her head. Gods forbid it should get wet. If the ink ran, it would silence her mother forever.

Careful. There are rocks underfoot. She set her feet gingerly. The water rose to her hips and then to her waist. Mid-stream, the current grew stronger. At Alonso's suggestion, she switched the donkey to her downstream side, a good precaution, because three-quarters of the way along, it lost its footing and stumbled into a hole.

Look out! Alonso shouted as the water closed over its head. It bucked for the surface and brayed. Ephraim choked and held on. The current swept them away.

Let go of the reins!

They jerked her off balance. She dropped them, afraid they would pull her under. She managed to right herself before she fell.

Don't worry! As long as he stays astride, the beast will fight to reach the bank.

Alonso was right. The donkey bucked and lurched, but it made it to the muddy shore. Ephraim slid from its wet flanks. Worried sick for him, she forced herself to move quickly. Her ankle turned on a stone. *No!* she thought as she wind milled. *The grimoire!*

Throw it!

She heaved. And then the river claimed her.

Water surged up her nose and mouth, clouded her eyes. The world turned a greenish-grey. She lost all sense of up and down. Through a trick of sunlight, a ray brought a large rock into view. She threw out her hands and shoved her head aside. The effort was enough to help her break the surface. She gulped for air and swept past Ephraim. The donkey was nowhere to be seen. The water carried her further downstream.

She had never learned how to swim, but the need to survive took over. Her arms and legs pumped. Her skirt thwarted her efforts. She was terrified it might snag on a rock and pull her down. Ahead, a partially submerged fir straddled the stream. Long skeletal fingers formed a sieve. If she clutched one of those branches, she might climb to freedom....

No! It's not safe! Alonso shouted.

His warning triggered a memory. Ondinas were water sprites that drowned foolish children. They disguised themselves as trees over streams. Of course, the stories were meant to keep the young ones away, but they served a purpose. Downed trees were deadly.

Angle yourself for the bank! Use the current to help you!

She kicked and struggled for all she was worth. The tree loomed ahead, too fast, too soon. It was going to catch her. Panicking, she adjusted her direction.

Not that way! Gods, Miriam! Something snagged at her skirt beneath the surface. She flailed wildly. Her body prickled. Alonso was adding what little strength he had to hers. A section of what looked like a demolished wagon spun away on the current and jammed. She wasn't going to make it. All she could do was to aim for the roots where they lay exposed on the bank. *Swim, Miriam! Reach!*

With a final lunge, she flailed, threw her hands before her.

She speared herself on cruel barbs. The current swung her legs out from beneath her, but she held on. Branches scratched her arms and face. Fear prompted her to climb. She clambered onto the roots like a drowned bee crawling up a thistle. Freed from the water's pull, she flopped onto the adjacent bank. She landed in mud. Her heart pounded in her chest.

Miriam, are you all right? Speak to me!

Her skirt was torn to shreds. One thigh suffered an angry gash. Her body felt as if it were composed of broken twigs, but these things were inconsequential. She had to find Ephraim and the grimoire.

Miriam?

I'm all right, she said. It wasn't true. Her leg throbbed, her tattoo burned. Had she reopened the cut? It didn't matter. *Where is Papa?*

Never mind him for the moment. Can you walk?

She rose painfully to her feet. She didn't think the river had taken them too far downstream. Alonso directed her. They chanced upon the donkey first. It munched on a patch of grass and eyed her balefully. She wanted to slap it but didn't. It had panicked, as she had. And it hadn't asked to come on this journey.

Alonso drifted off to find Ephraim. He returned shortly and led her to her father. Ephraim was on his feet and clutching a branch for support. When she saw him, he looked as if he were working up the strength to search for her. She stumbled through the trees. As he caught sight of her, he sagged in relief. She met him and they fell into each other's arms.

They were in plain view from the opposite bank. "We have to climb, Papa," she said. "We're too noticeable here. I'll help you on the donkey." Ephraim closed his eyes and nodded. His pale face changed her mind. "But maybe we can rest a minute."

She glanced along the muddy bank, hoping she might see the grimoire. It hadn't floated past her, but then again, its weight might have taken it to the bottom. She had no way of knowing. She peered into the rushing water.

I see it. Behind you.

Her heart skipped a beat. Caught in the lowest branches of a willow, her satchel and its precious contents lay. She scrambled for it, narrowly missing another dunking in the stream. She grabbed her pouch and held it to her chest like a baby.

"What's that?" Ephraim asked.

"My satchel," she said.

The trail was steep and slick. She had to shove the donkey from behind to make it climb. There were easier ways to reach the alpine road, but if the terrain was difficult for her, it would be harder for men on horseback. The trail leveled out and they stumbled onto a pitted road—the lower section of the Calipha Pass. She hesitated at the side of it. The surface bore ruts of recent travel.

Alonso?

It looks as if a number of wagons passed this way during the night. They're nowhere near, as far as I can tell.

How far could he move from her now? He seemed to be getting better at it every time he tried. Her stomach growled. She was thirsty and tired. Ephraim had to be exhausted, too. They needed to stop so she could redress his wounds as well as tend her own. Gods forbid that the plunge in the water had made them worse.

There's a spring not far from here. I'll warn you if anyone comes.

The donkey broke into a trot, smelling the water. "Don't fall!" she cried to Ephraim, as it bolted for the trees. She broke into a run, afraid he might. There was a crash and a groan.

She ran into the glade. Ephraim lay moaning on the ground. Not far from him, the donkey drank noisily. She glared at it and ran to his side. "Let me see." She set hands on his habit.

"Don't." He pushed her hands away.

"Oh, for heaven's sake, Papa. I've seen you naked. There's no need for modesty."

"Be that as it may, I'm still your father."

She turned and allowed him his dignity. When he had covered his manhood to his satisfaction, she unwound his bandages. Despite the falls, the river, and the blood, she was pleased to see that the worst areas had cleared of pus. He would scar, but his wounds were healing. She wrapped a clean poultice about him.

"How did we get here?" He watched her efforts with a practiced eye.

She nodded at the donkey. "Our friend, there. I stole him. We fled."

"Too simple. No one escapes the Guard. This was divine intervention."

She snorted. "You don't believe in divine intervention."

"I'm starting to. Our flight here was nothing short of miraculous. What *really* happened?"

She tied off the bandage and met his gaze. "Inara Gatekeeper happened."

He winced as if a secret pain were exposed. "You found it. Your mother's grimoire."

"Yes."

He ran a trembling hand across his brow. "I should've destroyed it. It was the last thing I had of her."

"It took me a few years to figure out that she and Inara were the same."

He pulled the habit over his head and they sat. He gazed into the trees. "It was safer to call her Mari," he said at last. "She was one of the most gifted healers of her clan."

"Mama was a healer?"

He nodded. "A *sentidora*. Like you."

She said nothing but turned the idea over in her mind. How different things were in the Diaphani world. Her mother had practiced as a healer among them. No one had prevented her, no one accused her of witchcraft as they would in Granad. A suspicion rose in her mind. If her mother had been a healer and a *sentidora*, how had she died from ague? She would have taken steps to combat the disease before it took hold. Yet this was the story Ephraim had told her. "How did she die, Papa? It wasn't from a fever, was it?"

He glanced away.

"Papa?"

He swallowed. "She died because I couldn't protect her." The pain was keen in his eyes. She reached out to steady his hands. His remorse struck her in a wave.

"One night, a boy came to our gate," he said. "His mother had gone into labour. Mari went to assist her. I was away, attending the Head Constable's wife. The birth turned out to be difficult. Mari had to cut the child from the woman's womb. There was no way she could save her without it involving a tattoo. The family was grateful, but a few weeks later, temple officials investigated. The woman's husband accused Mari of witchcraft. He said she had forced the tattoo on his wife. Mari thought she could trust them. She had saved two of their lives. But they betrayed her to spare themselves."

He took a deep breath. "The Solarium tortured her and then left her alone in a cell. She took a quill and carved herself with a curse. Three of the inquisitors died that night. One choked on a piece of bread, another drowned in his bath. The last was found in his sleeping robe, crushed beneath a piece of fallen mortar. Fearing more deaths, they set her on the stake." His voice broke.

She stared at him. Where had he been in all of this? How could he have let it happen? The accusation formed, tumbled from her lips. "So—they burned her."

He knuckled his eyes. "Yes. I wasn't around to see it."

She couldn't believe this was the father she loved. Was he a coward? "You didn't try to save her?"

"I tried, but every time I left the house, I found myself walking in the opposite direction with you in my arms. It was as if she'd also cast a spell on me, Miri! I couldn't break the compulsion. When I realized what she'd done, I had no will left in the matter. My feet led me away. I left Salerno in the dead of night, weeping."

"There's no spell like that in her grimoire."

"No. She thought some things too dangerous to set down. Magic like that demands lives. She paid for ours with her own." He gazed at her with haunted eyes. "And now it's your turn to answer my question, Miri. How did you rescue me?"

She pressed her lips together. She was no coward, either. She pulled her blouse loose from her waistband and revealed the tattoo.

He blanched. "I know that glyph! That's the sign of a priestess. What did you do?"

"I performed a resurrection."

"Gods! On whom?"

"On His Brilliance, the High Solar of Granad."

"And it *worked?*" He sounded astounded.

Don't tell him. He'll think I'm controlling you.

You're not controlling me.

No, but he might misunderstand. He's your father. He's bound to be protective.

"He came back to life and showed me the way out." It wasn't a lie, but it wasn't the whole truth, either. "He helped us escape."

"Then why is the Guard still after us? Surely, he would have called them off."

"He...he died, again."

Ephraim looked regretful. "He was a good man. He didn't deserve to suffer the way he did. I wish I could thank him."

"I'm sure he knows."

He glanced at her. "How can he know? You resurrected him and now he's gone."

She considered her tattoo. "I should put some garlic on this."

The distraction worked. He frowned. "Does it hurt?"

"A little. My leg hurts more." She spent a few moments setting garlic on her belly and thigh.

"Your mother had two tattoos on her feet. They crippled her for weeks."

"I remember them. But I never thought they were for anything more than decoration. I should have guessed."

"She said they gave her a deeper kinship with the sick. She knew you were gifted."

"Really? How?"

"Sometimes, when patients visited the house, they'd pat you on the head. You'd run away and tell us later what was wrong with them. 'Hot' or 'sick tummy', you'd say. Mari was so proud of you. She used to boast that no daughter of ours could do otherwise."

"But I don't have tattoos...well, I do now, but I never needed them to enhance my ability as a *sentidora*. If Mama was so gifted, why the need for them?" She set the garlic back in the pouch.

"They're a religious thing. They open a doorway into the spiritual world, invite the gods to come in. But they only strengthen what's already there. After her family died, she worried the knowledge would be lost. She meant the book for you."

"She did?"

He nodded.

"How did they die?"

"The town lynched them. They were blamed for a horse theft they never committed. Mari was visiting me at the time. We used to debate the uses of herbs and that sort of thing. I hid her away. With her family gone, she had nowhere to go. I'd like to think she would have married me, anyway."

"I have the book." It felt good to tell him.

"I'm glad. They'll use it as evidence against us if we're caught, but I'd rather have it."

"Tor Tomás is already convinced of my guilt, book or no. The grimoire is more of a godsend than a curse."

"Anything that comes from your mother is a blessing. You're my miracle, Miri. I wouldn't be here, if not for you."

She smiled.

There's an abandoned hut not far from here. I think it will suffice for the night.

"We should be on our way, Papa. There's a place ahead, where we can stay."

"Not like the last one, I hope." He frowned. "Wait. You've never been this far south. How do you know?"

She reached for the satchel. "The tattoo, perhaps. I just know."

They traveled the road until Alonso directed them onto another goat path. This time, the slope was easier. A wind sprang up, causing the pines to sway. Overhead, the sky was a deep blue. They broke from the forest and found themselves on the brow of a hill. There were no sheep, but the shepherd's hut had a door, walls, and a roof. Bales of hay crumbled in a corner. The donkey ambled into the shelter and munched on the straw.

"He thinks it's a stable," Ephraim said.

She watched to see if anything stirred in the chaff.

Don't worry. I would have warned you.

"No rats for company." Ephraim smiled at her.

They ate berries for supper, and she found an old well. After eating, they spent time washing. She threw on the monk's habit while her blouse and skirt dried in the sun. As twilight descended, she took Ephraim into the hut and made him lie down. They had survived a third night.

"Good night, Papa," she said as they settled in the straw. She heard a grunt. He was already asleep. *Good night, Alonso,* she added.

Rest well, Miriam.

He departed from her like a cool draught passing.

Where are you going? She had hoped that he would warm her like he had the night before.

He paused. *I should watch for the Guard.*

It was hard to suppress her disappointment. He sensed it, anyway. *I intend to watch over you, Miriam. It's the only thing I can do.*

She felt a stab of guilt. She had reduced him to this—her own personal watchdog. As he floated away, she wondered if anything more lay behind his words. What else might he want to do? The distance between them lengthened, but their link remained intact. She rose, unable to sleep. If Alonso didn't rest, then neither would she. She would wait and watch until he returned. She left the hut.

The moon shone over a far peak, nearly to its full. A dark speck flew past it, caught in its glow. A bat, most likely, but it might have been a bird. She shivered, felt cold.

She wanted...wished.... Alonso had been a handsome man in life. She reacted to him as if he still were. She sat on the brow of the hill and hugged her knees.

What do I *really* want? she asked herself. Alonso was an impossibility; he had no more substance than air. She had to accept it. In Granad, she'd wanted a stable life. She had given up on marriage, but if she and Ephraim made it to the Papal States, who knew what was possible? And maybe, just maybe, she'd find a community that valued her for who she was, that allowed her to exercise her gift. They were more tolerant there. Why not?

That's what I want! She jabbed a finger at the moon. *Even if I never marry, even if I die an old maid. I want to be valued for who I am, for what I can do. And I want the chance to do it. To be accepted, to exercise my power....*

Power? She paused, mid-thought. Was that true?

She had always wanted the power to rule her own life, to be free of the yoke of an external force, whether it was a society, a temple, or a man. *I want to be who I am. I want to succeed, to be given the chance to succeed. Life isn't worth living unless I have that.*

True enough. But there was more to it. She couldn't hide her innermost desires from herself.

She *did* want power. Not just the temporal kind, but real power, the kind the tattoos gave her, the ability to alter reality as she saw fit. The power to create, the power to protect, even the power to destroy....

Dangerous territory. She side-stepped it as she would a scorpion and considered the idea carefully. Perhaps that kind of power was too tempting, too likely to turn on its wielder. That kind of power might take more than it gave.

The wind keened about her. She rubbed her arms. There was no point in constructing arguments about things of which she knew little. Where *was* Alonso? If he hurried back, she could go to sleep and not worry about him. Yet, why should she worry? He was the closest thing to an angel she knew, and she didn't believe in those. But it was easy to imagine him with a halo and wings.

She savoured a moment of picturing him thus until an uncomfortable realization occurred to her. He would always be on guard, he would never know peace. She doubted he would ever sleep again.

And she had done this to him. Her power had called him forth. Guilt suffused her. The lesson was clear. With great power came great responsibility. It wasn't a question of dismissing things of which she knew nothing. She knew enough.

He was her responsibility now, as much as he thought her, his. She would never forget it again.

Chapter Twenty: Speaker

"THERE HE IS!" Rana pulled Kezia to one side. Anassa watched as the girls considered the camp's latest arrivals. Angél stood beside the Ferrara's *vardo* as he and his father unhitched their team. His mother, Leonora, added kindling to their fire.

"You're in luck," Kezia said. "The Ferraras have parked their *vardo* right next to yours."

Rana smirked. Without giving Kezia a second glance, she walked over to Leonora Ferrara. "Welcome, Bandoliera," she said. "Can I help you with that?"

Anassa prickled with irritation. Rana never offered to help her with anything unless something was in it for her. Leonora Ferrara glanced at Rana. "Some fresh water for cooking, if you're on the way to the stream," she said. "Rana, isn't it?"

Rana nodded. "Yes. Of Isadore clan." She indicated Anassa who hobbled up to them.

"Oh, of course!" Leonora said. "Matriarch! How nice to see you."

"And you, Leonora. You're looking well."

"I'm a little tired. It was a long journey from Tolede."

"Your business is thriving?"

"Oh, yes. Estaban is taking commissions, now. The Duke of Milano has been our biggest patron."

"That's wonderful."

"The work is grueling. Angél handles most of it."

At the sound of his name, Angél Ferrara glanced their way. Anassa watched as Rana tilted her chin a little higher. Angél was even better looking than she recalled. Work in the foundry had built muscles on his chest and arms. He looked more of a military man than a blacksmith. His dark hair hung over his eyes in a careless way. He set down the horses' harness and came toward them.

"I've unhitched the team," he said. "I'll water them in a minute. Do you need more firewood, Maré?"

"We have enough," Leonora said. "Angél, you remember Matriarch Anassa. And this is her granddaughter, Rana Isadore."

Angél lifted an eyebrow. "Little Rana? Truly?"

Rana nodded.

Kezia tugged at Rana's sleeve.

"And this is...?" Leonora asked, indicating Kezia.

"Kezia Amaya," Kezia said breathlessly. "Of the Amaya clan."

Rana winced. Angél smiled. "A pleasure." His glance drifted back to Rana. "Will you be dancing tonight?"

"I will," she said.

"I'll look forward to that."

"She won't be dancing until after the dedication ceremony," Anassa said.

Angél's eyebrows rose. "Ah. I'd forgotten. Hopefully, the new cuts won't prevent you from performing."

"Pain is nothing," Rana said. She walked away, dismissing his concern with a tilt of her chin....

At twilight, Anassa led the women into the caves, past the pools, and deep into the bowels of the mountain. Only those who had already dedicated themselves to Lys carried torches. The initiates, of which Rana was one, carried nothing.

"Here, we come face to face with Great Lys and our destinies," Anassa said, addressing the assembly. Behind her lay a fissure in the rock that led to a huge cavern. "Let us enter this place as we came into this world, faultless before our creator." She set her torch in a crevice in the rock and removed her clothes. The younger women who were not of Isadore clan gasped as they beheld her body. A great blue eye gazed out at them from beneath her throat—the mark of a matriarch and seer. Spirals of protection curled about her breasts and belly. For healing, red and blue snakes twisted about her arms. Brown hares and pale stags leapt about her legs, promising bounty.

"Upon entering, we must relieve ourselves of any burden, confess any offense we have committed against each other and Lys." This was the tricky part. In the past, some of the women had come to blows, particularly if one guilty party confessed to stealing another's man. "As Matriarch, I shall confess my greatest fault to you. As you pass into this sanctum, you will whisper your worst sins to me." *And pray no one hears what they aren't meant to*, she added silently.

She raised her arms. "Forgive me, Great Lys," she said, "for my transgression." She glanced at Rana who stood in the middle of the throng. "I have coveted something from You that I do not have. I have questioned your purposes." She stepped aside and bade the first woman to approach.

"I fear I'm barren," the woman said. "I want my sister's baby. Or I want her man to plant his seed in me."

Anassa shook her head. "Not a smart idea. Keep trying with your own man." She patted her on the shoulder.

The next woman came forth. "I spit in Carlos's food. I wish he would die."

The brute was rumoured to beat her. "Is that *all* you do to his food?" Anassa watched her shrewdly. The woman nodded, but Anassa doubted it. "Talk to your father and brothers. Have them speak to him. If they refuse, *I* will." The woman gave her a grateful look. "For anything else you've attempted, Lys forgives you."

Woman after woman stepped forward. The confessions flowed. "I set a curse on my cousin for tempting my man." "I slept with my brother-in-law." "I burned my uncle's *vardo*."

"Was that *wise*?" Anassa asked the woman who had whispered it. "What did he do?"

"It was an accident." She made a face. "Now he lives with us."

"Perhaps you need to build him a new *vardo*," Anassa said. The woman nodded.

Finally, Rana approached. Anassa waited. Rana smiled coolly and stepped past her.

Anger pricked Anassa like nettles. The rudeness of the girl! But now was not the time to confront her. *Let Lys deal with her*, Anassa decided. She followed Rana through the crack in the wall.

Inside, the cavern was dimly lit. Stalactites hung from the high ceiling in conical columns. In places, stalagmites met them half way. Some mineral made them glow with a cool phosphorescence. To Anassa, the cavern was a temple. She liked to think of the light as Lys's presence.

"In the darkness, there is light," she said. She stood near a shallow pool set in the rock floor. On its surface, reflections of the stalactites glimmered. "Tonight is the first night of reunion. Let the initiates who wish to dedicate themselves come forward."

A dozen girls approached her, including Rana.

Anassa stepped into the pool and disturbed the perfect mirror. She reached down and retrieved a stone dagger from its bottom.

"Upon each of you, I carve Lys's mark. In childbirth, she will protect you. She may also bless you with other gifts. Do you accept this?"

The girls replied in unison. "We do."

"Have no fear. The greater the blood, the greater the reward."

One by one, the girls stepped forward. Upon each girl's stomach, Anassa carved a circle within a circle, representing mother and child. Her own marking was barely discernable amid her other tattoos. Most of the girls whimpered as she cut them. A few slumped to the floor. Their mothers and aunts helped them regain their breaths. To each girl's mark, they applied a thick mud that they had collected from the cavern's walls. Rana shrugged off Anassa's help.

"I can do it myself." She rubbed the earth into her cut. "I've done it before." Anassa turned and watched the other initiates carefully. Now was the moment for new talents to appear. The girls struggled to their feet. Their mothers, sisters, and aunts helped them.

Anassa waited with bated breath. After five minutes of silence, she sighed. Nothing exceptional had presented itself. Another year, come and gone, and no one to take her place.

Dear Lys, she prayed. Surely, the goddess would hear her in this holy place. *You must know I won't last another year! Where is she? Where is the one you have chosen to lead our people after me?*

She waited, felt her yearning fill the cavern to its limits. Another minute passed. She set the stalactite dagger down. There was no dictating to the goddess. Lys's ways were her own. "Let us quit this place," Anassa said tiredly. "Lys's blessing upon you all." The women gathered near the crack in the wall and began to file out, one by one.

A shriek shattered the air. Like startled doves, the women drew back and rushed to help the girl who had collapsed. Anassa pushed through them. Rana writhed on the cave floor.

"Leave her!" Anassa cried. "The goddess is upon her! We must see how the gift manifests!"

Rana trembled uncontrollably. Her eyes drew back to show their whites. She mouthed something inaudible, and then bit down on her tongue. A stream of blood dribbled from the side of her mouth. Along with the blood came words, harsh and guttural. "The Seeress of Two approaches! The Flames of Sul dog her steps!"

Seeress of Two? Flames of Sul? What nonsense was this? "You speak in riddles. What do you mean?" Anassa demanded.

"New replaces old. Protect her, or all shall perish in the fire!"

"Tell us more about this Seeress of Two," Anassa pressed.

"She sees, but doesn't see. You must teach her!" Rana's voice began to fade. "Who is she? Where is she? When does she come?"

"Tonight. The moon's zenith. At the Neck."

Rana's eyes fluttered closed. Anassa took a deep breath. "Lift her by her arms and feet," she told the women. "She won't be able to stand for a few minutes."

"Is Rana our new seer?" Kezia asked the question in everyone's eyes. Anassa shook her head. Rana hadn't displayed the sight.

Rana smiled as if hearing something that pleased her. "Rana is Speaker," she said contentedly.

Speaker, yes, Anassa thought. Speaking was not as potent a gift as the sight, but it was a reliable talent when it presented itself. Unfortunately, it didn't occur by choice. The Ancestors spoke through their medium when they deemed it necessary—usually in times of threat.

Under the circumstances, the *fiesta* for their First Night would have to be postponed. The younger ones wouldn't like it, but that couldn't be helped. Lys had finally answered her. This Seeress of Two was her longed-for protégé, the seer who would take her place. Anassa wracked her memory. Which clan had not yet arrived? The Montoyas? The Escuderos? Who was the member among them that Lys had chosen? Whoever she was, they needed to reach her before the Torch Bearers did.

Chapter Twenty-One: Tribe

THE TOWN OF Elysir was not much different from Velez, Joachin considered, except instead of sitting on top of a hill, it squatted like a beggar at the foot of one. The locals eyed the Montoyas with suspicion as they rumbled their way past the market. Joachin met their hard stares, incensed that they should think he wanted their rotting meat or stinking fish. He fought the compulsion to search for the scarred priest. He could go, but if he did, it was unlikely he would find the clan again. This 'Womb' was their secret place. He would make inquiries about his mother's murderer at the camp. Someone in the Tribe must have seen something in their travels.

The band left Elysir quickly through the east gate. Soon, the procession struggled up steep hills. Ahead of Joachin, Guillermo's *vardo* lumbered from side to side like a drunken ox.

Casi appeared at the *vardo's* back window and leaned from it like a puppet. "Are you excited, *El Lince*? This will be your first time to the Womb."

He smiled. "Careful." The rig swayed. "You might fall out."

"I won't. There's going to be bonfires and dancing. *Maré* says your mama was the best dancer in the clan, but *Maré's* the best dancer I know."

"Casi, come inside," Luci called.

"I'm fine." She turned back to Joachín. "Do you dance, *El Lince?* I could teach you.

"A little."

"I'll show you more. *Paré* says we climb another league, then we squeeze through this narrow gap called 'the Neck'. After that, it's a scary way down, though I'm never as scared as *Maré* is."

"Casi, you're letting the dust in!" Joachín suspected Luci wasn't worried about dust at all.

"I'm just telling him," Casi insisted. The curtain fluttered down as she disappeared inside the *vardo*.

The procession finally came to a branch in the road. The main way turned north; the other was a weed-choked trail that slipped beneath a ceiling of rock, a lair for mountain lion or bear. It didn't surprise him that, other than the Diaphani, no one thought to pass here. As they rumbled through the Neck, the road narrowed to the point where there was little leeway between the caravans' wheels and the cliff's edge. As a single rider, he had no trouble, but half-way down, one of the teams shied at the pitch. The horses whinnied in fear. There was a scrabble of hooves on gravel, but other than that, no one made a sound. In amazement, Joachín realized that the women and children knew better than to scream. He watched as the driver jumped between the harnesses and grabbed the two horses by their halters. With soothing words, he steadied his team and coaxed them down the drop.

Ahead, the valley lay, littered with wagons. Campfires twinkled in the twilight, mimicking stars. With some surprise, the view tugged at his heart. Did all the Diaphani feel this way when they returned to this place? Perhaps it was the presence of the goddess, welcoming them home.

At the camp, Guillermo met another bandolier, a big man, Lorenzo of Isadore clan. Together, they parked the Montoyas' *vardos* throughout the camp. Many of their neighbours shouted welcome. Once their rig was parked, Casi ran to find friends. Luci introduced

Joachín to their nearest neighbour, a dumpy woman wearing a grimy black dress.

"Zara, meet my nephew, Joachín," she said proudly, drawing him forward. "Nephew?" the woman asked. Her dark eyes widened. "Not Estrella's son?"

"Yes! It's a miracle we found him."

"Is Estrella...?"

"With us in spirit, only," Luci said sadly.

"Oh, I am so sorry, Luci," the woman replied. She turned to Joachín. "Your maré was one of my closest friends. We were like sisters." To his alarm, she threw her arms about him and hugged him tightly. The moment lengthened.

"I think he's overwhelmed, Zara," Luci said.

"Don't worry, Joachín," Zara said, finally releasing him. "You'll get used to us." She waddled to her fire and scooped a bowl from her cook pot. "Here, have some stew." She handed it to him. He hesitated.

"Go on! Taste it!"

Not wanting to give offence, he tipped the bowl to his mouth and swallowed.

"Is it good?" Zara asked.

He nodded. "Delicious."

"I am famous for my cooking."

"I can see why," he said, although he didn't think the stew was that good. It had a strange taste.

"Where is everyone?" Luci asked Zara.

"At the Dedication."

"Oh, of course. We arrived late. Next year, we mustn't. Casi turns thirteen."

"She's still young, Luci," Zara said. "You could wait until she's fifteen and marriageable." She turned a speculative eye on Joachín.

Guillermo appeared from around the wagon's side with Iago in tow. "Joachín, we could use a hand," he said.

"Excuse me." Joachín handed Zara her bowl. "Thank you. That was wonderful." He brushed his hands on his pants, thankful to be released from the women. "What do you need?" he asked Guillermo.

"Just come. You'll see," Guillermo said.

"He's a handsome one," Zara told Luci as he followed in his uncle's wake.

Guillermo and Iago led him past a number of wagons until they stopped at a *vardo* with a bright red door. A group of men clustered about its back steps. They drew aside as the trio approached.

"Guillermo, you old rascal! Have a drink!" a portly man said. He lifted a clay jug and waved it. Another dozen jugs sat on the caravan's steps.

"Hector, this is my nephew, Estrella's son," Guillermo said. "Everyone, meet Joachín."

He was met with a chorus of hellos.

"You don't say?" Hector said. "Welcome, Joachín! Here, take my cup." He turned to a younger, chunky version of himself. "Tavio, get me another."

Joachín accepted the mug. "My thanks." He took a sip of what turned out to be excellent sherry. He turned to Guillermo. "So, this is the task you had to take me to?"

"Either that or Zara would have had your *cojones* within the hour."

Joachín sputtered. "Zara? She's old enough to be my grandmother!"

Hector laughed. "You have to watch the widows around here, Joachín. Whatever you do, don't eat anything they give you."

He blanched. "I already ate her stew. Only a mouthful," he added.

The men roared. "Not to worry, cousin!" Iago clapped him on the back. "There probably wasn't anything in it. I doubt if she's had time to prepare."

"Tell her you're full, next time," Hector advised sagely. "So, Guillermo, how did the trip to the coast go? Did you get that indigo shipment like you hoped?"

"No. Pirates took the ship off Tarrifa."

"Still, you must have picked up some trade along the way. You're looking well."

"Not as well as I'd like. On the other hand, you seem to be prospering, Hector."

"Oh, this." Hector indicated the jugs of sherry. "I keep drinking the profits."

The talk went on, mostly about business. Joachín met the Castros who were copper-smiths, the Gigas who were chandlers, and the Nardis who were coopers. He waited for an appropriate moment to ask for news of the priest, but two newcomers joined the group, sword makers from Tolede. They were introduced to him as Estaban and Angél Ferrara. Unlike Hector who was wealthy but didn't look it, these two wore expensive garb. The younger Ferrara's shirt was made from silk. *Pretentious for a blacksmith*, Joachín thought.

"We were sorry to hear about Talitha, Angél," Hector said. "Such a tragedy. She was a beautiful girl."

"Yes." Angél sipped his sherry. His face showed no signs of grief.

"Angél is seeking a new wife," Estaban Ferrara said. "We hope to arrange something while we're here."

"There are plenty of girls, none of whom are interested in me," Hector said. "You shouldn't have a problem, Angél."

Angél shrugged. "I'm in no hurry."

"We want a girl with talent," Estaban said.

Silence descended on the group. Joachín read the uneasiness in their faces. Luci told him that when Estrella left for the sake of his father, her loss was doubly felt by the Tribe. Estrella had also been a dreamer as he was. Ferrara meant to deplete the Tribe.

There was something about Angél he didn't like. "There's always Zara," he said.

Everyone but the Ferraras burst into laughter.

Angél glared at him. "You're more her type. Stinking and ugly."

Joachín went very still.

"Now, now." Guillermo placed a tight hand on his arm. "Let's not lose our heads over Zara. Joachín was making a joke, Angél. He didn't mean it. Your words were uncalled for. Perhaps you didn't mean them."

Angél looked down his nose at Joachín. "I was joking, also." He didn't smile.

"So, we are all friends!" Hector said with false cheer. "I'm thirsty. Everyone, hand me your cups." He reached for a fresh jug.

"You'll get me drunk, Hector. My wife'll never forgive me," Miguel Nardis said.

"You dance better when you're drunk, Miguel." Hector winked at him. "Sonia likes that."

"To me! To me!"

The men looked up. A crowd of women stood on a ledge half-way up the nearest hill, at what looked to be the entrance to a cave. Many of them bore torches. The crone in front lifted her arms as if to embrace the camp.

"That's Anassa, our Matriarch," Guillermo told Joachín. "Something's got her in a knot."

"Riders to the Neck!" the old woman shouted.

Joachín watched as she hobbled down the steep trail. Behind her, several wives carried a young girl by her shoulders and feet. The big man he had met earlier, Lorenzo, ran to meet them. He spoke with several of the women, turned, and charged down the hill like a wounded bull.

"Which of you has a fast horse?" he shouted, coming up to them.

"What's happened, Lorenzo?" Hector asked.

"Rana's turned Speaker. She says we must ride to the Neck before midnight. Something about rescuing a new seer."

"Rana is Speaker?" Angél Ferrara asked.

Lorenzo ignored him. "Who can go?"

"I will," Joachín said. His Fidel was the fastest horse he knew. "What am I to do?"

"Find a young woman on the run. Possibly two. They may be part of a clan, or maybe not. They're being chased. Bring them here. I'll also need men to remain at the Neck, on watch."

Joachín nodded.

"I'll come with you," Iago said.

By the time they had mounted up, there were half a dozen men in the rescue party. Joachín wasn't pleased to see Angél Ferrara among them.

Chapter Twenty-Two: Rescue

THE MOON WAS at its zenith. Miriam lay on the brow of the hill. A dream held her fast; Alonso was an eagle. A grey cord bound them by wrist and foot. He spread his great wings and leapt into the air. Their string lengthened and stretched. She watched as he rose higher and higher, becoming a faint speck against the night. He wanted to test their limits, see how far he might fly before their bond pulled him back.

She squinted to get a better view. Something dark built behind him, a roiling black cloud. She shouted a warning, but he didn't hear her. Nor did he see it right away. When he finally did, it towered above him, ready to collapse. He banked and swooped to avoid it, but it chased him, sending out gusts of wind to buffet him and tear at his great wings. He fought and spiraled. The cloud closed in. She watched as it blotted him out.

No! she cried, unable to move. The storm rolled over her, snuffing out the stars.

Miriam! Get up! She bolted upright, startled by the urgency of his voice. The wind was fierce.

Tomás and the Guard are on the path we took to get here. They'll be here in minutes. We have to run!

Her heart fluttered like a bird in a trap. She raced to the hut to retrieve Ephraim.

I'm sorry! I should have warned you sooner! I was trying to see how far I could go!

Ephraim lay like a dead man. Fear wrapped her in a tight cloak. She grabbed him by the shoulder and shook him hard. "Papa! Get up!"

He opened his eyes and looked dazed. She hoisted him to his feet. They stumbled for the door. *Which way, Alonso?*

Into the trees ahead. There's a dry bed. I'll direct you.

How do we know they won't see us?

We don't.

Half way there, she realized she'd left the grimoire. With a cry of dismay, she released Ephraim to retrieve it.

You can't! They're about to break from the trees.

Alonso, it's the only thing I have of my mother! I have to get it!

Keep going! He'll stop to read it. It'll buy us precious time.

Her eyes filled with tears. How could she have been so stupid? She may as well have delivered her mother into Tomás's hands. With the book at his disposal, he'd be more dangerous than ever.

It can't be helped. Think of your father, now. You have to run.

They entered the woods and stumbled down a steep gulch. Ephraim clung to her weakly. She had pulled him up too fast. The habit beneath her arm was damp with his blood. His foot snagged on a rock and he tripped, knocking them painfully to their knees. A shower of rock skittered down the wash before them. The crash of stones echoed in her ears like cannon fire.

Tomás is circling the hut.

She helped Ephraim to his feet.

Head to your right. The trees will help you down. The horses can't come this way. It's too steep. He'll have to go back the way he came. They're dismounting. He's entering the hut. He's seen the donkey and the pouch. Good. We'll reach the road before they do.

The road? But we'll be out in the open, Alonso!

The trees hide us. If we get far enough away without being seen, he may think we're further along.

She had to use extra caution with Ephraim, but thankfully, the moon lit their way. As they tumbled onto the road, she hazarded a glance to the brow of the hill. A swarm of torches jigged back and forth across it. Ahead, the road disappeared into nothing. She hefted Ephraim against her side and whispered encouragement. They had taken twenty steps when Alonso shouted, *Go back! There are bandits!*

From out of a black wall, men on horseback appeared like riders from a crypt. She choked on a cry and pulled Ephraim to the side of the road.

The front rider saw them. He galloped toward them, his horse's hooves pounding. The men behind him followed suit. Soon, they were surrounded. She set herself in front of Ephraim to protect him. There was nowhere to hide.

"We mean you no harm," the front rider informed her. He was a large man, well-muscled and lean. He reached from the saddle to grab her by the wrist. She pulled her arm out of reach, too frightened to scream. Another man, with the grace of an acrobat, leapt from his mount. He approached her open-handed, as he might a nervous horse.

"*Serina*," he said. His voice was light and his eyes were earnest. He had a gash on his cheek that gave him a rakish look. "I'm sure you'll find this hard to believe, but our Matriarch sent us to find you. We were expecting two women. Are you traveling with another?" His jaw dropped as if he'd been pole-axed. "You!"

She didn't know what to make of him. He set a hand to his chest. "I am Joachín de Rivera Montoya," he said, as if reciting a prayer. "I am at your service, *Serina*. Believe me when I say I mean you no harm."

She eyed him warily. *Alonso?*

He's beside himself for some reason, but not by us, I think.

"We waste time here." The first man was as impatient as his stamping horse.

Do we go with them?

They're Diaphani. They have no reason to wish us ill. With Tomás behind us, I think we have to.

"You will ride with me," the big man said.

The other man, Joachin de Rivera, shot him a dark look. "Let her decide." He turned back to Miriam and waited. Of the two, he had the bigger horse. Ephraim would ride easier with him. "Can you take my father?" she asked.

His expression fell, but he nodded. Had she disappointed him, somehow? She had no time to ponder it. She released Ephraim into his arms.

The larger man grinned and pulled her onto his horse. "I am Angél," he said, as she settled behind him. "And you are?"

"Miriam."

"Hold tight, sweet Miriam." He tucked her hands about his waist. His familiarity made her blood rise. "We're about to make a tricky descent. I don't want to lose you."

"Where are we going?"

"You'll see."

She didn't like the dismissal. He didn't notice and spurred his horse for the rock wall. To her surprise, a hidden trail lay there, invisible in the dark. They entered a cave and traveled its length. Soon, the roar of water pounded in her ears. A river churned far below. The rock cleft opened, and the night sky reappeared. A moonlit valley spread before them. She caught a hint of sulfur on the air.

Angél pointed. "Normally, you'd see a hundred fires from here." Without warning, his horse stumbled, throwing her hard against his back. His muscles were firm and well formed. She flushed as he shifted to accommodate her. "Our Matriarch ordered them doused."

"What is this place?"

"We call it the Womb. A site of pilgrimage for my people."

"How do you know about me?"

"Our Speaker foretold you."

Confusion clouded her like a draught from the depths. *Alonso?*

They're Diaphani. They have strange powers.

They reached the bottom of the trail. Another group of men waited there, armed with knives and clubs. As Angél passed them, they eyed her uneasily, their regard unsettling. Did they know about the Guard? Or were they posted here as a regular practice, she wondered?

Lumpy blocks took form in the dark. Caravans, she realized. Beside each one, women and children stood as still as stone. Their whispering followed her like a breeze.

Angél brought her to a wagon at the far end of the camp. Another crowd of people waited there. As she dismounted, she looked for her father and Joachín de Rivera. Several people were helping him lift Ephraim from his horse. A stab of guilt pricked her. She hadn't waited to see how Joachín would manage it. It would have been a difficult descent. The trail was steep. She ran to Ephraim and knelt by his side. He looked grey in the moonlight. The right side of his habit was soaked. His breathing was laboured.

A shadow loomed over her. "Don't worry. We will care for him."

Behind her, an ancient woman stood. Her white hair framed her head like an untidy halo.

"You're safe now, child. I am Anassa, Matriarch of this Tribe."

"I am Miriam."

"So Angél told me.... Sweet Lys!" she cried. Her look of welcome disappeared. She straightened as if she'd been slapped. People stared at her in alarm. She grabbed the bumpy necklace about her throat and snagged Miriam with a claw. "What are you?" she demanded. She shook her by the wrist. Her hand squeezed like a vise.

Miriam yelped, more frightened by this change in mood than by anything she had experienced. The crone's eyes burned into hers. They were intense, pitiless. She tried to pull her arm free and couldn't budge it.

Gods! Alonso said. *I feel like she's choking me! I can't breathe! Make her stop!*

The crone leaned into her face. "Who's in control? You or him?" She whispered it as if she didn't want her Tribe to hear. All about them, people shifted from foot to foot, ready to rush to her aid should she need it.

"Please, you're hurting me!" Begging for release was the only way to deal with her. The power emanating from her was daunting. Had her mother been this strong? She couldn't imagine it. "You're hurting him!"

Some of the fire went out of the old woman's eyes. She drew in a deep breath, released her hold, and then, in a complete change of mood, patted Miriam's hand as if she were a favoured grandchild. "It's all right!" she announced to her people. "She *is* as foretold. "Our Seeress of Two!"

Miriam rubbed her wrist. What had they fallen into? How did the old woman know about Alonso?

"You will come with me," Anassa Isadore murmured in her ear, her false cheer gone. "We have much to talk about." She addressed her people. "No fires until the morning. It's probably safe for us to sleep, but I want sentries kept. Double posts at the Neck."

Alonso, what is she talking about?

As if she heard the question, the old woman turned and beckoned to her. Few people cowed Miriam, but this grand dame did. "My father?" she asked, hating the quaver in her voice.

"He will be cared for." Anassa pursed her lips. "As for you and your *companion*, you have some explaining to do."

She sees me! Alonso said in astonishment.

Chapter Twenty-Three: Seer

THE TRIBE DISPERSED to their caravans or to their assigned sentry duty. No one accompanied them to Anassa's *vardo*, but Miriam knew it was useless to run. She and Ephraim were well and truly caught. They were foreigners here, likely prisoners as well. Anassa's people appeared to mind their own business, but she knew many wondered and watched.

These were her mother's people. They were strange, different. Their clothes were unusual—patterned and colourful, as if they chose to wear them that way to remind themselves of who they were and how they distinguished themselves. Many of the women wore their wealth on their arms and ears. Bangles and hoops glinted dully as they moved. She had always assumed she would look as they did, but she saw now that her appearance was a muted blend. She had the dark eyes and high cheekbones of the Diaphani, but she was a softer version compared to these *puros*. They were darker, more exotic and extreme. The women wore their hair down and wild. Perhaps that reflected the biggest difference of all. They were free. They expressed themselves as they chose. And Anassa was the wildest and most powerful member of them all.

Her caravan, or *vardo*, as she called it, was no less a reflection of that strangeness. Multiple glyphs had been painted on its walls. Miriam recognized a few from her mother's grimoire. To the uninitiated, they would have appeared senseless scrawls.

Anassa climbed the steps and opened her door. Inside, a lone candle flickered on a night stand. The *vardo* was so well shuttered, it shed no light. She waved Miriam inside. "Quickly," she said.

Miriam hesitated.

"Do you want them to see? I'm not going to bite you! Come in and sit down!"

There was no escaping it, no point in arguing with her. Miriam understood the need but she didn't like being told what to do, particularly by a querulous old woman who had just overpowered her on some invisible level. The promise against biting wasn't a reassurance, either. She entered the *vardo* and sat on a bench before the candlelit table. The place smelled of spices: cinnamon, pepper, and clove. She found it reassuring. There were so many quilts strewn on Anassa's bed that it resembled a nest.

"Tea?" Anassa set a hand to a copper tea service to test it. "Good. I brewed it before the dedication, but it's still warm. I think you'll find it refreshing." She didn't wait for Miriam to answer and poured her a cup.

Miriam frowned. Again, the assumption that the old woman knew best.

"Take it! Drink!" Anassa motioned.

Miriam sniffed the cup. It smelled of lemons. It seemed benign enough, but she wasn't about to trust the crone on her say so.

"Why would I poison you, if I could have told the Tribe to finish you off moments ago? This is your first visit to my *vardo*. It's proper to offer...oh, never mind!" Anassa waved the explanation aside. "How is it you're carrying that ghost?" She pointed at the empty space beside Miriam.

She means me, Alonso said.

Miriam said nothing. "How is it you can see him?" she asked at last. "*I* can't even see him."

Anassa smiled. "My dear, I am a *clara vidente*, the most clear-seeing of all of our Diaphani. Shall I describe him to you? A handsome man, tall and hale. He has blonde hair, fringed like a monk's. If I were a temple-goer, I'd say he was a priest, a Solarium official of high rank... yes! He confirms it. He's nodding!"

She stared at her in awe.

"I can see now, that he's no longer a threat. But the question remains, *why* is he attached to you? What did you do?"

She didn't want to tell her. If she explained how the resurrection spell went awry, about why she had to save her father....

"I know the Torch Bearers are after you, even if the Tribe doesn't. Our Speaker foretold you—'Seeress of Two' she called you. Now it makes sense. But I still need to know. If you tell me the truth, you have nothing to fear from me. I've been waiting for you for fifteen years."

What should I do, Alonso? She didn't know what to make of her.

Best tell her. She'll have it from us, one way or the other.

He wasn't keen to relive the coercion.

Strangely enough, as she shared her story with Anassa, the pressure in her chest lessened, as if her confession relieved a burden. Who else might better understand what she had been through? Who, other than her mother, had such a wealth of knowledge? Miriam bared her torso and showed Anassa the resurrection tattoo. Anassa pursed her lips.

"That's a rare glyph. Not generally known. How did you know to make it?"

"My mother. I should have mentioned her before. She was Diaphani. I copied it from her book." The loss of the grimoire still pained her.

Anassa's brows lifted, as if she recognized the markings of race. "She was Diaphani? Of course! I see it in you, now! Who was she, child? From which clan?"

"I knew her as Mari. She called herself Inara. I don't know from which band she came. You'll have to ask my father."

"Was she gifted?"

"She was a *sentidora*, like me."

"You're also a *sentidora*?" Anassa reached for her hand again, but this time there was no sense of being trapped. Instead, their energies mingled, merged. "What do you feel?" she asked.

Her right hip flared with a dull pain that radiated down her legs and to her feet. She had an ache in her neck from sleeping badly. Anassa's mind was clear and sharp, her presence was powerful, but her physical condition was poor. Miriam gazed at her sympathetically. "I think," she said, finding it strange to be on the giving end of advice, "that you should drink more willow tea. Perhaps get someone to ease that soreness in your hip with an oil rub or a hot bath. A pleasant walk in the morning would also do you good."

Anassa smiled and released her hand. "I'll keep," she said, patting it. "It's late. Let's get some sleep. I'll clear you a space. In the morning, we'll continue our conversation."

Miriam felt filthy, her clothes were torn to rags. She hated to set her body down on Anassa's clean quilts. "Don't worry about that." Anassa waved off her objections as if she had heard them. "I have water, here. You can wash your hands and face."

"Can you hear my thoughts?"

"No. But your expression tells me enough."

"What about my father?"

"Cared for. You can check on him in the morning."

There was nothing for it, but to do as she was told. Given the choice between her mother's people and the Torch Bearers, she and Ephraim were better off. But as soon as he was well enough to travel, they would go.

Assuming Anassa would *let* them leave. Something in the old woman's treatment of her suggested otherwise.

The morning began without preamble. Miriam was allowed to relieve herself, wash her hands and face, and eat a breakfast of gruel sweetened with honey. After that, Anassa shuttered them away in her *vardo* where their dialogue continued. She was not allowed to see Ephraim, although Anassa reassured her that Eva, their clan healer was looking after him. Miriam bit down on her frustration, but at the same time, she thirsted for knowledge. No one else had the background to explain things to her as Anassa did. She wanted to learn. She hungered for it, in a way she had not thought possible. They could afford a few hours.

"Have you always been able to do that?" Anassa asked her, in regards to her talent as a *sentidora*.

Miriam nodded. "But I don't really understand it. I thought it might be a type of healing ability."

Anassa set her tea down. "Being a healer and a *clara sentidora* aren't the same thing. One can be a healer without being sensitive. *Clara sentidoras* experience other people's emotions and physical states through touch. The few I've known call it a curse, as much as a gift."

Miriam nodded. That had been her experience.

"Being both is helpful," Anassa added. "Your diagnoses are never wrong."

That was also true. "I've heard there are other talents, although they're usually dismissed as madness," Miriam said. "Hearing voices, for example."

"Yes. Those are the Speakers—the *clara oradoras*. An Ancestor speaks through them. They're the true mediums, they prophesize. My granddaughter foretold your coming. That's how we knew."

The idea of someone using her body like a town crier was disturbing. "Do these special talents always fall to women?" she asked.

"Not always. Seers and Speakers tend to be female. Dreamers and Remembers are usually men."

"Dreamers and Rememberers?"

"As the names suggest, it's what they do."

Miriam knitted her brows together. She wasn't sure if Alonso made her a seer. "But I don't have visions," she said. "I don't see Alonso. I only hear him."

"That's because you're so new to his presence, I expect. Would you be willing to experiment?"

"What would it involve?"

"Nothing dangerous. I just want to determine the extent to which he can help you."

"That's been changing. At first, he didn't want to leave me, but now, he can leave for a short while to see what others are doing. He tells me about it, but I don't actually see."

Anassa set a finger to her lips. "That could change."

A knock came at the door.

"Wait!" Anassa cautioned whoever was outside. She turned to Miriam. "Ask His Brilliance to show you, not tell you, who is standing outside the door."

Alonso, can you do that? Miriam asked.

I don't know. Maybe if I concentrate hard enough.

She felt a tightening in her brow like the onset of a headache. It grew worse. *Ow. That hurts.*

Do you want me to stop?

No. It would be good if I could see.

Maybe if you closed your eyes?

Anassa and the *vardo* fell away. The pain intensified. She breathed through it. An image appeared. Blurry. She choked in surprise, which made it vanish. Vexed, she shook her head, took a deep breath and allowed the pain to build once more. The point between her eyebrows felt as if it were on fire. One of the energy foci she recalled, from her mother's grimoire.

Are you sure?

She suspected Alonso felt the pain as she did.

Just do it! She gritted her teeth, caught her breath, and controlled the intensity. Once again, an image built. And then, without warning, it flowered briefly in her mind. She gasped. It faded again almost immediately, but she retained it.

A Diaphani girl of about fifteen stood on the wagon's steps. Her hair was black and curly and interwoven with daisies. Like all Diaphani women, her face was tanned, her cheek bones sharp. Her expression was anything but pleased. She waited with her hands on her hips.

"A girl," Miriam told Anassa. "Pretty, about fifteen. She has daisies in her hair. She's wearing a pink blouse decorated with white dots, like moons. Her skirt is black and embroidered with roses." She opened her eyes. Anassa smiled at her.

"Come!" Anassa called to the visitor.

The door opened. The girl she described stood in the doorway. Miriam caught her breath. The ache between her eyes receded beneath the flush of success.

"So, you *are* a seer, after all!" Anassa patted her on the shoulder. "The Ancestors don't lie. Miriam, meet my granddaughter, Rana. She's the one who foretold you."

"Can we have fires this morning? Everyone wants to know," Rana said.

Anassa looked exasperated. "Didn't they see mine? We've already had our tea."

Rana turned to leave.

"Rana, stay." Anassa restrained her with a hand. "You two girls should get to know one another."

Rana pursed her lips.

"Sit for a moment." She patted the spot beside Miriam. "Both of you have something in common. Miriam's not only a seer but a speaker."

Miriam turned to her in surprise. A speaker?

Rana wrinkled her nose, as if smelling something off. "That's very interesting, *Puri*. Two gifts, instead of one. How did you learn this? Did she prophesize for you?"

"No."

"Then how is she a speaker?"

Miriam shifted uncomfortably. It was clear that Rana wasn't pleased with the news. It could only be that Anassa considered Alonso a type of ancestor. In a way, he did speak through her.

"There are different levels of speaking, just as there are variations in the sight," Anassa said. "What *is* important is that you both benefit the Tribe."

"I need air," Rana said. "It's stuffy in here."

"Perhaps you can introduce Miriam to some of your friends?"

"Perhaps." Before Anassa could say anything more, Rana opened the door and tripped down the steps.

"Don't worry about her." Anassa dismissed her with a wave. "She'll come around when she sees you're both useful. Let's determine your reach. See how far that priest of yours can go."

"I should check on Papa, first."

"Eva came and told me about him this morning. He's recovering, but he needs plenty of rest. Let him sleep awhile. Come."

They stepped from the *vardo*. Behind it, a path snaked up the mountain's side. A thin stream of water trickled beside it.

"Can you see what's hidden in that slope there? " Anassa pointed.

Miriam closed her eyes. Alonso showed her without having to be asked. This time, the pain was less. Would practice make it easier? The yellow trickle was a give-away, but instead of a sulfur spring bubbling from a cleft as she expected, she saw dark caverns and emerald pools, ponds that steamed in the dark.

"Oh!" she said. There was more than one of them. Women soaked in the nearest cavern. Men swam in another, higher up. She told Anassa what she saw.

"You did say you thought I should slip into a warm bath," Anassa reminded her, smiling. "Why don't we go together?" She took Miriam's arm and they climbed the path. When they reached the cave's mouth, Miriam paused to survey the camp below. Beside Anassa's *vardo*, Rana stared up at them. As they made eye contact, Rana walked away.

She's not happy with you being here, Alonso said.

She won't be unhappy for long, Alonso. We'll leave in a day or two, when Papa's better.

She and Anassa entered the cave. As they approached the green water, Alonso drifted away from them like a man heading out for a pleasant walk. *I'll leave you two ladies to your baths*, he said.

Miriam watched as Anassa followed his retreat. The old woman nodded. "And a gentleman, too," she said approvingly.

Chapter Twenty-Four: Dreams Come to Life

AFTER SPENDING A cramped night on the floor of the Montoya's *vardo*, Joachin woke at dawn before the rest of the family. He left the caravan quietly and headed for the river. Last night, he'd done what was necessary. He'd set his needs aside for the sake of the girl and her father, but this morning, he was his own man. Miriam had chosen Ferrara, not him. Perhaps his dreams had meant they would meet and nothing more. Very well—they'd met. It had been a mistake to read anything into it. He kicked at a stone and watched it skitter. Word passed that Torch Bearers were stationed in Elysir. They were a ruthless lot. It made sense that his nemesis might be among them.

He found Fidel cropping grass beside an olive tree. He swung his leg into the saddle.

"*El Lince!* Where are you going?" Casi appeared from around the tree, as inquisitive as a ferret.

"Go back to the *vardo*, Little Cat." How had he missed her? He'd been too distracted.

"I want to go with you!"

"You can't."

"Why not?"

Because you mustn't be near me when I get blood on my hands. Because this is something I do alone. As much as Guillermo and Iago had promised to help him avenge Estrella, he didn't want them involved. They were family. If they helped him, Luci and Casi would be at risk.

Casi's lips trembled. She looked as if she were about to cry. An uncomfortable thought occurred to him. *Does she suspect what I'm about to do?* "I'm just going for a morning's ride," he said. "Fidel needs the exercise."

"Let me come with you! You carried the new seer's father, last night. I'm no problem. I'm lighter."

Her eyes pleaded. She was so small. He tried to harden his heart, but he couldn't. Perhaps the bastard didn't ride with the Torch Bearers. Perhaps he could put off his search for another day. What was the harm in waiting until the Tribe quit the Womb? Guillermo said they would stay another two days. Casi's lower lip trembled. No wonder Luci found her such a handful.

He extended his hand. Casi whooped as he drew her into the saddle.

"I know of a place that has sparkle stones," she told him excitedly. "I'll show you. They bring good luck."

He needed good luck. "Point the way," he said.

He spent the rest of the morning helping Guillermo with chores. The horses needed re-shoeing, one of the *vardo's* steps had to be replaced. By mid-morning, Casi pestered him to teach her how to make a coin disappear. Sleight of hand wasn't much of a stretch for her. After a few attempts, she managed the trick. She did it so well, he questioned whether he'd been wise to show her.

"Don't tell your mother," he warned.

"I won't!" she replied, a natural conspirator.

Iago approached them where they stood in the sun. "*Maré* says it would be nice to have some coneys for supper. Want to go hunting?"

He preferred knives. "I'm not good with a sling."

"I'll show you. It's easy once you get the hang of it."

He doubted he'd develop a feel for it, but he sensed his cousin wanted to talk. "I'll get my horse," he said.

He headed to the river to retrieve Fidel. He ducked out from beneath the branches of an olive. A girl sat on the river's bank. He hesitated, not wanting to startle her. She glanced his way over her shoulder.

She was no longer wearing the filthy skirt and bloodied blouse he remembered from the night before. Now, she wore an embroidered top and a deep blue skirt. She had brushed her hair. Not that it mattered. Caked in mud, she would have been beautiful. She lifted a graceful hand to push aside a strand of silky hair.

"Oh!" she said. "You!"

He nodded awkwardly.

She rose and came toward him. Instead of the determination that usually marked her face, she looked nervous. He hardly blamed her. He was anxious himself. "I want to thank you for last night," she began awkwardly, "for taking such good care of my father. That was a hard journey. I didn't realize how difficult it would be when I asked you."

A frog took up residence in his throat. "How is your father?" he managed.

Her brows knitted together. "He'll get better now that he has a place to rest." She offered him a tentative smile. "Your name is Joachín? Did I hear that right?"

He nodded.

"I am Miriam. We didn't have a chance to talk last night."

"No." Gods, around her, he could barely put two words together. His pulse was racing. What kind of magic was this, that she should affect him so? He was good with women. Better than good. It had always been a point of pride with him. The moment lengthened, turning awkward.

"Well, thank you, again." She turned to leave.

"Wait! The people say you're a seer. Is that true?"

She pursed her lips. "Anassa says so. It's something that's come to me lately."

He felt like a leaf tossed in a storm. The dreams had been one thing, but now that he was in her presence...a woman like this could make a man forget everything he was about. "It's a potent gift," he stammered.

She nodded.

"Last night...." He faltered. She had the face of a goddess. Everything the priests said about heaven was true. "I meant what I said. I...I am at your service, Miriam. I would never hurt you."

A line of worry creased her brow. What a thing to say. Now, he'd scared her. Gods, could he get nothing right? "I'm not a seer, but I have a talent, too," he said quickly. "I dream. I'm a dreamer. I don't dream regular dreams, but I have those, too. I dream of people I've never met. I dream of their present and sometimes their future. I've dreamt of you."

Her eyes widened.

He stepped toward her. "The first time, you drove a donkey cart and wore the habit of a Luster monk. Later, you hid from Torch Bearers, between two houses in a village."

She grew very still.

"No one knows it, but you're still running from them."

"Only Anassa knows this," she whispered. "She asked me not to say anything until everyone meets tonight at the *divano*. She wants me to stay, but I think we should go. I'm afraid I'll bring the Guard down on everyone's heads."

"You won't. Your presence here is a blessing."

"I'm hardly a blessing if Tor Tomás finds me."

"Who is he?"

"The Grand Inquisitor."

"What does he want with you?"

"I foiled his plans.

"He murdered the High Solar. He tried to blame Papa and me, but we got away. He's a beast, inhuman."

Joachin nodded. A devil like that would attract others. Maybe his nemesis was part of the Grand Inquisitor's retinue, a lesser demon. "Did you, by any chance, see a priest in his company, one who bears a scar? Across his face, as if someone had cut him there?"

"Yes," she breathed. "The Grand Inquisitor, himself."

Time stopped. His heart didn't beat, he didn't breathe. And then life surged through his veins, again. They had come together closely, as if pulled by unseen strings. He needed to mount Fidel and ride off. He needed to stay exactly where he was. He drank in her eyes and lips. She wasn't a woman. She was Lys come down to earth. Insanity. His heart hammered, his lips burned. What he really wanted to do was to kiss her.

"Did he hurt you?" The idea infuriated him.

She gazed at him with huge, dark eyes. "No. Papa struck him over the head in time."

"What do you mean?"

"He tried to rape me." She flushed, looked away.

"He'll die for that, as well as other things. I will kill him."

She regarded him as if that made perfect sense. "You know him?" "He murdered my mother. I was the one who gave him that scar."

The world slipped away. There was just the two of them, bound together by a past so terrible and a future so heavy that it was beyond reckoning. Her lips parted. She *was* his dream and his future. Did she see it? It didn't matter. He would show her. Let his mouth confirm it.

She stepped back, broke the spell. "Will you tell me if you dream of me again?" She looked flustered, ready to run. He didn't blame her. They'd been drawn together like two planets spinning about a sun. What two people spoke as intimately as they did, after knowing each other for five minutes? What kind of a bond was that? Surely, she could see they had a common destiny, that they were part of a bigger plan.

He took a deep breath to clear his head. "I will." He wasn't sure of the wisdom of it.

"Thank you. I have to go." She fled.

He watched her leave. When she slipped out of sight, Iago sauntered up to him. "You were a while," he said. He glanced at him sidelong.

Joachin clawed a hand through his hair. "I ran into someone."

"I know. I saw."

At nearby cook fires, members of the Tribe chatted, stirred pots, and washed dishes. They looked as if they were minding their own affairs, but Joachin knew better. Nothing passed in this place unnoticed, especially when two people gazed into each other's eyes as if they had found lost love.

Iago nudged him in the ribs. "She's gorgeous. I don't blame you."

Joachin grimaced.

"How do you do it?"

"Do what?"

"Attract the girls. I see how they watch you. When you pass, they follow you with their eyes."

"Women watch rogues, too."

"Exactly! I want to project that."

Joachin snorted. "That doesn't always help." Now that Miriam was no longer close by, he wasn't so addled. "That last one couldn't leave fast enough."

"She'll come around."

Joachin wasn't so sure, but he hoped. One thing was certain. He needed to kill the priest first. He would follow where his heart led after.

Chapter Twenty-Five: Lessons

MIRIAM FORCED HERSELF to walk, not run. She knew Joachín watched her. He had been going to kiss her. She had stopped it. Who knew where things might have led, had he roused her further? Gods, what madness was this that she should be so attracted to a man she'd just met? She didn't believe in love at first sight. There were a lot of things she didn't believe, but they seemed to exist in spite of her. She had to calm down.

She thought of Angél Ferrara and their ride together from the night before. She had been aware of the hard roll of his muscles as they moved back and forth beneath his shirt, but fortunately, her clothing had protected her. Angél was handsome, yes, but he didn't unravel her like Joachín de Rivera. What *was* it about him?

I don't like either of them. Alonso sounded put out. *That Joachín is dangerous. His energy emanates in red waves. He finds you attractive.*

She flushed. She'd felt the attraction too, but Alonso didn't need to know that. *He said he dreamt of me.*

He's lying. He said that to impress you.

But he described the situation perfectly, Alonso—how we were on the run from the Torch Bearers, how I hid in Batos....

All guesswork. He's very clever. Don't trust him.

He seemed reluctant to say anything that might put Joachin in a good light. It bothered her, but she decided not to dwell on it.

They made their way back to Anassa's *vardo*. The old woman wanted her to return by noon so that they might share a meal and talk at length. She'd been on her way to do that when she felt the need to gather her thoughts by the river.

What do you think Anassa wants to talk to us about, Alonso? she asked.

Gods if I know, he replied, irritated.

"If we hold hands, I might be able to hear His Brilliance directly." Anassa set their plate of bread and olives aside and cupped Miriam's palms with her own. Miriam found her change in attitude unsettling. Last night, she had been a terrifying crone, today, a kindly grandmother feeding her tea and tapanade. At Anassa's touch, she noted the old woman's hip didn't ache so much. "Your Brilliance?" Anassa inquired politely.

Here, Alonso said.

Miriam caught a flash of him before he faded from view. He wasn't adorned in his robes of office, but looked like a simple Luster monk in brown homespun. Her heart quickened. The last time she'd seen him, he'd been a corpse. The headache she'd come to associate with her increasing sight was only a dull throb this morning.

"Oh, good! I can see *and* hear you! I hoped this might work." Anassa squeezed her fingers. "This is exciting, isn't it? Now, you must both understand that having the sight is of great benefit, but there are pitfalls."

Miriam straightened, intrigued.

"Of course, you remember how cautious I was when I first learned of you, Your Brilliance. I had to be sure you weren't a threat."

Miriam suppressed a smirk. Anassa spoke of their meeting as if it had occurred months ago, rather than last night.

"We Diaphani know better than to treat with the dead," Anassa continued. "Those who die peacefully shouldn't be bothered in their repose. As for those who die violently, they tend not to go on, but to float."

So, I'm floating. He still sounded out of sorts.

"Yes, you float. But not like an ordinary ghost. You're in transition. I think you choose to remain that way."

He said nothing. Miriam felt him tense as if he didn't want to acknowledge it.

Anassa drew in a deep breath. "The spiritual world is not how either of you imagine it. It isn't a place where angels sing or devils torment. There are any number of levels between the heavenly and the damned. How we choose to act determines the grace or evil we encounter."

I know that much.

"No offence, Your Brilliance, but you don't. You're in limbo. Despite your devotion to Sul, you've had no experience of him."

I beg your pardon?

"You haven't spoken with him, have you?"

Of course not! I never expected that. When I was alive, I prayed and read scripture, but I never assumed....

"You studied ancient texts that may or may not be accurate."

Are you telling me I spent my entire life...?

"That's exactly what I'm telling you. You already know it. Let me ask you a question. If you were to actually speak with Sul, wouldn't you be convinced of the correctness of your insights?"

I...no! I wouldn't trust any voice in my head.

"But you're a voice in Miriam's head. She trusts you."

That's different. Religion isn't about personal experience, it's about faith. That's what faith is—a decision to believe in things that have no proof. Even if I've lost mine, there's virtue in blind hope.

"Nonsense. Why should anyone have to settle for that?"

He sputtered, at a loss for words. Anassa supplied a few. "It all comes down to relationships—the ones we pursue and the ones we don't. Why should the gods talk to you, if you don't talk to them?"

What is prayer, if not talking to the gods?

"Prayer is different things to different people. If you did nothing but mumble platitudes in my ear, I don't think I'd reply."

Miriam felt him pull the shreds of his dignity about him like a tattered cloak. *What is the point of this conversation?*

"I am establishing credentials," Anassa replied smoothly. "We Diaphani speak to our Ancestors and to Lys directly. They, and She, speak to us. Therefore, we have a greater knowledge of the spiritual world than you do."

Miriam came to Alonso's defense. "I don't believe in the gods, either."

Anassa regarded her balefully. "Wasn't it Sul in his earthly incarnation who said, 'He who has ears to hear, let him hear?' You brought Alonso back from the dead. Isn't that proof that the gods might exist, that the world is bigger than you thought?"

"It's certainly bigger. But until Sul or Lys actually speak to me...."

"There are mysteries. The world of spirit is the greatest mystery of all."

"Then enlighten me, Anassa. Papa and I attended Mass to maintain appearances, so I know some of what the priests taught. But as for the goddess, I know nothing."

Sul is the Creator, Alonso said. *He blesses the dutiful and damns the lost...* his voice trailed off.

"I don't think it's quite as simple as that," Anassa said. "Sul and Lys are two parts of a whole. We Diaphani see them as having different functions: Sul creates the universe while Lys interacts with it, like a mother tending a child. The Solarium doesn't like her, of course. The temple can't allow a personal bond with any god. It takes away their role of intercession."

I wouldn't give it that much credit, Alonso said. *It's more about position and power.*

That word, again. Power. Anassa seemed to suggest that the kind of power she sought was spiritually based. Yet, if one had to have faith.... *I dabbled without believing*, Miriam thought, *but I also dedicated myself to a goddess.* Had that been an act of faith?

"I didn't want to suggest that, Your Brilliance, but if you say so, then it must be," Anassa said primly.

"It's not just about position." Miriam felt the need to defend him. "It can also be about good works. You planted parks, Alonso. You used temple funds to do it. And the new aqueduct for Granad—you were the moving force behind that."

True. Much to the displeasure of my Exchequer. He didn't like me using the treasury to fund them.

"So, like anything, there is the good and the bad." Anassa lifted a finger to the ceiling. "Which brings me to my next point. Pay close attention for it affects you both. There are entities of good and evil in the spiritual world. For those of us with one foot in the spiritual realm, we are much more susceptible."

Miriam felt Alonso cringe. "How so?" she asked.

"Spirit is a vast ocean. Many things swim in it: the living, the dead, and other entities that are neither one nor the other. Ghosts drift between survival and extinction within the tides of time. Those who *do* accept the transition of death head for deeper waters—the life-giving realm of the reefs or the murkier voids of the depths. It's the depths of which we must be wary."

No one said anything for a moment.

Miriam finally spoke. "When you say 'depths', what exactly do you mean?" The word was fraught with menace. It hinted of dark potentials beyond their control.

Anassa drew in a breath. "Forgive me. Sometimes I forget to put it in simpler terms. I hadn't wanted to get into this today, but I suppose we must. Most people think that emotions are nothing, impotent, without substance. That isn't true. They are forces, energies that can be used. I use the word 'depth' to describe those places created by the darker emotions. It is in the depths where entities of destruction feed."

"Entities of destruction?"

"Demons, if you will, although the term is misleading. 'Malignancy' might be a better choice. Usually, they stay where they are, unless something stirs them up. They feed upon negative emotions like hatred, pride, or lust—the more intense the feeling, the greater their interest. In our world, evil acts attract them. They nose around, like leeches after prey."

Miriam frowned. When she called him forth, Alonso had been ablaze, a fiery elemental bent on seizing her. But had that been his only objective? Had he also been fleeing something? "Are these entities always dark?" she asked.

Anassa shook her head. "No. They can appear in any guise. A priest might see a fiery hell, a Diaphani, something else. They aren't particular. They borrow ideas from the thinker's mind and appear in ways he expects. They're dangerous and take delight in annihilating their victims."

"How likely are we to run into these?"

"Certain people and places draw them. They're easy to sense. Their presence is a blight, they shrivel everything they touch. Those who aren't sensitive are less likely to feel them. But for those of us who see, speak, sense, or dream—we're far more vulnerable."

"So, you're at risk because you're a seer, and Rana, because she's a speaker."

"Yes. And you, because you are both, as well as a *sentidora*. Alonso is in even greater peril, because he's a spirit."

Miriam felt a chill in the air despite the noon-day heat of the *vardo*. "How do we protect ourselves?"

"Avoidance is best. Don't allow dark emotions to dictate your actions. But if you can't evade a dark entity because of what someone has done, calling on the Ancestors often works."

But I don't have any Ancestors, Alonso said.

"Of course you do!" Anassa replied. "Anyone who has loved you and passed on is an Ancestor. Any spiritual master is an Ancestor. And there are entities of light that have never seen human form, but when called upon, will come to your aid."

Angels? Alonso asked.

"Your term. A man with wings doesn't always apply."

Alonso was quiet for a moment. Miriam could see him again. The ache between her eyes was barely discernable. He sat beside her, studying his hands as if considering his past. The planes of his face were smooth and unlined, but his eyes were troubled. *What if one has never been loved?* he asked softly.

Oh, Alonso! She wanted to reach out to him. He had served the temple but had never experienced any genuine human connection. How sad to be respected by all and loved by none.

"Everyone has been loved," Anassa told him gently. "As a last resort, we can call on the gods. Theirs is the purest love of all."

Alonso didn't feel that any more than she did, Miriam knew. But in the end, maybe all one needed was one person, one special soul who saw the good in you and appreciated the uniqueness of who you were, someone who made the days pass pleasantly and the night's soar.

She took a deep breath. All of that—especially the last—was impossible with Alonso. She couldn't be that person for him, or he, for her.

But they could be the best of friends. Perhaps that was enough.

Enough for whom? her conscience demanded. *For him or for you?*

It was a dangerous question. She set it out of her mind, not trusting herself to answer.

Chapter Twenty-Six: Ephraim Knows Best

EPHRAIM OPENED HIS eyes and blinked. Miriam sat beside him on the bed. "How are you feeling, Papa?" she asked. "Can I get you anything?"

She watched as he gazed blearily about the *vardo*. His glance rested on Eva.

"This is Eva, Papa. She's a healer. We're in her caravan in a Diaphani camp."

He found his voice. "Hello. My wife was a healer, also."

Eva nodded, gave him a quiet smile. She handed Miriam some clean strips of cloth. "I changed his bandages earlier, but here are more if he needs them. Try to get some water into him." She indicated a bucket on a shelf.

"Thank you." Miriam glanced back at Ephraim as Eva left them to their privacy. His colour was better.

"The last thing I remember was falling down a stream bed," Ephraim said. "The Guard was right behind us. How did we escape?"

"We ran."

"I know that. But we were asleep in the hut. The next thing I know, you're shaking me awake and telling me to go." His hand tightened on hers. "I know you, Miri. You're not telling me everything."

She fingered the edge of his blanket. *I have to tell him, Alonso.*

Tell him, then.

"The High Solar is still with me, Papa. When I resurrected him, he didn't return to his body. He's in mine."

Ephraim stared at her, dumbstruck. "Gods. Possession?"

"It's not like that. He helps me. It's because of Alonso that we're here."

"He brought the Diaphani?"

"No. He warned me about the Torch Bearers. He saw them in time."

Tell him that I'm sorry this has been done to him.

"Alonso says he's sorry you've suffered."

If I could help him in any way, I would.

"He says if he can help us in any way, he will."

"He's not manipulating you?" Ephraim asked.

"No. We've been through that." She smiled. "He's a well-behaved guest."

Ephraim fixed his gaze on the ceiling. When he met her glance again, she couldn't read his expression. "There is something the High Solar can do for me, if he's truly part of the spirit world," he said. "Mari. Can he talk to her for me?"

He wanted to speak with her mother. Alonso recoiled. *I don't think I can do that.*

"He says he doesn't think he can."

Ephraim sighed, gazed back at the ceiling. "So, what are our plans?"

"We stay until you've recovered. Then we leave."

He nodded. "I think that's wise. These are your mother's people. It was kind of them to help, but we put them at risk."

"Anassa wants us to stay. She thinks we'll benefit the Tribe."

"Anassa?"

"Their Matriarch."

"I see. That doesn't surprise me. They like to hold onto their own."

"There's a *divano* tonight, a tribal meeting. Anassa knows about the Torch Bearers, but I think the rest of the Tribe should know."

"Tell them we'll leave as soon as possible."

She nodded. It was best they go before they felt a connection to these people. She thought of Joachín de Rivera. His teeth had been so white, his eyes so brown as to be nearly black. Had he kissed her, his beard would have prickled, but his lips would have been soft. Or... perhaps not. Maybe his kiss would have been deep and hard. She caught her breath.

"What is it?" Ephraim stared at her.

Her face flamed, as much from embarrassment as from desire. She wiped her hands on her skirt.

"Nothing," she said, turning away.

Chapter Twenty-Seven: Divano

TO LUCI'S DELIGHT, Joachin and Iago brought home six hares. Later, Joachin complimented her on her stew. She brushed his praise aside. "You boys outdid yourselves. This, anyone can do."

"Thank Iago," Joachin said. "He caught five of them."

Iago grinned. "It takes awhile to get used to the sling, cousin."

Joachin shrugged. "I only caught the last because Fidel nearly stepped on it." Iago laughed. As Casi collected their plates, a runner approached their *vardo*. He had a thin face and a long nose. Despite his lanky limbs, there was something refined about him.

"Bandolier Lorenzo asks that we convene," he told Guillermo. "He'd like to start the *divano*."

"Thank you, Jaime. We'll be there," Guillermo replied.

Jaime inclined his head and jogged for the next group of caravans.

"Jaime is the son of Donaldo Franco," Guillermo told Joachin. "They're musicians and will play for us. Luci!" he called. "We should go."

She emerged from behind the *vardo* where she'd been scouring plates. Casi appeared with her. "We're heading off to the *divano*," Luci told Casi. "Stay here. Or visit the Ortega girls, if you like."

"I'll make biscuits for breakfast." She hazarded a quick glance at Joachin.

The three of them walked across the camp to where a cluster of caravans featured guitar motifs on their walls. As they passed by, Joachin glanced at the matriarch's *vardo*, hoping to see Miriam there. According to Luci, the Francos weren't only musicians, but builders of fine instruments, stringed, but also percussion. In two and threes, members of the Tribe approached the same spot.

The women found stumps and sat on them. The men stood behind their wives. Each group represented their respective clans and dressed to indicate their bands. Luci and Guillermo wore indigo. In front of their *vardo*, Donaldo Franco waited with his son. Like Jaime, Donaldo looked as if he were constructed from cat gut. His limbs were long and bony, his fingers thin and resourceful. Appropriate for a musician, Joachin thought. Donaldo cautioned the crowd for silence. Joachin looked around again for Miriam, but he didn't see her. As the crowd quieted, Donaldo spoke.

"Once again, we are well met. It's been a year since most of us were here. To start, let's hear the words of our Rememberer, Ximen, who reminds us of our roots."

A small, blind man stepped forward. He was oddly dressed. His cloak looked as if it had been constructed from swatches of cloth, representing all those present. His eyes shone like pale marbles. He took a moment to scan each face in the crowd as if he saw every person clearly. He paused a moment when he came to Joachin, blinked, and then moved on. He lifted his arms and spoke.

"Let us imagine the Himals, mountains so high that they have the audacity to leach the sky of its blueness. And this blueness turns to the whiteness of snow, melts, and becomes icy, frothing water. Streams form, cord, and twine. As the land falls toward the sea, the river broadens into a wide plain. Every spring, it floods its banks, leaving rich silt for the people who have settled there. This is the Andu valley, where we began, where our roots reach beyond the sediments of time. I ask you to remember. Who are we?"

Joachín listened as everyone in the Tribe recited the litany. "We are the Diaphani. People of the Mist."

"And like mist, we vanished into the earth and the water when the barbarians came, some of us to the mountains, some to the desert, some to the sea. Eventually, we found each other, coming together like the tributaries of the vast Andu River. Look about you. We are the remnants of a once great nation. We have suffered much, but we endure."

"We are the Diaphani. People of the Loss," everyone intoned.

"We must honour who we are. Preserve who we are. We must never forget! So say I, Ximen, Rememberer."

"We are the Diaphani. We do not forget," the Tribe finished.

There was a moment of silence. Joachín felt strangely moved. It seemed as if the Diaphani paralleled his own unhappy past.

"Let us begin with those who stand to my right, the Francos. What have you to report, Bandolier?" Ximen asked.

Donaldo Franco stepped forward. "After last year's meet, we traveled through the passes of Andor to southern Franca. We didn't stay long. There was trouble."

"What kind of trouble?" Angél Ferrara demanded.

"The Cathara were being prosecuted for heresy. We passed through Franca quietly and made our way to Genoa where we stayed with the Count of Novell. The count welcomed us as fellow artists. He is a poet of renown. I name him a friend to the Diaphani."

"Good to know. Anything else?" Ximen asked.

"Jaime, as you know, has come of age. We seek a bride for him."

Several families within the circle nodded. Likely, they had eligible daughters.

In succession, each bandolier or his wife contributed to the report. Ximen turned to the Montoyas. Luci stepped forward.

"We thought we had nothing to tell, but we have wonderful news." She placed a possessive hand on Joachín's shoulder. "Our family has grown by one. This is Joachín, *El Lince*. He is Estrella's son. He's come home."

All eyes were on him. Some showed their amazement, a few their distrust. Angél Ferrara regarded him with open hostility.

"Where is your *maré?*" Estaban Ferrara demanded.

No mention of his father. So, this was how it was to be. "My father died in a bar fight when I was nine," Joachín said. "My mother died two years later."

Silence met this announcement. Angél muttered something in his father's ear. The elder Ferrara made a face and nodded. The implication was clear. *This is what comes from running off with riff-raff.*

Ximen spoke, his blind eyes fixed on Joachín. "By rights, it is his option to claim the title of bandolier. As Estrella's son, he's the eldest remaining male of the Montoya line."

Angél Ferrara erupted. "How can you offer that? He's half blood!"

"Guillermo is bandolier of the Montoyas! What does he say?" Estaban Ferrara demanded.

All eyes turned to Guillermo. He shrugged. "It's not like I'd lose my standing. I took Luci's surname after marriage to preserve it. I'm the eldest Gonzales, so I forfeit nothing. Besides, Joachín isn't married yet. He'd be bandolier in title, only."

"What about Iago?" someone called.

"If Joachín takes the title, I revert to Gonzales, too. I don't mind," Iago said.

There were a few nods at this reminder.

The blood rushed to Joachín's face. Diaphani law was too convoluted for him to follow. For years, he'd been without a family and had resented it. Now, he was being acknowledged as a leader of a clan.

"Well, *El Lince?*" Joachín didn't like how the elder Ferrara handled his name. "What do you say? Are you ready to live as one of us?"

Luci stood. "He *is* one of us!"

"Only if he chooses to be. His father never wanted that," Ferrara said.

"Perhaps it's too soon for him to know."

Joachín glanced at the ancient woman who spoke, the matriarch of the Tribe. Her multiple tattoos made her look fierce, but her tone was gentle. Everyone turned to her with respect. "Consider how he must feel," she said, regarding him. "He doesn't know us. All he's known is that we didn't come looking for him when Estrella died. I should have kept my eyes on her, but I didn't. Now, we ask him to make up his mind. Perhaps, we need to prove ourselves to him."

He caught Ximen the Remember watching him. "Also recall that *El Lince* has survived without the benefit of the Tribe," Ximen announced. "For nine years he's not only endured, but he's thrived. There's a gift in that. He is a man of means."

Joachin glanced at him sharply. The way in which the Rememberer emphasized *gift* made him wonder how much the blind man knew.

"At eleven he nearly killed his mother's murderer, a false priest. I've seen it and more," Ximen said.

Joachin stared at him. The blind man saw the past in the same way he dreamt the future. Ximen was more than a historian. He was a judge. His talent allowed him to confirm the truth or falseness of any claim. Joachin took in the reactions about him. Several members of the Tribe looked upon him with new respect. The phrase 'a man of means' had made an impact.

"Forgive us our initial distrust," Donaldo Franco said, "but if the Rememberer endorses you, then so must we. Welcome *El Lince*. We leave it for you to decide if you will stay or go." Luci hugged his arm. No one expected him to reply.

Ximen spoke. "Where did we leave off? Ah, yes." He acknowledged the head of Isadore clan. Bandolier Lorenzo stepped forward.

"As you all know, last night we met our new seer. She's asked to speak to us," he said.

Miriam stepped forth. Joachin watched as she took a deep breath to steady herself before the crowd.

"I want to thank all of you for rescuing my father and me," she began. "Your kindness and generosity have been overwhelming. My father is doing better. We hope to leave as soon as possible."

"Leave?" Anassa interrupted.

"I must tell them, Anassa." Miriam faced the crowd again. "You're an amazing and wonderful people. I'm honoured that you would have me as your new seer. I would love to serve you, but my father and I are on the run...."

Anassa grabbed her by the arm. "Don't."

...from Torch Bearers who have accused my father of murder. He's committed no crime, but if we stay here, we put you all at risk."

"We're harbouring fugitives?" Bandolier Ferrara demanded. "What madness is this?"

"Miriam, this wasn't the time!" Anassa said.

"You would keep this from us?" Estaban Ferrara glared at her. He turned to survey the Neck, as if expecting to see an army of Torch Bearers riding down it. Some of the women whimpered in fear.

"There is no reason to panic!" Anassa shouted in a stronger voice than Joachin would have given her credit for. "We have always been hounded by the Guard! This is nothing new! That our new seer is also pursued makes her one of us!"

"She's not of the blood!"

"And your blood is so pure, Estaban Ferrara?" Anassa rounded on him. "You and yours, who live in a town and travel once a year?" She spread her arms wide. "What matters more? From whom we are borne or how we live? I say the gods dictate who is blood and who isn't! Lys chose *her*!" She pointed at Miriam. "Our Speaker confirms it!"

"We must consider outcomes...," Ferrara began.

Anassa cut him off. "I am considering outcomes! How many seers can we count among us, other than me? If I die tomorrow, who will watch for us? Which one of you has displayed a new talent this past year? Tell me!"

No one spoke.

"We need the gifts of as many as possible. Having our new seer with us is a greater boon than a drawback."

"What does *Serina* Miriam say?" Ximen the Rememberer turned his white eyes to her. His face was serene. Joachin watched as Miriam met his regard solemnly. *She looks as if she carries the weight of the world on her shoulders*, he thought.

"I don't want to put any of you at risk," she said.

"We are already at risk," Anassa repeated tiredly. "More so, without you."

Miriam considered the crowd of faces about her. "What do all of you say? Would you have my father and I stay with you?"

Joachin wanted to shout 'yes!' but he held his tongue. Most of the Tribe didn't accept him yet, either. To his relief, Luci and Guillermo both nodded, but they were in the minority. Many of the Tribe looked unsure.

He had to say something.

He stepped forward. "I've dreamt of her." All eyes turned to him. "I am a dreamer. Twice, I saw her on the run from the Torch Bearers. She isn't here by coincidence, but by divine plan. I don't dream of anything that is insignificant."

"True," Ximen confirmed, nodding.

"Estrella was also a dreamer," Luci said in awe.

Anassa nodded. "So, our speaker foretells her, and this one, Estrella's son, has dreamt of her. That is *twice* the goddess has shown us. Do we turn our backs on Lys?"

Most people shook their heads, although some remained unconvinced. Joachín thought Miriam looked troubled.

"Much has been presented for discussion," Ximen said, his milky eyes bright. "We remain at the Womb for another two days. Let us convene tomorrow night to hear what's been decided." The crowd dispersed. Most of the bandoliers formed clusters to talk over events while their wives headed for their caravans.

Luci turned to Joachín. "Why didn't you tell me you were a dreamer?" she asked.

"It never came up." He looked over the retreating crowd.

"Leave him be, Luci," Guillermo said. "It's a private thing. Maybe he doesn't like to talk about it."

"Yet, you confessed it tonight." She eyed him speculatively and followed his gaze. Miriam stood talking quietly with Anassa. "Are you hungry?" she asked. "I could make you something."

Joachín shook his head. Guillermo clapped him on the arm. "I think you need a drink. Let's go find you one."

Joachín turned to Guillermo as they walked away. "I didn't come here to take your place as bandolier."

Guillermo shrugged. "You won't take it. If you stay, I'll give it up. It's the right thing to do."

"I think I prefer being a Gonzales," Iago said. "It follows the line of patriarchy and gives me more status. Don't tell *Maré* I said that, though." He glanced behind them. Luci was out of sight.

Joachín frowned. "How is it I'd be bandolier, anyway?"

Guillermo lifted his eyebrows as if the answer was obvious. "You're the eldest surviving male of the Montoyas."

"But you...."

"I'm a Gonzales. When I married Luci, I became the Montoya so the clan name wouldn't die out. Now that you're here, you're the Montoya. It's custom."

"Quite the night!" Hector waved a bottle of sherry in their direction as they approached his *vardo*. "Our new seer on the run and Joachín, not only the new Montoya, but a dreamer!" He winked at Joachín. "Word has it you spent time with her this morning."

"Word travels fast," Joachín said bleakly.

"You're a nosey old souse, Hector. Anyone ever tell you that?" Guillermo asked.

Hector chuckled. "Often." He poured sherry into cups. "Pay me no heed, Joachín. I have no life. She is a beauty, though." He sighed. "If I were ten years younger, I'd be on her like a stag on a hind."

"You think she'll stay?" Iago asked. "Become our next matriarch?"

"If she does, Joachín, here, will be lead bandolier, providing he marries her. I'm half tempted to try for it, myself."

"You like your life as it is, Hector," Guillermo said. "No one tells you what to do."

"True. I'm comfortable. But if I could find a good woman who likes fat men and rich food, I'd be a happy man."

"What about fat food and rich men?" Iago asked.

Hector nodded. "That would work."

A thrum of guitars came from across the compound. The Francos were tuning up. The opening strains brought the women from their campsites.

Hector grinned wolfishly. "Ha! Entertainment!" He grabbed a second jug. "Better take this with us. Dancing is thirsty work."

As the men made their way to the Franco's caravan, Luci and Casi appeared, wearing russet and indigo skirts. Casi sported daisies behind one ear, making her look more the cat-in-the-posies than ever.

"I've been waiting for this all year," Luci said with enthusiasm. "Do you dance, Joachín? Your mother used to be the best dancer of us all."

He considered the wooden planks the men had set on the ground. There was plenty of room for everyone to dance, but the floorboards created a space for those who wanted to display their virtuosity. He straightened his shoulders. He would show the Tribe he was one of them, not the outcast the Ferraras claimed. His ability might also speak silently to Miriam. He hoped she understood dance the way most women did—the best dancers made the best lovers. It had everything to do with one's comfort with their body, with one's confidence in what he could do. And of course, exceptional ability only came after a great deal of practice in both spheres.

He took a deep breath. It was bad luck to brag.

"I do all right," he said.

Chapter Twenty-Eight: Newfound Son

THE FIRST FEW dances were for everyone's participation. The Francos opened with a lively and cheerful tune. Jaime strummed the rhythm while, in complicated triplets, Donaldo plucked the strings. Joachin's feet twitched, but it was better to wait. These first songs were for the Tribe to celebrate their reunion, not for a lone dancer to show what he could do. He surveyed the spectators on the outskirts of the circle and frowned. Miriam was nowhere among them.

Casi fluttered past him. Luci spun not far behind. His aunt held her hands out to him. "Join me, Joachin!" she called.

Smiling, he shook his head. "I'm happy watching you!" She waved and didn't persist. As the set ended, everyone clapped and shouted. Jaime and Donaldo took their bows, paused to take a drink, and then they started again.

This time, Donaldo stood to sing while another guitarist took his place. "That's Rico," Luci said, pointing him out to Joachin. She had come to stand beside him to catch her breath. "He's not as good as Donaldo, but then, few men sing as well as Donaldo does."

"A man of many talents, is he?"

She nodded. "He's about to sing a *Trienso*. Not my forte, but others like it."

Joachin nodded. A *Trienso* was a difficult *palo* in both song and dance. The form expressed great longing or passion. To some extent, the words determined the steps, but the singer often chose the lyrics for the dancer. A *Trienso* was usually a solo piece.

"Who's dancing?" he asked.

"I'm not sure. We'll have to wait and see," Luci said.

Jaime and Rico strummed the opening chords. The introduction was solemn and hinted of introspection. On the edge of the circle, a dancer appeared. She strode to the middle of the dance floor with her eyes downcast. When she reached the centre, she posed with her back to the audience. Slowly, she raised her arms, her wrists curling into *flores*, her fingers beckoning as if she wanted to stroke the night. Donaldo followed with the expected intro—"Le re lee, lee, lee...."

The dancer swayed, as if unaware of the audience behind her. Then, as Donaldo cried of unrequited love, she turned suddenly and picked up her skirts. Her feet tapped an insistent beat. She didn't look at the audience, but seemed engrossed in her steps as the dance picked up speed. As Donaldo sang of unmet needs and loneliness, she responded to each verse as if acknowledging that was how she felt. Faster and faster her feet moved until she reached a crescendo. Then as abruptly as she had begun, she stopped. Her head snapped up as if to confront the audience.

The crowd responded with enthusiasm. Even Joachin had to admit the girl was good, better than most. Her footwork was precise and her arm work, smooth. She evoked a sense of silent desire. And this, by the end of the first half of the song.

Jaime stood, tapped his father on the shoulder. Surprised, Donaldo smiled and sat down to pick up his guitar. With an outstretched hand, Jaime began the second verse. Startled by the change in singers, the dancer turned abruptly to regard him. Never dropping their shared gaze, she began to dance once again. Her arm curled up as if she were considering him, her face taut. Her second arm beckoned, as if in invitation. The audience hooted with excitement. Beside him, Luci crowed with delight.

"That's Kezia!" she said. "I almost didn't recognize her. She's grown up so much over the past year! Jaime just informed her of his intentions. Look! He's singing to her!"

It was true, if the lyrics had anything to do with it:

Oh, little bird,
Teach me to fly.
For I've never found Love
until now.

As they finished, the crowd clapped and laughed. The girl looked flushed and excited, Jaime pleased.

Donaldo set down his guitar and addressed the audience. "We've had a request for a *Zabira*. I hope the dancer will forgive me if I'm a little rusty, but I'll do my best."

"You may be old, Donaldo, but the rest of us aren't! *Zabira!*" Hector shouted.

With enthusiasm, the men in the audience took up the call. The women looked on, some tolerant, some askance. "*Zabira! Zabira! Zabira!*" the men shouted.

It wasn't often one witnessed a *Zabira*. Joachin watched the stage with interest. Done right, the *Zabira* was one of the most seductive dances performed. Only certain women could execute it properly. The allure was the unspoken promise of what came after. The girl had to be sure of herself, confident in her appeal.

The guitars started up, accompanied by a tambourine. Again, the rhythm established a slow walk, but this time, the melody teased. From the edge of the floor, a new girl appeared.

Her face was veiled, but not much else. She had covered her breasts with scarves. Her midriff was bare, except for the ink of a new tattoo. Her hips were wrapped in a shawl. With each step she took, the shawl's tassels swayed, heightening her movements. Placing each bare foot before her like a tigress stalking prey, she moved to the centre of the floor, her hips fluid and undulating. When she reached the middle of the stage, she lifted her arms and stretched her hands to the stars. Her fingers snapped, bringing together a pair of hidden zills. Their sound left a sharp 'ting' upon the air. No one in the audience spoke.

Joachín felt his blood rise. None of the men could take their eyes from her. Cat-like, she performed a series of slow twists that made her look as if she pulled herself from the inside out. Her hands came up, stroked her ribs, reached for her face. With a flick, she pulled the veil away and let it fall to the floor. She began to dance, her hands caressing her sides, suggesting that she might pluck the scarves away also. Her hips wove to and fro, her torso slid up and down. Her flexibility was amazing; she had no spine. More than one man rubbed his hands against his thighs as she shimmied and arched. When her dance came to its end, she stood stock still. Then she turned to boldly stare at one man in particular—Angél Ferrara. As she ran from the stage, the men groaned and shouted for an encore. The women clapped appreciatively.

Donaldo spoke again. "Our speaker does more than speak! Right now, I'm practically speechless! Thank you, Rana! Some one, hand me a drink! We poor men need to gather our wits." The audience laughed. He waved his hands. "All right, let's be fair. Give the women something to ogle. Angél, come here. Show us what you can do."

A few of the younger girls squealed. Shaking his head to protest it, Angél Ferrara stepped onto the stage.

Acting like he's humble, Joachín thought. Angél spoke a few words to the musicians, struck a pose. Bored, Joachín glanced to the side of the floor. Miriam stood there, as beautiful as a star plucked from the sky. She must have come forward while the last girl danced.

She watched Ferrara with cautious interest. As if sensing her regard, Ferrara glanced her way and smiled. Joachín felt the sherry curdle in his gut.

The guitars started up. Ferrara surveyed the audience as if reviewing troops. He poised one hand on his hip as if resting it on a sword. Joachín snorted. A few people frowned at him before returning their attention to Ferrara. Without warning, Angél broke into a flurry of footwork followed by a moment of stillness. Then he dropped into a lunge meant to astonish because of its breadth. People gasped.

Joachín swore under his breath. This wasn't dancing, this was posturing. The fool had no sense of how to put it together, how to speak from the heart. He wanted to spit. What did the son of a rich Diaphani family know about being destitute, about fighting for food with rats? Had he ever been spat upon? Kicked for being in the way?

Dancing wasn't about looking impressive. It was about opening one's veins, about pouring out one's soul.

Outperforming him wouldn't be difficult. As Angél finished to enthusiastic applause, Joachín headed for the stage. "Do you know a *Guiridilla?*" he asked Donaldo tersely. "Something that speaks of overwhelming loss? The death of a great love?" He thought of Miriam. "Or the yearning for one?"

Donaldo lifted his hands. "Don't all *Guiridillas* deal with those themes?"

"If you'd sing one, I'd be grateful."

Donaldo eyed him appraisingly. "If you dance like your mother did, the gratitude will be ours." He turned to the audience. "Joachín has asked if he can dance for us. Let's give him a warm welcome."

There was a smattering of applause. Luci clapped enthusiastically. From the side of the stage, Miriam watched him. Her face was a mix of emotions. He would have given anything to know what they were. *This is for you*, he told her, holding her gaze. She blushed and looked at her feet.

Forget her and focus, he thought, not wanting to be distracted. *I must pour the past into the dance, show them where I've been, what I've endured. Let the magic take me.*

He bowed his head as if in prayer.

Prodigal daughter, abandoned son. I have returned.

In an explosion of footwork, his feet pounded his passion, his heels hammering the counterpoint. Three resounding stamps, as if to emphasize his determination, his hands slapping his chest in rapid succession as if to say, *I–am–Joachín!* Then a single clap to cue Donaldo to begin.

Donaldo sang the traditional opening—a long and drawn out cry of pain, the lot of the Diaphani. "Ayeeee, ayeeee, ayeeee!" Between each wail, the guitars strummed.

Joachín started slowly, as if to explain what his life had been. His movements were controlled, his arms strong with pride. Then he stiffened, as if burdened by the weight of sudden grief. He remembered his mother and her sad demise, her broken spirit after his father died. In every sweeping movement, in every abrupt pause, he expressed his pain. Tears came, unbidden. He shook them away, defiant of his sorrow.

Lys forgive me,
if I should forget,
my maré's
gentle smile.

Her pain...
was my pain,
yet hurt...
would she be,
to see...
what I have...
...become.

The lyrics were a gift; Donaldo knew his heart, exactly. Joachin's footwork built, sharp and determined. Soon, the floorboards began to lift beneath the battering of his boots. With a plunge, he struck the wood as if driving a sword into a priest, and then he spun away from that moment, feverish, crazed. Part of him realized that his feet had never moved so fast. His eyes burned. Droplets of sweat flew from his brow. In a final outburst of grief, he clenched his fists and slammed his body to a halt, holding his head high. He panted heavily, his stance saying he was done but undefeated, a survivor who did not submit.

There was a stunned silence and then a roar. En masse, the Tribe swarmed him. The women cried their passion. The men shouted their support. He stumbled beneath the pounding of his shoulders, endured wet kisses on his cheeks. The bitterness in his heart receded. He was one of them—no, their adoration told him he was more. He was their hero, the quintessential essence of who they were: the Diaphani, the Proud, the Undefeated, the Strong.

"Gods above, I've never seen anything like that!" Hector yelled.

"He's Estrella's son! And *my* nephew!" Luci said. All about her, heads nodded.

In the midst of the crowd, Joachin turned to acknowledge Donaldo and the guitarists. "Thank you," he said over the crowd's enthusiasm. "I have never danced like that before."

"And you may never again, my friend!" Donaldo called back, smiling. "That was a special moment. A gift from the gods. Not to be repeated."

"People will talk of it for ages," Jaime said, coming up to him with his guitar in hand. "It was a pleasure to play for you, Joachín. The thanks are ours."

"Cousin!" Iago wrapped an arm about his shoulder. "You must show me how you do that step." He tried to mimic the lunge and failed.

Joachín laughed. "Of course!" He glanced about for Miriam. He wanted to see her face, to read how his performance had affected her. People crowded in and out. She was nowhere to be seen. His smile faded, the sweetness of his victory, lost.

Chapter Twenty-Nine: Enamorados

THE DANCING HAD been exciting, but Miriam was exhausted. Joachin burned across the stage like a fire unchecked. He had been an element of nature, as pure as the night air, as fluid as water, as certain as stone. She had been caught up in it, but her own hidden flames disturbed her. As the crowd congratulated him, she retreated. She needed solitude, calm.

She passed a stand of pines and headed for the river. The moon shone brightly, its reflection glimmering upon the water. The night smelled of pine sap. She found the fragrance soothing.

You're reacting to their energy as well as their smell.

She jumped. She'd been so distracted by Joachin that she hadn't sensed Alonso's approach.

The what?

The pines. You're reacting to their life force. It emanates in their scent. You pick up a little when you're near them. That's why sitting beside them is so rejuvenating.

Is that why? She smiled. Had he been like this as a boy, excited to share his latest find?

I've been walking through them. They tickle, did you know? And I touched the mind of a squirrel. I've never been so dizzy, Miriam! Branches flying at my head, the ground gaping beneath my feet, and me, with my fear of heights!

Alonso, afraid of heights? She couldn't imagine it. He laughed, a clear buoyant sound. She had never heard him laugh before. It pleased her immensely. *If I didn't know better, I'd say you'd been drinking with the men,* she teased.

In a way, I have. Life is intoxicating, Miriam. I never noticed it before. Everything has a glow, the trees, the plants...and everything vibrates, even the rocks! If we could sense it like this when we're alive, we'd have so much more reverence for it.

Rocks vibrate?

They do. I haven't decided yet whether they're so slow that we don't notice them, or whether they vibrate at such a high frequency that we're unable to see it. And you....

Yes?

You shine with a soft green light.

I do? Do you shine, too?

Well, sort of. I'm grey. I think it's because I'm dead. The lack didn't seem to bother him. *I wonder if the moonlight augments it. If I look at members of the Tribe, they look like a rainbow. Every person has a different colour associated with them.*

I wish I could see it.

Close your eyes. I'll see if I can show you.

She did as he bid. A puff of warm air wrapped itself about her fingers. *If I hold your hands, that might make it easier.* She thought he stood in front of her, but as she concentrated, she felt him at her back. He'd come close and had wrapped her arms with his from behind. Her neck prickled.

Now, he said, *look at that pine in front of you.*

There was no pain, but there was a pressure. She opened her eyes and gasped. The tree was still a pine, branched and needled, but instead of being a black shadow against the bright night, it was outlined by a dim yellow glow. As she gazed about her, all of the trees and plants were.

Oh, Alonso! How beautiful! The trees weren't as bright as the moon, but he was right. Everything glowed.

That's what the spirits of trees look like.

She wanted to see him, to look into his face.

Allow me, he said.

To her amazement, he stepped through her so they might stand face to face. She felt a momentary buzz; his passing crackled through her like the air before a storm. And then he was before her. She caught her breath.

Alonso wasn't grey. He gleamed like pewter. His hair was spun silver. His eyes retained their original blue, although they were much paler than they had been in life. They reminded her of two precious aquamarines set into the face of a god.

Well? he asked softly. *What do you think?* Something burned in his eyes that she dared not name. For a moment, she was too overcome to speak.

He swallowed, as if he, too, felt the moment intensely. *Miriam,* he said, *I have to tell you something. I don't know what's possible for us. At the same time, I don't know what isn't possible. I know you've felt...that is to say, that we.... I've also felt–oh, for bloody sakes! Another love-sick swain! I find a moment alone with you, and they swarm like flies. Go away, why don't you?*

She stared at him and then followed the line of his sight. Someone walked toward them.

"Miriam?"

Alonso faded away. Her headache came back. She shivered. She knew that voice. Angél Ferrara's.

He hesitated a few feet from her as if afraid she might take flight like a nightingale. He looked even more imposing in the moonlight than he did during the day. He seemed made of inky shadows.

"I was worried." He held out his hand, entreating her for understanding. "I saw you leave the camp. I thought someone should accompany you, make sure you're safe."

Why on earth would she not be safe in a Diaphani camp? Who would accost her, unless the Torch Bearers found them? "I'm fine," she said, wishing he hadn't intruded. "I needed some time to myself."

"Oh. I see. Well, I won't bother you, then." Sounding affronted, he turned to go.

"No, don't leave." She regretted her words. He had rescued her—for that, she was grateful. "I didn't mean it the way it sounded."

"You're certain?"

"No, please." She sat and indicated the grass beside her.

He joined her without waiting for further assurances. They both fell silent and gazed over the water. The moment lengthened. Where had Alonso gone? She suspected he watched them. What *had* he been going to say before Angél interrupted?

"I know what you mean about needing to be alone." Angél glanced at her from over a shoulder. "One needs to get away to clear their mind. Especially in a Diaphani camp. We're never by ourselves. Family is always around, telling you what to do." He pulled at a blade of grass and tossed it to the sparkling surface. "It's good to find a place where the trees mind their own business."

She could no longer see the trees' glow. Disappointed, she met Angél's gaze. He held her glance overlong. She looked back over the water.

"What did you think of the dancing tonight? Did you like it?" he asked.

She thought of Joachín. "It was wonderful. I've never seen anything like it."

"Do you dance?"

She shook her head. "No. Mama died when I was very young. Papa never had the time for it. I thought Rana danced well tonight." Perhaps if she reminded him about Rana, he might leave her alone.

"She did." He tossed a pebble into the water. "Tell me, what's it like to be a seer?"

She frowned. "It's a little strange."

"Have you had the gift for long?"

"Not long."

"So, you see things in your head? You hear what people say?"

"I see some things." He seemed overeager. She shouldn't have invited him to sit.

"Forgive me, am I prying?"

To suggest he was would insult him. To say he wasn't only encouraged more questions. "No. It's just that I'm new to it. Yes, I can see things in a way most people can't. I described Rana to Anassa as she waited outside the *vardo* today. Sometimes, I hear...." She stopped. That line of discussion led to Alonso.

"Conversations?"

"No."

"What, then?"

She thought of Alonso's last words regarding love-sick swains. "Warnings."

He nodded. "Those would be helpful. So, you're a speaker as well as a seer."

"So Anassa says."

"Those are valuable talents to have." He shifted closer to her. "Allow me to apologize for my father. What he said, about you not being of the blood. He's an old man, set in his ways. He doesn't see the future as I do."

She was almost certain it had been Angél who had accused Joachin of being a half blood. She was no different. "I'm not sure I see it, either."

"You're a valuable asset, Miriam. As Anassa said, blood is about how we live and to whom we dedicate ourselves. Tribe is family. You should be a part of it."

"That's kind, Angél. But Papa and I are wanted...."

"By the Torch Bearers. That's nothing new. They barely tolerate us as it is."

"Which is why we have to leave."

"True. But consider this. Instead of going on your own, you could come to Tolede with my parents and me. We're settled. We don't travel. Mother thinks you're wonderful. You needn't worry about Father. He'll come around. You could pose as my cousin...or perhaps, my wife."

It was out of the question. "I couldn't."

"They don't know we're Diaphani in Tolede. We run a thriving business. We temper fine swords and other weaponry. Noble families, from as far away as Inglais, commission us."

"I...it's not a good idea, Angél."

"You don't need to make up your mind right away. But give it some thought. We're an important family in Tolede. I guarantee the Guard won't bother you."

He pointed at the dark sky. "Look! The Matriarch is rising, above the horizon."

Relief swept through her. She didn't want to talk about traveling, or worse, living with him in Tolede. One bright star shone above the lip of the Womb. "We call that star the Vela," she said.

He quirked an eyebrow. "The candle?"

She nodded.

"Now that you mention it, I've heard it called that, too. What about that group of stars?" He stood and offered her a hand to rise.

"The Swan." She took it for a second and released it. She didn't want to feel what he was feeling. There had been a flash of heat, but it faded.

"We call it that, also. And those?" He set a hand on the small of her back.

"The Twins. What do you call them?"

He stared down at her, his face intent. "The Lovers. For the two are never parted and always together. They say that if they ever separate, the world will come to an end."

Dismay flooded her. She muttered a protest as his mouth came down on hers. His lips were hot and tasted of wine. His desire wrapped itself about her like pig iron, molten, stinking, foul. She couldn't breathe. She shoved him away. As they broke apart, the fiery smelt running through her veins cooled.

"Don't *ever* do that, again!" she said.

He grinned at her. "You liked it."

She wiped her mouth.

He laughed. "Don't deny it. You did."

Mute with embarrassment, she turned to leave. He caught her by the arm. "Don't be angry with me, *querida*. I promise I'll never do that again without your permission. You're beautiful and in trouble. That's a potent mix for any man."

She yanked her arm from his grasp. He caught her by the sleeve. "Please, I apologize." He released her. "I couldn't stand it if we never spoke again. I meant what I said about you coming to Tolede. If you do, it will be on your terms."

"That isn't likely. I have to get back."

"Do you forgive me?"

His earlier brashness was gone. It was better to accept his apology than question it. The last thing she needed was for anyone in the Tribe to think ill of them. "I forgive you," she said grudgingly. The words tasted sour. She wanted to spit them from her mouth.

He straightened, smiled as if nothing untoward had passed between them. "Then allow me accompany you back to your *vardo*, *Serina*. You never know what rogues lurk in these bushes."

His grin told her he thought himself one. She refused to meet his smile, knowing it would encourage him further.

As the music started up again, Joachín pulled away from his well wishers. A coldness had crept into his gut. Miriam was nowhere to be seen. It was possible that she had retired to her *vardo*, but Ferrara was also missing. His motives were clear. He wanted a gifted wife. He would seduce Miriam if he could.

Joachín strode for the river, thinking she might have gone there to find some peace. He headed for the olive where he had encountered her earlier. Fidel nickered at him as he drew close. He patted the horse and scanned the banks. Nearby, a couple stood in a tight embrace. His heart jolted and then steadied as both faces turned to stare at him. Not Miriam with Ferrara, thank the gods. The girl looked flustered, the man, annoyed.

"Sorry." Joachín left them to walk upstream. The water rushed by. The night breeze cooled his face. A stand of pine loomed in the darkness. As he approached the trees, he heard, "Don't *ever* do that, again."

Miriam. Angry.

"You liked it. Don't deny it."

Joachín slipped his knife from its sheath.

"Don't be angry. I promise I'll never do that again without your permission."

Blood pounded in his ears. He gripped the blade. If Ferrara had done anything to her, he would pay with his life.

"I have to get back." She sounded strained, annoyed. *Good.*

"Do you forgive me?"

A pause. "I forgive you."

"Then allow me to accompany you to your *vardo, Serina.*"

Ferrara said something more, but Joachín didn't hear what it was. She hadn't allowed him to take advantage—that was all that mattered. As they appeared, Joachín withdrew into the trees so they wouldn't see him. To his surprise, someone scrambled away from him like a startled cat—Rana Isadore. Her eyes were rimmed with tears. There was only one explanation for it. She'd seen Ferrara and Miriam together.

Joachín followed Miriam and Angél at a discrete distance. Angél escorted her to the *vardo* where her father stayed. Miriam stepped inside and the door closed. Angél sauntered off, whistling.

Too angry to speak, Joachín slid away like a lynx in the night.

Chapter Thirty: The Lodestone

THE DANCING WAS all right for the young people, Anassa thought, but as matriarch, her responsibility was to watch for the Tribe, not enjoy herself. Even though the folk of Elysir claimed that the Womb was a haunt for demons, it might occur to the Grand Inquisitor to return to where he'd last found traces of Miriam.

Anassa settled her quilts about her, closed her eyes, and let her vision float into the sky like an owl on the hunt. Beneath her, the Tribe's fires burned brightly. Beyond the Womb, nothing moved on the dark road to Elysir. She turned her attention to the Solarium and passed through its thick walls. In the temple, Luster monks fed the eternal flame. Others scurried along corridors, bent on various tasks despite the hour. Unsure of which way to go, she mouthed a prayer to Lys for guidance and followed a burly monk down a marble hall. He carried a tray holding a small flask of wine and cutlery. He knocked at a gilded door.

"Come," someone said.

The monk entered. In the room, the Grand Inquisitor sat at an ornately carved desk. A large book lay open before him. He didn't bother to glance up from his reading. The monk set the tray at his elbow and left. Tomás traced one of the markings with a forefinger. Anassa recognized the glyph. The 'Lodestone' compelled its target to come to the bearer. The flask contained ink, not wine. The cutlery consisted of knives.

He would have one purpose in cutting himself with such a tattoo, and she knew what it was. Blinking like a mole, she struggled to rise. Her legs resisted. With a squawk, she fell onto her bed in an untidy heap.

◗◖L◗◖

To Miriam's surprise, Ephraim was awake and chatting with Eva. His bandages were fresh, his colour, better. Miriam commented on it.

"Eva's taking good care of me." He smiled at the Diaphani woman who sat across from him. "She's an excellent healer. I doubt if I'm as good a patient." He shifted his weight and winced.

"Oh, you're no bother at all." Eva squeezed his hand. Her fingers lingered a moment before she withdrew them. Ephraim blushed and looked away.

Miriam eyed the two of them. Were they developing feelings for one another? Patients fell in love with their physicians all the time. Ephraim had usually been on the receiving end of those associations. A number of widows had found him appealing in Granad. He and Eva seemed as snug as two caterpillars in a cocoon.

"You're eating well?" she asked, breaking the awkwardness.

"I spooned some soup into him," Eva said.

"Awful stuff. She adds too much garlic."

"Don't complain, Ephraim. It's good for you."

He pursed his lips in amusement. "It *is* good for me, but it makes me a terrible wagon mate." He glanced at Miriam and patted his belly. "Gas, you know. The *vardo* reeks to high heaven."

"Oh, Papa! It doesn't!"

"All right, it doesn't. I was worried it might, but Eva airs it."

Eva smirked. "Better to stink from garlic than wound rot."

Miriam smiled at her. She liked this woman. "I think you've been out-doctored, Papa."

"Maybe I have." He winked at Eva and glanced back at Miriam. "What have you been up to?"

"I went to the *divano* earlier."

"Ah, yes. And how did that go?"

"Anassa wants us to stay. She knows we're a threat to the Tribe, but she's convinced we're a bigger boon than a risk."

That sobered him.

"The Torch Bearers have no love for us," Eva said. "Ephraim tells me you're a *sentidora* as well as a healer. If that is so, Anassa won't want to lose you."

"Not everyone shares your opinion, Eva."

"Then they're fools. I know of what they complain. They say you're not of the blood. We are too inbred, as it is."

"Actually, Miriam *is* a half-blood," Ephraim said. "My wife was Diaphani."

Eva's eyes widened. "From which clan?"

"The Manzanos. She was Inara Manzano."

"I remember them. So sad! They died in Salerno."

"Yes, all but Inara. I sheltered her. She became my wife."

"You never married, again?"

"No. It was too important to take care of Miriam."

"Every girl needs a mother."

"True, but there wasn't anyone suitable."

She wished they wouldn't discuss her as if she weren't there. Ephraim had liked some of the widows who had pursued him, but he had broken off the relationships. Why? Had she made it difficult for him to remarry? She shifted uncomfortably. She hadn't liked any of them, so she had been the perfect brat. She hadn't wanted to share him with anyone.

Eva held up three fingers. "I see three reasons for you to stay. One, you're both healers, and we are in short supply. Two, Miriam is a seer. Three, Miriam is the last remaining Manzano. Lineage passes through the mother's line. Miriam is the Manzano matriarch."

Miriam stared at her. Ephraim looked at a loss for words.

Eva turned to Miriam. "Anassa didn't tell you this?"

Miriam shook her head. "I didn't know Mama's last name!"

The healer pursed her lips. "Three is the number of foundation. The goddess means for you to be here."

"Eva, I don't think...."

"It isn't about thinking, Miriam. It's about recognizing patterns, about seeing synchronicities."

She didn't need another Anassa-like lecture. Ephraim rubbed his neck. "Perhaps we should speak of this later," Miriam said.

Eva misunderstood. "You're right. Your father looks tired. Ephraim, you should rest."

Ephraim looked bemused. Miriam stood. She had been wrong to keep him from others as she'd grown up. She had been selfish, but children often were. She kissed him on the cheek. Ephraim's and Eva's interest in each other put things in a different light, but it was best if she and Ephraim didn't stay long with the Tribe. "I'll check on you in the morning," she said. She thanked Eva for her care and left them.

Candlelight flickered from Anassa's caravan. She was glad the old woman was awake. A lone guitarist strummed by the fire. Couples swayed in close embrace. Miriam climbed the *vardo's* steps and opened the door.

"Thank Lys!" Anassa sat on the floor in a rumpled heap. Had she fallen? "Come in, child. There isn't a moment to waste." She struggled to stand. "I must cut you."

"Cut me?" Miriam froze.

"The Grand Inquisitor is reading your grimoire. He's about to use a particular tattoo against you. I must ward you with another."

Her stomach tightened. She hadn't liked cutting herself. "What will he do?"

"Nothing if we prevent it in time. If we don't, the effect will be harder to control, but don't worry. I have the advantage. He's new to this. I'm not. Bare your torso."

Alonso?

Better do as she says. I looked in on him and couldn't make sea or sky out of what he was reading.

She rubbed her arms. Anassa lurched past her, reached into a cupboard and pulled out a vial of ink and a knife. She handed her a flagon of brandy that sat on the table. "Drink this," she said. "It will dull the pain."

Miriam drank. The liquor burned her throat. Anassa pressed her to the bed and tugged at her waistband. Miriam pushed her hands aside. "If you show me how to make the mark, I can cut myself," she said. The idea of anyone, even Anassa, slicing her stomach, made her ill.

"There's no time for that." Anassa stopped her from baring herself past her hips. "That's far enough. I'll put this second tattoo beneath the first one."

Cuts on her lower belly conjured even worse images than a carving higher up. "With this, no one can coerce you," Anassa said.

"Coerce me to do what?" She gripped the quilts and tried not to think of the knife. "Why would my mother have such a tattoo in her grimoire?" Had she read about it and forgotten? It was so long ago.

"She may have known it, but never used it." Anassa splashed brandy over her belly. "Take another drink." She handed her the flask.

Miriam's cheeks flamed. The brandy burned, but it also eased her fear. She trusted Anassa. The cut would be clean. It wouldn't hurt as much as when she had done it herself. She closed her eyes, felt dizzy.

She expected to feel the edge of the knife, but instead, she felt Anassa's hand on her navel. She opened her eyes and wished she hadn't. The old woman was poised over her with the blade. The point came down. The room spun. Anassa's hand didn't move, but wet flowed beneath her fingers. *My blood*, Miriam thought. Curiously, her fear dissipated; Anassa's palm seemed to widen and grow warmer. The room floated away into darkness. She became aware of a presence, then a weight. Someone lay on top of her. A man. Naked. Tor Tomás leered at her, but before she could flinch, his image faded and Joachín was there, closer than life.

"*Cielo*," he whispered, calling her 'heaven'. He pushed a strand of hair from her face with such tenderness that she felt herself melt. Belly to belly, his skin slipped against hers. They were both bare. His closeness dizzied her. She caught her breath. "You are mine. I am yours. Don't be afraid," he said.

He kissed her and she returned his kiss hungrily. He pressed his body against hers. The tautness of his muscles against her breasts set her on fire, turning her limp and then fierce with need. There was an ache in her belly, a heat in her loins. She clasped him, curled a knee about his hips. He was hard and firm and hot. She wanted to possess him, to claim him entirely and be claimed. From a long way off, someone cursed, breaking the spell. Someone else shouted in alarm.

The world tilted and dipped. Joachín vanished. She bit her cheek and tasted blood. The light of the *vardo* blinded her, harsh and immediate. Coming to, she scrabbled at the sides of the bed. Something wet dribbled down her belly. She tried to stand. Boney hands pushed against her chest.

"Miriam! Lie down!"

She fought. A slap brought her to—Anassa struck her hard across the cheek. She gasped, blinked in shock. Between clouds of grey, Anassa faded in and out of her vision.

"Forgive me," the old woman muttered, her face ashen, "but I thought you were about to charge the door. Lie still, Miriam. I have to staunch the blood."

"What happened?" she asked, feeling faint.

"He nearly had you, but I finished the tattoo. He won't be able to affect you that way again."

Her tongue felt thick.

"Did you see the Grand Inquisitor?"

"For a second." She thought of Joachín and swallowed. "He turned into someone else." She pushed her gorge down, knowing she might injure herself if she vomited.

Anassa dabbed at her belly with a cloth. "What you saw wasn't real. A spell like that takes whatever desire you have and twists it to the caster's purposes. The Grand Inquisitor made you think you were with a man you want. Whoever you saw won't know you dreamt of him. That's not the way a tattoo like that works."

Maybe it wasn't, but the sense of being with Joachín upset her. She hadn't realized the depth of her attraction for him. She had wanted them to...mortification swamped her in a hot tide. Tomás had sparked that lust. She had never desired a man like that before. Her body felt bereft.

"You should sleep." Anassa rubbed salve onto her stomach. "I'll wake you in a few hours and apply more of this. Don't worry. The Grand Inquisitor can't force you now. Not even in your dreams."

"Does he know where I am?" She felt drained, limp.

"I don't think so. That spell was designed to compel you to go to him, not the other way around. He won't get a fix on you unless he finds something else in your mother's grimoire." Anassa noted her dismay. "Don't worry. He won't get past me. I'm watching him."

Miriam closed her eyes and tried to ignore the burning of her belly. Why Joachin? Why any man? Joachin was a complication she didn't need.

But you do need him.

She came fully awake. The voice was a woman's. Anassa sat meditating with her eyes closed.

I'm hearing voices, now, she thought. Perhaps it was an after-effect of the tattoo or the brandy. *Who are you?* she demanded.

The voice didn't reply.

Alonso?

He also failed to respond. *Strange,* she thought. *Why doesn't he answer?*

She reached for him. Their link was intact, but he was a long way off. She frowned. She could use the comfort of his presence right now. She didn't feel safe without him, although considering what she had gone through, perhaps it was better he was away.

An awful thought occurred to her. *Gods, had he witnessed...?*

She sincerely hoped not.

Chapter Thirty-One: Vertigo

JOACHÍN JERKED FIDEL to a halt. Jagged rocks threw stark shadows across the road leading to the Neck. Behind him, campfires flickered on the Womb's plain like embers in a hearth. Fidel stamped and snorted. He patted the beast's neck to soothe him. They were both pent up.

He let the horse find its way to the river where it dipped its muzzle into the water. As it drank, the water broke into moonlit shards. Seeing Miriam with Ferrara had stabbed him as surely as if Angél had knifed him in the gut. It was fortunate for Ferrara that Miriam had rebuffed him. *Not that I wouldn't like to murder him on principle,* Joachín thought.

He splashed his face. He had wasted too much time here. Reuniting with Luci and Guillermo had been wonderful, but it had caused him to delay. His mother's death debt was due.

Family. Community. Relationships. They were complicated things.

He mounted Fidel and rode for the Neck. If he did things right, neither Miriam nor the Tribe would know of his absence. He would infiltrate the Solarium in Elysir. He'd be silent and quick. Without the Grand Inquisitor to oppress them, the Tribe would be safe. He'd return to the camp a hero and woo Miriam properly. Ferrara didn't stand a chance.

As they climbed the narrow trail, Fidel became edgy. The River Gemilla crashed along its course far below them. The horse didn't like the noise or the dark.

"Almost there." He patted Fidel's shoulder. "Soon, we'll be out of it." The black mouth of the Neck loomed ahead. A short trek through the chasm, and they would be on the road to Elysir.

As they entered the rift, the rock walls closed in on either side, leaving a narrow gap where he could see the stars. Soon, even those were lost to the ceiling of stone. His ears rang; the river roared. Fidel leaned close to the wall on their left. Riding blind, Joachin marveled again at how the *vardos* struggled up and down the incline. It was hard enough for a lone rider at night.

I'll be glad to be out of here, he thought. He felt unaccountably hot which made no sense; the night was cool. He didn't like enclosed spaces but attributed his anxiety to a thief's dread. He took a deep breath and swayed. *Gods*, he thought. *What is wrong with me? Am I sick?*

Grey swaths passed before his eyes. Sudden vertigo assailed him. He grabbed for the pommel and missed. As he slid from the saddle, a small part of his mind registered that he was falling, but his fear of the cliff's edge faded as he hit soft ground. To his surprise, Miriam lay beneath him, nubile and willing. Stunned to find her there, he did what his body demanded and kissed her passionately. She wrapped her arms and legs about him. Desire rose in him in a blaze, ready to combust out of control. He wanted to devour her, to sink himself into her until they merged as one.

And then, as if she had been wrenched from his grasp, she was gone.

He curled in on himself and groaned. The river's din rattled in his head. His tongue felt thick. He tasted blood. His cheek prickled, pitted with small stones. Fidel nuzzled his ear.

A waking dream? He'd never had one of those before. He wasn't sure they were possible. A wave of nausea washed over him. He fumbled for Fidel's reins and stood unsteadily, like a newly birthed foal.

Perhaps his plans for murdering the Grand Inquisitor were best put off for the night, he considered. There was no point in killing someone, if one wasn't in his best form. He climbed shakily into the saddle. Ever insightful, Fidel carried him back the way they had come. Joachín was relieved to see the lights of the camp appear as they emerged from beneath the thick walls of the Neck.

The horse picked its way carefully down the decline. Joachín drew in great lungfuls of air. What kind of magic turned a man wild with desire, then barred him from heaven when he was at the gates? Who would be so heartless as to do that? He didn't know much about love spells, but any fool knew they were designed to consummate not aggravate.

When he was a short distance away from the camp, he dismounted and walked off the rest of his frustration. Ahead, the river bowed into a wide arc and turned shallow. He considered jumping into the water for a swim. It would cool him off. He left Fidel on the shore and pulled at his shirt. As he stepped out of his boots, he heard a rustling. It came from a nearby ring of bushes. Fidel snorted and stepped back.

Within the circle of shrubs, a couple lay on the ground, rocking in a tight embrace. The girl's legs were about the man's buttocks. He had pushed his pants to his knees. He grunted and thrust into her repeatedly, like a stag in rut. Joachín couldn't see who the girl was, but from the back, he recognized Angél Ferrara.

His heart stopped. Miriam had returned to the healer's *vardo* to look in on her father. He had seen her go there. This wasn't she.

Ferrara arched his back and groaned. The girl bit down on a cry.

As quietly as he could manage, Joachín stepped back into his boots, pulled his shirt over his head.

"You'll talk to him, won't you?" the girl asked.

Joachín paused. It wasn't his business, but his instincts prompted him to listen.

"If you like," Ferrara said.

"So, we're engaged?"

"I suppose."

"I love you, Angél."

"Get up."

"Do you love me?"

Ferrara laughed, adjusted his pants. "How could I not with those tattoos on your breasts?"

Joachín led Fidel away. He didn't wait to learn if Angél Ferrara or Rana Isadore heard him.

Chapter Thirty-Two: Viper

MIRIAM OPENED HER eyes. Judging from the pale light seeping in through the curtains, dawn was breaking. Anassa snored in the bunk beside her. She turned her attention from the old woman and felt for Alonso.

Here, he replied.

He sounded strained. She was glad he was back. Her stomach ached where Anassa had cut the new tattoo.

You should put more salve on that.

She reached for the tin pot that lay beside her on the night table. Without looking at her belly, she smeared a thick layer of ointment over her cuts. She winced. *How does it look?* she asked.

Angry in places.

She glanced down. The new tattoo consisted of two quarter moons, one prone, the other supine, intersected by a wavy cross. The arms of the cross were actually two snakes passing each other, as they might in a melon patch.

I'm glad that didn't push me out.

She wiped the remainder of the salve from her fingers. *Why should it? It's meant to ward against interference. You don't coerce me.*

No, but it repels. I'm very aware of it.

Other than a dull sting, she didn't sense any repulsion emanating from the tattoo. Why would he be so conscious of it?

He shied away from the question. She caught a flash of his face as he turned from her. He looked helpless and upset.

What is it, Alonso?

He was silent for a moment. When he turned to face her, he was as flushed as the rosy dawn. Other than last night, she had never seen him so clearly. Did he take on the quality of light around him? He drew in a deep breath as if to steady himself.

What's wrong? Have I done something? she pressed.

He shook his head, looked down at his balled fists. He kept tensing and releasing them. *Nothing. You've done nothing.*

She wanted to touch him, reassure him. *Alonso, please tell me.*

Forgive me. He gaze was distant, as if he beheld a place she didn't see. *I was about to tell you last night, but I had no idea how much.... You've ignited things I haven't felt for a very long time.*

She stared at him.

I'm sorry. He stood as still as a reflecting pool mirroring the sunrise. *I'm a fool.*

Why was he so upset? His eyes were a troubled blue, hinting of deeper waters. They drew her in—she felt a yearning so intense that it stunned her. Alonso wanted.... Sweet gods, he couldn't want that, but he did. Impossible! She surfaced, felt overwhelmed by the pull of his desire. It wasn't simple lust that held him. It was passion, love. How could he feel such things when he was only a ghost? Last night, he must have felt them when Tomás nearly snared her. Or worse, when she thought she'd been with Joachín.

He winced as if reacting to the thought. *Forgive me.*

You felt me...respond? She wanted to die of embarrassment. Of course he had. He had no choice but to feel what she did. Tomás's meddling and Anassa's tattoo had turned him into a voyeur.

It's not that. It's just...you. He came close, as if he could no longer contain himself. His expression was earnest, his eyes as blue and as encompassing as the sky. *Last night, I felt you, needed you, wanted you. I can't deny it. You're life to me, Miriam. You're my breath, the beat of my heart. How can I not love you? I'm a priest. You're my temple. I worship you in a way I've never done before.*

Dismay suffused her, as well as a strange quickening in her chest that she didn't want to acknowledge. Tentatively, he reached out to her, a lover plucking up his courage. She felt the warmth of his hands merge with her own. His fingers were as soft as rose petals. They slid up her arms. He closed in to kiss her. As his face filled her vision, she stiffened, gently forcing him away.

I am so sorry, Alonso, she said. She meant every word of it. She felt him deflate. He felt no more substantial than a summer breeze. *I don't mean to hurt you.*

The moment was lost. The sun had gone behind a cloud. He seemed to coalesce into himself. He dropped his hands and turned away. *I know you don't. I also know that you don't love me the way I love you. I had hoped...I thought...forgive me. I can't seem to help myself.* He faded from view.

She wanted to weep. There were no barriers between them; they were too vulnerable, too exposed to one another. He hadn't asked for this. Neither had she, but their differences were insurmountable. How did one make love to a ghost? It hurt to feel him suffer. She hated being responsible for it. More than anything, she wanted to take his hurt away. *I've never had a friend like you, Alonso,* she told him. *You are the best and closest friend I have ever had.*

He hadn't disappeared. He was still there, but not as present as he was. Her words didn't comfort him.

You think I give you my second best? She was afraid he might go. She couldn't bear the idea of life without him. *I think friendship is better than love, Alonso. It's nobler, more pure. It isn't marred by anger, or jealousy, or possessiveness. We offer the best of who we are to our friends. We accept them completely, flaws and all. Please, don't be unhappy. I can't stand it if you are.*

He brightened a little. She caught a flash of his face. The hurt had diminished, he was less aggrieved. She hadn't given him what he wanted, but she had convinced him that he was important to her, that he meant a great deal. *At least I don't have to hide it, anymore*, he said.

Anassa stirred in her sleep.

We can't stay here, Miriam said. *Anassa will know something is amiss, and I don't want to explain it to her. This is our business, not hers.* She also knew that the moment the old woman awoke, her instruction in the ways of the Diaphani would continue. She rose hastily and pulled on her blouse and skirt. She stepped into her boots and slipped from the *vardo* as the sun spilled into the valley.

Are you going to be all right, Alonso? She tripped down the steps, worried as to how he was taking her rejection.

I'll be fine. As long as we're together.

She nodded, wanting that as much as he did. She felt him bask in the sentiment like a flower opening to the sun.

A few early risers were up and sitting by their cook fires. As Miriam walked by, one woman approached and offered her a steaming bowl of porridge. "For you, *Serina*," she said. Miriam wasn't hungry, but not wanting to offend, she accepted the bowl and thanked her hostess.

"I am Luci," Luci said. She pointed to a brawny man who juggled a crate at the side of their *vardo*. "That's my husband, Guillermo."

Miriam smiled at him. Beneath his large, thick mustache, Guillermo bore an expression that suggested the morning had come too early. He nodded at her and then turned his attention back to the empty cage in his hands. "Which of the birds do I give to the matriarch?" he asked gruffly.

"It doesn't matter." Luci looked exasperated. "Any three will do."

"It does matter," he countered, "if we travel as far as the Port of Bispo."

"Choose the best flyers, then."

"And which ones are those? Some of these are five years old, Luci. They could die on the way."

"Oh, for Lys's sake." Luci glanced at Miriam and shook her head, one woman complaining about a man to another. "He doesn't feed them, so he doesn't know which ones are the strongest. Those two." She pointed to a pair of mottled pigeons. "And that one." She indicated a smaller white.

Miriam stared at her in surprise. She and Ephraim had kept birds. They had sent them to Gaspar, and he had sent them back. "But you travel. How do they know where to go?"

Luci regarded her earnestly. "That is a great mystery. I have no idea how they find us, but they do."

"It has something to do with the matriarch's sight." Guillermo set the pigeons into their cage. "She imprints the birds, somehow. If she sees a threat, she releases one to warn us."

"Would you like me to take these?" Miriam asked. "I'll be returning shortly to Anassa. I could save you the walk."

Guillermo inclined his head. "That would be welcome."

The *vardo's* stairs creaked. Looking as if he hadn't slept well, Joachin appeared from around the corner of the caravan. His hair was disheveled. He had pulled on his pants, but his torso was bare. Miriam swallowed. He was well-muscled and lean, exactly as her dream had shown him. Her heart began to pound.

"Aunt, have you seen my shirt?" He stopped short when he saw Miriam.

"I washed it," Luci said. "It's hanging on the line. What on earth did you do to it, Joachin? It looks like you rolled in the mud."

"Something like that." He didn't take his eyes from Miriam.

"Of course, you know who this is." Luci indicated Miriam. "*Serina*, this is my nephew, Joachin."

"We've met." Joachin sounded as if he'd swallowed a fish.

"Oh, you have?" Luci glanced between the two of them. Miriam flushed. She reddened even more as Guillermo's bushy eyebrows rose in speculation.

Iago appeared from around the corner, looking like a younger, rumpled version of Joachin. "*Maré*, do we have any bread?" he asked. "Oh! It's you!" His mouth fell open.

"Don't be rude, Iago. Have either of you seen Casi this morning?" Luci asked. "I told her to start the fire, but she's disappeared."

"She probably went to find more of those stones she likes to play with," Joachin said.

"That girl." Luci sniffed. "I wish she wouldn't run off."

Miriam returned her bowl to Luci. "Thank you for the breakfast, Bandoliera. It was very good." Guillermo handed her the cage.

"I'll escort you back," Joachín said.

"Take your shirt!" Luci yanked it from the clothesline. He grabbed it and tied the laces as he caught up with Miriam.

"Did you come by to see me?" He sounded hopeful.

She kept her eyes on the camp ahead, afraid her face might give too much away. "No. I was just passing by." She glanced at him sidelong. "Why do you ask?"

"I thought...never mind."

The road held a fascination for them both. Joachín ran a hand through his hair. "I want to apologize for yesterday. I'm not usually so blunt. It was a strange thing for me to tell you...about my dreams."

She nodded. "Things have been strange, lately."

"I'm sure they have, with you being a seer. Here. Let me carry that." He took the bird cage from her. As their eyes met, a smile touched his lips. He had beautifully curved ones, a little full, but not too much. His nose was long and aquiline, strong like the Roma senators of old. His eyes were as rich as the earth itself. Fertile ground. She glanced away.

"Have you given any more thought as to whether you'll stay?" he asked.

"With the Tribe?" She shook her head. "No. I'm not convinced we should." She thought of Angél Ferrara's proposal to take her to Tolede.

"Well, I hope you do."

She met his eyes again, touched by his sincerity. "It might be better if we go, Joachín," she said frankly. "I hate putting so many at risk."

"That isn't your fault. Maybe it's better to deal with the threat than to run away from it."

She stiffened. What did he mean? That she should confront Tomás directly and save everyone the trouble?

"I don't mean that *you* should take care of it," he said. "I mean we should. The men of the Tribe."

She shook her head, held up her hand. "I don't like killing, Joachín, no matter what the justification. I think it's better if Papa and I leave."

"But where will you go?"

"I don't know. One of the families has offered to take us in. We might stay with them for a while."

His glance hardened. "Forgive me, Miriam, but there's one thing I *must* say. If you are speaking of the Ferraras, don't trust them. Angél Ferrara,"—he formed the name as if he wanted to spit it—"is a self-serving, arrogant bastard. He doesn't care about the Tribe. He doesn't care about anyone but himself. He wants a wife who will bring wealth to his family. With your gift, he'll use you to do that."

She frowned. Had Joachín seen her with Angél? She wasn't sure whether to laugh or be insulted. "You mean to say that Angél is only interested in my talent?"

"I don't mean it like that. Of course, he wants you because you're beautiful and smart. Any man would want that. But he also wants a wife with a gift. And the more potent the talent, the better."

"Let him marry Rana Isadore, then."

"She may want him, but I doubt if he wants her." He set the cage on the ground. "Listen to me, Miriam. Last night, I saw them together. Don't believe anything he tells you. He's a liar."

"That's a strong accusation, Joachín."

"I know a liar when I meet one."

"Oh? And how is that?"

"Call it a gift."

She shrugged. "I have no interest in Angél."

"Good." He picked up the bird cage.

An older couple approached them. The man had his arm about the woman's waist for support as she helped him walk. For a second, Miriam didn't recognize them, and then it dawned on her who they were. Ephraim and Eva.

"Papa!" She ran to him, pleased to see them. "You're walking!"

Ephraim waved. Then he winced and clutched at his side. Eva chided him. "Getting some air after breakfast," Ephraim said. "I keep forgetting not to move too fast."

"That gash over his right rib concerns me," Eva told her. "I thought it best to get him on his feet. I'm taking him to the hot pools. They'll help him."

"She's the doctor." Miriam marveled at how contented Ephraim looked.

A scream cut the morning air. From all around the camp, heads turned. At the Montoya's *vardo*, Luci shrieked and leaned over a small form in her arms. Iago ran toward them.

"Healer," he stammered, coming up to Eva. "My sister's been bitten by a viper. Please come!"

"Little Cat!" Joachin set the bird cage into the dirt and set off at a run behind Iago. Miriam followed at their heels.

Guillermo pulled Casi from his wife and placed his mouth over one of her forearms. He sucked, turned, and spat. Casi's arm was red and swollen. Two deep puncture marks scored her flesh at the elbow. Guillermo unsheathed his knife.

"That won't help!" Eva said as he was about to cut the girl. "Get her into a sitting position. We must stop the poison before it reaches her heart." She turned to Luci. "I need something to tie off the blood." Distraught, Luci handed her a dish towel. Eva dismissed it and accepted the Iago's handkerchief instead. She knotted it tightly about Casi's upper arm.

"Get that limb into hot water," Ephraim told Luci, "but not so hot as it will scald. The heat breaks down the poison." He turned to Eva. "Do you have any oldenlandia?"

"What is that?"

"A remedy for snake bite. Some call it tongueweed," Ephraim said.

As Luci submerged Casi's swollen arm into a tub of water, Casi began to shake. Miriam set a hand to the girl's clammy face. As she touched her forehead, the world turned red and black. She gasped from the intense heat, feeling as if she stood in the core of a volcano. Venom, like lava, crept along Casi's veins in a slow moving flood. Her capillaries curdled into clots. *Gods, Alonso!* Miriam said, finding it hard to breathe. Casi was dying by inches.

Alonso didn't answer her. She realized he was holding back the wall of poison, a dam soon to break.

She focused her attention on Casi's stuttering heart, the final place where the girl's battle for her life would occur. With some surprise, her sight offered a clear image. She saw Casi huddled in her core, a frightened wisp of an urchin clinging to a finger of stone.

Don't be afraid, Miriam told her. *I'm here to help. Take my hand.*

Casi ignored her, rocked in tandem with her heartbeat.

Casi! Miriam said firmly. *If you don't reach for me, I can't help you. I'm going to pass along some of my strength to you. If you want to live, you'll accept it.*

I can't! she wailed. *If I let go, I'll die!*

Then don't let go! It was best not to panic her further. If Casi wouldn't reach for her, she would have to go to the girl. That meant a complete surrender of her strength, and she wasn't sure Alonso could save her. It didn't matter. Healers sacrificed themselves every day. *I will come to you,* she said. *Get ready for me.*

She reached for her. As her own spirit merged with Casi's fading glow, she collapsed, shocked that such a thin waif should carry so much mass. Alonso's hold on her disintegrated like a wall under cannon fire. *Alonso!* she cried, afraid she had lost him.

He brushed her fingers, scrabbling for a hold. He had no more substantiality than melting sand.

The world swayed. The island within the lava slipped away. She had the sensation of falling, burning. The shock was painful, and then she was out of it. She landed, condensed, became aware of her own body. She was no longer in Casi. Instead, she lay in the dirt. The sun scorched her eyes as she cracked them open.

"Gods!" someone swore. A forest of legs stood about her. A pair of hands tried to lift her by the shoulders. She rolled to her side and vomited.

"Leave her a moment," Ephraim said.

She caught her breath and tried to sit. Joachin knelt at her side. He had wrapped an arm about her shoulders. Her heart fluttered as she regarded him. Her chin and bodice were wet. Her mouth tasted sour. *I must look a sight,* she thought, thinking that Luci's gruel decorated her blouse. *How awful.*

She wiped the spittle from her jaw. "How is Casi?" she whispered.

Not far from her, Luci rocked Casi in her arms. The girl no longer convulsed. Her colour was returning to normal. Her arm, which still floated in the tub of water, was less bloated. She had not yet returned to consciousness, but her chest rose and fell. She breathed. Luci's face

was wet with tears. Guillermo wrapped his arms about his wife and daughter.

"Are you all right!" Joachín examined her with concern. How could he bear to be near her? A line of worry creased his brow.

Eva knelt beside them. "You Medinas are a cause," she said. She laid cool fingers on Miriam's forehead. Her touch was soothing, like clear water. "Joachín, take her to my *vardo*. When I'm done here, I'll look her over."

"I don't need to be checked over." She struggled to stand. "I'm all right."

"You are not all right. You fainted. You have a fever."

Joachín helped her to her feet. They heard a gasp.

"Sweet Lys!" Luci stared down at Casi in her arms.

Casi was awake. She regarded Miriam as if she were a saint.

"Casi says the seer healed her," Luci whispered. "She says she spoke in her mind and stopped the venom."

"Anassa healed her?" Eva asked.

Luci shook her head. "No, not the matriarch." Her eyes shone with gratitude and awe. "She means the *Serina*. Our *new* seer."

"Is this true?" Eva turned to Miriam.

"Thank you, *Serina*. Thank you for saving me," Casi said.

"How did you do that?" Eva demanded. The crowd began to mutter. "No one does that. Not even our matriarch."

"She's a *sentidora*," Ephraim said.

"Even so. What she did went far beyond that scope."

"Then she must be a spiritual healer as well as a seer," a woman said.

"Lys be praised! What gifts she brings to us all," another added.

Miriam sagged against Joachín. "Take me to Anassa," she said, fearing she would faint again. She and Alonso might have saved Casi, but the aftereffects of the poison were about to make themselves apparent a second time.

"Of course." He slipped his arm about her waist. "It'll be faster if I carry you." He swept her into his arms as if she had no more weight than a broom. It surprised her; he was all wire and muscle. "She wants to see Anassa," he told the group. "Come or stay. Either way, the matriarch must be told."

Miriam wasn't sure if she preferred being carried. Her stomach revolted with every step. Half-way there, she lost the rest of her breakfast. "Don't worry about it," Joachín soothed. "You saved Little Cat. I owe you her life. Besides, it's an old shirt."

She hid her face in his shoulder, mortified. *Alonso? Are you there?* she asked.

Mostly.

How are you?

He sounded shaky. *Not so bad this time around.*

She sagged with guilt. How could she have forgotten? He had died by poisoning. Would that be his lot from now on? He would endure whatever she forced upon him?

It's all right. We survived. The child is safe.

A shadow fell across her as if something blocked the sun. Joachín tensed.

"What the hell have you done to her?" A one-man army barred their way. Angél.

"Get out of my way, Ferrara." Joachín's voice had an edge to it. "I'm taking her to the matriarch." He swept her aside. Her stomach roiled.

Angél grabbed him by the arm. "I asked you a question, Half Breed."

"Remove your hand or lose it."

She didn't doubt him for a second. Angél was a fool to underestimate him.

Ephraim appeared. "Everything is fine, Angél," he reassured him. "There's been an incident. Joachín is taking Miriam to the matriarch. Come with me. I'll explain."

Joachín and Angél eyed each other coldly, and then Angél released his hand. Miriam glanced up at Joachín. His eyes had turned jet, his face was tight. Behind him, Angél and her father fell into a hushed discussion. Their intimacy bothered her. When had Ephraim become familiar enough with Angél to call him by his first name? Joachín ignored them and trudged along.

As they came within sight of Anassa's *vardo*, Rana approached them. The closer the girl came, the more Miriam found her proximity unsettling. Rana was rough wool on wet skin. "*Puri* is waiting for you," she said, wrinkling her nose. She smiled at Angél behind them.

The door to Anassa's *vardo* swung open. The old woman stood framed in her doorway. "So!" she announced with relish, pointing a crooked forefinger at Miriam. "Our new seer has worked a miracle! None of you witnessed it, but I saw her go into the body of Casi Montoya. I watched as she destroyed the spirit of the snake. Which one of you questions the importance of Miriam Medina, now?"

She grinned as if she had just released the sun into the sky.

"Will she recover?" Angél Ferrara called.

"She will, but after such an incredible feat, she must rest. Bring her." She waved Joachin inside. Joachin climbed the steps and settled Miriam onto the bed. Anassa closed the door behind them. "Thank you, *El Lince*," she told him. "You can leave us, now."

There was creak on the steps and a tapping at the door. Anassa pursed her lips. "That's Ephraim Medina," she told Joachin. "Tell him he can visit his daughter in a few hours."

Joachin nodded and regarded Miriam. "I'll come back to see how you're doing." He reached down and clasped her hand. She blushed as the warmth of his ardor grew apparent. She wished he would stay so she might bask in it. Anassa cocked an eyebrow. "Tell me how Casi fares, when you come back," she said.

Joachin gave her fingers a squeeze and then released them. "She'll be fine, thanks to you."

As he left, Anassa eyed Miriam. "So, you and Joachin. Spinning around each other like butterflies in the spring."

"We aren't...."

"Oh, don't deny it. It's as clear to me as the tattoos on my arms. Still, he might be all right." She set a finger to her lips as if considering the potential. "I knew his mother, Estrella, of course. If he's as good a dreamer as she was, you two would make a fine pair. His father, I never thought much of. Let me guess. Joachin was the one you saw last night."

Miriam closed her eyes. She felt shaky, sick.

"We can talk about that, later. For the moment, we must restore your energies." Anassa retrieved ginger and cinnamon from a cupboard. "What were you thinking, Miriam? Throwing yourself at the venom like that? You took a big risk. The poison might have taken you, as well as Casi Montoya."

"I didn't know what else to do."

"Well, I suppose you must trust your instincts."

"What did you mean about destroying the 'spirit of the snake', Anassa?" The idea of fighting something intangible was upsetting.

"Oh, that? Nothing. There is no 'spirit of the snake'. I needed to reinforce to the Tribe how valuable you are."

That was disturbing. Even Anassa wasn't above grandstanding if it furthered her purposes. Deceptions had a way of being found out.

"Drink this." Anassa held a cup to her lips. The flavour burst upon her tongue. "Next time," she advised, "don't draw upon your energy. Ask the goddess for help. If it suits her, she'll channel her power through you. That way, you come out unscathed."

"How do I do that?"

"Just ask. It's no more difficult than that."

"But I don't believe in the goddess, Anassa."

"Even now?" Anassa sighed. "I see I have my work cut out for me. There's so much I have to teach you."

Miriam made up her mind. She had to tell her, make her accept for once and for all, that it was better for the Tribe if she and Ephraim left. Joachín had hinted that he might round up the men to storm the Solarium in Elysir. After what had happened with Angél, it was likely. Joachín was too rash. She suspected most of the Diaphani men were. "Papa and I can't stay."

Anassa stared at her.

"I know we'd be useful here, but there's still the problem of the Grand Inquisitor. What if Tomás learns I'm here? What good would I be if all I did was to bring destruction down on our heads?"

"We can set more wards, increase the watch. We'll hide you."

"Wards are fallible. So are people."

Anassa sighed. "We can't always prevent the evil men do, Miriam. We can only decide how we will contribute to the good. Have faith. The goddess will never allow us to be obliterated. She protects us, looks out for us. Even if we suffer, we always endure. Spring follows winter. Life follows death. Everything has its cycle, including the Diaphani. We need you."

"Anassa, I would never forgive myself if I...."

Anassa cut her off. "Miriam, I am dying. I feel it in the way my bones ache as I wake each morning and the way my legs bow a little more each season. I've six moons left to me, maybe a sun's cycle at most. I can't leave the Tribe bereft. I mustn't. That *would* be the end of us. Someone has to watch. I believe Lys means for that person to be you."

"How can you be so sure?"

"Look at how you came here. Lys has been manipulating events all along. She sent you running from Granad."

"The Grand Inquisitor sent me running."

"If not him, then she would have found another way. He was a convenient tool."

"Convenient?"

"I'm not saying he isn't dangerous. But don't you think the luck you've had in escaping him and coming here isn't a little...unusual? Rana foretold you. Joachín dreamt of you. He's another one I have my suspicions about. What are the chances of him running into the Montoyas like he did, after nine years of being without family and not knowing they existed? As for you two, you've known each other three days, and already you have a strong attraction."

Miriam coloured. "Those things are coincidences."

"There are no coincidences, Miriam. Only destiny."

Anassa took her hands in hers. Her body felt like worn burlap, a dried sack held together by little more than brittle, thinning bones. She felt parched, as if her blood were drying inside her veins. "If you can't believe in the goddess enough to answer her call," Anassa whispered, "then answer mine. Take pity on me, Miriam. Let me die knowing you'll care for my Tribe. Will you do it?" she asked fiercely. Her old eyes welled with tears. Her fingers shook.

Gods, Alonso. What do I say?

I think we say, 'yes'.

His confidence was as solid as the earth. With some surprise, she realized that he wanted this. It gave him a purpose.

It tempted her, too. But what if it was the wrong decision? If Tomás found her, the Diaphani would pay. But would it occur to him to look for her among them? They were insular, they kept to their own. And what better life could she have? In Granad, she'd been Ephraim's assistant and barely tolerated as it was. Here, she could care for these people, openly and without condemnation.

She wanted a community, had yearned to be an important member of one. Ephraim and she didn't need to travel to Roma to find it. Anassa would teach her, show her the ways of true power. She had cast seed upon rich ground.

"Yes," Miriam said, feeling as if the shambles of her life had finally reassembled themselves into something coherent, as if she had come home. Alonso's elation mirrored hers like a stream bubbling down a mountainside. A chip from the wall of time fell into place, pinning her to this new responsibility. It seemed as much of a promise to her, as she was to it. "Yes," she said, more sure. There was no turning back. She had given her word.

Fate shifted, altered its course. In a realm both impossibly distant and at the same time near, the embodiments of divine love and creation smiled.

Chapter Thirty-Three: Protegida

"*I KNEW IT* would come to this," Ephraim said, as he and Miriam spoke privately in Anassa's *vardo*, hours later. "Does Anassa know about the High Solar?"

"She does."

"And what does His Brilliance think of it?"

"He wants to serve. I suspect once you've been a High Solar, you're always a High Solar."

Alonso laughed. His happiness buoyed her.

"I think this gives him a reason for being. He's doing what he's always done. Tending his flock."

Ephraim regarded her with pride. "And now, you're a leader, too. Such ambition."

"Anassa says she has much to teach me."

"I'm sure she does. Come and see me if she tires you." He kissed her on the cheek.

She hugged him. "I'll see you at the *divano*, tonight, Papa. I'm glad you're willing to take this chance."

She watched from the door as he and Eva walked away, arm in arm. He had accepted her decision readily. Perhaps his innermost desire had been answered, as well. Eva would make a good wife. She rubbed her arms, thinking of the desolate years he must have spent—she had been too self-absorbed to notice, but now, his loneliness was gone. Surely, his quick recovery was because of Eva.

She stepped from the *vardo* that was to be her home. Her idea of stability had changed. Home wasn't so much a place, as it was a purpose. It was people to care for, and being with people who cared for her.

From the bottom of the trail, Anassa waved. They would bathe in the pool and have an afternoon nap. Anassa insisted they sleep so she might be fully refreshed for the *divano*.

"This is a functionary mantle," Anassa said hours later. She flicked a few specs of dust from it. "I only wear it for betrothals and baby dedications. Now, it's yours." The robe was a bright blue. The hem was embroidered with black and white moons. The work was ornate and beautiful.

"Are you sure?" Miriam asked. "The Tribe hasn't decided whether Papa and I should stay."

"The news of what you did for Casi Montoya is all over the camp," Anassa said. "Tonight, you'll be acknowledged as my protégé and Tribal Seer, as well as matriarch of the Manzanos."

"After my mother," Miriam said.

Anassa nodded. "Slip it on."

Many of the Tribe waved at them as they made their way to the *divano*. As Miriam escorted Anassa to the meeting, she felt awkward wearing her mentor's tunic.

You have every right to wear it. It's your robe of office, Alonso said. *By wearing it, you tell them that you serve them.*

It might've been better to wait until my position is official, she replied.

Nonsense. You know your worth. They'll see your display as an affirmation of it.

She nodded to Estaban Ferrara as she and Anassa passed their *vardo.* The bandolier inclined his head. Angél's mother, Leonora, dipped into a curtsey. Miriam found her deference foreign, something a commoner might do before a noble, but never one Diaphani to another. *How strange,* she thought. A day ago, Estaban Ferrara had called her a half-blood. He had accused her of bringing the Torch Bearers down upon them. Pray to Lys that never happened.

I know his type. Hidden claws within silken paws. He'd do well at the temple, Alonso said.

"For you, *Serina.*" Angél's mother offered her a bouquet of daisies. "I have one for you, too, Matriarch," she told Anassa.

The gift was a peace offering. Leonora was trying to make amends for their poor behavior from the night before.

"Please place those as an offering to Lys," Anassa told her. "It was kind of you, Leonora, but we're on our way to the meeting. We've nowhere to put them."

"Oh, of course." Leonora flushed.

Estaban Ferrara scowled at his wife. Miriam looked at her sympathetically. "That was thoughtful," she said, wanting to both irritate him and support his wife. "I'm surprised you found them so late in the season. Did you pick them?"

"Angél did."

"Oh. Is Angél coming to the *divano?*" It was a lame attempt at conversation, but she had to say something.

"Nothing, save death, will stop him from attending, *Serina,*" Estaban Ferrara said. "You may be sure of that."

Miriam gave him a wan smile. What an odd thing to say. The man bothered her, even when he was trying to be pleasant.

As she and Anassa headed for the Franco's caravan, many of the Tribe had already converged there. Luci and Casi were the centre of attention. Casi looked pale, but she stood stolidly as if determined to be treated like an adult. Guillermo and Joachin spoke quietly to one side.

How relaxed Joachin looks, tonight, Miriam thought. He had an aura of command about him. The effect was subtle. It was in the way he held himself, as if he took his status for granted. He had put on a clean, white shirt. His dark skin contrasted against it nicely. Desire unfurled in her belly like a cat flexing its claws. *Stop it,* she told herself. She looked away, hoping she wasn't transparent.

On the other side of the crowd, Rana Isadore, Anassa's granddaughter, held court amid a cluster of girls. Rana eyed her coldly. It was nothing Miriam wasn't used to. Many of the girls from Granad had done the same thing. Ephraim had maintained they were jealous, but that had done little to lessen her feelings of isolation. She scanned the crowd for her father. He stood near the back of it with Eva. Seeing her, he waved.

Ximen the Rememberer stepped onto the wooden boards of the dance floor. The blind man lifted his hands for quiet, and the crowd fell silent. Like Joachin, he seemed larger than his stature suggested, as if his body barely contained him.

"Last night," Ximen said, "we gave ourselves a day to decide whether or not we would accept Miriam Medina as our new seer. Under the circumstances, I doubt if there are any objections. Does anyone object?"

Rana looked as if she was tempted to say something, but at the last moment she changed her mind. No one uttered a word.

Ximen spread his hands. "Excellent! That's it, then." He smiled.

"And *that's* what I can't stand about Ximen," Hector Cortez said loudly. "The man never stops yakking. He goes on and on. I get thirsty listening to him. I need a drink." The crowd tittered.

Ximen grinned good-naturedly. "We still have to put the question to the *Serina,* of course. On behalf of the Tribe, do you accept us, Miriam Medina? Will you be our new seer?"

"Please say 'yes'," Hector said. "You can travel with me, girl. I have plenty of sherry. I'll do everything in my power to make you happy. I'll even marry you, if you like."

Anassa scoffed. "Such a proposal! She'll travel with me, as is proper, Hector."

"Pah! There is too much 'proper' in the world."

Many of the men agreed. Guillermo clapped Hector on the shoulder. The Rememberer lifted his hands for quiet. Everyone turned to Miriam.

"I am honoured that you would have me," she said. "Anassa suggested I wear this mantle. I hope I don't appear above myself."

The crowd protested. Anassa waved the comment aside. Miriam smiled. "I'll do all in my power to serve you. Both my father and me." From the corner of her eye, she caught Ephraim nodding. "I will watch for you. Under Anassa's tutelage, I'll learn best how to do that."

Ximen spoke. "This is an important occasion, one that occurs only once in a lifetime. As is *proper*,"—he gave Hector a measured glance—"each of us must come forward and offer our allegiance to our new seer. As she bestows her blessing upon us, she'll come to sense who we are."

Miriam glanced at Anassa for explanation.

"Don't worry," Anassa whispered. "Accept their homage as they present it. Repeat their names as they give them to you."

Ximen was the first to turn to Miriam. Behind him, the Tribe formed a line. He held out his hand. Miriam accepted it. Again, she felt that mass of ancestral memory he held.

"*Serina*, I am Ximen, Rememberer, as you know," he said. "What you don't know is that I am also at your beck and call. So it is, between Rememberers and Seers. If there is anything you need to know about the history of our people, or about anyone's past, ask me. Between the two of us, we'll learn the truth of any matter."

"Thank you, Ximen," Miriam said.

He's a good man. He'll make an excellent right hand.

He's a little alarming, Alonso.

That's why I like him. He knows too much.

The line of people passed her by, each member expressing his or her support. Mid-way, Rana appeared. Once again, Miriam's back itched.

Rana lifted her chin. "I am Rana and Speaker," she said loftily. Her tone was as icy as the winter wind. "I speak for the Tribe. The Ancestors speak through me."

"Rana," Miriam repeated. She held out her hand.

Rana narrowed her eyes and turned on her heel. Anassa sputtered in annoyance. Miriam kept her expression composed.

She doesn't like you.

She dismissed his concern. *It doesn't matter. We're equally useful to the Tribe.*

She thinks you've usurped her. You'll need to watch her.

Oh, Alonso. Caring for the Tribe will take enough of my time without having to worry about Rana. She may not even travel with us if she marries Angél.

Let's hope she does.

Joachín appeared before her. He smiled warmly, clasping her hands in his before she could prevent him. At his touch, her desire spun out of control. Her eyes drooped and her lips parted. She forced herself to breathe. Their mutual attraction entwined them like two coils of a spring. Lys forbid he should suspect the effect he had on her. Thankfully, he released her, after giving her palms a squeeze.

"*Serina* Miriam," he said, setting a hand to his heart. "Protocol dictates that I tell you I am Joachín de Rivera, but I'm also pleased to say that I'm the new Montoya Bandolier." He watched her expectantly.

Joachín, a clan leader? So, her instincts weren't wrong. He *had* accepted the title, which meant several things. He would stay with the Tribe, take his place as an important member of it. But had he accepted because of her? Was he staying because she was?

"That's wonderful, Joachín!" she said enthusiastically. And then she burned with embarrassment. How transparent. To anyone watching, she would look like a silly girl, not the matriarch they needed her to be.

He nodded happily. "Guillermo gave it up. He's reverted to Gonzales." He smiled again. His teeth flashed whitely, dazzling her. "I may be a clan of one, but I am well connected."

She felt light-headed. "So, you'll be traveling with the Gonzales' after the Tribe quits the Womb?"

"Actually, I thought I might travel with you and the matriarch. I hoped you'd find me useful."

She swallowed. "Indeed, I..., yes, we would. It would be of great benefit to have a dreamer with us."

His expression fell.

"It's rude to monopolize the *Serina's* time. Other important people must speak with her." Miriam glanced over Joachín's shoulder. Angél glowered behind them like his avenging namesake. Instead of his usual attire, he wore an ornate shirt embroidered with roses. The blouse was a work of art. Each flower had been sewn by an expert hand. Stiff with anger, Joachín stepped aside.

I've seen a few of the men wear them, Alonso said, *although none so dandified as this.*

She was inclined to agree. "Angél," she said, sobering.

He lifted her hand and kissed her palm. He may as well have groped her. With revulsion, she pulled her hand away and fought the urge to slap him. She was a matriarch now, Anassa's protégé. How dare he do that? She forced herself to calm. Angél pursed his lips as if he found her annoyance entertaining. Anassa glared at him, but he didn't appear to notice. "*Serina* Miriam," he said, "you bring much good to the Tribe. Your talent as a seer would honour any man." A few people chuckled behind him. He trapped her hand again. His need to possess her wrapped itself about her like a trap.

"I would speak with you, privately," he whispered, "after this homage is done."

"I don't think that's wise." She retrieved her hand. "We won't have time. Anassa tells me there is other business over which we must preside."

"You know the protocol, Angél." Anassa watched him with cool eyes.

He inclined his head. "Very well. We'll speak later." He leaned in to her ear. She drew away, fearful he might kiss it. "Until then, *mi vida.*"

He stepped aside. She felt soiled, wanted to wash herself. Zara, the widow, waddled forward. "You're the lucky one," she said, smirking.

Miriam frowned.

"Oh come now, don't play coy." Zara winked. "Angél is both handsome and rich. I see what's going on between you two. Just because you're a seer doesn't mean you're not human."

Miriam bit her tongue.

"Don't make assumptions, Zara," Anassa warned.

"Well, he won't be announcing *me*," Zara said. "My potions aren't strong enough."

Alonso, what is she talking about?

I have no idea, he replied.

"I'm at your service, Miriam," Zara said, "though with your looks and talent, you won't need it." She lumbered away like a barrel on legs.

One by one, Miriam greeted the rest of the Tribe. By the time she was through, she had calmed down enough to realize that Anassa was right. Each member did have a unique imprint, a distinct energy unto themselves.

They're your people, now, Alonso said.

Our people, Alonso.

Yes, he breathed. His contentment steadied her.

Ximen stepped to the centre of the planked floor. "We come now, to my favourite part of the pilgrimage," he said. People all about him smiled and nodded, as if they knew what was coming. "Every year, I am reminded of my darling Conchita and how beautiful she looked on the day we were betrothed. She's with me, still." He set a hand to his heart. The crowd murmured in sympathy. He smiled fondly. "So," he continued, clapping his hands, "two young men have advised me of their suits. All the parents are agreed. In the romance of the moment, does anyone else feel the need to declare their undying love?"

A number of the young girls giggled. Ximen glanced over the crowd. No one spoke. "No? Very well, then. Jaime Franco, come forth."

The young musician stepped from the crowd. He wore an elaborate blouse similar to Angél's, except instead of roses, his shirt was emblazoned with guitars and drums.

"You have something to say?" Ximen asked. All around him, men grinned while women whispered. To Miriam's surprise, Jaime loosened the ties of his shirt.

"I say," Jaime began, "that I have found the love of my life." The crowd cheered. Jaime began to walk toward a girl—Kezia Amaya, the young dancer he had serenaded the night before. Kezia lifted trembling fingers to her lips as if she were too overcome to speak. Beside her, Rana watched like a tolerant queen supporting her best maid.

"If she will have me," Jaime continued, "I will love Kezia, serve her and protect her for the rest of our lives. I will be her husband, and she will be my wife."

He slipped his shirt from his arms and stood bare-chested before the girl. Then he dropped to one knee and tied the blouse about her hips. Demurely, Kezia looked down.

Why doesn't she say anything? Miriam asked Alonso.

I suspect it's all been pre-arranged. The Amayas and Francos look happy enough. It was true. Both families seemed pleased.

"This blouse is a symbol of our betrothal," Jaime announced, rising. He took Kezia by the hand. "Tomorrow morning, we will hang it from our *vardo*, blooded, as a sign of our marriage."

A great shout of approval rose from the crowd. Miriam watched as Kezia flushed with embarrassment. As Jaime wrapped his arms about her, she hid her face in his shoulder.

Blooded? she asked Alonso.

Surely, you don't need me to explain.

Oh, she said, embarrassed by the lapse. Amid wishes of good luck and the odd suggestion for successful love-making, Jaime led Kezia away.

Ximen lifted his hands for quiet. "We have one more troth to plight. Angél Ferrara, come forth."

As Angél stepped forward, Rana straightened. A small smile played upon her lips. She held herself proudly. Meeting Miriam's eyes, she tilted her chin into the air. She looked triumphant, a queen who had won her crown.

Miriam cringed, overcome with an inexplicable foreboding. *Why do I feel this is about to go wrong?* she asked Alonso.

Not to worry. Ximen said all the parents have granted their permission. Just as well. I can't stand Angél.

You don't like Joachín, either.

Neither one of them is good enough for you.

"Angél Ferrara, you have something to say?" Ximen prompted.

Angél unbuttoned his shirt. "I say I have found the best woman to grace my side. She is beautiful and gifted. She will benefit my family as well as assist the Tribe." He headed toward Rana. "I say," Angél continued, "that I will love her, serve her, and protect her, if she will have me. I know what lies in her heart, though she hasn't said in so many words. She is too modest, too polite. So, I will speak for her. I will be her husband. She will be my wife."

Removing his shirt, he strode past Rana and ignored her. To Miriam's horror, she realized who his intended target was.

Estaban Ferrara's words echoed in her mind. *Nothing, save death, would stop him from attending, Serina. You may be sure of that.*

Angél stopped before her.

"No," she muttered.

Rana shrieked, her voice cutting through the shocked congregation like a sword. "No! It was supposed to be *me*, not her! You promised me, Angél!" Crying, she shoved her way through the crowd and disappeared. Anassa hobbled after her.

"Don't do this!" Miriam told him. "I did *not* agree to marry you." He ignored her as if she hadn't spoken. Without saying another word, he tied his shirt snugly about her waist. Cheers went up. Over the crowd, she caught Joachín's stricken gaze. He looked as if she had dealt him a fatal blow. His eyes found hers; they were dull with bewilderment and pain. His lips trembled. He looked as if he wanted to say something. Then abruptly, he turned away.

Gods! Did he believe this insane charade? Angél threw an arm about her shoulders and shouted to the Tribe. "She agrees!"

She threw off his arm. The crowd shouted its support and applauded. Joachín disappeared among them. She wanted to scream after him, 'Don't believe this!' but too late, he was gone.

"I did not agree to this!" Miriam tore the shirt from her waist and threw it at Angél's feet. "Papa!" she demanded, as Ephraim approached them. "How could you consent to this?"

Ephraim spread his hands. "Angél came to me this afternoon saying you agreed to it," he said. "I didn't know he assumed that you would! I thought it was a good thing. The Torch Bearers won't look for us in Tolede. The Ferraras are a highly respected family."

"Is there a misunderstanding?" Frowning, Ximen came toward them.

"There is," Miriam said. "I did not agree to this farce!"

"Miriam, you must see the sense in this," Angél told her. She didn't like his tone. He spoke as if she were a child throwing a tantrum. "I offered to take you and your father to Tolede to protect you. I didn't offer to make you my wife, but that's the honourable thing to do. Why not? We'd make a good match. If you don't love me now, you will." He lifted an eyebrow. "I assure you."

"That is unlikely in the extreme!"

"You're upset. Forgive me. I should have made it more romantic." He turned to address the waiting crowd. "It's all right," he said, waving to placate them. "Just a lover's spat." He laughed.

She wanted to strike the smugness from his face, but decided that dirtying her hands wasn't worth it. "There is *nothing* to work out," she said heatedly. "I am not marrying you. Get away from me. You've ruined everything." She pushed past him and ignored the well wishes from the crowd. Angél had the sense not to follow her. As she approached Anassa's *vardo*, she heard stormy crying from within. Rana, of course. Anassa would be with her.

She fidgeted. Where could she go? The only place she would find peace was at the women's pool. She headed for it and trudged up the steep path. The acrid smell of sulfur filled her nose. Below her, the strum of guitars lifted on the evening air. It was a special night for one couple—Jaime and Kezia. The Tribe would join them in their celebration. At the top of the path, she looked out over the Womb. Twilight painted the caravans in soft ambers and pinks. Beyond the camp, a red plume of dust trailed behind a lone rider heading out. She ached at the sight of him.

How could he believe she would marry Angél Ferrara? Had he no faith in her judgment or himself? Why would she choose such a self-satisfied lout? Was it because Angél was rich? That he could give her a better life and Joachin thought she valued that? She clawed at her hair in frustration.

I don't want that, Joachin! I want...! She choked off the thought. Alonso hadn't said a word, but he was near.

She rubbed her arms. If Joachin chose to leave and go his own way, that was his choice. There was nothing she could do about it. She couldn't live his life or direct his fate. She wished—no. She was done with wishes. Men were problems, and Joachin, the biggest problem of all. Better he was gone.

We're not all problems, Alonso insisted.

"Yes, you are!" she shouted in a temper. Her voice echoed throughout the cavern. *You are, are, are!*

He didn't argue it. She ignored him, shed her clothes, and stepped into the warm pool.

Chapter Thirty-Four: Invocation

"*I WANT HER* dead!"

Anassa recoiled at Rana's words. "You don't mean that." She hugged the girl tightly by her shoulders. "Miriam isn't to blame. If anyone is, it's Angél."

"He was mine until she came along. He wouldn't have looked at her if you hadn't made her Seer. Let me go!" She shoved Anassa aside.

"I didn't make her a seer. Lys did," Anassa said. "Where are you going?"

"Nowhere that concerns you, *Puri*." Rana spat the endearment and slammed the door behind her. Anassa flinched. A dull pounding began behind her forehead. She rubbed at the ache. Angél hadn't approached Lorenzo to ask for Rana's hand. She should have known something was amiss.

Young men, she sighed. *Their passions rule their heads*. She thought of Joachín. There was another who was enamored of Miriam. He had to be the one she saw. That compulsion snare had been a near thing.

She took a deep breath to steady herself. When had she last eaten? She couldn't remember. She deliberated returning to the communal fire. The wives would have food, but she didn't want to leave the *vardo*. There were biscuits in her cupboard. She could eat those. But before she did that, the Womb needed checking, the Tribe had to be safe. Afterwards, she would look in on Miriam and Rana.

She lay on her bed and closed her eyes. Around the fire, dancers swirled beside the flames while spectators clapped and sang. Sparks spun into the night in tight spirals. Along the river, a tangle of children waded in the moonlit water, one of them astride a horse. She smiled, remembering she'd done the same thing as a girl. Beneath the trees, couples murmured and caressed. She floated higher, searching for whatever might threaten the Tribe's peace.

All was well. Nothing stirred on the roads except for a lone rider who galloped to Elysir. She dismissed him.

Like a bee drawn to a rose, she focused her attention on Miriam. She found her soaking in the women's pool. The water spread from her neck in an emerald cape. *In trouble, she seeks the comfort of Lys's embrace*, Anassa thought. How could she know this was the best place for her? The water was curative. It relieved burdens.

Miriam's eyes were closed. Anassa doubted if she drowsed. She looked strong and serene, as if the day's worries were dissipating into the mist. Anassa nodded to herself. *Miriam will make a fine matriarch,* she decided. *The goddess chose well.*

She withdrew from Miriam and searched for Rana.

Her granddaughter wasn't in any of her usual places, but that was to be expected. Rana was too proud to talk with friends about the fire. She wouldn't cry herself to sleep in Kezia's *vardo*. Besides, Kezia was a married woman this night. Anassa sent her sight scouting over the banks of the river. Not finding her, she pulled in her focus and waited. The Ancestors would show her the way.

After a moment, she saw Rana standing within a ring of jagged rock. Anassa knew the place; she had warned the Tribe about it. Rana had shed her clothes. She gripped a knife. Her body was slick with blood. Two dark gashes ran from her bare shoulders to her waist in a vulgar cross. A series of long slashes fell from her thighs to her knees like the claw marks of a great cat.

She was panting heavily. She pointed at an unwieldy mass that hung between the rocks. "Pain is nothing," she muttered, as if to convince herself.

"Stop!" Anassa shouted, rising. "Don't do this!"

Rana held her shaking hands steady. "*Hymenoptera*, I invoke you," she whispered, her tone fierce. "I offer my blood as a promise of sweeter meat to come."

She stumbled forward and plunged the dagger into the dark sack. A black swarm spilled from the tear and engulfed her in a thick cloud. She let out a scream as the insects covered her from head to toe, but she didn't flail. She shuddered and remained upright, jerking and trembling, as if their stings were somehow bearable.

Anassa stumbled for the caravan's door, her sight locked on Rana. The girl had become a vague shape of rippling black. Her arms, legs and torso were thick stumps. A hazy glow emanated from her writhing body. In places, yellow streaks formed within it, in others, inky stripes blotted out the night. Beneath it, Rana wept and squealed. The thing hovered over her head for a moment and then floated away, drifting like a foul stench on the night's breeze.

Anassa blinked. Her vision cleared. She pushed open the *vardo's* door and fell down the stairs. She picked herself up, hobbled for the trail and managed three steps along the path before her legs gave out from beneath her.

Chapter Thirty-Five: Hymenoptera

SOMETHING IS...OFF.

Miriam opened her eyes. Shimmers of green light wavered along the cavern's walls. Alonso had left her to the privacy of her bath, but now he was back. He stood at the entrance, obscured by the mist.

What is it? she asked.

I'm not sure. Can't you feel it?

There was something—a prickling in the air that set her teeth on edge. It was an unpleasant energy, toxic and furious. It made her want to slide beneath the surface of the pool. She reached for her dress instead. A vision filled her mind. At the bottom of the moonlit trail, someone had fallen. People ran to help. Miriam recognized Anassa the same time Alonso did.

Oh, no, Alonso! Is she all right?

I don't know. I hope so...gods! he shouted. A black and yellow cloud filled the cave's entrance. From it, dark clots materialized and flew at his head. He swatted at them, but they settled onto his arms, legs, and face. He bellowed as they bit and stung. A second swarm flew at her. Wherever a clot struck, her skin puckered and burst. She flailed and twisted to avoid them, but she couldn't strike them away. Wherever the things landed, they attached. Each one drilled its way to her core. The pain became excruciating, beyond bearing. Overwhelmed by it, she retreated inside herself.

In the deepest place of who she was, she found Alonso. He had grown thin and indistinct, a sputtering candle about to burn itself out. He was praying, beseeching Sul to save them. She had never believed in the gods, but desperation drove her. *Lys*, she pleaded, finding faith in a final act. *Help me! Help us!*

No voice responded, but an image broke through her tortured thoughts—the sea, as green and as glowing as life itself.

She toppled into the pool.

Water coursed down her throat and into her lungs. She couldn't breathe. It didn't matter. She was drowning, but that was preferable to enduring that thing out there. The water snuffed the terrible hurt. The pool lulled her, filled her pores.

Farewell, Alonso, she said, feeling a lingering regret when he didn't answer her. Perhaps he had already gone on. Her vision dwindled to a point. She released her hold on life and waited for death to claim her.

Chapter Thirty-Six: Necessary Arrangements

MIRIAM FLOATED ON the water, face down. He dress drifted about her like a sodden sail. "Pull her out!" Anassa shouted.

As the men set Miriam on the rocky edge, Anassa surveyed her body. The water had nullified much of the damage, but the bites were apparent. She hoped Miriam would live, but whether she did or not had no bearing on her responsibility. Rana would be tried at dawn.

"Force the water from her lungs!" she told Lorenzo. He pushed on Miriam's chest. No water spouted from her mouth. He pushed harder. The water erupted in a gush.

"Give her breath!"

Lorenzo hesitated. Iago Gonzales, Guillermo's son, stepped forth. "I'll do it." He set his mouth on Miriam's and blew a lungful down her throat. After a few moments, she choked and coughed up more water. Iago wiped her face and rolled her onto her side.

Anassa turned to Lorenzo. "If she hasn't run, you'll find Rana in those rocks near the wasp's nest. Fetch her and lock her in my *vardo*."

A flicker of dismay crossed Lorenzo's face. He looked reluctant.

Anassa lost her temper. "You question my judgment? I *saw* it, Lorenzo! She invoked a demon! She has to be punished!"

He nodded, exited the cave. "Go with him," Anassa told the rest of the men. "He'll let her go." They exchanged glances. She knew what they thought—that her sense of duty was absolute. She wouldn't spare her own blood when it came to the Tribe's safety. Without a word, they filed out after him.

"Iago, stay." She set a boney hand to his shoulder. "I need you to carry her."

He hoisted Miriam into his arms. "Where do I take her?"

Rana would be held in her caravan until day break. "To Eva's *vardo*. Her father will want to be with her."

They made their way down the steep trail to the camp below. A crowd surrounded them half way up and peppered them with questions. "I'll explain everything at dawn," Anassa said. Despite her reticence, a ragtag parade followed them to Eva's wagon. Candlelight flickered from behind the healer's windows. Hearing them, Eva opened her door. "What is this?" she asked. Anassa waved Iago inside. He swept past Eva and carried Miriam into the *vardo*.

"In a moment," Anassa told her. She paused at the top of the steps to address her people. "There will be a *divano* for judgment at daybreak. I expect the heads of the clans to attend."

She ducked into the *vardo* and shut the door firmly behind her. On a rumpled bed, Ephraim leaned over Miriam. His fingers were at her neck, checking her pulse.

"Thank you, Iago." Anassa dismissed him. She wondered where Joachin was. If anyone should be here, it was he.

Iago paused at the door. "Can I tell my *maré* what happened? She'll insist on knowing."

Anassa nodded. Guillermo had been in the party she'd sent to collect Rana. He would tell Luci. "You can, but she may already know." News spread quickly about the camp.

Iago nodded his thanks and left.

"What happened to her?" Ephraim asked. Deep lines etched his forehead. Eva set soft fingers against Miriam's cheek and studied her intently.

Anassa sighed. "She was attacked by an hymenoptera."

"A what?" Ephraim frowned.

"Sweet Lys!" Eva looked at her round-eyed.

"It's a type of demon. A *noxience*, we call it, the toxic embodiment of a living thing." Anassa spent the next few moments explaining what had occurred and why.

"I hardly believe this is possible," Ephraim said at last. "I'm a man of science. I've never heard of such a thing. What can we do for her? Will she be all right?"

"The danger has passed. The pool did much to nullify the attack, but if we hadn't pulled her out in time, she would have drowned."

"The marks are disappearing. They look less red, now. I have some ointment that will help." Eva reached into a drawer and withdrew a tin.

"She needs to be immersed in the pool a few more times," Anassa said. "We'll have to stay after the Tribe leaves. Perhaps for as long as a week."

"I don't mind, Matriarch. I was planning on traveling with you, anyway." Eva glanced at Ephraim.

"This thing," Ephraim said. "Is it still at large? Can it come back to hurt her?"

"It's out there, but I doubt if it will return. Noxiences rarely revisit the person who repels them. It may fly back to Rana, but it's more likely to cause trouble where ill deeds occur. Tonight, I'll ward the camp. I don't think it'll come back to bother us. In the meantime, we should sleep."

"There doesn't appear to be much room." Ephraim glanced about the *vardo*. Moving Miriam was out of the question.

"You will sleep with me, Ephraim," Eva said. "There's enough room for both of us on my bunk. When Anassa finishes the warding, she can settle beside Miriam."

He reddened.

"It can't be helped." Eva folded her arms.

Anassa glanced at the two of them. Neither seemed to dislike the idea, although Ephraim was embarrassed. A private man, he was at a disadvantage in a Diaphani camp.

"I snore," he said.

"I know."

"I won't be long." Anassa rose to her feet as ungainly as a stork. She reached for several clumps of sage that hung from the ceiling. "I'll take care of the camp while you two decide on sleeping arrangements."

Over the next hour, she smudged the compound, scratched protective glyphs into the dirt, and muttered petitions to Lys. Sage floated on the night's air. When she returned to Eva's caravan, her back ached. The *vardo* lay in darkness. Eva and Ephraim were spooned together beneath Eva's quilts.

She glanced down at Miriam. The girl's chest rose and fell shallowly. Anassa was exhausted, but she knew she couldn't sleep. Until Miriam was out of danger, there would be no rest for her this night.

Chapter Thirty-Seven: Incubus

MIRIAM FLOATED IN a black ocean without a shore. She expected the tiny light to wink out, but it remained where it was. After an eon or so, it grew larger or she floated toward it, she wasn't sure. She rose and fell in a rhythm, carried by waves. A whooshing filled her ears. It reminded her of what a mother's heart beat might sound like to a baby in the womb. *I'm the baby*, she thought. Up and down, higher and lower, she bobbed. The water brightened, life coursed through her veins. Above her, a white surface rippled, became distinct. Her head broke free. She gasped and opened her eyes.

Darkness lay about her. Her eyes adjusted, focused. Inky clumps hung from a slatted ceiling. The familiar aromas of calendula, rosemary, and wintergreen told her where she was. Eva's *vardo*. Anassa's words floated through her mind like a trail of sea wrack—*Spirit is a vast ocean. Many things swim in it: the living, the dead, and other entities that are neither one nor the other.* And then they were gone.

Someone snored. She turned her head to see who it was and wished she hadn't. Her neck burned. Her arms, legs, and back hurt, too. Tiny bumps lined the inside of her throat. She had been stung, over and over. She'd fallen into the pool. The water had been a relief.

She lay without moving to assess the damage. As far as she could tell, she had no broken bones. The pain was skin deep, but something else wasn't right. The knowledge of what it was swamped her in a tide.

Alonso.

In a panic, she reached for him, refusing to believe he wasn't there. Nothing. She bit down on a wail.

Please! I can't live without him! She wasn't sure to which god she appealed. No divine voice responded to her plea, nor did the one she most wanted to hear. Tears slid down her cheeks. He had been her friend, her guide. In truth, Alonso had been more. He had loved her and she had loved him, although not as he had hoped.

What difference did that make? She rounded on herself. Love was love. Why confine it to such a narrow definition? The best kind of love was broad, encompassing. It didn't matter that they had never loved physically. Alonso had been her beloved from the start, from the moment she regarded him as he lay dying. She hadn't recognized it when she should have. And now that she had, he was gone.

The words felt hollow. Only three words to describe his absence, yet they spoke volumes. Without him, she was a shade of herself. She was no longer whole. She was broken, shattered, lost. Three words, followed by three words, then another three—what was it with threes? She stared at the ceiling, her throat tight. If she couldn't have him, she hoped Sul did, that the god had answered his prayers. Pray to heaven that he hadn't gone to that fiery hell from which she had called him. She closed her eyes. Her heart was broken. It would never heal. Another thought occurred to her.

I am no longer a seer.

She recoiled from it as if it were vulgar. It was a selfish concern, unworthy of Alonso's memory. She hated the regret she felt, not for him, but for herself. She had taken pride in the ability he had given her. Now, she was nothing, less than nothing. She was the outsider she had always been, first in Granad, and now, here.

Did Rana think she liked being Angél's choice, the centre of his attention? Beauty was a threadbare blanket that left you cold. It lacked substance. Alonso had loved her for who she was, not how she appeared.

I should have died with him, she thought miserably. *Life without him is nothing. I am nothing. He made me whole.*

No, a faint voice stirred, like a puff of wind promising rain. *I wouldn't have wanted that.*

She gasped, reached for him like a child her favourite toy. *Alonso! I thought...!*

Her need to hold him and never let him go, unleashed a storm. His lips found hers, their touch electrifying. It was not like kissing another human being, a man, solid and warm. Embracing Alonso was like clasping pure energy. Wherever his kisses touched her, her skin tingled with sparks. His hands left trails of heat. The deeper kisses charged her, made her feel as if she were about to burst forth with light. Her heart thudded. She suspected it pounded for them both.

It wasn't so much a question, but a hesitation. Within the tempest they had become, Alonso paused. For the briefest fraction of a second, like a charge building before a lightning strike, he held back. And in that moment, she knew he was waiting for her answer, yes or no. She wasn't so naïve as to misunderstand, but she wasn't sure if their consummation meant her death. It was possible. She couldn't imagine him wanting to kill her. Did she trust him or not? Did it matter?

She clutched at him and surrendered to the moment. *I love you, Alonso!* she cried.

Light split the darkness. His presence overwhelmed her. He was inside her in a way she had never experienced before. Their prior connection had been limited to his voice in her head, his emotions touching her heart, the brush of his hands upon hers like a summer breeze. Now, they were merged in a chasuble of passion—he, divine lightning, and she, mortal sky.

She no longer knew where she ended or he began. They were one being, charged, molten, glowing. For a second she felt as if they commanded the universe. They were the holy spark, the birth of all things. And then, the edges of that ultimate realm fell away. She condensed, contracted, and exploded with light.

Aching pleasure rippled from her core, radiating through her belly and lancing down her arms and legs. She gasped, caught her breath and wanted to laugh and cry at the same time. She was still aware of Alonso. The culmination of their coupling hadn't forced him aside. But now, they were half merged, as if her climax had shaken them to their foundations. He was depleted, yet, replete. The storm had passed. He seemed more contented than ever.

So was she. They lay without speaking, as if words were beyond them. She didn't need his reassurances. His love nourished her, like rain on parched earth. The sweetness of it was almost too much to bear. She was afraid that if she spoke, her words would break their peace, like stones disturbing a perfect pond.

A wave of warmth washed through her. *My* alma, *my soul. I should have said so before, when you told me you loved me, but I was so overcome. I do love you, my Miriam. I always have. I always will.*

Joy filled her to the brim. She savoured its cup until curiosity distracted her momentarily. How was it possible to feel such pleasure when Alonso had no physical body? *Is it always like that?* she asked. *Love-making, I mean?*

It's never like that.

She turned the thought over. How was it with normal men, then? She couldn't imagine it being better. Their coupling had been divine, not of this world. What was Alonso, now? An angel? An incubus? It didn't matter. All that mattered was that they were together.

He lay beside her, watching her with his perfect blue eyes. He was naked, as beautiful as she had imagined him to be when she had seen him in his bed chamber, so long ago. He would have made a fine subject for any sculptor portraying the god. His pose was far from Sul-like, though. One crooked arm pillowed his head. The other lay across her waist, his hand warm against her buttock. He glowed faintly, as if radiating bliss.

I thought I was going to die, she said.

He smiled, traced a finger along her waist. *Sometimes, it's called that— the little death. But I would never do that to you, my Miriam. What kind of a lover would I be, if I took your life?*

How did you know you wouldn't?

I just did. Having been through death twice, I think I'd know.

Twice?

He nodded. *I died again, after that thing attacked us. But this time it was different. I'm not sure I can describe it.*

Try. If he told her he'd flown with hippogriffs, she wouldn't have cared.

I called out to Sul. I didn't see the god, but a blast of light rescued me. The wasps fled before it. From out of it, beings of radiance came. They surrounded me like planets around a sun. They were heady, Miriam, liberating. And then, they left me, like a comet with sparks in its wake.

She caught her breath.

And that was the second amazing thing. One of those sparks turned into my old mentor from seminary, Luminant Silvio. He's been dead for fifty-two years. He beamed at me as he flew by. Then my grandmother, Jade, swept past, laughing and waving. Finally, my own mother, Nina, swirled about me. She gave me a look of such tenderness that I found my heart beating again.

You didn't follow them?

I couldn't. I had to come back. You needed me.

He had sacrificed his place with the high ones for her. He had honoured her beyond belief.

Given the choice between them and you, I know which one I'd choose. You're my paradise, Miriam, he said. *You always will be.*

He kissed her and set her alight once again. She was happy for him, overjoyed for herself. But their new life together would be fleeting. His existence was not the natural order of things. How many times could one die, before the gods intervened?

I love you, Alonso, she told him. She would not allow her fear to come between them. Let their passion burn again before he sensed it.

Chapter Thirty-Eight: Ruse

ELYSIR'S GATES WERE closed for the night, but it was only a matter of time before Joachin found where he might break in over the outer wall. Like any town in Esbaña, municipal complacency gave him an advantage. It took money to maintain the walls and pay for a Watch. The *Reconquista* was decades past, the Moori long ago converted or killed. At night, the constabulary manned the four gates, but that was all.

After scouting for half an hour, he found a promising spot and tethered Fidel to an oak. The horse eyed him accusingly. He had spurred him mercilessly as they had galloped from the Womb.

"Sorry, old friend." He stroked the beast's neck. He felt calmer now. Miriam had distracted him, but he had regained his focus—her betrothal to Ferrara had seen to that. He'd been a fool to think that her blushes meant something, that she'd found him attractive. Fine. Other women found him appealing enough. Once he collected his mother's death debt, he'd celebrate with a new woman at his side. No, *two*.

The tree provided a good boost. Others used this place. Hand and foot holds were chipped into the wall. He'd have to be careful. Thieves' guilds were becoming more prevalent in the towns. They'd object to an interloper using their routes. He climbed to the top of the wall and peered over the edge.

A low tiled roof lay beneath him. From the smell, a blacksmith's shop. He slid to the tiles, careful not to make a sound. On a far edge, the top of a ladder protruded, confirming his belief that he passed along an illicit way. He made his way down the ladder and stepped into an alley.

No assailant accosted him from the shadows. As he slipped from the lane into the main road, the sound of strummed guitars emanated from a tavern. He turned away from the music and headed for the temple. Hopefully, the Grand Inquisitor had not yet quit Elysir. Gaining admittance to the Solarium would be a much greater challenge than getting into the town.

He walked quickly and reviewed his options. He could abduct a Luster monk and disguise himself, but he didn't know the temple protocols well enough. One small mistake would expose him. There would be a morning Mass, but he didn't want to wait, not sure if the Grand Inquisitor would officiate. Besides, murdering a man in front of parishioners was a bad idea. Escape would be next to impossible.

The spires of the Solarium rose above the roofs in the moonlight. He turned a corner and regarded the great edifice from across its square.

The words of his old mentor, Guido, long dead, struck him. *When you can't approach the mark with impunity, make the mark come to you.*

Strange that he should think of Guido, now. He hadn't thought of him in years. It was almost as if the old man stood beside him, wheezing into his ear. He frowned, glanced behind himself. Other than a small dust devil chasing leaves in the gutter, the street was empty. There was no way to make the Grand Inquisitor come to him at this hour. He was better off breaking in through a window.

A pebble skittered across the cobblestones and struck him on the ankle. Guido used to kick him when he was being dense. He stared at the stone, and then he knew.

Gods, he thought, glancing at the Solarium. *Could it work?* He gave a short bark of laughter.

It *would* work. The audacity of it excited him. He'd enter the temple by its front doors. He'd whisper a few words in the right ears and be ushered to the Grand Inquisitor's side. Before his retainers could blink, he'd twist a dagger into the bastard's heart. And then he'd run as they recovered.

He trotted across the square and ran up the Solarium's broad steps. He grasped the great brass ring and knocked. His hammering boomed through the wood and beyond it. He waited. No one answered his summons. He knocked harder.

A wicket, set within the great door, opened a crack. An ancient Luster monk stood there. Beneath his brown cowl, his face was papery thin and looked covered in dust. Joachín wondered what corner of the temple they kept him in. "What do you want?" the monk asked, scowling.

"I need to see the Grand Inquisitor," Joachín said.

"Come back in the morning. He's not available at this time of the night."

Joachín forced the wicket wide. "He'll see me, I think."

"How dare you?" The priest glared at him in outrage.

"Oh, I dare," Joachín replied easily, stepping through the door. "I have something he wants, something he'll pay for. I know the whereabouts of Miriam Medina."

The monk led him down several long corridors of grey marble, inlaid with sun motifs of alabaster and gold. Works of art covered every inch of the walls: Sul creating the world, Sul setting the stars into the sky, Sul, multi-rayed and golden, welcoming the dead into paradise. Of the goddess, there was no trace. Joachín noted the larger works and considered where the side halls led. It was crucial to remember the way back, as well as potential routes out.

Other than his doddering guide, few clerics wandered the halls. The monk brought him to an alcove more opulent than the rest.

"Wait here," he said. Joachín nodded.

A golden statue of the god stood before the ornate doors. *How appropriate*, Joachín thought. *The god waits in the hall, while the demon sleeps within.* He slipped his knife into his sleeve and smiled grimly. *Soon, Maré*, he promised. *There will be once less devil in the world tonight.*

The monk reappeared at the door. "Come," he motioned.

Joachín stepped into the suite. On either side of the portal, two of the Inquisitional Guard stood at attention. In a doorway leading to a bed chamber, another henchman towered, as big as a bear. In the centre of the room, Tor Tomás sat upon a throne-like chair. His white habit looked as if it had been freshly starched despite the lateness of the hour. He regarded Joachín with the hooded scrutiny of an asp.

He had aged a bit, but the golden eyes were familiar as were the faint lines of scar across his face. Joachín met Tomás's gaze without flinching. He would have to strike fast and true. There would be no time to enjoy it. The guards would attack as soon as he moved. He considered the thickness of the window glass and calculated the drop to the ground.

"You have information about Miriam Medina?" Two bright spots appeared on Tomás's cheekbones. His scar gleamed in the candlelight.

"I do." Joachín stepped forward.

"Stay where you are." He held up a restraining hand. The giant henchman shifted his weight. "Your name?" Tomás asked.

"Guido Sanchez." Why not? Might as well do his old friend proud.

"You're a citizen of Elysir?"

"No, Madrone."

"What is it you do?"

"I procure and sell goods."

Tomás and the giant exchanged a look. "So, now you wish to sell me information about Miriam Medina. Let's hear it."

"There's a reward?" He hoped he looked greedy enough.

"That depends on the quality of your information. I pay nothing until your story is verified."

"Very well. I'll whisper it into your ear."

Tomás barked a laugh, an ugly sound. "You think I let filth like you within five feet of me?"

Joachín coloured. "I want what is my due. I tell you, and these others might take advantage."

"My retainers are trustworthy. You, however, I doubt."

The situation was sliding out of his control. He'd been a fool to assume it would be easy. Perhaps if he convinced them he could lead them to Miriam, he'd get close enough to stab the bastard. "I can take you to her," he said, "but it's dangerous."

"Why is it dangerous?"

"She's in a tavern run by brigands. Thieves and murderers, every one of them."

"And you know this, how?"

"I'm one of them. A thief, I mean. I want to turn from my wrongful ways."

Tomás smiled tightly. "So—let me make sure I understand you, correctly—you want to repent of your sins? If you think to impress me with that, you're wrong. More likely, you want to betray your friends so you can claim the whole reward for yourself." He leaned forward and gripped his arm rests. "*Where is she?*"

"At the Raging Bull, near the edge of town."

"How did she come to be there?"

"I don't know." Sometimes lies were better if they weren't too elaborate.

"He doesn't know. How disappointing." Tomás set a finger to his lips. "What do you think, Barto? Has he anything to tell us, or is he like the rest who have come here?"

"He's a liar like the rest of them."

Joachín didn't wait to hear what else they might say. In a moment, Tomás would have him clapped in chains. He pulled his dagger from his sleeve and threw it at him. It spun end over end in a blur. The second before it reached him, Tomás dodged. The blade struck bare wood.

It missed him, how? Joachín reached for the second knife in his boot, but Barto intercepted him. Joachín stabbed the big man in the chest. The knife bounced off his habit—he wore armour underneath. Barto caught his wrist and knocked the knife aside. The two bodyguards leapt from behind him and pinned Joachín by the arms.

Like a spectre of death, Tomás rose from where he'd fallen. He brushed off his habit. "Bring him," he said. He swept into the adjacent room.

Joachín was strong-armed into it. It wasn't a bed chamber as he thought. The room was mostly bare, except for two long tables. The biggest had chains with iron cuffs dangling from its corners. A book lay on the second, with several knives and other unpleasant looking objects.

"Tie him down," Tomás said.

He thrashed and kicked. Barto loomed before him with a fist held high. As the punch connected, Joachín felt his nose crack. Pain lanced through his skull. Someone kneed him in the gut and he doubled over. Soon, it became hard to distinguish between the kicks and the blows. He blacked out. When he came to, they had spread-eagled him across the large table. Iron rings encircled his ankles and wrists. His nose was broken. His mouth was filled with blood. He swallowed, choked. It was hard to breathe.

"There you are." Tomás slapped him smartly across the cheek. "Sometimes Barto overdoes it. I was worried we might lose you." He smiled grimly.

Joachín closed his eyes to shut him out.

"No, no!" Tomás grabbed him by the chin. "You mustn't sleep. I need you clear-headed. Do you know what this is?" He held up the leather-bound book for Joachín to see.

"A book." One of his molars shifted. A spear of agony stabbed along his jaw.

"Not just any book. A grimoire. Prohibited, but useful. Some of the tattoos in it actually work. I'm going to try one on you. If it's effective, you'll never lie to anyone again."

"Not that he'll live long enough to test it," Barto said.

Tomás chuckled. "True, but let's not get ahead of ourselves. Now, I expect this will hurt," he held up a knife for Joachín to see, "but what's a little more pain, hmmm? I expect you're used to it by now."

Joachín flinched as the blade pricked his breast bone. Tomás was playing with him, relishing his fear. In another second, he would stab him through the heart. He closed his eyes again, unwilling to give Tomás the satisfaction of seeing his terror. He waited for the knife to finish him, but the cut only burned. The wound was superficial. Tomás rubbed something into it, which was more alarming than being stabbed. The world tilted, turned grey. He felt faint. The blade nicked him under the chin. He wished it hadn't.

"Don't move," Tomás said.

Something wet dribbled into the base of his neck.

"There," Tomás said. "In a few seconds, that should take."

"If it works," Barto said.

"Well, if it doesn't, we'll do it the old way."

A cool lethargy overcame him. The room had an unusual but familiar tang to it, sweet and green. He had smelled that fragrance before. He was so tired. Whatever Tomás had drugged him with was leaching the strength from him, but the pain was lessening. He wanted to sleep, to dream.

"You say you have information about Miriam Medina. Is that true, or was that a lie?" Tomás wavered above him.

"True," he whispered. The table rose and fell. Dartura. They had rubbed Dartura into his cuts, the same herb he had wrongly used when Iago and Guillermo caught him.

"Where is she?"

He fought the compulsion. It was hard not to say. "Not far from here," he replied.

"Is she at the Raging Bull as you claimed?"

"No."

"Ha! I knew it. Where is she, exactly?"

"At the Womb."

"The Womb? What nonsense is this?"

It wasn't nonsense. It was true. He felt no need to repeat it.

"A brothel?" Barto suggested.

"No. I know them all in the area. What is this Womb?"

"A place."

"What kind of a place?"

"Hidden."

"Where is it?"

"Down a road."

"What road?"

"A long road."

"Gods, this is getting us nowhere. He's talking in circles." Tomás turned to the old monk who had escorted him from the front door. "How much of that herb did you give him?"

"Only what the book said, Radiance."

"You've given him too much."

"If I'd given him too much, he'd be unconscious by now."

Tomás ignored him and turned back to Joachín. "How do you know Miriam Medina?"

"I met her." He could see her, now. The *vardo* lay in darkness. She was sleeping. Anassa snored beside her. On a bed across from them, a couple slept beneath blankets. Eva the healer and Miriam's father, it looked like. Joachin frowned. He didn't think they had coupled, but the dream suggested otherwise. Miriam opened her eyes. "I love her," he added wistfully.

"You love her," Tomás said. "Yet you betray her. You make no sense."

She was muttering something now, as if talking to someone he didn't see. He liked the way her lips moved. She had such beautiful ones. Soft and full. He wanted to kiss them. Someone slapped his face.

"Wake up! Where did you meet her?" Tomás bent over him.

"At the Neck."

"The Womb, the Neck! What are these places?"

"It's what they call them."

"Who calls them?"

"The...," he didn't want to say it. He had to say it. "The Diaphani."

"She's with a band of Diaphani?"

The word was vile. He couldn't prevent it. "Yes," he said wretchedly, his betrayal complete.

For a moment, there were no further questions. He hated Tomás, hated himself. The Grand Inquisitor was frowning, studying the grimoire. "What is your involvement in this?" he asked dryly.

Joachín licked his lips. "I came here to kill you."

That caught his attention. Tomás loomed over him, his face round and pale like the moon. "Why? We've never met."

"We've met." He tasted blood. "Nine years ago, when you raped and murdered my mother."

Tomás stared at him as if were trying to remember. "Where?"

"In Taleda. In a brothel. She was a whore. I was her son."

Tomás touched his face. His eyes glittered, like beetles on a corpse. He dropped each word slowly, as if shoveling dirt into a grave. "You... did *this*...to me?"

"Yes." The word didn't feel so bad this time.

He straightened. "Well, you've made a great mistake in coming here, Guido Sanchez, or whatever your name is. You'll tell me the whereabouts of your beloved, and when I find her, I'll do the same to her as I did to your sweet, pleading mother. Then I'll come back here and deal with you. Where, exactly, is this Womb?"

"Not far."

"In the town?"

"No."

"Outside it then? Which direction?"

"East."

"How far east?"

He fought as hard as he could, but after two hours of questioning he told them all he knew. He could barely hear Tomás over his own weeping. He'd been such a fool to think he could take him unawares.

"When I come back," Tomás whispered in his ear with such venom that he thought he might bite him, "I'm going to carve your face to look like mine. Then I'll gouge out your eyes, slice off your nose, and cut out your tongue. I'll flay the flesh from your scrawny buttocks, and then I'll take you from behind, like I did your poor, pathetic mother." He turned to his giant henchman. "Barto, watch him."

As Tomás left with the remaining guards, Joachin nearly broke from despair. His pride had brought him to this. He had betrayed Miriam. He had failed his mother. He deserved whatever the gods sent him unless there was a way to change the odds.

His only option was Barto.

I have gold, he wanted to say, but his lips refused to make the offer. *Lys save me*, he thought. How could he talk his way out of this, if he couldn't lie? He tried a second approach—a Diaphani curse. *Release me, dog, or scorpions will share your bed, locusts devour your food.* Nothing. He'd have to find another way.

It was a laughable idea, but the less he resembled a captive, the better. Perhaps the giant might give him some information he could use to his advantage. He cleared his throat, thankful that the effects of the Dartura were wearing thin. Pain sharpened his focus. "So," he began, "have you worked with the Grand Inquisitor long?"

The giant settled himself against the window ledge. "Not long." He leaned against the glass.

"Must be hard, keeping such long hours."

Barto snorted. "I'll say this for you. You have *cojones*."

He took it as a compliment. "You're from around here?"

"What's it to you?"

"Nothing. You just remind me of some of the hill folk I've met in my travels. Hardy types from up north. They wrestle wolves and bear."

"I'm from Andor. You've a good eye."

What's left of it, Joachín thought. He could only see out of his right one. "You're a long way from home. What brings you here?"

"Work. Grand Inquisitor said he could use a man like me."

"I see. Have you always been a...priest?" He'd been about to say 'torturer'.

"No. I farmed. I wanted better for my woman."

"Woman?"

"I wear the habit, but I don't live like one."

"She travels with you?"

"She's dead."

"Oh." Not a good line of inquiry to pursue. "How long have you worked for the Grand Torch...?"

"Shut up." Barto settled against a wall. "I need to sleep."

Joachín lay in the cold and stared at the ceiling. He didn't doubt that Barto would beat him again if he irritated him further. As long as he didn't kill him outright, Tomás wouldn't care what Barto did.

Tomás and the Guard would reach the Womb in less than two hours. By dawn, they would attack the Tribe.

Joachín strained at his bonds. They refused to give. His only way out was if Barto released him.

He slept fitfully. At one point, he slipped into a dream. It was day. Barto stooped to enter the door of a cottage. Inside, a dark-haired woman stirred a pot over a fire. She reminded him of Miriam. They might have been sisters or cousins. She smiled as Barto entered.

"Are you hungry?" she asked. "I've made stew. Here, eat." She handed him a bowl.

He sat down at a table and shoveled in a spoonful. "It's good," he said.

She settled on a stool beside him. "I have news."

"What?" He took another mouthful.

She set a hand to her belly. "I'm with child."

He stared at her in amazement and set down his bowl. "Maia!" He pulled her onto his lap. "When?"

"October."

"A boy or a girl, do you think?"

"A boy, I'm thinking."

"We'll name him after my father."

"Grimwald? Such a stern name for a baby!"

"Nothing wrong with it. He'll grow up to be a strong man like me."

A slap woke Joachín. He opened his good eye but couldn't focus.

"Drink this. You better not die on me. I'll be tanned for leather, if you do."

The wine coursed down his throat and hit him like strong drink. His vision blurred and went black.

Now the girl, Maia, was alone. From the look of her, she was eight months pregnant. She lay in a dirty cell and stared fearfully at the door. The sound of footfalls approached her from down a hall. She whimpered and crawled into a dark corner on her hands and knees.

The door opened. Tomás stood in the frame. "There you are," he said as if locating a lost cat.

"Please." She hugged her belly. "Let me go. I promise, I won't say anything. I'll say I lost my senses, that I wandered off. I'm huge, ugly. There are others, younger, prettier. You can't want me."

"But I *do* want you." He crossed the cell and toed her with his boot. "It amuses me that you're down here. Upstairs, Barto thinks you're dead. Get up."

"No!"

He hauled her by the arm.

"I am too close to term!"

He slammed her face into the stone wall. "Lift your skirt and bend over like the slut I know you are. If you don't, I'll stomp that belly flat."

She dissolved into tears. She hiked up her dress with shaking hands. He thrust her over as far as she could go, lifted his robe, and fumbled with himself. Crying all the while, she set her palms against the wall to brace herself. He gripped her by the hips and began to pump.

His voice was a harsh rasp as he thrust into her. Her belly scraped the wall. "I would've thought...," he said, getting into a rhythm, "that a village wise woman...like yourself...would have ways...of stopping this.... You're hardly...worth...my while...."

Joachín forced himself to wake. He was breathing hard. "Maia!" he said, staring at Barto. "Your wife!"

The huge man shuffled from his place by the window. "What did you say?" His attitude suggested Joachín avoid that topic.

"She's alive," Joachín said. "I dreamt it. She's here, in the temple."

"Don't you speak of her!" Barto lifted a fist to silence him.

"There are cells beneath us! The Grand Inquisitor is keeping her there. He's been using her. I dreamt it! I have a gift!"

"You're lying!"

He was beside himself. "I can't lie! I have a truth tattoo carved into my chest, remember?"

Barto's fist hovered. "How did he take her?"

"I don't know! All I know is, she's down there!"

The big man's eyes bore into his. Without another word, he turned and stormed from the room.

"After you find her, come back and release me!" Joachin shouted. His reply was a slam of the door.

Minutes crawled by. An hour. Two. His limbs stiffened. Thirst plagued him. Beneath the clots, his tattoos throbbed with a pulse of their own. He wished with all his heart that he had Miriam's skill as a seer. He needed to know what was happening to her and the Tribe. Dawn slipped past the window sill and sent bright shafts into the room. He closed his eyes. Barto had forgotten him. The gods were just. He had betrayed Miriam, he had forsaken them all. He received no better than what he deserved.

But if that was so, why had he dreamed? He gave it up, too miserable to think.

The outer door creaked. Someone closed it softly. Whoever it was didn't want to be heard. Hope blossomed in his heart. He gave silent thanks to the goddess as Barto entered the room. The big man dropped a habit at his side.

"Any minute now, and the bells will call for morning prayers," Barto said. "That's our best chance to leave. Can you walk without support?"

Relief swept through Joachin. His aches and thirst washed away. "Release me, and I'll walk on coals if I have to. Did you find your wife?"

Barto sprang the cuffs from his arms and legs. "I did. I took her to a safe place."

"What did she tell you?"

"She confirmed what you said." He grimaced, struggling against an inner rage. "You best wipe that blood off your face."

Joachin tried to stand. Barto caught him and held him steadily. "We have a common purpose, now," he said. "That piece of scum won't get away with what he did to my Maia."

Joachin nodded and regretted it. His nose felt twice its normal size; his legs kept melting beneath him like wax. Two lone men against an army dedicated to the Grand Inquisitor—their chances of succeeding were next to none.

On the other hand, considering the state he was in two hours ago... his luck was changing. The goddess was on his side.

I'll take those odds, he thought.

Chapter Thirty-Nine: Blight

ANASSA WATCHED AS Lorenzo and a number of the men brought Rana to face the *divano*. Dawn was upon them, although the sun had not yet risen beyond the Womb's eastern edge. Far above, clouds clustered, their bellies a mottled red.

Beside Anassa, Ximen waited, his blind eyes fixed upon the small group that approached them. Wordlessly, the Tribe parted as Rana was escorted into their midst. There was no talk except from a few mothers who shushed their children or nursed fussy babies. Anassa knew there was little need for preamble. Everyone understood why the court had been called. On a stump behind her, Miriam sat. She was still weak. Beside her, Ephraim Medina and Eva stood.

Every inch of Rana's skin was covered in angry red welts. Her face and arms were bloated like sausages about to split. Despite the pain she had to be feeling, she struggled against her captors like a lioness in a net. Did rage empower her alone? Anassa clutched her bone necklace to be safe.

"You think to judge *me?*" Rana saw the gesture for what it was—a ward against demons. "Judge her!" She pointed at Miriam. "She was the one who forced me to it!"

"Be quiet," Anassa said.

Rana shrugged the hands from her. "You chose her over me, yet I'm Speaker! She's not even one of us!"

"Silence! You'll have your chance to talk. This hearing will be conducted in a proper manner."

Rana scoffed. "I doubt that. You've already made up your minds." She turned to the crowd. "Have a care, all of you. What I called into being, I can call again."

Anassa stiffened. "How dare you! You threaten us?"

"You're threatening me, *Puri!*"

Ximen raised his hand. "I've seen the events," he said gravely. "Rana Isadore, the evidence rests against you. You called an *hymenoptera* into being. You directed it to attack Miriam Medina. Fortunately, she survived. I see that as a direct intervention by the goddess."

Rana sneered at him. "So, what will you do, Rememberer? Exile me from the Tribe? Execute me? Try it, and you'll have a wrathful ghost in your midst. I'll hunt you all you down. I'll strike whoever lifts a hand against me. I'll...."

"Stop!" In spite of his size, Ximen's voice echoed throughout the compound as if he spoke for all the Diaphani, past and present. "We will act fairly," he said, struggling for calm. "No act, however heinous, is without its reasons or its source. Now is your chance to tell us what your reasons were. Why did you try to kill Miriam Medina?"

Rana spat in Miriam's direction. "She's a blight upon us! Everyone thinks she's wonderful, but she's not! She's wanted by the Torch Bearers. They'll learn we're harbouring her. She'll bring misfortune upon us all!"

"That's not the reason. You were jealous."

"How can I be jealous of her? She's ugly, scrawny!"

"You wanted to marry Angél Ferrara. He chose her over you."

"She bewitched him! He would have chosen me, if not for her!"

Ximen turned to Miriam. "Did you bewitch Angél Ferrara?"

Resentment roused Miriam to life. She glared at Rana. "I did not."

Anassa glanced at Angél who stood with his parents to one side of the circle. He refused to look at either girl.

"Then she did something! She gave him a potion!" Rana said.

Miriam stood shakily and clenched her fists. "You'd like to think that, wouldn't you? That he chose me because I took unfair advantage. Maybe he saw you for who *you* really are—a girl so poisoned by envy that she resorts to black magic to have her way. I don't blame Angél for not wanting you! Look at you! Your sorcery reveals you for what you are. What will you do when he marries someone else? Attack her, too?"

Rana shrieked, lunged at her with her fingers clawed. The men held her back.

"Enough!" Anassa shouted. She had expected more from Miriam, but perhaps Rana had exposed old hurts. Miriam was beautiful. Most people saw that as an advantage, but among her peers, she might have been resented for it.

"He wanted me! He promised! We lay together!" Rana told the crowd.

Anassa stared at her, aghast. How could she have been so foolish as to lie with Angél? Tribal taboos were strict—no woman coupled with a man until they were married. The bridal shirt was hung after the couple's first night together, a display of virtue and virginity lost. Ximen looked at Angél gravely. "You made a promise to Rana?" he asked.

Angél met his eyes. "I made no promise," he said stiffly.

Ximen studied him, his pale eyes probing. A flash of disgust flickered over his face. "I think you did," he said flatly. "When you lay together, she asked if you were engaged. You told her, 'I suppose.' That suffices as a promise." He turned to the solemn faces about him. "I think I have a solution to this problem, if the Tribe will permit." People nodded. Angél and the Ferraras did not.

Ximen regarded Rana, once again. "Rana Isadore, you are guilty of the attempted murder of our new seer, Miriam Medina. In most cases, such a deed is met with execution or exile, but there are extenuating circumstances. I don't believe you'll be a threat to the Tribe if we give you what you want. You will continue to act as our speaker. You will prophesize when the moment comes upon you, and warn the Tribe as befits. You will also marry Angél Ferrara, this day. He'll take you from here, and you will live with him and his parents in Tolede."

"No! I don't want her!" Angél shouted.

Rana crumpled, all of the fight taken out of her. "I'll get better, Angél!" She lifted a hand to appeal to him. "I'll heal!"

"I am *not* marrying that witch!" Angél said.

Lorenzo caught Rana by the shoulders. "You've lain with my daughter. I think you will," he said.

Angél glanced at the accusing faces about him. "So be it," he said angrily. "She can work in the foundry until she drops." He turned on his heel and stalked from the assembly. Bandolier Estaban pushed after him. Angél's mother, Leonora, followed them like a beaten dog.

"Angél! I love you!" Rana reached out to him. When he didn't respond, she began to cry.

Anassa felt torn. Despite the terrible thing Rana had done, she was still her granddaughter. Invoking the *hymenoptera* had cost Rana much; she hadn't been healed by the pool as Miriam had. It was possible her scars would be permanent. It was also clear now, what had sparked this whole debacle. Angél had deflowered Rana, and then, as if she were nothing, had cast her aside.

I should've seen this the night she came home floating on clouds, Anassa thought. At least Lorenzo seemed relieved by this turn of events, if no one else was.

"We'll make it right," he told Rana as she blubbered into his shoulder. "I'll make sure he takes good care of you. If he doesn't, he'll have to answer to me."

"Yes, *Paré*."

"Send me a bird if he mistreats you."

"Yes...." Rana stiffened. She pushed Lorenzo's arms aside and stood tall and straight, as if another mood claimed her entirely. Her eyes gazed into the distance, to the plain beyond.

"Rana?" He set a hand to her elbow.

Slowly, she lifted her arm and pointed. "They are upon us!" she cried, her voice growing shrill and ringing out. Rana had stabbed a finger at the Neck. From what Anassa could tell, nothing descended down the narrow trail.

"The Hounds of Sul approach! Death rides to claim us!" Rana shouted. All about her, women cried out in fear, grabbed for their children. Not understanding, the little ones began to wail.

"How soon?" Lorenzo demanded, shaking her. Rana ignored him. Men ran for weapons.

Anassa peered at the Neck. Dust billowed from it. Mounted men emerged from the cave's mouth in a cloud. Heedless of the decline, they rode down it and galloped toward them.

"To the caves!" Anassa cried. "We must go deep and pray that Lys hides us!" The women and children would heed her. The men would fight. She watched as Ephraim and Eva helped Miriam to the path. Lorenzo ran to collect his knife. Rana stood where she was, still in her trance. Anassa cursed her shaking legs and stumbled for her granddaughter.

Chapter Forty: Apprehended

MIRIAM FOUGHT OFF Ephraim and Eva. She couldn't flee while Anassa and Rana faltered. "Let me go!" she said. "I have to help Anassa!"

"You're not in any shape to help anyone!" Eva insisted.

"I'll get them," Ephraim said. "Take Miriam up the hill."

"No, Papa! I'm not leaving until we all are!"

Ephraim hadn't waited to hear her protests. He ran to Rana and tried to draw her away.

Rana snapped out of her daze. "Get your hands off me!" she shrieked. She clawed at his face and drew blood. Ephraim set a hand to his cheek and stared at her in astonishment.

Miriam slipped an arm about Anassa's waist. The old woman seemed confused. "Come," Miriam murmured. "We have to hurry." From the corner of her eye, she watched as her father limped in the wrong direction with Eva at his heels. "Papa!" she called. "Where are you going?" There wasn't time to retrieve anything from Eva's *vardo*. What were they thinking?

"My heart...!" Anassa clutched her chest.

"It's only fear," Miriam told her. People ran every which way. "Once we get to the pool, you'll catch your breath, and we'll scan to see what happens. *Alonso!* She reached for him, needing the steadiness of his presence. *How many of them are there?*

A cavalry.

One hundred and twenty men. Armed with spears and swords against half as many Diaphani. She didn't dare look. *How far away are they?*

They're on the plain. The men of the Tribe have armed themselves. They'll meet the army head-on, past the camp.

Where is my father? Can you see him?

He's run to get a blade, too.

The fool! Where is Eva?

She's trying to pull him away.

The rumble of hooves approached them, like growing thunder. Anassa's face was ashen. Without warning, she moaned and slumped in Miriam's arms.

"Anassa!" She struggled to lift her. They had come to the base of the path leading to the pools. How was she to carry her all that way? Beyond them, the men of the Tribe roared as the riders swept among them. Miriam heard the whistle and thump of swords as they plunged into flesh, the screams of horses, the grunts of dying men as they fell. Knives were hopeless against the weight of heavy steel. Fear propelled her. She hoisted Anassa into her arms and staggered up the path.

Behind you! Alonso shouted.

She turned to confront her attackers. Too late, she saw her mistake. Two horsemen bore down upon her; the first one with his sword aloft. His arm descended. The blade sliced Anassa crudely, gutting her as if she were no more than a sack of grain. Blood spattered Miriam's arms and face. With a cry, she dropped the old woman and shielded her eyes with scarlet hands.

"Hold!" an imperious voice ordered.

The second blade never fell. In shock, Miriam gazed up to see who had spared her. The sun crested the rim of the Womb, throwing her rescuer into stark shadow. He brushed a cowl from his gleaming head. She recognized the familiar scar that jigged across his face like a bolt of lightning.

"Miriam Medina," Tomás said pleasantly. "How nice to see you."

She stood her ground, hating the scarred priest with every ounce of her being. She would kill him with her bare hands if she had to. Anassa lay dead at her feet. Who knew how many others had died because of this man? She should have killed him in Granad when she'd had the chance.

"You're a monster!" In a fury, she threw herself at his legs to tear the flesh from them. He booted her in the chest and knocked her to the ground. She landed on Anassa, the breath knocked from her lungs. "I can see why you might think that," he replied. "Get her," he told the guard.

Alonso! Help! she cried.

Gloved hands clapped themselves about her shoulders. Alonso threw himself at the guard, but he passed through him. There was nothing he could do. How was it that he could be so present in their love-making and have no effect, now? She clawed at her captor. He knocked her hands aside and cuffed her across the head. Tomás spurred his mount ahead of them, his interest fading now that his prize was won. The guard settled her roughly in front of him and squeezed her breasts. She screamed in protest. Tomás glanced their way, but the guard removed his paws before he saw.

"We have the witch! Leave the rest!" Tomás shouted. The soldiers who had been sent to ferret the survivors from the caves reappeared. "They'll all die of starvation, anyway." He cast her a backward glance and laughed. Before him, *vardos* burned like funeral pyres. Flames twisted and roared on the morning breeze. Fallen men dotted the plain. She stared in dumb misery at every corpse she passed, hoping she wouldn't see Ephraim. She didn't, but she still felt as if she were eroding away. She was a sand woman, scoured to bone. She closed her eyes and felt numb.

We shouldn't have come here, Alonso.

He said nothing, too sickened to speak.

A dim hope snagged her. *Can you see any of them? Are there ghosts?*

It took him a moment before he composed himself to answer. His voice was ragged. *No. They've all gone on.*

Is Papa all right?

I don't know. I...I can't see him among the fallen.

It was a small comfort. She clung to it. Pray to the gods that Eva had taken him to safety. The wind picked up. Grit peppered her face. *It hurts, to leave them like that,* she told Alonso. *They should be buried.* A great pressure pressed down on her heart. It hurt to breathe.

Last rites are for the living, he said dully. *I think they'll understand.*

Wraiths of smoke followed them as they ascended the Neck. Her guard wrapped a stiff arm about her to keep her from falling from the saddle. She did her best to ignore his filthy thoughts and wondered about Joachin. He had missed all of this. She hoped he was safe somewhere.

I am with you. Always, Alonso reminded her.

I know. But you may not want to be. If we don't escape, I'll burn.

He said nothing for a long moment. She caught his emotions as they twisted past her—his despair over his inability to help, his fear for her worst of all. *We mustn't lose hope,* he said at last, grasping for shreds.

Chapter Forty-One: Cárcel

THE CAVALRY POUNDED past them. As Joachín caught sight of Tomás and then Miriam, he spurred his horse from the glade.

Barto grabbed the halter and pulled him up short. "Not yet."

"I can't leave her!"

"You have to. Make the brave charge now, and we'll burn for fools."

"But he'll kill her! And before that, who knows?"

Barto took his meaning. He grimaced. "Women are stronger than we give them credit for. Deal with it. You're useless to her dead."

Joachín clenched his teeth. The hardest thing to do was to bow to logic.

They let ten minutes pass before they nudged their horses from the trees. To any of the cavalry glancing behind, they seemed nothing more than two Luster monks heading to Elysir on temple business.

Our best chance will come when we pass the market, Alonso said. *Droop a little in the saddle as if you've given up, but not so much as to make him think you'll fall.*

She slumped. The guard tightened his grip about her waist, but he soon relaxed it. She'd been thinking the best time to throw herself from the horse was after they passed the town's gate, but Alonso was right. They needed a large crowd. She could flee between the tents. He would warn her of any blocked routes. If they escaped, she would climb the town's walls and make her way back to the Womb.

Tomás galloped ahead of her. His dark cape billowed behind him like the wings of a great bat. The town guards saw them coming and shouted at those milling at the gate. One farmer barely managed to pull his team of horses out of the way in time.

The market wasn't far. As Tomás trotted past it, Miriam lifted her knees high and leapt from the saddle. The guard let out a shout. She landed painfully on her knees. Hooves pranced about her head. She lurched to her feet and stumbled away. Her guard swore and vaulted from his horse.

"You fool!" Tomás yelled. "Grab her!"

Miriam, look out! Alonso shouted.

A merchant with a wide girth stepped into her path. She darted past him, but not fast enough. He snagged her by an arm and held her firmly. His broad face creased into a grin.

"Let me go!" she cried.

Rough hands clamped her about the wrists. "I'll take it from here, citizen," the guard said.

The merchant released her and wiped his hands on his doublet. "Glad to help. Is there a reward?"

"You have the thanks of the Solarium," the guard said gruffly. As he escorted her back to his horse, he shook her like a rat. "You think to cost me my post, you stupid *puta*? I'll toss you to the fires, myself."

She ignored him. Any retort would earn her a blow to the head.

We'll find another way, Alonso promised.

They rode toward the Solarium and bypassed it, heading instead to a low white-stuccoed building on the opposite side of the plaza. The place displayed few windows. Those it had were barred.

"Escort her to the women's section," Tomás told her captor. "I'll attend her there, shortly."

The guard marched her through the *cárcel's* front doors, gave a brief explanation to the corporals on duty, then pushed her past a number of cells inhabited by Elysir's more disreputable citizens. She ignored their catcalls. She was ushered into a second chamber that consisted of a narrow aisle with a barred cell on either side. In one of the holds, a putrid pool lay stinking. The guard pushed her into the cleaner one and locked the cell's door. He leered at her through the bars.

"I'll be back, once the Grand Inquisitor's done with you." He left the hold smirking and shut the door behind him.

She made a face, tested the bars. They refused to budge. The walls of the jail felt as if they were closing in on her, as if they barely held back the weight of the earth. Her fingers started to shake. *Alonso, how do we escape?* she asked, tamping down her panic.

We must wait and see what presents itself. Perhaps, when they come to take you.

The door opened. Tomás paused beneath the frame. He chuckled as she cringed. "How charming. My very own canary, perched in a gilded cage," he said.

He sauntered toward her. She backed away and watched him warily. He leaned against the bars and trailed a finger along one of the rails as if to tickle it. "You know," he said, "I've often wondered how you escaped me the first time. For a while, I actually thought you walked through walls." He held up a hand as if she might protest it. "Oh, yes, I thought you'd performed a wonder. I realize now that someone must have helped you. You'll tell me who that was, but I must say, what a good thing it all turned out to be."

He waited for her to reply. When she failed to, he cocked an eyebrow. "Aren't you wondering, 'why this change of heart?' Well, it's very simple, really. I had no idea of what you were capable. So, instead of killing you, I'm offering you employment. We'll work together. What do you think of that?" He smiled hugely, as if he had offered her the stars.

"I say," she said, hating him with every fibre of her being, "that because of you, my teacher lies dead, gutted like a fish and left to rot in her own blood."

He pursed his lips. "I would've spared her if I'd known what she was."

"She was a helpless old woman!"

"Not helpless. A sorceress. Like you."

"I am not a sorceress!"

"Witch then. Whatever term you prefer. The only reason she wasn't able to prevent her death was because she was so close to it. I've studied enough arcane texts to know it works that way. If it hadn't been *me*, it would have been something else. We all have our place and season."

She couldn't believe the nonsense he was spouting.

He lifted a hand as if to placate her. "I understand why you're upset. I don't blame you. She was valuable and had an extensive background we could have drawn upon. But aren't you even interested in what I have to offer? I'm giving you a chance. If you hadn't run off and spent the night in that hut, I never would have found your book."

The grimoire.

"I've read it thoroughly. I even tried a tattoo on myself and it works quite well, although it does make me curious." He beetled his brow. "Have you actually cut yourself with all of them? I can't fathom carving so many. The risk from infection would be great."

Any indication that she knew of her mother's book would damn her for a witch, although he was already convinced of her guilt. "I don't know what you're talking about," she said.

"Oh, don't be tedious. I can see you haven't used the truth tattoo on yourself, but that would defeat its purpose, I suppose." He pointed at her. "What you really need is a tattoo to make you a convincing liar. I couldn't find that spell in your book, however. Disappointing, but I suppose like any art, if you're talented enough, you can create the spell yourself."

He spread his arms wide as if to embrace her. "Don't you see, Inara? You have nothing to fear from me. There is so much we could do together. We could be partners, like Felipe and Maria. Who knows how far we might go, to what heights we might climb?"

His exuberance was genuine, but he was delusional. He thought she was Inara, her mother. And he had just compared them to the king and queen consort of Esbaña.

"I'm going to tell you something." He leaned toward her as if his confession were a gift. "I've never trusted anyone. But with your help, no one would be able to hide from me. I'd be privy to all secrets. Nothing would be beyond my grasp."

He glanced at her ruefully. "I can tell. You already think I'm too powerful. My influence isn't as strong as I'd like. I have enemies who whisper lies about me into important ears. I need to silence them for once and for all. With you by my side, we could benefit one another."

His strange yellow eyes had darkened to amber, his pupils had grown huge. "But why stop there?" he asked softly. "Why limit ourselves to mere worldly concerns? You have an arcane knowledge that I lack. You must appreciate how difficult this is for me to admit to you. But I need to understand more. I want to learn, to experiment. You could be my teacher. We could accomplish great things, unheard-of things. I could make you my queen. Together, we could find a way to rule and live, forever."

He held his breath.

"Well, perhaps not forever," he amended as if her silence suggested he retain sense, "but for a very long time. Life is far too short. Tell me—what, exactly, did you hope to accomplish in tattooing the High Solar? I've pondered it and pondered it. You attempted a resurrection spell. Obviously, it went awry. As annoying as he was, Alonso isn't up and walking among us. Still, I can't help think that it did something. I've read enough of your book to know that tattoos don't just fail. There's always some kind of a result. What was it?"

"As you suggest, the spell didn't work. If it had, the High Solar would have accused you of his murder."

He smirked. "I'll give you this—you are clever. You knew it was me from the start. I'll bet you don't know what I used, though."

She glared at him.

"Want to hazard a guess? No? Oleander leaves. Taken from the very bush in his room."

Gods! I want to throttle him!

"I liked the irony of it. He took care of that plant, and it took care of him. But in all seriousness, there *is* something more about this Alonso business you're not telling me." He pursed his lips. "I can almost taste it. Is it something to do with you? Have you extended your life, somehow?"

I told you that's what he's after! Immortality!

"Only the gods can grant that."

"Hmmm. I wonder. In any event, we can't stay here discussing it. I might be persuaded to let you live if you cooperate. Of course, I'd expect additional benefits." He paused to regard her. "You'd be my mistress. I can shelter and clothe you as if you were noble. I'll tell everyone you're my sister. Not that it would make any difference. They'd all turn a blind eye."

If he touches you, I'll kill him! I'll find a way!

If she agreed to it, it might provide them with a chance to escape before he expected her to fulfill her side of the bargain, but she couldn't stomach the thought of being near him. Anassa's death was seared into her memory. Even now, she saw the Diaphani men littering the plain. She gave Tomás a withering glance. "I'd rather couple with a ghoul."

All traces of his good humour disappeared. "I see." He smoothed down his gown. "Shall I tell you a secret, *Serina*? I used that truth tattoo on your beloved, and do you know what he did? He betrayed you. He told me where I could find you and the rest of the Diaphani. And just so you know? He came to me in the first place. He wanted a reward for selling you out. How much do you love him now, I wonder?"

Who was he talking about? Joachín?

"He's in the Solarium, indisposed. I have other plans for him, but eventually, he'll burn alongside you. I think it would be nice for the two of you to go together. I'd like to see that. Lovers consumed by the flames of their passion."

He smiled coldly. "You should have said 'yes'. You're such a beautiful young thing. I suppose it'll give me some comfort to watch your hair burst into sparks and your skin crack to char."

He was hoping for a reaction. When she didn't respond, his expression turned menacing. "But before all that, I will have some satisfaction."

He pulled a key from his robe and jammed it into the lock. With a clang, he jerked the cell door open.

She backed away, but there was nowhere to run. He leapt at her. She ducked past him, but he was horribly fast. Did her mother's book have a tattoo for speed? She thought it might. He caught her by the shoulders and threw her to the floor. The breath went out of her as he pinned her to the straw. *No!* Alonso bellowed, his voice a roar in her ears. Tomás clawed at her blouse. As his fingers touched her flesh, she flared with such sick need that she wanted to vomit. She fought him, but he was too strong. He forced her legs apart, fumbled with his habit. His penis was stiff and hard. For a second, it probed her, and then it shriveled into a limp, dead worm.

Horrified, he reached down and cupped himself. "What have you done?" he cried. She shoved him aside and stumbled for the door. He growled and snagged her by the ankle. As she kicked his hand away, she fell. He was on his feet again with a speed that went far beyond the norm.

"Force me and it falls off!" she shouted. Panting, she pointed at the tattoo that lay exposed beneath her blouse. "See this? It stops you." Anassa had said that no one could coerce her, but she doubted that went beyond sex. He could hurt her in other ways.

He glared at her, his expression warring between fury and disbelief.

"You can't kill me, either!" Pray to Lys he believed it.

"We'll see." He rose to his feet with as much dignity as he could muster. He was closer to the door than she was. She considered rushing past him but saw the futility of it. She would never get past him or the guards. She had a better chance once they escorted her from the jail.

"Send a messenger to the Solarium!" he shouted at the guard outside the door. "Make the plaza ready!"

He regarded her coldly. "I may not have had you as I would like, Witch, but the fires will. Unless you can thwart death, as you claim. I look forward to seeing if that is so."

A chill breeze swept past her as the door boomed shut behind him.

She sagged to her knees, the silence too complete.

At the market, Joachin spurred Fidel forward as Miriam tried to escape, but once again, Barto had prevented him from interfering. "Not yet," the huge man insisted as the guard took custody of her. They followed at a cautious distance. Barto argued against storming the *cárcel*. Of course, he was right, but it didn't help to admit it. "How can I think clearly, knowing what might be happening to her in there?" Joachin demanded.

"She'll endure." Barto glanced away. "Don't think about it."

"I'll kill the bastard. Twice. First for my mother, and then for her."

"We'll kill him when the time is right. Look." Barto pointed at a throng of Luster monks emerging from the Solarium. They were loaded down with planks, saws, and hammers. They congregated at a spot adjacent to the temple.

"They'll build a pulpit and a pyre. Tonight, when the Grand Inquisitor preaches about the evils of witchcraft, they'll march her there." Barto nodded at the larger of the two platforms being erected. "The whole town will attend. We can grab her between here and the jail."

Joachin conceded, but he didn't like it.

Chapter Forty-Two: Adrift

THE CROWD GROWLED, at other times, it cheered. Alonso would leave her for short periods only to return more distraught than ever. Miriam caught glimpses of what he saw: a thousand people filling the square, a pyre with twin pillars, the giant Orb of Sul passing on the shoulders of a dozen Luster monks as they made their way through the throng. While they waited, he told her again of his encounter with the Beings of Light, as if it might console her. It didn't.

The Host you encountered, she asked, unwilling to accept her fate. *Can they help?*

I don't know. I'll try to reach them. I will ask.

He faded from view. It had been three hours since Tomás's visit. The cell was cooler. The sun was setting. It wouldn't be long before the guards arrived.

The walls of the *cárcel* fell away. Alonso turned his attention inward. When the *hymenoptera* attacked him, he had withdrawn to a featureless, grey place, a refuge point that balanced between the earthly and immortal worlds. He hadn't known to go there, but he had nonetheless, as if fleeing by instinct alone. Sul hadn't responded to his pleas, but those who shone with the brightness of heaven had. He hoped the Host would hear him now. More than anything, he needed to help Miriam.

"Please." He beseeched the silence about him. "You heard me before. There must be some way you can save her."

He heard nothing, felt nothing. There was no great show of light, no comet of High Ones rushing past. If they dwelt in the same universe he did, they were distant. He was alone—a ghost in a void.

What was he doing wrong? When the Host had chased away the wasp demon, they'd been real, present. What was different about his reaching out to them now as compared to then?

Before, he had been in the direct line of attack. He'd been the one at risk. Was that the difference? He wasn't in danger even though Miriam was? They couldn't respond to her? Was it a question of authority, of responsibility in the spiritual plane? Hierarchy, he understood. He'd dealt with it his entire life. Did they have no influence in the mortal realm?

He turned in every direction and called them until his throat grew raw. He felt the shock waves of his voice ripple into the distance. He was adrift, a ship lost on a barren sea.

Then, from a long way off, he thought he heard, *You are floating, Your Brilliance.*

Anassa? he shouted. He peered through the mist, held his breath. No reply came. Had he imagined it? Or were her words a memory of what she had once said?

They had been in her *vardo.* She had told him he was in limbo, in transition. That much was obvious. Without Miriam to anchor him, he was lost, nowhere. Anassa said he had to choose. The talk had strayed into something about the ocean. Dear Sul, he had to remember. What was it?

How you choose to be, determines the evil or the grace you encounter.

That was it, yes! But what did she mean by it? He struggled with the thought like a fish on a line. He had to choose. He'd been too frightened to go on. How was this of any help to Miriam?

If he chose grace, he would encounter grace. If he chose evil...he wasn't about to do that. Evil was what he was trying to prevent. He had called to the embodiment of grace, but the Host had failed to respond. Why did he feel he was failing a test?

I don't know the answer to this riddle! he shouted. *I would answer it if I could, but I don't know what to say! Tell me what to do, and I'll do it!*

The silence was deafening. He felt as if the fog contained a multitude of invisible presences, all waiting, all watching. What good was the Host if it refused to appear?

He had been away from Miriam for too long. He had to go back to her. If there was nothing for it but to die with her on that pyre, then so he would. She was his life, his love. He couldn't imagine existing without her.

She won't face death alone, he thought. *If we must, we die together.*

But how could he let that happen? What was love if the lover expected as much from his beloved as he did from himself? Love gave everything it had, nothing less. It wasn't about being equal. It was about uplifting one's beloved, raising her above oneself. He couldn't allow her to suffer and die. He would not.

There had to be a way to save her. Pray to Sul he found it, before she was put to the torch.

Chapter Forty-Three: Foiled Plans

AS THE AFTERNOON plodded on, the plaza became congested. Amid the sawing and hammering, criers announced the burning every half hour. A parade formed as the town's guilds marched about the square. Joachin recognized the various brotherhoods: money lenders, silk merchants, metal smiths, glass blowers. Each group waved their pennants proudly. They also carried the gold and white flags of the Solarium. Food sellers conducted a brisk business. Near sunset, a dozen Luster monks brought forth the multi-rayed Orb of Sul. The heavy disk caught the last vestiges of the sun as it circled the plaza. Members of the clergy marched behind it, singing hymns. Joachin hated the sight of it all.

"Soon," he told Barto grimly. The large man nodded.

The air stank of pitch. In the centre of the largest platform, two pillars stood. The priests had painted them with tar. At their bases, mounds of kindling were stacked. Joachin wondered who the second pillar was for and realized with a start that it might have been him. The priests lifted the Orb up the temple's steps. As they disappeared inside, trumpeters blasted a fanfare. A phalanx of hooded Torch Bearers cleared a path through the crowd. Tomás descended the steps and strode for the pulpit.

If I kill him now, no one will expect it, Joachín thought. He could strike and flee. In the mass confusion that followed, there would be no burning. He stepped away from Barto and pushed through the crowd.

"Don't!" Barto shouted.

Tomás had climbed the narrow stairs to his pulpit. Joachín shoved people aside. They grumbled until they saw who pushed them, a cowled Luster monk in brown. A ring of torches marked a space where the mob wasn't allowed to cross. Beside each torch, a priest in gold and white stood with hands clasped.

He wasn't far now. In front of him, the spectators stood two-deep. Another fanfare of trumpets blared. All eyes turned to look at the *cárcel.* The crowd gave a collective shout. At the top of the jail's steps, Miriam stood, surrounded by guards.

Alonso floated above the square. The dislocation bothered him. He had wanted to return to Miriam but instead, he hovered over the pyre. The sun had set. Dark clouds piled on the horizon. Torches flickered along the periphery of the platform. In a pulpit looming over the people, Tomás stood.

There was a fanfare of trumpets. The jail's back door opened. Catching sight of Miriam, the crowd roared. Her wrists were bound, she had been forced to carry a candle. The flame wavered, her hands trembled. Alonso flew to her.

Have you thought of anything? she asked dully.

Shame crushed him. How could he tell her he hadn't?

Tomás is about to preach his sermon. After that, he'll list my sins against the temple and Sul. And then.... She didn't finish the thought.

He remembered the flames that had torched him, the agony following his first death.

Alonso?

I'm here, he said. Would it be the same, this time? He suspected it would be worse.

Were you able to contact the Host?

Not yet.

She sagged, close to defeat.

Guards set hands on her forearms. A priest prodded her from behind. She flinched and swore at him from over her shoulder. Alonso took heart that she still had a spark of fight left in her. She held her head high as they forced her down the stairs.

Joachín fought his way back through the crowd. There wasn't enough time to kill Tomás. He needed to save Miriam first, kill the bastard after. *Forgive me, Maré,* he thought, knowing that his mother would understand. He found Barto. They forced their way through the onlookers, intent on intercepting Miriam before she reached the pyre.

They were ten feet from her when she blinded one of the guards. The candle's flame did little harm, but the wax was another matter. The crowd roared and hemmed her in as she tried to bolt. The rest of the guards rained blows upon her head until Tomás bellowed at them to stop. Joachín cursed his ill luck. They would be doubly vigilant now. She'd stolen away his element of surprise.

Think, Joachín, he told himself. *All your life, you've lived by your wits. What won't they expect?*

He considered his nemesis, watching from the pulpit. Tomás looked sure of himself, confident of the night's outcome. He turned his regard from Miriam to gaze serenely at the Solarium as if he were in silent conversation with Sul. Beyond the open doors, the nave glowed, lit by its eternal flame.

You are soul burdened, my son. Let me relieve your darkness with light.

The memory of the Solar's words, spoken so long ago in Herradur, seemed to come from nowhere. Joachín's mouth fell open. He shut it as quickly. "Come," he told Barto. "I know what we must do. It's time to pay our respects."

Barto eyed him dubiously. Then understanding dawned on his face.

Faith is a wonderful thing, Joachín thought as Barto's expression reflected his newfound belief.

Chapter Forty-Four: Sacrifice

JOACHÍN WAS IN the crowd, Alonso! I saw him! He was dressed as a Luster monk!

I'll see if I can find him. He floated above her and scanned the crowd. He couldn't see Joachin anywhere, and gave up after a number of tries. Beneath him, spectators milled like ants. The guards pushed Miriam up the pyre's steps. The mob screamed as a priest bound her to a post. Alonso panicked. They'd run out of time.

Please! he beseeched, looking at the dark sky. *Show me a way!*

There was a disturbance at the pulpit. A Luster monk approached Tomás and whispered something into his ear. Tomás's head snapped up at the news. He stared at the temple. Alonso ignored him and floated higher. Beneath him, torches wavered with cruel intent. Despairing, he looked to the hills.

Far away, above the Womb, a heavy wall of cloud built.

Alonso caught his breath. With a bolt of insight, he knew what he had to do. Anassa had said it, her words were an echo in his mind: *How you choose to be determines the grace or evil you encounter.*

It wasn't about goodness intervening or wickedness destroying, he realized. It was about choice—his choice. The Host couldn't operate here, at least, not to the extent that he needed them. He, however, had the freedom to act. He had an advantage Miriam did not. Death granted him the ability to choose whatever he wanted to become.

It meant annihilation, irrevocable change. He would lose himself completely. There were no guarantees. He might not retain any memory of who he was. He hadn't crossed the threshold the first time. He realized now, he had created his own hell and had been trapped in it. The fires were of his creation. The flames had been borne from his outrage, his need to avenge his death. Miriam had called him forth, had given him a second chance. She'd given him much more—a moment of passion he would cherish for as long as he could. But now, he would save her.

She was a better person than he had ever been—beautiful, wise beyond her years, practical, and honest. He would do this for her. Already, he could feel himself changing. Tears pooled in his eyes with such substance that he felt their wetness, something he thought he would never feel again. It was time to bid her goodbye.

Miriam. Even to his own ears, his voice sounded slurry. *My love.*

She leaned her head against the ugly post, closed her eyes to shut out the torches.

Alonso?

I have to go.

The words struck her like a blow. How could he suggest such a thing? They would die together! *Don't leave me, Alonso!*

I will always be with you, my heart. You'll understand, I think. I've never loved any woman like I've loved you, Miriam. And I always will. But I must do this. It's the only way. Farewell.

Alonso!

Her fear and helplessness tore at his heart, but he couldn't tarry. Tomás was nearing the end of his sermon. *Every word that spouts from his mouth is an affront to grace,* Alonso thought. He would wash that filth away. He would save his Miriam, his love. He had no more doubts about his place in the world.

He lifted his arms and embraced the sky.

Chapter Forty-Five: Fire and Rain

JOACHÍN AND BARTO slipped into the Solarium via a side door. They ran down empty halls and slid around a corner to enter the nave. A lone monk toiled at the eternal flame, tipping oil into the great basin that fed it. Above him, the Orb of Sul hung like a golden spider.

"Umberto! There you are!" Barto said jovially. Joachín ducked his head inside his cowl. As the aging cleric shuffled up to them, Joachín realized he was the same doorkeeper who had drugged him a night ago. Barto stepped in front of him to bar his view.

"Where else would I be?" Umberto asked.

"Well, here, of course," Barto said. "I've come to relieve you, Brother. Tor Tomás thought you might like to witness the proceedings."

"That doesn't sound like him."

"No, but he's in a fair mood. Go on. We'll tend the flame for you."

Umberto peered around Barto to squint at Joachín.

"If you don't hurry, you'll miss the burning!" Barto waved him on. "He's nearing the end of his sermon."

"Well, if you're sure...." The old man hesitated.

"Come back and tell us about it."

"I'll do that!" he conceded. He smiled wolfishly. "It's been a long time since I've seen a witch sizzle. A great victory for us! We'll send her screaming back to her evil consort!" He waved and hobbled for the great portal.

As soon as Umberto was out of sight, Joachín ran for one of the tapestries that hung beside the altar. Barto made for the other. Between them, the Orb of Sul hung from ropes suspended from the high ceiling.

Joachín found his cluster of pulleys behind the cloth. He glanced at Barto to see if he had located his. With a nod, they released the ropes, straining not to let the Orb fall too quickly. "How long do you think it will take to catch?" Joachín called.

"It's gilded wood," Barto replied. "As soon as the gold melts, it should go up like kindling."

Joachín's muscles screamed with complaint, but they managed to lower the thing without dropping it. As the Orb settled onto the sun altar, Joachín tied off his ropes. The plan was to keep it upright so that it caught before the ropes gave. He darted out from behind his tapestry. Barto did the same. They watched for a moment as the lower part of the Orb curled into flame. Soon, the main body was engulfed. Tongues of fire ran along the Orb's legs and up the pulley lines. The heat of the conflagration grew intense. The Orb swayed and crashed. Barto ran to the temple's landing. "Fire!" he shouted. "The Solarium is on fire!"

With grim satisfaction, Joachín watched as hundreds of faces turned their way. Beyond the crowd, priests held torches, but they hadn't thrown them at Miriam yet.

"Fools! Don't stand there gawking!" Tomás shouted at the crowd. "Get water! Douse it!"

The mob began to move. Joachín didn't wait to see how they would handle the flames. Thunder rumbled overhead. As the crowd surged, he fought his way to Miriam.

They hadn't immediately set her alight as she thought they would. Instead, the priests stripped her and gagged her with a garrote. The crowd screamed with excitement as they beheld her tattoos. She was a witch—the demon marks proved it. She closed her eyes during this indignity, not wanting to acknowledge Tomás's open lust or his approval of the priests' handling of her. At the last moment, she opened her eyes and gazed at the night sky. Where was Alonso now? Tears trickled down her face. Without him, life had no meaning.

She didn't blame him. There'd been nothing they could do. She knew that as surely as she knew she was about to die. The pain would be terrible, but in death, she would join him. Perhaps he waited for her on the other side. Together, they'd enter paradise. She hadn't believed in a heaven. Now, she hoped.

A crash came from overhead. Thunder. She felt a smattering of wet against her skin. Rain. It was raining.

From across the square, someone shouted, "Fire!"

Of course, there was fire. She was about to burn. Torches were going to fall at her feet.

"Don't stand there gawking! Douse it!"

Tomás wasn't leering now. Instead, he waved his hands at the mob as if he might move them. Across the square, flames billowed inside the Solarium. Yellow streamers writhed at the door and wavered behind windows. People ran, formed a line. A crack of lightning split the sky. She squinted through the growing wet. The rain came down with a roar.

Several priests threw their torches onto her pyre. One torch smoked at her feet, but the kindling failed to catch. The downpour continued unending.

No one watched her now. She saw her chance and shook the fuzziness from her mind. She squeezed her neck from the garrote. They hadn't clamped it tight—all the better to watch a witch scream and writhe. She struggled against the ropes and managed to free her feet and knees, but the cords binding her chest were too tight. She kept fighting, not caring how the ropes cut her. She thought of Ephraim and how he had suffered. Her wounds were nothing compared to what his had been. She thought of the mother she barely remembered, who had burned on a pillar. Her family was dead, her Tribe, lost. She hoped that some of the Diaphani survived. For them, she would endure. She would escape and find the living. She would honour their dead.

Alonso! It's raining! We have a way out! She held her breath, hoping for a response. There was none. She'd felt their link break. He was gone.

Why couldn't he have waited another minute? She tasted rain on her lips. Salty. The sky's tears mingled with her own. Tears streamed down her face, merging with the rain. She couldn't see through the downpour. The Solarium was a bright smear.

Lightning lit the sky. The air was charged; she felt the buzz of it on her flesh. It reminded her of the intimacy they had shared, as impossible and unexpected as that had been. Where was he now, her love? What would he say about the rain?

The revelation struck her in a flash. The sudden illumination left no room for doubt. Alonso hadn't left her, but he *had* changed. He was still with her, beating down. She let out a wail, realizing what he had done.

Gods! Alonso! You did this for me? Why?

The rain pelted, made her skin slick. She knew why. He had loved her more than he had loved himself. He had given her this chance. She couldn't waste his gift. She wriggled, hoping to squeeze past the last ropes. A Luster monk noticed her attempt and leapt onto the platform. He grabbed her with wet hands. They were hot, unpleasant. She was too panicked to recognize their touch. She fought him off.

"It's me! Hold still! I'll cut the cords!"

Joachin. She gasped, held her breath as he did so. Strangely enough, her nakedness before him didn't bother her. What mattered was the attention they would draw as they tried to leave. "They'll see us," she said.

"They won't." As the last rope gave way, she sagged into his arms. His fingers burned. Desire lifted its unwelcome hood—she choked, affronted. How could she feel such a thing for Joachin after losing Alonso? Grief and the instinct to survive were impelling her. That had to be it. Joachin pulled the habit from his body and dropped it over her head. His face was a mess and his shirt was soaked in blood, but he seemed to be moving without pain—his own body's need to survive. "Quickly, now," he said. He jumped from the pyre and pulled her after him.

Hope suffused her, honing her mind to cut through any loss. "My grimoire," she said. "It's a book of tattoos. Tomás has it. He said you were in the temple. Do you know where it is?" She would need it to guide her, to serve the Diaphani.

Joachín looked uncomfortable.

"We have to find it. It's the only thing I have that will show me the ways of the Tribe."

"Let me get you to a safe place, first."

"No! We go now, Joachín, while their attention is on the fire!"

"Miriam, I don't think...."

"And don't ever leave me again! There have been too many deaths. I have to make amends. We are family, Joachín."

His face twisted with passion, remorse—she wasn't sure what. "All right," he replied. "I pray you don't regret it." He took her by the hand. His dedication felt as strong as her own. "Let's go."

They took a less frequented route through the Solarium. He and Barto had used it on their way to set the fire. He made it a point to never forget any path he had taken.

They encountered no one as they ran through the halls. The priests still battled the blaze. They came to the alcove that led to Tomás's quarters. Joachín made sure the way was clear, and then he drew her into the recess. The door was unlocked. He eased it open to listen for anyone who might be inside. Satisfied that no one was there, he pulled her into the darkness but left the door ajar.

"Wait here. Watch the outer hall. Let me know if anyone comes," he said.

She nodded.

He moved with calm assurance past bulky shapes that loomed in the darkness, the suite's desk and chairs. Before him, the black entry to the second room gaped like a pit from hell. He flinched, remembering the punishment he had taken there. He glanced back at Miriam. She had moved away from the light, but not so far that she couldn't hear anyone approach. He could just make her out standing beside a crenellated window. The long drapes had been pulled aside. *Good*, he thought. *She's also keeping an eye on what's happening out there.*

He slipped into the second room, which was as dark as pitch. The book had been on the smaller table behind the door. He turned and felt for the table's edge, passed his hands over it. The surface was bare.

He fought for calm. If the book wasn't there, someone had taken it. The obvious choice was Tomás. If he had returned here after capturing Miriam, he would've discovered him and Barto gone, although he might have thought that Barto had already disposed of him. *Let that be the case,* he hoped.

He felt his way to the larger table. Other than some scattered pots and dried blood—his—the surface was clear. The other obvious spot was the desk in the adjacent room.

As he turned, his boot caught on a black lump that leaned against a table leg. He reached down and felt the pyramid trapping his foot. The grimoire. He picked it up. It had fallen. Why? Surely, Tomás wouldn't be so careless as to drop his precious book, unless....

Unless he had dropped it in his hurry to hide.

His skin crawled. He pulled his knife from its sheath. A chill curled about him like the onset of winter. He made no sound as he stepped softly into the first room. Miriam stood by the window, but she wasn't alone. A shadow pressed tightly against her side. A knife glinted at her throat, catching the reflection from the window.

"There you are," Tomás said pleasantly in the darkness. "You caught me at a bad time. Luckily, I heard you, before you barged in here." He shook Miriam. "Give me the book, or I'll slit her from ear to ear."

Joachín didn't move.

"You have something I want. I have something you want," Tomás said patiently. "Lay the grimoire on the desk, and I'll let her go."

"You're lying," Joachín said.

"Well, you'd know, wouldn't you? Tell you what. Drop the book, and I'll release her. You save her before I stab her in the back."

They were too far apart. He couldn't reach her fast enough. Tomás would kill her the instant she moved.

Or would he? Maybe he was bluffing. Maybe Miriam was more valuable to him alive. But why put her on the pyre, if that were so?

Unless Tomás didn't think she *would* die. Maybe he put her there to force a miracle, to see if something intervened to thwart her death. The fire in the nave had saved her. So had the rain, as well timed as that had been. Perhaps Tomás needed her *and* the book. The only way he'd release her was if he thought he might lose one or the other.

"Poor odds," Joachín said. The truth. He took a step for the door as if to leave, praying his insights were correct.

"What are you doing?" Tomás pressed the knife's point beneath Miriam's ear. She yelped. Joachín hoped the bastard hadn't cut her.

"I'm leaving."

"But she's your beloved! You love her!" He shook Miriam. "Ask him if he loves you! He can't lie."

"You're insane!"

"Ask him or I'll cut your wretched throat!"

She cried out. "Do you love me, Joachín?"

He needed to distract Tomás, to get between them. Maybe the truth spell would allow him to say what he needed as long as he kept the truth fixed firmly in his mind.

I don't just love you. I adore you.

"I...ah...dore...don't...." The words tripped unwillingly over his tongue. "I'm stealing this book." He slid past them for the door, knowing he looked like scum for leaving. He hoped the taunt would force Tomás to move. It did.

With a growl, Tomás lunged at him with the knife, holding Miriam before him like a shield. Joachín blocked the knife and thrust at his ribs, hoping for a killing strike beneath the arm. The blade struck, but not where he had planned. Some force turned the point from where he meant it to go. As Tomás clutched himself, Joachín grabbed Miriam by the wrist and pulled her out of harm's way.

"Guards!" Tomás shouted. He stumbled after them, clutching his side. A dark stain spread between his fingers.

Flee! You won't have a second chance!

Maré? Joachín asked. The voice had been female, but it hadn't sounded like his mother.

One more strike and he'd finish the bastard, rid himself of her death debt. He thrust the grimoire at Miriam and raised his knife.

"Joachín!" she gasped. The book fell to her feet. Blood dripped from a line across her throat.

"You're cut!" The decision was made. Given the choice between a dead girl and a dead priest, he knew which one he had to choose. He caught her as she crumpled. The grimoire would have to stay where it was. He only had two hands.

With Miriam in his arms, he bolted for the alcove. Tomás leaned against the doorframe and screamed. Red bloomed on his habit. "Guards!" he hollared again. The effort proved to be too much for him. Groaning, he slumped to his knees.

Joachin charged back the way they had come. His heart thudded with suppressed fury, his veins flowed with ice. He had failed—again. He hadn't collected his mother's death debt, but some things took priority, some things were more important than his honour and his pride.

Like the lifeblood staining his hands.

He had to get her somewhere safe, had to see what damage Tomás had wrought. Someday, he would return to kill him, but today was not that day.

His boots pounded against the marble. From behind them, the sound of pursuit built like thunder.

Chapter Forty-Six: Destiny

THANKFULLY, THE CUT was shallow, but the shock of everything that had occurred made Miriam's mind fold in on itself like a bird tucking its head beneath a wing. A cold lethargy settled over her as she and Joachín made their way through the streets of Elysir. When she tried to recall their flight later, snatches of memory came: Joachín setting her on her feet, the streets filled with blurs of people, the town constabulary knocking heads to clear the square. She had to climb a slippery wall. Her legs kept wilting beneath her. Joachín set her astride a horse. They galloped through the cold and wet. Eventually, they lay shivering beneath the eaves of a tree. She couldn't stop shaking despite his warm arms about her.

He kept repeating her name, over and over. She wished he would stop. His voice pierced the grey fog. Was he afraid of getting lost? Her neck burned. He rubbed her arms and back. The blood returned to her limbs and after a time, she felt warmer. She fell asleep and knew nothing more until they woke the next morning, tangled together like two moths in a web.

She opened her eyes to find him watching her, his pupils dark beneath slitted lids. Had he slept? His face was a mass of cuts, his nose bloody and askew. She pulled herself free from his arms and headed for the stream to wash her face. The cut at her neck was tender, but it wasn't deep. Dawn broke through the trees in thin pink bands. Raindrops glistened on the branches. The rain had stopped.

She was more herself now than she'd been last night, but she still felt numb. She hadn't met her death on a pyre, but she felt dead nonetheless.

Alonso.

She reached for that place where he had dwelt and found an empty room, its hearth cold and forsaken. She covered her face with her hands and drew in a ragged breath. The lump in her throat swelled. A wrenching pain tore at her heart. With a wail, she fell to her knees and wept without shame. She clawed at the gravel in the stream. Her body ached. She wanted Alonso. She was an empty husk without him.

Strong arms wrapped themselves about her. Joachin muttered words of comfort. At first, she didn't understand him, but finally, two words made sense. *The Womb.*

His voice was strange, faltering. "You can stay...gone half an hour at most, maybe some escaped...I need to know."

She stood on shaky legs. She was spent, tired—it was the aftermath of her grief, she knew. She wiped the tears from her face. Alonso was gone, but he had given his life for her. She couldn't waste his sacrifice. She had to endure, had to be strong for her Tribe. "No. We go together, Joachin. They're my people. I have to see."

"They're my people, too," he said sadly.

He looked as if he had survived a battle, but it steadied her. "You should wash your face," she told him. A trivial thing, but she needed someone, other than herself, on whom to focus. He knelt at the stream's edge as if to please her and dabbed at his face as best he could. When he was done, she asked him how he had broken his nose. He waved the question aside. It wasn't a concern. They found Fidel and mounted up.

The view from the Neck devastated her. She had known what to expect, but the stark reality of it pushed her close to a breaking point again. Instead of *vardos*, blackened timbers pointed at the sky, their ribs exposed and smoking. In many places, clusters of carrion crows perched and squabbled. There was little doubt over what they fought. Joachín mouthed an oath and spurred Fidel into a gallop. The horse leapt beneath them and bore them down the slope, churning the gravel to dust. As they drew close, the birds reeled into the sky. The air was fetid. Relief came with a puff of breeze.

The first corpse lay on its side like a dead ox, its eyes pecked away. Flies crawled over the multiple stab wounds. Miriam recognized the blood-drenched waistcoat.

Hector.

She bit down on a cry. The sherry merchant had been so full of life, so buoyant. He had offered to marry her, a joke to be sure, but he would have treated her like a queen. She swallowed against the lump in her throat. Hector hadn't liked 'proper'. This was what came from the Solarium's idea of propriety. He should not have been cut down to this sad, sorry lump. "We have to bury him, Joachín," she said.

He didn't speak. He seemed stricken beyond words. She understood it, but the depth of his grief surprised her. He felt the loss as keenly as she did.

They moved to the next corpse and scared away the birds. Donaldo Franco died with a sword run through his throat, silencing his fine voice forever. Not far from him lay his son, Jaime. Jaime's back resembled a carcass of beef, riddled with stab wounds. In a parody of love, he lay sprawled over his dead bride, Kezia. Their spilled blood had formed their bridal bed. To the last, Jaime had tried to protect her.

They found two corpses inside a charred caravan next. The bodies curled in on themselves like torched kittens. Perhaps the two had hidden, hoping to elude the invaders. Miriam hugged herself tightly, sickened.

"Come away." Joachín set an arm about her shoulders. A wave of anger pricked her. She needed to know who these two were. She had to know who they all were. She shrugged him aside.

"Let me go! I have to see...." The words caught in her throat. From the look on his face, he knew exactly who these two were. She caught her breath and stared at the torched *vardo*. An appalling possibility occurred to her. She shied away from it, stared about the compound in a panic, hoping to find something that negated the terrible truth.

There was no avoiding it.

Papa and Eva. This had been Eva's *vardo*.

With an agonized cry, she fell to her knees and dissolved into great, wracking sobs. Her wails turned foreign; they hammered her from the inside, battering her ribs until they threatened to break. She couldn't stop crying. Joachín tightened his arms about her. Finally, after what seemed like a lifetime of grief, she pushed him away. She didn't want to be held, didn't want to be contained, even by someone who cared. Her whimpers grew thin, like the calls of a tern lost at sea. An ocean could not contain the tears she shed.

After a while, Joachín wrapped his arms about her again. This time, she let him stay. Despite the heat of the morning, she felt cold. He was comforting, a piece of driftwood to which she could cling. He was solid, not about to slip away. She leaned on his shoulder, grateful for his steadfastness.

"I never should have come here," she whispered. "If I hadn't, everyone would be alive."

He shifted slightly. "It wasn't your fault."

"Of course, it was. This wouldn't have happened if not for me."

"What I meant is, you didn't do this. Tomás did. May he rot in hell."

She thought of Tomás and shivered. Once he recovered from his wound, it wouldn't be long before he was after them again. He had said that Joachín had told him where she was, that she was being harboured by the Diaphani, but that was unlikely. "How did this happen?" she asked. "I thought we were safe. I wanted to believe it."

He stiffened.

"Joachín?" She turned in his arms.

He set his forehead on her shoulder and let it rest there. She felt a swirl of emotion in the contact, so tormented that she couldn't make out what it was.

"What is it?" Of course, it had to be grief. They hadn't yet found Guillermo or the Montoyas. His family lay dead with the rest.

He shook his head, hid his face in her hair.

"Joachín?" She drew away from him.

He finally met her gaze. His eyes were blacker than she had ever seen them. A memory haunted them, held him captive.

"I did this." He swallowed as if the taste were bitter. "All of this is my fault."

Tomás's words rang through her head in cruel mockery. *Shall I tell you a secret, Serina? He betrayed you. He told me where I could find you with all the rest of the Diaphani. He wanted a reward for selling you out.*

"I thought I could fool him," Joachín continued miserably. "I was going to murder him to avenge my mother and then return to you. Instead, I betrayed everyone."

She stared at him.

"He carved me with a truth tattoo. I told him everything—where you were, where the Tribe was, how to get to the Womb. Later, I convinced his henchman to let me go."

His words turned her cold. Behind them, her father was a shriveled, blackened husk. "You told him?" she demanded. He didn't have to repeat it. She felt his betrayal like a stench on the skin.

He closed his eyes as if the truth were too painful to bear. "I didn't mean for any of this to happen, Miriam. When I left, my blood was up. I couldn't stand the thought of you marrying Ferrara. I told myself it didn't matter. I convinced myself that I had wasted my time with you, that I needed to collect my mother's death debt. My pride got in the way. I've destroyed everything."

She lifted a hand to silence him. It didn't matter that he was telling her the truth. The truth was too terrible to excuse. She stood.

"Miriam, I am sorry. You have no idea how sorry I am."

She refused to look at him. It would have been better if were dead. Why hadn't he died, instead of Alonso? "Don't ever speak to me, again."

"Forgive me! If I must, I'll spend the rest of my life making it up to you!"

His words set her ablaze. "You think you can make this up to me, Joachín? You can *never* make this up to me! Don't you understand? You've killed my father! He died a terrible death because of you! All of the Tribe did. None of them are left! Do you see anyone walking around? Talking? Everyone I see is *dead*. Everyone! All because of you!"

"That may be, but you're still alive. I won't leave you."

"Well, I can leave you!" She set off for the stream. The water sparkled in the morning sun as if nothing wrong had occurred. She would leave the Womb. She would never speak to him again. She wished he would take Fidel and ride away.

In the meantime, there were bodies to which she had to attend. The rocks lining the stream bed were of a suitable size for burial. She would cover Papa first, and then the rest. Later, she would light a candle to remember Alonso. Her face twisted with disgust. Where, in this destruction, would she find a candle? She waded into the stream and filled her skirt with stones.

A crack and a snap split the air. Joachin was pulling charred planks from Eva's *vardo*.

She dropped the rocks. They tumbled into the water with a splash. What did he think he was doing? In a fury, she clawed up the stream's bank, drenched to the waist. She ran back to him and yanked his hands from the blackened timbers. "Don't you touch them!"

He regarded her dismally. "I'm making them a pallet. I was going to hang them in the trees."

"You will do no such thing!" She had never heard of such rubbish. What did he mean to do, dangle them like cocoons?

"It's a Diaphani custom," he said dully. "I may be half Diaphani, but I know some of the rites. *Maré* told me. Lys's elements are air and water. Sul's are fire and earth. They revere the goddess. I think it might be more appropriate to build aerial graves."

She glared at him.

"If we were near the sea, we could release their remains to the water, but scaffolding is also an acceptable form. I don't think they'd like to be left in the ground."

There was so much she didn't know. She was half Diaphani as he was, but he knew more of their customs. "Do what you will then, but not with my father. He isn't Diaphani. I'll bury him." Without another word, she turned to Ephraim's corpse. She touched his scabbed skin. Her fingers shook. She blinked hard to keep the tears away. She would not cry, not anymore. And especially not in front of Joachin.

"Allow me," he said. "I'll pull him free."

"Get away from him! I can do this!" She had done it before with Gaspar.

He stared at her as if seeing her for the first time. Then he nodded and stepped aside.

A sharp cry floated on the wind. It seemed to drop from the sky, like a kestrel giving voice. They glanced in the direction from which it came. High above them, at the entrance to the women's pool, a small figure stood. It set a hand to its mouth and waved. "*El Lince!*" it shouted. "*Maré!* He's come back for us!"

"Little Cat!" Joachin said, astounded.

From the cave's mouth, a woman appeared at the child's side. She lifted a hand to shield her eyes.

"Dear gods! They're all right!" He ran to them with his arms outstretched. Luci and Casi met him half way and caught him in a crushing embrace. Iago, his cousin, appeared at the cave's mouth and clambered down to meet them. They had gone deeply into the mountain, far beyond the Guard's reach. Guillermo had insisted that Iago accompany Luci and Casi into the caves. Someone had to protect them. As Iago relayed events, other women and children emerged. They had hidden and had waited until now to come forth. As the women fanned out to find their fallen men, wails rose from about the burnt camp. Miriam did what she could to comfort them.

As the sun set, all those who had fled or died were accounted for. A quarter of the Tribe had survived. Some members weren't present among the living or the dead, Rana and the Ferraras among them.

"Where are the Ferraras?" Joachin asked. The Tribe sat around a fire in the lee of a boulder.

"Gone," said Ximen. As well as protecting his mother and sister, Iago had rescued the blind man and had led him into the caves.

"How did they manage that?" Joachin demanded.

Miriam regarded him sourly. Other than Ximen who was infirm, Joachin and Iago were the only surviving adult males. Being the more mature of the two, Joachin had taken on the mantle of leadership. He had dried tears and organized scaffolding parties. He'd sent the children fishing for supper and authorized cook fires. Without questioning his role, the women deferred to him. Their regard sickened Miriam. Joachín had no business playing patriarch.

"There's another way from the Womb," Iago said. "It's a hidden tunnel through the caves—a long, difficult trek. It's too small to accommodate the *vardos*, but we've always known of it. They went that way. Back to Tolede, I expect."

"They didn't fight with the rest of the men?" Joachín asked.

Iago sneered. "They said they had to take Leonora and Rana to safety."

"So, Rana is gone, too." Miriam didn't know what to think. Obviously, Rana didn't share her sense of responsibility.

"We are bereft," Ximen said sadly, his pale eyes watching the flames as if he saw the past unfolding there. "But all is not lost." He surveyed the host of glum faces about him. "We shall endure as the goddess pleases. We have our seer and our dreamer." He smiled faintly.

Miriam wouldn't speak for Joachín, but her conscience dictated that she speak for herself. "I am here to serve you," she told them, "but I'm no longer a seer." The loss of that was painful. She missed Alonso more than ever. "That which made me so is gone."

"How can that be?" Casi's eyes were wide. Luci shushed her.

"I was a seer because I carried the spirit of a dear friend," Miriam explained to them. "I resurrected him through a tattoo. He showed me everything I needed to know. He died yesterday, with the rest of our men."

She would not cry before them. Luci nodded as if understanding. Her eyes were damp. Some things were too precious to share.

"But how could he die, if he was a spirit already?" Casi asked.

"Casi," Luci cautioned.

"I don't know," Miriam replied. "I think I held him here, or perhaps he chose to stay with me for a while. He's gone, now."

"May he rest in peace." Ximen's solemn gaze met hers. Somehow, he knew. The old man lifted his hand in blessing.

"I, too, have something to confess," Joachín began haltingly. Miriam glanced at him. She didn't want to hear his confession. She couldn't forgive him, she never would. She doubted if the women of the Tribe would excuse him, either. Would they stab him or stone him, once they knew? He was a dreamer and valuable to the Tribe, but his betrayal had cost them dear lives. Fathers, husbands, and sons had perished.

She rose from the circle and walked into the night. The wind came up, smelling of rain. In the trees near the stream, the bodies of the dead fluttered in their shrouds. She had helped to set them there. Silently, she walked past the scaffolds and came at last, to Ephraim's grave. She knelt beside it and rested her brow against his headstone. She had carved a six-sided star on it. Ephraim had never lived openly as a Juden, but there had been times when his faith had expressed itself. He had once explained the star's significance. The two entwined triangles meant 'as above, so below'. She hoped that was so—that he existed 'above' somewhere. Overhead, the stars shone brightly.

The breeze brought her news—small cries of dismay. Joachín was telling them. She wanted to block out his voice, a low drone that seemed as poisonous as the *hymenoptera* that Rana had called into being. Joachín didn't deserve to be heard, he didn't merit forgiveness. But perhaps he didn't deserve to die, either. There had been too many deaths. Maybe the women would vote to banish him. She could agree to that. His pride had brought the Tribe to ruin. It had killed her father, and it had killed Alonso. In his arrogance, Joachín thought he could outwit Tomás, and he had been wrong.

And yet, you, too, are guilty of pride.

She startled at the voice. Was that true?

How can you fault him entirely, when your own vanity made you stay?

Before Alonso had gone, she'd thought she could serve the Tribe as both healer and seer. She had always wanted to be recognized as a healer, even before she and Ephraim were on the run. She had liked the recognition. And she had wanted power—the kind Anassa wielded. Anassa had made her an important figure among her adopted people, but their association had been a mistake. She and Ephraim should have left the Tribe when they were able. Like Joachín, she had brought disaster upon them all. Even if he hadn't been involved, Tomás would have found her eventually.

And was it not pride that had enticed you in the first place? the relentless voice asked. *The idea that you could resurrect the High Solar in order to save your father?*

Her face reddened. She felt as if she were being taken to task by a relentless tutor. Fear had spurred her, but fear hadn't been the only factor. From the very beginning, her actions had determined her destiny as well as the fate of everyone she met. She was as much to blame as Joachín was. Maybe more so.

Destiny, Anassa had said. She didn't want to believe in it. Destiny was the purview of the gods. Yet, in that first act of carving Alonso's flesh with a resurrection tattoo, she had invoked a goddess. She had dedicated herself to Lys, not Alonso. The goddess's mark was on her stomach. Such an allegiance had its price.

If all of this was destiny, then Joachín was also a part of it.

"I don't like this!" she said, glaring at the moon. "You don't play fair, Lys! You take more than I'm willing to give!" She clenched her fists. Had she known, she never would have made the bargain. Her father was dead. He hadn't died in a torture chamber, but he had died here, on this moonlit plain. Lys had granted him days, not years. That wasn't fair. The goddess's purposes were not her own. And then, there was Alonso....

He had been another unforeseen development, but in the end, the greatest love of her life. She would never love another. She missed him more than Ephraim. She felt so alone without him.

She rubbed her arms. It was getting cold, but she didn't want to return to the fire. Unlike Joachín who had told Tomás that he didn't love her, Alonso had. What if she and Alonso had met without the restrictions of priest and parishioner, or noble and commoner, separating them? Would they have married? She would have been honoured to have been his wife. He had been the perfect man—the other half of her soul. How could she carry on, being half of whom she was?

Instead, she'd been left with Joachín—who *didn't* love her. She'd been foolish to think that he did.

Why dwell on this? She hated Joachín. He would never be the man Alonso was. She had been attracted to him, true. He was handsome, rakish, unreliable, and more than a little dangerous. Her stomach churned whenever he touched her. All right—admittedly, not her stomach. He was warm, smelled of the earth, but that was animal magnetism scenting the air, nothing more. The thing to remember was, he had betrayed her.

He came back to save you, the annoying voice said.

Out of guilt, she told it.

A shooting star cut across the sky. She heard the crunch of a boot on stone. She didn't turn. She knew who it was. Joachín.

Why couldn't he leave her alone? He didn't love her any more than she loved him. Whatever she felt had been infatuation, made worse by Tomás's meddling. It wasn't the deep love she felt for Alonso.

"Miriam?"

She glared at him.

"They've forgiven me." He spread his hands in mock humility. "They said we're too few to hold blame or grudges. They know the power of tattoos. They understand the compulsion I was under. They said too many of us have been lost. They don't want to lose you or me, no matter what's happened."

You or me. Why couldn't he speak for himself?

"Ximen thinks your sight may come back. He says it's been known to happen. They want my guidance as their dreamer."

She shrugged.

"So, there remains one final thing I have to ask." He paused. "I said I wouldn't leave you, but it's not only up to me. Do you still want me to go?"

"I bow to the Tribe's wishes."

"That's not what I'm asking."

"That's my answer."

"It isn't enough."

"It'll have to be."

His face twisted. "You said we were family, Miriam. Tribe. Has that changed now that you know the truth?"

"You are part of the Tribe, Joachín. What's left of it," she said bitterly. "I didn't lie about that."

He looked away. "I don't lie, either." He glanced back at her, taking in her face in the moonlight. "I've lied to many people, but I've never lied to you." She flushed. "Did you believe me when I told Tomás that I *didn't* love you?" he asked.

"That doesn't matter."

"You must have heard how garbled my words were, how hard it was for me to say!"

"You said you were stealing my book."

"Which I would have done! But I didn't, to save you!"

She didn't want to hear anymore. She swept past him and headed for the campfire. He was too...she didn't know what he was. Too frustrating to listen to? Too hazardous to trust? He'd brought disaster upon them all. She was also to blame, but that was of less account. She was still furious with him.

"Miriam, I *do* love you!" he insisted, following at her heels. "My passion for you has been there from the beginning. Everything you say or do, I react to, like tinder set alight! You're life to me, Miriam. You're my breath, the beat of my heart. How could I not love you? If I were a priest, you'd be my temple. I worship you in a way I've never done before!"

A warm swell filled her with such presence that it seemed to come from the stars. Alonso had said those same words after Anassa had cut her belly with the repulsion tattoo. Had Alonso just spoken through Joachín? Was it possible that he was still with her in some way? A wind sprang up. It began to rain. An ache wrapped itself about her heart.

"Not only do I love you, Miriam, I adore you." Joachín caught her by the shoulders. She felt the truth of it in his touch. The rain pelted down with a vengeance. In the distance, figures ran from the campfire. The Tribe was retreating to the caves. "That's what I was thinking when Tomás asked me," he said, holding her firm. "I can't help it. I feel you, need you, want you, in a way I can't explain. I think Lys has decreed we be together. I'm almost sure I heard her speak to me when we were running from Tomás. She told me we had to go, right then. That we wouldn't get a second chance."

He held her tightly, as if afraid to let her go. Her heart quickened. The repulsion tattoo was *not* working. He looked as if he wanted to kiss her but was waiting for her to decide. One kiss would mean all was forgiven. All was not.

She pushed him away angrily. "That's ridiculous. You were hearing things. I'm getting wet."

She walked away from him in the downpour, aware he wasn't following her.

She turned, exasperated. He was waiting for her acceptance. Fine, she could give him that. The Tribe needed him, even if she did not. She beckoned to him to come.

He stood his ground.

For a moment, she had the feeling that he was about to turn away, to leave her forever. She caught her breath, angry with herself for being dismayed. Would he always run off when things became difficult? She hated him for it, hated herself for suspecting there was more to it than what she was willing to admit. Most of all, she hated Lys for meddling. Why would the goddess choose her and Joachin to lead the Tribe? Two half-breeds, one a dreamer and the other, a fallen seer. Poor choices for a poor people.

"You can stay!" she shouted at him. He stood there like a post, which annoyed her immensely. They were soaked to the skin. Her monk's habit hung from her like a soggy rag. She bit her lip. "Very well, *I* want you to stay! The Tribe needs you."

She watched as he came back to life. He trudged toward her, a man given a reprieve. Water streamed down the planes of his face. She reminded him of Sul in his depiction of savior of the world. Yet Joachin was no Sul. He was infuriatingly mortal and weak. On the other hand, she was no Lys, either.

He glanced at her sidelong as they climbed the path. The trail was slick with mud. He hesitated, offered her his hand.

She couldn't touch him, too afraid that the unwelcome desire she felt for him might return. She shook her head, unable to speak. He dropped his hand and followed her into the cave.

How is this fair, Lys? she asked the goddess. *Where is my will in the matter? Have I no say?*

No voice answered her. She hadn't expected it would.

They entered the grotto to the women's pool. In the darkness, the Tribe huddled miserably in a tight group. Luci rose when she saw Joachin.

"Iago collected some wood, but I forbade him...," she began.

Miriam cut her off. "There's no reason for us not to light a fire. The cleft above us will draw the smoke."

"But this place is sacrosanct."

"The goddess doesn't mean for us all to die."

Ximen lifted his hands placatingly. "I think it's all right," he said, his voice a balm. "We enter a new era. I suspect the goddess will pardon many things." He gave Miriam an admonishing look.

Joachín nodded. "We can have a fire tonight. But at daybreak, rain or shine, we find any horses that remain, and we quit this place. It won't be long before the Torch Bearers return. I didn't kill Tomás, unfortunately. He'll stop at nothing now, to find us."

"Where will we go?" Zara's anxiety was obvious. For once, the potion maker had other things on her mind than men.

"South, I think," Joachín said. "The winter snows are coming, so we mustn't linger. We'll head for the coast. Make new lives for ourselves as fishermen."

"But that means we give up our life of travel!"

"For a time. We need to reestablish ourselves, make some money."

"No."

Everyone turned to look at Miriam. "We need to go further," she said, feeling a rare clarity in her words, as if some agency inspired them. "As long as we stay in Esbaña, we're at risk. We must travel beyond Tomás's reach. Trade has opened across the great Ocean Sea. We will head for the new world."

Gasps filled the cavern. The idea of traveling such a vast distance astonished them.

Joachín nodded. "Yes," he said. "Our matriarch speaks the truth. That is exactly what we must do."

As she tried to sleep, she thought of the plans they had made. They would find the horses and travel the cavern route from the Womb rather than risk the road past Elysir. According to Ximen, it would take five days without food to come out on the other side. It would be a difficult trek, but they had water. They would survive.

She listened to the sobbing around her. There would be many nights like this—of women pining for their men. Not far from her, Joachín lay. He was awake, staring at the cave's ceiling.

Grief made people want impossible things. She dismissed her desire to crawl over to him and settle her head on his shoulder. She hated herself for being weak, for wanting to feel the comfort of his arms about her, and more, so that she might douse her grief for Alonso in his embrace. Her need for Joachín betrayed her, urging her to seek new life, to choose passion over death. Once again, she cursed the goddess for making her endure such an unreasonable attraction.

You asked me if you had a say in the matter. You do.

She startled. *How is that?* she demanded, unwilling to be swayed by a grace so pristine that it settled upon her like soft, golden down.

Joachín is my chosen. I need him to lead the Tribe as much as I need you.

And my choice in the matter would be…?

Love him or deny him. That's your business, not mine.

She glared at Joachín and swallowed. Her body ached, and not from lying on the hard ground. It didn't help to admit that perhaps the goddess had her reasons. Lys chose him because he was a survivor with few scruples. Not a charitable thought. But had she also chosen him because Lys knew that the two of them together, might be a formidable force? That they might not only lead their Tribe to the new world, but help it thrive?

Miriam rose from where she lay, stepped around bodies, and headed for the cavern's mouth. Streams of wet fell from the lip of the overhang. She paused for a moment to stare over the Womb. The valley was shrouded in rain. She couldn't see to the far side. Not caring about the cold, she stepped from the cave and descended the trail to the spot where Anassa had died. The downpour drenched her to the skin.

She stood there, forlorn. The man she truly loved was gone. The raindrops pelted her face. Her brow creased, she choked on a sob. *I can't hold the rain, Alonso!* she cried, lifting her hands to him as if he were the sky. *Couldn't you have done something else? Been something else?* More than anything, she wanted him to find his way back to her, to stop her before she became unfaithful to his memory. She didn't care how he managed it. She cupped her face in her hands and wept.

She finally cried herself out. The wind was cold; she was frozen to the core. She hadn't noticed when she had begun to shiver, but now, she shook uncontrollably. It seemed a betrayal of him to leave.

"Miriam!"

Trembling, she turned. Joachin stood at the cave's entrance. The flickering light of their fire shone all about him.

He beckoned to her. "Come out of the rain. You'll catch your death."

His words were a portent, an inevitability. There was one path to take, and he stood in the middle of it. She could remain where she was, childish and stubborn, or accept the fate that the goddess had chosen for them.

She trudged up the path and met him at the entrance. He held out a hand to help her climb the last few steps. She resisted the temptation and ducked past him.

"Will you ever forgive me?" His voice was raw with yearning.

She hesitated. She was too spent to deal with him now. In truth, she had forgiven him. She had cried away her fury while mourning Alonso.

"If it helps you to know, I'll carry the guilt for what happened for the rest of my life," he said.

She nodded awkwardly, her throat thick. She took a step.

"Miriam!" His tone pleaded.

"I do forgive you," she whispered, "but that doesn't change the fact that this still hurts." She clasped her hands to her chest.

"I'll do whatever I can to make things right. Not that I can ever make them right. So many have been lost...." He trailed off.

She closed her eyes. *Goodbye, Alonso,* she thought. *I will love you, forever.* She turned to Joachin.

He stood there in a torn shirt, half of his chest bare, the blood stains from the tattoo Tomás had given him leaching into the cloth. Beneath the shadow of his beard, his face was scratched, his nose swollen. As scarred as he was, he was still attractive, perhaps more so because of it. He was a dark night to Alonso's day, a moonlit sky to the noonday sun.

"Life is too short to carry such a burden, Joachin," she said.

His dark eyes sparked with hope. His lips trembled, but his jaw tightened with determination. She read his intention. He would woo her and win, no matter how long it took. Eventually, she would be his. Against her will, she flushed and her heart quickened.

Love him or deny him, Lys had said.

She turned away, afraid that he might see the desire she so carefully hid.

And Joachin, Dreamer and bearer of a truth tattoo, saw her denial for what it was and followed her into the cave, a palmer on a pilgrimage for love.

Afterword

THIS BOOK STEMS from a family myth. My mother's side of the family, the Frankos, claimed we were once Spanish nobles who were kicked out of Spain by the king. As a teenager, I accepted this without question and took great pride in thinking we came from nobility. Years later, a little study helped uncover the truth. In the middle ages, the only people who were evicted from Spain were the Moors, Jews, and gypsies. In 1492, the same year Columbus sailed to the new world, the last Moorish stronghold in Grenada fell. Catholic Monarchs Ferdinand and Isabella issued a royal decree where anyone who wasn't Catholic had to convert to the true faith or leave. My family might have left Spain at that point, or possibly, we converted and fled later, when it became too dangerous for us to stay. Further investigation showed me that Franco (the Spanish version of Franko) is a converso or Jewish convert's name.

In *The Tattooed Witch* trilogy, I take liberties with the history, reflecting it and using it to my purposes, rather than remaining completely true to an accurate time-line or actual people. The Spanish

Inquisition's main function was to ensure religious orthodoxy and seek out heretics. My story focuses on witchcraft which was of a lesser concern in Spain, although there were cases. I've also taken creative license in other ways: in the mid-sixteenth century, gypsy caravans (vardos) didn't exist. They appeared later, in the 1800's in England. Flamenco dance, as I describe it, has only been around for 200 years although its roots go back much farther; the palos (dance forms) reflect real dances, but I've made up the names. Tomás de Torquemada (whose first name I borrow for my Grand Inquisitor, Tomás) lived from 1420 to 1498 and would have died before Miriam's time. Because I wanted the freedom to play with events and tell the story in a romanticized way, I created a parallel world.

I'd like to think that there's something to be said about presenting a romanticized version. Perhaps those things that touch us most deeply, that strike us as most true, aren't always tied to the accuracy of people or events.

Susan MacGregor, Spring, 2013.

About the Author

SUSAN MACGREGOR IS an editor with *On Spec* magazine and edited the anthologies *Tesseracts Fifteen: A Case of Quite Curious Tales*, (Edge Books) and *Divine Realms* (Ravenstone Press). Her short fiction has appeared in a number of periodicals and anthologies, including *A Method to the Madness*, (Five Rivers) and *Urban Green Man* (Edge Books).

Currently, she's revising a non-fiction book, *The ABC's of How NOT to Write Speculative Fiction* (Third Printing) and working on the third book in her *Tattooed Witch Trilogy*, a paranormal romance/fantasy set in Spain during the Inquisition and colonial expansion into the New World.

Susan keeps a blog at http://suzenyms.blogspot.ca/, and can be found on Facebook at: https://www.facebook.com/susan.macgregor.

Books by Five Rivers

NON-FICTION

The Terriers of Scotland and Ireland, Bryan Cummins

Al Capone: Chicago's King of Crime, by Nate Hendley

Crystal Death: North America's Most Dangerous Drug, by Nate Hendley

Dutch Schultz: Brazen Beer Baron of New York, by Nate Hendley

John Lennon: Music, Myth & Madness, by Nate Hendley

Motivate to Create: a guide for writers, by Nate Hendley

Stephen Truscott, by Nate Hendley

The Organic Home Garden, by Patrick Lima and John Scanlan

Shakespeare & Readers' Theatre: Hamlet, Romeo & Juliet, Midsummer Night's Dream, by John Poulson

Elephant's Breath & London Smoke: historic colour names, definitions & uses, Deb Salisbury, editor

Stonehouse Cooks, by Lorina Stephens

FICTION

88, by M.E. Fletcher

Immunity to Strange Tales, by Susan J. Forest

Growing Up Bronx, by H.A. Hargreaves

North by 2000+, a collection of short, speculative fiction, by H.A. Hargreaves

A Subtle Thing, Alicia Hendley

The Tattooed Witch, Book 1, by Susan J. MacGregor

Kingmaker's Sword, Book 1: Rune Blades of Celi, by Ann Marston

Western King, Book 2: The Rune Blades of Celi, by Ann Marston

Indigo Time, by Sally McBride

Wasps at the Speed of Sound, by Derryl Murphy

Things Falling Apart, by J.W. Schnarr

And the Angels Sang: a collection of short speculative fiction, by Lorina Stephens

From Mountains of Ice, by Lorina Stephens

Memories, Mother and a Christmas Addiction, by Lorina Stephens

Shadow Song, by Lorina Stephens

YA FICTION

Type, by Alicia Hendley

Mik Murdoch: Boy-Superhero, by Michell Plested

A Method to Madness: A Guide to the Super Evil, edited by Michell Plested and Jeffery A. Hite

FICTION COMING SOON

The Runner and the Wizard, by Dave Duncan

Kaleidoscope, by Robert Fletcher

Cat's Pawn, by Leslie Gadallah

Cat's Gambit, by Leslie Gadallah
The Loremasters, by Leslie Gadallah
Old Growth, by Matt Hughes
The Tattooed Seer, Book 2, by Susan J. MacGregor
The Tattooed Rose, Book 3, by Susan J. MacGregor
Broken Blade, Book 3: The Rune Blades of Celi, by Ann Marston
Cloudbearer's Shadow, Book 4: The Rune Blades of Celi, by Ann Marston
King of Shadows, Book 5: The Rune Blades of Celi, by Ann Marston
Sword and Shadow, Book 6: The Rune Blades of Celi, by Ann Marston
Bane's Choice, Book 7: The Rune Blades of Celi, by Ann Marston
A Still and Bitter Grave, by Ann Marston
Diamonds in Black Sand, by Ann Marston
A Quiet Place, by J.W. Schnarr
Forevering, by Peter Such

YA FICTION COMING SOON

My Life as a Troll, by Susan Bohnet
A Touch of Poison, by Aaron Kite
Out of Time, by David Laderoute
Mik Murdoch: The Power Within, by Michell Plested

NON-FICTION COMING SOON

The Terriers of England and Wales, by Bryan Cummins
Pub to Pub, Coast to Coast, by Bryan Cummins
China: the New Superpower, by Nate Hendley

YA NON-FICTION COMING SOON

Your Home on Native Land, by Alan Skeoch
The Invisible Ape, by John Steckley

The Prime Ministers of Canada Series:

www.fiveriverspublishing.com